golden state

A Novel

stephanie kegan

SIMON & SCHUSTER

New York London Toronto Sydney New Delhi

Simon & Schuster
1230 Avenue of the Americas
New York, NY 10020

This book is a work of fiction. Any references to historical events, real people, or real places are used fictitiously. Other names, characters, places, and events are products of the author's imagination, and any resemblance to actual events or places or persons, living or dead, is entirely coincidental.

First Simon & Schuster hardcover edition February 2015

SIMON & SCHUSTER and colophon are registered trademarks of Simon & Schuster, Inc.

For information about special discounts for bulk purchases, please contact Simon & Schuster Special Sales at 1-866-506-1949 or business@simonandschuster.com.

The Simon & Schuster Speakers Bureau can bring authors to your live event. For more information or to book an event contact the Simon & Schuster Speakers Bureau at 1-866-248-3049 or visit our website at www.simonspeakers.com.

Manufactured in the United States of America

1 3 5 7 9 10 8 6 4 2

Library of Congress Cataloging-in-Publication Data

Kegan, Stephanie.
Golden State : a novel / Stephanie Kegan.
pages cm
1. Brothers and sisters—Fiction. 2. Bombings—Fiction. 3. California—Fiction. 4. Psychological fiction. 5. Domestic fiction. I. Title.
PS3611.E355G56 2015
813'.6—dc23
2014040473

ISBN 978-1-4767-0931-4
ISBN 978-1-4767-0933-8 (ebook)

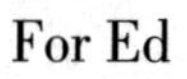

For Ed

Acknowledgments

I am indebted to the memory of Les Plesko, whose wisdom and generosity made this book possible, and to Joan Sullivan, for more than I can say.

My deepest gratitude goes as well to Barbara DeSantis, Mollie Glick, Millicent Bennett, Terry Gillen, Sandra Irwin, Laura Simko, Steven Charnow, Marisel Vera, Karen Karbo, Greg Hrbek, and Nora Linneah Gregory.

golden state

chapter one

THE BAY AREA was in the midst of an autumn heat wave, hot, dry, and unnatural. The air electric against my skin, I had the sense that a single match could ignite us all.

On the front porch, last night's Halloween pumpkin was collapsing in on itself—as much, I imagined, from the sound of jackhammers as from the heat. Yet another house on our street was being rebuilt into a mansion. It made me fear for the soul of our family neighborhood at the base of Berkeley Hills.

Downstairs, Eric was shouting at Julia, hysterical in a school-morning drama of her own making. Behind my bedroom door, in front of the bureau that had been my grandmother's, I fastened on a necklace of bright beads and tiny skulls.

It was the first of November, the Day of the Dead.

As if I had nowhere else to be, I reached for a small silver-framed photo from the clutter on my dresser top—the little boxes that held a piece or two of jewelry, the handmade knickknacks from the kids, the old photos I barely looked at anymore. I had other snapshots of the three of us, but this one was my favorite. My brother, sister, and I were lined up against the door of our old garage, squinting into the sun. Bobby was in the middle in a zippered jacket, his jeans rolled up at the ankle, an American boy of the fifties. On his right, Sara, in a starched dress, looked as if she was ready for anything the third grade could dish out. I was the littlest in the family, no more than three, perched in my mother's high heels next to my big brother. I brushed the glass where

Bobby's hand rested on my shoulder. There was no special day of remembrance, I thought, no sad, sweet, shared mourning for those who were not dead, but simply gone.

On the stairs, Lilly called for *mommy*. I put the photo down. I had two kids to drive to school, twenty-two more to teach, and no more time for my private sorrows.

Julia rode shotgun, not speaking to her little sister or me, her head bent over a stack of smudged three-by-five cards. She was debating in a tournament at Stanford and had dressed in her most college-worthy outfit—a little gray skirt, a striped preppy blouse, a long cardigan with just the right amount of sag, and a pair of new flats that looked like they pinched her feet. I'd known better than to suggest a more comfortable pair.

Outside her school, Julia bolted from the car without saying goodbye. I watched her run from us, my small, slender fifteen-year-old with bouncing red-gold hair and an IQ so high it scared me. I could barely admit how relieved I was to see her go, to be alone with Lilly, who at seven still believed I could do no wrong. We love you both the same, we told the kids: a half lie—the love yes, the sameness impossible.

I drove south through the hills, away from Julia's expensive school for intellectual superstars, down toward Mountaintop. Despite the lofty name, the little elementary school where I taught and Lilly was a second grader was wedged into a commercial street in the Berkeley flats. My husband and I had helped found the school. We'd raised money, painted walls, and planted trees, transforming a warehouse on San Pablo into a dream we'd had for our children. When Julia started first grade here, I was suddenly free. I had bigger aspirations than returning to my old teaching job. I was going to be a professor with an office and students who could sit still. But Lilly popped up unexpectedly, Mountaintop needed me, and here I was—for now.

My third-grade classroom was one of the larger rooms, with a wall of windows catching the morning light. As customary, we started the day on the floor, my students and I in a circle on the rug, the kids with their legs crossed, mine folded under my denim skirt. I read to them about *El Día de Los Muertos*, the holiday of the dead. This morning we were going to make our own small altars, I explained, paint them bright Aztec hues, decorate them with marigolds and clay skeletons we'd make ourselves. In the afternoon, we'd take a field trip to a cemetery.

As usual, Ben's hand popped up.

"What if you don't know any dead people?"

I was surprised, but I shouldn't have been. My students were so young, their parents and grandparents still so young themselves, this seemed entirely possible. Then you can make an altar for a pet, I suggested. Our class goldfish, Kramer—after the character on the Thursday night show—had died the week before.

A hand rose slowly. I called on Annie.

"Did you know it's so hot out because the globe is warming?"

A couple of the boys tittered. I shot them a look, but Annie had already dropped her head. I was surprised the kids knew anything about global warming.

"Annie has brought up something really important," I said, improvising. "So important, I think our class should study climate change."

I didn't want to think why I was plunging into a subject that had no curriculum. All that work to make Annie feel better? Or was it in some way for Bobby?

Annie's head came back up. I dismissed the kids to their seats. It was nine ten, and we were on a roll.

LILLY AND I stopped for an ice cream after school. Julia off debating at Stanford, it was just the two of us on gummy Shattuck Avenue in the unseasonable warmth, feeling carefree. At home, Lilly played in the backyard while I sliced carrots and potatoes to the news on NPR. When I finished, I turned down the volume to sit with my feet up, reading the newspaper I'd had no time for in the morning. I was deep into a story about the terrible war in Bosnia, civilians killed in the market, hardly listening to the radio at all. Yet I heard the newscaster say there'd been an explosion on the Stanford campus.

By the time I reached the radio dial, the report was over. I turned on the television in the family room and started flipping through channels.

The story might have been breaking news, but I had to wait until five o'clock to hear it.

Less than an hour before, an explosion of unknown origin had ripped through an academic building in the heart of the campus. The building had been evacuated. There were casualties.

I told myself that Julia was safe, that all the kids were, that casualties didn't mean them, but I was frantic as I phoned my husband. As soon as Eric picked up I blurted out the news. "Just a second," he said calmly. I heard a click and understood I'd been on speakerphone. "You're in a meeting." I pictured his office, lawyers in grays and blues. "I'll call you back when I know more." My tone was even, but I wanted to punish him. I wasn't even sure what he'd done wrong.

The phone rang almost immediately. It was one of the other debate mothers, who hadn't heard from her daughter either. She was so agitated that she made me sound calm. "The students aren't together," she said. "They're spread all over the campus, moving separately from building to building to debate all these kids from other schools." Before we ended the call, I tried once more to reassure her, but I couldn't even reassure myself.

Lilly emerged from the backyard hungry. I could barely think. I gave her a graham cracker, and told her she could watch TV in my bedroom. Julia would have been suspicious of my breaking of the no-eating-upstairs rule, but Lilly took the cracker and ran off before I might change my mind. On the news, they still didn't know what caused the explosion, but they had an unconfirmed report on the casualties: a professor and a graduate student in critical condition. Two other employees wounded less seriously.

I shuddered but I couldn't help my relief. Not a high school debater among the injured. I was about to let Eric know when the phone rang again. Julia was on the line making little sense.

"I can't understand you," I said, the fear in my daughter's voice making me desperate.

"I don't know where I am," she said. "It's dark out. I can't find anyone."

I got her to calm down, tell me the story: She'd been away from the center of campus and hadn't heard anything. When she'd moved to her next round, the building was locked. She'd waited for what seemed like forever, then gotten lost trying to find her way back. Finally she'd found a public phone, but now she didn't even see any people around.

My panic was so palpable, she recoiled from it.

"I shouldn't have called," she said. "There's nothing you can do."

It was clear she didn't know about the explosion. My only thought was to keep her where she was.

"Give me the number on the telephone. I'll get the campus police to pick you up."

"I see somebody," she said. "I'm going."

She left me holding the phone.

Lilly came downstairs asking for more graham crackers. I gave her the box and sent her back upstairs. I'd forgotten dinner, the vegetables and chicken still in the refrigerator. I was shoving the pan into a cold oven when Eric walked in. He'd been listening to the updates on the radio on the way home.

"There must be someone we can call," he said.

I threw up my hands. "Who?"

"The campus police for a start."

"For a start?" I heard the shrillness in my voice, but I couldn't contain myself. "What are you implying? That I didn't think of that? She said she saw someone."

Eric looked exhausted. "Don't give me a hard time, Natalie."

"A hard time?" I shouted. We traded accusations, making little sense. Suddenly there was Lilly in the shorts she'd worn to school, her still-baby-chubby knees bare.

"Why are you guys fighting?" She had her feet planted on the linoleum as if she were going to take no more childishness from us, but her eyes were wary.

What could I tell her? That for a moment the heavens had parted to show us a future in which we'd lost one of our babies? "Daddy and

I are being stupid," I said, a hand at my eyes. "No, I'm the one who's being stupid."

Eric pulled me next to him. Lilly squeezed between us.

"Dinner is going to be really late," I said, clinging to them both.

WE TRIED not to make a big deal out of picking up Julia when the bus arrived at her school. It could have been any night, parents waiting for their kids in the dark parking lot, just another thing that had to be done. Except that no one spoke or even looked at anyone else, each family grabbing their child and spiriting him or her away.

Two hours past the usual time, Eric put Lilly to bed. I sat with Julia while she picked at her dinner and told me about her day. After all that had happened, what she wanted to talk about was how upset she was that she hadn't done better in the final round.

At eleven, with Julia safely in bed, Eric and I collapsed on the couch. Eric clutched a glass of red wine and wrapped his free arm around me. I rested my head against his shoulder. We'd panicked earlier, but now we'd returned to ourselves, loving and loved, safe in our togetherness. I turned on the late news with the remote, and finally got the full story.

That day, a little after four o'clock, the head of the computer science department at Stanford University had opened a package addressed to him. The blast from the incendiary device inside had blown off his arm and half his face. The graduate student chatting with him had died on the floor from the massive wound to his chest.

There had been no malfunctioning generator at Stanford, no chemistry experiment gone awry. It had been a bomb that had caused that afternoon's devastation on the campus where my daughter had been walking in her new shoes. Someone, some person had done that.

"I can't listen anymore," I said. I clicked off the set and turned to Eric. "Bed," I said, longing for the sleep that would return us to the safety of our ordinary lives.

chapter two

A STORM ten days into the month brought the strange November heat wave to an end. The rain meant no outdoor recess. Lunches would have to be eaten inside, my students and I tethered to one another like convicts on a chain gang. On the fourth day of downpour, the kids grew shifty-eyed, the boys itching like desperadoes who'd been forced to check their guns at the saloon door.

At the store after work, feeling clammy and sorry for myself, I spent too much on groceries for dinner—a rack of lamb and an extravagant bottle of wine. Once I was past the cash register and home, it seemed worth it, the kitchen filled with the smell of rosemary and garlic sizzling in fat. Lilly drawing in the steam on the window.

The phone rang, and I knew before answering that it was Eric. When I heard his weary *hey*, I understood he wasn't going to be just late. He was going to be ten or eleven o'clock late. I tried to push down my anger, my disappointment. More than good food, I'd been craving conversation, adult life, the pleasure of lingering at the table over a second glass of wine. Eric must have wanted some of that, too. When he apologized, he sounded defeated.

It was starting. I knew the cycle of Eric's overworking as well as I knew the seasons, the back-burner cases heating up, the trial dates looming. At first he'd dread the unreasonable hours, the time away from home, the fatigue, but in time he would give in to the drug of overwork, fingers drumming, his gaze gone from us. The children and I would dismiss this stranger, draw into one another until it was over and he turned to the task of wooing us back. The girls would give in at the first sign their real father had returned. It took me longer to forgive the betrayal of all those hours.

I ate with the kids, feeling sorry for myself. Julia made a show of clearing a few plates before taking off to study. The rain picked up. I sent Lilly to get ready for bed. She came back, reporting a leak in her bedroom. I grabbed a soup pot and followed her upstairs,

There was no end to the things that needed repairing in our old house. We'd been fearless when we bought it fifteen years before, a 1920s, two-story, Spanish-style stucco, with worn hardwood floors, stairs that creaked, leafy views, and young families up and down the block. We'd updated the kitchen to suit my idea of myself as a cook, and left everything else as it was.

I moved Lilly's dollhouse away from the damp spot on her ceiling, put the pot on the floor to catch the leak, and read her bedtime story to the plinking of water on metal.

"What are we?" Lilly asked, stalling when I reached to turn off the light.

I asked what she meant.

She ticked off on her fingers. "Mexican, Jewish, Asian, Catholic."

"We're Californians," I said.

"But what else?"

"There is nothing else," I said, kissing her good night. Another time, I'd tell her the stories from my side of the family: my mother's forebears crossing the Sierra Nevada just ahead of the Donner Party; my father's great-great-grandfather arriving for the Gold Rush and never telling anyone where he'd come from or what he'd left behind.

After I'd said good night to Julia, I graded papers exactly the way I told my students never to do their homework: in front of the television. A report on the eleven o'clock news made me put down my red pencil. The FBI had tied the bombing at Stanford two weeks before to a serial bomber they'd nicknamed the Cal Bomber for the state in which he operated. Our state. Years on the FBI's most wanted list, and all they had on him was the composite drawing on the screen. A man in a baseball cap and sunglasses. He looked like everyone and no one. Until Stanford, he hadn't sent a bomb anywhere in six years. Now he was back.

I turned off the set.

Eric opened the front door at eleven twenty, his pinstripe suit rain spattered, the fresh shirt I'd watched him button this morning now limp and clinging to him. He sat next to me, his briefcase sliding to the floor, leaned his head against the couch, and shut his eyes.

"That bad?"

"That bad," he said. "I'm sorry about dinner."

"I hate your job." I meant it. The incessant hours, the every-man-for-himself mentality in the guise of congenial partnership.

"When the kids are through college . . ." His voice trailed off.

We'd crossed this territory before. Eric's conviction that he overworked for us, and mine that we never asked this of him. I never cared about money. My parents were lofty thinkers who drove old cars and took us on vacations to a dusty cabin in the Sierras. My first job out of college was as a temp for two dollars an hour. It got me to an attic room in Paris, with yogurt and French bread for dinner. When I finally trained for a career, it was as a teacher. When I married Eric in my parents' backyard, my sister and I barefoot with wildflowers in our hair, he was a part-time high school athletic coach. I'd never felt like we needed anything more.

I brushed Eric's face with my fingers, and felt the deep creases spreading from his eyes. We were the same age.

I was quiet for a moment. "Remember when my dad was alive and my mother still had Thanksgiving, when we'd sing 'Over the River and Through the Woods to Grandmother's House' with Julia? And then she'd ask if every pair of trees along I-80 was the woods?"

He laughed, no memory about the kids too corny for us. I asked if he was hungry. He said he was famished, no time even for lunch. In the kitchen, he picked up the wine bottle I'd bought and looked at the label. "I'm sorry," he said again. I'd left the bottle out so he would be, but I was finished with that game.

"Open it," I said. He ate his reheated meal as if he'd never tasted anything as good. It was nearly midnight, but we talked as if we didn't have to get up at six in the morning. Together, we'd always had that, the ability to forget about tomorrow.

I told him what I'd heard on the news.

"Jesus," he said.

"Julia was there."

He took my hand. "She's okay," he said.

We weren't talking about a terrible crime anymore. We were talking about Julia, our high-strung daughter, who wailed day and night as an infant, who later couldn't tolerate a broken crayon, a wrinkled paper, or the seam on the toe of her socks. Our firstborn read by three, played chess at six, and began writing a novel at seven. Even now, we had to limit the hours she studied, enforce days off. Another mother might have bragged. I worried, and Eric reassured.

We got in bed, listening to the water dripping in Lilly's room. "You know what this means," he said. "We can't put off getting a new roof another year."

I nodded supportively but I didn't agree. All the roof needed—all I needed—was for it to stop raining.

Eric reached out his arm. I moved next to him, patted down the hair on his chest, and laid my head there. He was asleep immediately. I don't know how he did that, awake to dead asleep in an instant, no drifting off.

I didn't want to go to sleep. I wanted to stay here, this hair pressing my cheek, the rhythm of this strong heart at my ear, the sound of rain on the window, punctuated by the night groans of an old house leaking at the seams.

chapter three

THANKSGIVING loomed and I still hadn't made a single plan. The simplest and the hardest thing would be to start with Sara. Although my sister and I lived less than a hundred and fifty miles apart, we hadn't seen each other in two years. Sara didn't do holidays. She hated driving to the city from her place in Potter Valley. She hadn't much liked my husband since he put on a suit sixteen years ago to go work as a lawyer. She'd say no, but I'd feel good about inviting her, as if the gulf between us were not wide, as if one day she might join us, and Bobby, too.

I called from the wall phone in the kitchen while the kids and Eric watched TV in the family room. My sister and I had both been playing our parts for years. Sara did the aging hippie on her plot of land miles from anywhere, rewashing plastic baggies. I was the corporate lawyer's wife with the evidence of our careless consumption overflowing the bins at the side of the house.

A few minutes into our conversation, though, Sara threw me a curve. "I thought I'd go down to Mom's this weekend for her birthday. It's her eightieth. You should come, Natalie. Mom would like that. The three of us together."

"Mother isn't turning eighty," I corrected. "She was born in 1916. She's going to be seventy-nine."

We argued for a few minutes, but the number was hardly the point. Seventy-nine, eighty-four, a million. What did it matter? We both knew that all Mother really wanted for her birthday was to hear from Bobby.

* * *

Eric insisted I drive his Lexus to my mother's even though I was more comfortable in my old Honda. There was something about his car, the padding of the seats, the quiet climate control of the ride, the way the windows demanded to be rolled up, that made me feel not quite present. I was driving from Berkeley to Sacramento, but I was in no way connected to the road.

I pulled off on Stockton Street, the exit for the house I'd grown up in, swearing when I realized my mistake. I'd have to drive through traffic and turn around to get back on the freeway. But, really, what was the rush? There wasn't any set time for us to gather in the gated community where my mother now lived.

Maybe it wouldn't hurt to drive by the old house, I thought, wondering if that had been my aim all along. I turned off the air conditioner, rolled down the windows, and headed toward Forty-Sixth Street. In a car that was not my own, parked in front of the house where my mother no longer lived, I remembered the summer heat of my childhood. Valley heat so intense it burned the grass and shimmered the air, sweat dripping onto my cotton top, my father coming up the walk, his white shirt stuck to his back, his fingers hooked into a jacket thrown over his shoulder, my mother behind drapes drawn to keep out the sun.

When the heat became unbearable, I'd go across the hall to Bobby's room in the coolest corner of the house. He had a *Boys' Life* room with brown-on-brown-striped bedspreads, shelves crammed with books, a built-in desk stretching under the window, and a small, shady sun porch stacked with more books. He never seemed to mind it when I showed up in his space. He'd let me read from his collection of Superman and Batman comics. I'd sit on the floor between the second twin bed and the wall, a tall metal glass of icy Kool-Aid at my side, my back against the bed, my bare feet resting on the cool plaster wall. I remembered the smell of those comics, the feel of them on my fingers, my big brother building his model planes or playing a solo game of chess, the two of us quietly together.

A car horn sounded up the street. I snapped to attention, as if the honk had been directed at me. Then I started my own car, and headed to where I was supposed to be.

THE GUARD at my mother's complex waved me through. He wasn't doing much of a job guarding, but then I didn't look like much of a robber, a middle-aged woman in her husband's shiny car, a present for her mother gift-wrapped on the seat beside her.

Even though my mother had lived here four years, I still struggled to find her condo among all the other pale-colored units surrounded by artificially green lawn.

"You shouldn't have come," she said at the door. "I told Sara not to, but she had a bee in her bonnet." My mother had graduated first in her class from Berkeley, traveled the world, and danced at the White House, but at heart she was still a girl from the Sacramento Valley. She looked like an advertisement for the golden years—tall, broad shouldered, and smooth faced, her once-salt-and-pepper hair now a stylishly cut white. She wore expensive slacks, a crisp white blouse, and a red cardigan with gold buttons. A pair of heavy gold bracelets jangled on her wrist.

I felt suddenly sloppy in my jeans and T-shirt and the unbuttoned, flowing blouse I'd grabbed at the last minute. I lacked what my mother had always had, the ability to dress well without thinking about it. She waved me toward the bone-colored couch. "Sit, I've made iced tea." She refused to let me help her, and I felt like what I was, a visitor in my mother's house.

When she went for the tea, I circled the living room. I still couldn't get over her new place, the white walls, the sterile rooms, the absence of family history. My mother had taken almost no furniture from the house where she had lived with and without my father for forty years. She'd put the photographs away, the framed black-and-whites of my parents' life in politics: my mother and father with Governor and Mrs. Brown, with Adlai Stevenson, with John F. Kennedy. My father a young man beside Eleanor Roosevelt, who is smiling at him instead of the camera.

"I miss the old stuff," I said when my mother returned.

"God, I don't," she replied, putting our iced tea on coasters on the pristine coffee table.

I looked at my mother. She could have stepped out of a 1940s movie. She was never like the other mothers, nagging, waiting for you to come home. She spoke to five-year-olds as if they were college graduates. As usual, I didn't know what to say.

When Sara barged through the door a moment later, I was actually relieved.

"Man, I don't know how you do it," she said to me. "I just can't do traffic anymore." She waved her fingers. "All those people in their miniature tanks." She knitted her brows. "That's not your car parked outside, is it, Nat?"

"It's Eric's," I said, repressing the urge to curry favor with her by adding that I still had my same old Honda.

She looked older than when I'd last seen her. The long, wavy hair she tied behind her neck was now more gray than brown. The lines around her eyes were deeper, the flesh on her neck looser, but her body looked as lithe as it had been in her high school cheerleading days. She wore a short, khaki-colored cotton shift, her legs tanned and muscled, a T-shirt, a bulky sweater, and flip-flops. Only Sara could drive for two and a half hours working the stiff clutch of an old Volvo in those floppy rubber sandals.

My sister had started college as a sorority girl and finished as an earth mother dishing up brown rice to a houseful of hippies. She graduated, bought a skirt and blouse, and the next thing I knew, she was a social worker with a car and her own apartment overlooking Lake Merritt. Her new life had seemed so glamorous to me that I fantasized about getting a county job of my own when I got out of college.

After a few years, Sara moved north for a succession of jobs in ever more remote towns, until she settled in Potter Valley. I wasn't even sure how she lived anymore—whether she worked or not. Sara didn't like explaining herself any more than she liked getting mired in the quotidian activities that burdened the rest of us.

"You look good, Natalie," she said after our embrace. "Prosperous."

It was her way of saying I'd gained a few pounds. I tried not to feel hurt. Sara was Sara. She had her nightgown stuffed in a brown paper bag to spend the weekend with our mother.

We had lunch in the dining room on my mother's new blond-oak table. She'd divided the contents of the old house among her three children according to a plan that was hers alone. The Oriental rugs, Stickley dining table, and the china went to me, the matching sideboard, the glassware, and Roseville pottery to Sara, the framed etchings to Bobby, who lived alone in a one-room shack without electricity or plumbing.

Out of old habit, I pressed my thumb against the handle of my fork, but there was no embossed flower to imprint into my flesh. This wasn't my great-grandmother's silver, I suddenly realized, the silver my mother had taught me to polish because Sara always refused. She said it was a waste of time. But I loved watching the tarnish go away, working next to my mother as she passed on the family stories: how my great-great-great-grandmother Kristin had crossed the Sierras in a covered wagon carrying a silver spoon from her mother. How years later, her granddaughter Lillian had swept into Gump's in San Francisco with the same spoon and ordered the pattern remade in a service for sixteen. One day, my mother used to tell me, the set would be mine to pass on to my own daughter.

Until that moment, I hadn't understood it was gone.

I took a bite of salad, but I couldn't swallow. Four years after the fact, the cold logic of what my mother had done choked me. She might have bequeathed me the story of Kristin and Lillian, but she'd handed over their sterling to Bobby. She'd given him what he could easily sell.

"You're not eating," my mother said.

I was forty-eight years old. There was nothing to say. I took another bite.

We had coffee and cookies for dessert. Neither Sara nor I had thought to pick up cake—not that my mother would have cared about one. She hated fuss.

I kissed my mother good-bye at the door, and Sara walked me to the car. "Did you ever think Mother would choose to live in a place with a little guard and an up-down thing?" Sara waved her arm like a crossing bar.

"I never thought she'd move from the old house," I said. "I never thought she'd do a lot of things."

Sara squinted at me. "What's up with you today? Where'd you stash your usual Chatty Cathy self?"

Her remark caught me off guard. Sara wasn't particularly attuned to other people's emotions. If I ever had to survive the crash of a small plane in the Alaskan tundra, there's no one I'd rather have at my side. But I wasn't bleeding, freezing, or starving. I was standing beside Eric's Lexus parked behind a bed of perfectly maintained pansies.

"I don't know," I said. I doubted that Sara would understand. I'd believed my mother when she told me the story of the spoon that Kristin brought with her into California from a home and a family that she would never see again, a spoon remade into a set that passed from daughter to daughter. I'd believed it meant something about family and the history we pass on. Maybe I'd confused it with love.

Sara gave me a quizzical look as she pulled a small purple pipe and lighter from her shift pocket and cupped them in her hand. She checked behind her. Then she lit her pipe and took a deep, pungent drag.

I stepped back from the pot smoke, agitated, aggrieved. "Did you know Mother gave Bobby the family silver?"

"Maybe she wanted him to set a lovely table," she said when her lungs had cleared.

My laugh was dry. I wished I hadn't said anything.

"You need to let it go," she said. "They're just knives and forks. And Mom will never accept that Bobby is what he is."

"What he is, is a monumental loser," I said, surprising myself. I never spoke about Bobby that way.

"He's not a big-time lawyer. I'll give you that."

I let that go. "Don't you think about him?"

She shrugged. "He's just some person out there. I cultivate my own garden."

I pictured her in a straw hat, holding a hoe. It made me smile. But neither one of us was being truthful. There was a vanishing at the center of our lives, a brother gone so far from us that he had all but disappeared. Not just some person out there. Not a loser, but painfully, inexplicably lost.

chapter four

I WAS TEN YEARS OLD, and my world was about to end. I had one brother and Princeton was taking him from me. They were going to pay his way. They'd even pay for his toothpaste. A professor from the math department called our house in Sacramento to tell Bobby he'd have a ball there.

At another house, the invitation might have been a bigger deal. At ours, going to Princeton meant you couldn't go to Berkeley.

Berkeley was an idea to my family as much as a university, the summit of a statewide system second to none, a place where kids arriving on Greyhound buses with thirty dollars in their pockets could get the finest education the country had to offer. It was an idea my father, as a political strategist and a top aide to Governor Pat Brown, had helped make real. The proposal he shepherded had a dull name, the Master Plan for Higher Education, but there was nothing dull about the outcome: the best in public higher education, accessible to all Californians tuition-free, four new state colleges, three new university campuses, Berkeley rated first in the country. But my brother chose Princeton. "Smaller classes," he said.

"You'll hate the snobbery," my father said.

"He's only sixteen. I worry about him going so far away," I overheard my mother tell my father. But neither parent said he couldn't go.

Since they weren't going to stop my brother, the job fell to me. When I wandered casually into his room, Bobby was at his built-in desk under the window, constructing one of his model planes. He made his models from scratch with balsa wood, using the instructions printed in a book with minuscule type. He hung the finished planes from the ceiling, even the one that Mother hated. It was a red-nosed Japanese Zero. He'd constructed the cockpit from tiny bits of plastic, and I'd been in his room for the argument. "Those planes attacked us at Pearl Harbor," my mother said. "I don't want to see one displayed."

"It's not the plane's fault it belonged to the enemy," Bobby had said.

The Zero with the bright rising suns stayed. Bobby was the only person in the family who could ever win an argument with Mother.

I readied my case as I sat crossed-legged on his bed in shorts, the raised stripes of the bedspread pressing against my bare legs.

"What's up, chipmunk?" he asked, his pale, steady hands affixing one tiny sliver of balsa to another.

"It's about Dad," I said.

"What?" Bobby sounded surprised, as if I might know something he didn't.

"He's going to be really hurt if you don't go to Berkeley."

"Dad will be fine," Bobby said, turning back to his plane.

I arranged the pillow behind my back, lifted my head to the planes suspended from the ceiling. Bobby was right. Dad never seemed anything but fine. Aiming for nonchalance, I watched the models on their slender wires float slowly in the breeze. "I heard that at Princeton the rich kids smash the model planes of the poor kids."

His head bent over his work, Bobby nodded. "Thanks for telling me. I'll leave them here."

I recognized the tone. It was my father's: kindly, amused, a tone used exclusively on me, the permanent youngest. If my brother moved far away, I wouldn't be able to bear it, but I suddenly hated him the way I hated Sara, who never let me near her room, her friends, or her things.

"Mom says you're too young to go to Princeton, and nobody there will be your friend."

I spoke like that to my sister every day. I'd use anything on her, stuff I'd overheard, made up. But Bobby wasn't Sara. My chest heaved from the weight of what I'd said, the truth at the heart of my lie.

"I was thinking you could visit me sometime," he said. He didn't seem angry about what I'd just said. He sounded the way he always did, serious, thoughtful, and easy. "Fly out alone when you're twelve or thirteen."

You could build a nation on Bobby's promises. I pictured it: me flying across the country by myself, sitting by the window, eating lunch off a tray, carrying my suitcase off the plane. I'd wear nylons and straighten them on the tarmac.

I let Princeton have him. When he came home at Christmas, my mother said he was too thin. I asked him if we could move up my visit by a year. He said he'd think about it.

When Bobby returned for the summer, I went with my parents to the airport. He didn't look like himself anymore. His hair was scraggly, his neck so scrawny that his Adam's apple looked enormous, his skin gray in the fluorescent light of the terminal. When I rushed to throw my arms around him, he didn't laugh or call me chipmunk or squirt. At home, he slept late into the day, and I no longer read comic books in his room.

"Bobby's different," I complained to my mother.

"That's just the way college kids are," she said.

My father didn't seem to think so. He wanted Bobby out of bed and doing something. I heard my parents arguing about it.

Sara said it was Bobby's problem if he was unhappy at college.

When I went to Girl Scout camp, Bobby wrote that he envied my sojourn in the wilderness. It was the first time he'd ever said he envied something about my life and I wanted camp to last all summer. In September, Bobby went back to college, Sara began her new life as cheerleader, and I started sixth grade.

Two months later, Bobby came home.

"It's not Christmas," I said to my mother. "It's not any other holiday. How come Bobby's home?" I should have been overjoyed, but instead I was cautious. Something was wrong with my big brother, and I didn't understand why no else noticed.

"He needs to rest," my mother said.

The next week, his belongings came in boxes in the mail.

He stayed in his room all day. His door was closed to me, but I didn't care as much as I once would have. I had my own life now. I hung out at the shopping center with my friends and wore lipstick behind my mother's back. My mother was now someone I had to get around.

Sara was hardly ever home. She was either at school, cheerleading, or going somewhere in a car driven by a boy.

At night, Bobby ate with us silently, looking only at his plate. Other than Sara and me, no one in our family had ever done much arguing. Now Bobby and my father battled constantly, their voices loud and desperate.

I argued with my mother about wearing makeup, about going places with my friends. We fought about my hair, the red hair I hated. Finally, I bought a six-pack of black dye capsules and used them all at once. I was on my way out the door with my new raven hair when my mother stopped me.

"You're not going anywhere until you wash that crap out of your hair." She actually said *crap*.

"It's my hair," I said. "You can't stop me."

When she ordered me back upstairs, it drove me over the line.

"You're just jealous because your hair is gray and ugly. You look like Daddy's mother."

It wasn't true. My mother may have refused to dye her prematurely gray hair, but she was still young and beautiful. But there was something special about my father. His looks, his effortless glamour, had an immediate effect on women. They lit up for him. Even I had seen it.

I'd wanted to hurt my mother, and I sensed I had. I blamed her for the changes in our family I couldn't even see had taken place.

chapter five

I BURROWED DEEPER under the covers. Sunday meant I could sleep as late as I wanted, as the girls would permit. But there was so much to do. Christmas vacation was only a week away. I had to finish shopping, get started on the cards, order Lilly's doll. I needed to firm up holiday plans with my mother. We might have let her back out of Thanksgiving, but there was no way she was getting out of Christmas.

I heard Julia's footsteps on our bedroom floor. She climbed in next to me. "Mom," she said, touching my shoulder. Her voice was tremulous. I turned over, looked at her. She'd been crying. I asked what the matter was.

"I wish I could still believe," she said. "It's so sad when it's gone."

"When what's gone?" I asked, brushing the hair from her face. My mother said we indulged the kids too much. I didn't remember ever crawling in bed with my parents. That bedroom door was shut.

"The magic," she said.

I wanted to laugh, but she looked so serious. I pulled her close, and said I understood, sensing she was going to keep this up for a while. No one could suffer a loss of faith like Julia. What she needed was an older sister like Sara to toughen her up. Sara once had told me every gift I was getting for Christmas. I don't know how she knew. I'd had my hands over my ears but she couldn't be stopped. At Julia's age, I wore high heels to Christmas dinner, my father and brother in jackets, my mother and sister in dresses and pearls.

I couldn't remember the last Christmas my parents and the three of us kids had all been together. I must have been in college. The holiday wasn't remarkable. I had no idea that my brother would soon stop coming, that I'd barely ever see him again. In the past fourteen years, I'd seen him just once, by accident, six years ago.

My mother was still living in the house on Forty-Sixth Street, the house I thought she'd never sell. The girls had coveted these velvet Christmas dresses we'd seen at Macy's. I'd wanted them, too. Holly red for two-year-old Lilly, midnight blue for nine-year-old Julia. The finery had led somehow to a visit with my mother. The girls and I drove from Berkeley to Sacramento, to the old house on a Saturday, just for the day, the kids decked out in their new dresses.

We had lunch in the dining room where I'd eaten as a girl, a lady's lunch with china, embossed silver, and white lace, Lilly eating without a spill. Afterward, we went into the living room. The girls banged on the piano. The doorbell rang, and suddenly there was my brother standing at the edge of the room, a slight man, stooped, in a threadbare jacket, his hair graying and wild.

The girls stopped their banging to stare. I rose from the couch. Bobby and I hadn't seen each other in years. He'd refused to come home even when our father was dying. It astonished me that he'd left his cabin in the wilderness to come here.

He didn't move from his spot beside the door. I couldn't move either, but our mother was a frenzy of animation, her eyes crazy with joy. "Bobby, what a wonderful surprise," she said. "You're here, and Natalie and the children! Come in, come in."

Our mother, a dignified woman who did not laugh easily, was carrying on like a southern belle, giddy, flushed, scampering to the kitchen to gather refreshments. I went to my brother, throwing my arms around him. His clothes smelled of his unwashed life. His arms stayed at his side. As I pulled away, humiliated, terrified, he lightly touched the top of my hair.

"Sit," I said, pointing to the overstuffed easy chair. When he did, I realized he was in our father's chair.

"I can't believe you're here," I said. "What brings you? I mean to California," I added too quickly. As far as I knew, he still lived three states away in Idaho on land none of us had seen, purchased with his share of the inheritance from Dad.

"Research," he said, as if he still were the assistant professor he once had been.

I suspected he'd come to ask Mother for money.

"Julia," I said brightly, motioning to where she stood aloof, "come say hello to your uncle." I didn't add, although she knew, *and godfather*. She moved partway to stand beside me, a Victorian child in a fancy dress, long red hair down her back. She was clearly condemning, not of Bobby but of me. I hadn't provided her with an uncle like the ones other girls had.

"Hello," she said, afraid to approach him.

"Math is Julia's favorite subject," I chattered as if he were some friend of my mother's who'd dropped by unannounced.

"It is not," she said.

I turned to her. "You can watch TV in Gram's room."

Lilly toddled over, a red velvet cherub. She planted herself in front of Bobby, stuck a finger up her nose, and studied him. She was trying to get a reaction. The finger thing always worked at home, but Bobby barely looked at her.

"You my uncle?" she asked.

"And take your sister with you," I said to Julia, who hadn't moved from my side. Lilly protested as she was carted off, the only one of us in the room who wanted to stay.

I dropped to the couch across from him, my heart pounding. My brother gazed at the rug, his handsome face collapsed. I could see that his teeth hurt. His eyelashes were still long. I used to touch them. Make a butterfly, I used to say, and he would, batting them against my chubby fingers as I laughed.

"Why haven't you answered any of my letters?" My voice shook. I was afraid to hear him say he cared nothing about me, never had.

When he finally spoke, his voice surprised me. His answer took that long. "It's better that you don't write," he said.

I rubbed the face of my watch. Bobby had taught me to tell time. He let me wear his watch to school. Even then, the mechanics of hours and minutes meant nothing to him. He talked about trains in outer space, fathers younger than their children, the universe in the tip of a pencil.

All I could say aloud was "It's been so many years. Are you okay?"

There was another silence before he said, "I've made my choices."

Finally, my mother returned, pushing a mahogany trolley with a glass top. My parents had served their cocktails on that cart. As much as I had ever wanted anything, I wanted a drink right then, but instead the trolley held my mother's rose-patterned china coffeepot, the matching cups and saucers, and, incredibly, her three-tiered plate stuffed with cookies and chocolates.

"Black?" my mother asked Bobby. He didn't answer. "Black," she repeated cheerfully. "I taught all my children to drink their coffee black."

Bobby reached for the cup, his hand shaking—the same hand that had drawn me a map of the United States, from memory, freehand, as I watched. Every state line perfect. Every capital named. He was fourteen, two years away from being a National Merit Scholar. I was eight. Forty years later, I still had that map in my dresser drawer.

Bobby gulped his coffee as if he were freezing inside. My mother placed mine on the end table next to me, but I knew I could not lift the cup. I joined Bobby in staring at the rug as Mother kept on chattering. The rug was Oriental, large enough to fill the room, deep blue with black and red geometric flowers. We'd played trains on it, Bobby and I, his set handed down to me, with pieces of wood track that notched together, the trains going this way and that.

"Do you remember the trains?" I asked, using my hands to describe them.

When he didn't answer, I said, "I loved those trains." It was the closest I could get to telling him how I still felt, would always feel about him.

He stared at his lap, saying nothing, a ghost with warm breath. I wanted to plead: *tell me what happened to turn you into this strange person.* Instead I looked away, my eyes and throat burning. I was afraid of not being able to rise to my feet, but then I was up. "We have to go," I said.

My mother looked stricken. I realized, a moment too late, as I stood there, that she'd just been saying she didn't want Christmas presents from us, that this afternoon was her present, her oldest and youngest together, both of us visiting for no special reason.

There was nothing I could do. I couldn't stay. I collected the girls, who were more than ready to leave. We said good-bye to Gram, and made a show of saying good-bye to Uncle Bobby.

I stood above the chair where Bobby sat, his hands on his bony thighs, my father's chair. I leaned down, touched the side of his face, his gray stubble bristling my fingertips, and kissed him on the cheek.

My arms still wrapped around Julia, now dozing beside me in bed, I counted back. That kiss on the cheek was the last thing my brother and I had shared in six years.

Yet, Bobby was always in my life, in memory, in the waiting that I no longer recognized as waiting, in the dream of his return, my brother magically restored, everything as it should be.

chapter six

I WAS FIFTEEN MINUTES and two years late for a mammogram, flushed and breathing hard. My doctor's office had called to inform me about my two-year tardiness. Cowed, I accepted the first available appointment. Two days before Christmas vacation, I took the morning off from work.

I signed in at the reception desk and sat in a line of gray, padded armchairs. I tried to focus on all I had to do to get ready for Christmas. Lilly's doll was on the way, and I'd taken care of Eric's family, but I had nothing for Julia, Eric, or my mother. Sara and I no longer exchanged Christmas gifts since we'd given each other the exact same sweater four years ago and Sara said, "It's a sign to cut the crap." The last gift I had gotten Bobby was ten years ago. A flannel shirt. He'd sent it back unopened.

A television tuned to a morning talk show hung from the ceiling. A pair of high-cheeked, short-skirted women who were probably never late for their mammograms chatted on the set. I turned to the pile of magazines on the table next to me, chose a *Newsweek*, and flipped through its wrinkled pages. I stopped at a story about the Cal Bomber. Over twelve years, this terrorist with a grudge against the modern world had killed three California academics and maimed sixteen others. Fingers, hands, whole arms, parts of faces, eyes, ears gone. His latest attack so close to where Julia had been. I couldn't read any more. I put the magazine back.

A nurse in a flower-printed smock opened the door and called my name.

"Are you ready for Christmas?" she asked brightly as she squashed my right breast between the X-ray plates.

My eyes watered from the pain.

"Did everything look all right?" I asked when she was finished.

"Your doctor will notify you," she said.

I walked toward the door, holding my paper smock to keep it around me. "No," I said. "I'm not ready for Christmas."

It was ten thirty when I got home. I spooned chocolate ice cream from the carton. I didn't have cancer. I'd be ready for Christmas.

I thought of calling Eric just to hear his voice, to talk about nothing. We could plan dinner. But he was so busy. I had two hours before I had to be at work, just enough time to write some Christmas cards. I'd toss in a school picture of each girl. *Everyone doing well, no big news*. Tucked in with last year's cards, the ones I'd kept to answer this year, was Bobby's letter.

It wasn't addressed to me. My brother hadn't written me in fourteen years. I doubted he ever even thought of me anymore. But at the end of last year, he'd sent my mother a six-page missive in a tiny, cramped scrawl, detailing his thoughts about the assault of technology and the desecration of the environment six years before the approaching millennium. My mother had xeroxed it and sent it to Sara and me as if it were a Christmas letter from a brother in the army. I hadn't taken the time to more than glance it. All those nearly impossible-to-decipher words that told me nothing about how my brother was doing.

I needed to get going on the Christmas cards. I don't know why I started reading my brother's letter instead. Maybe it was out of guilt that I hadn't read it in the first place. Maybe it was out of the same old desire to find something I knew wasn't going to be there, even in a glimmer.

My brother began with complaints about his health, his creaky knees, his sensitive stomach, his failing eyesight. The inadequacy of drugstore eyeglasses. He moved on to the pettiness of daily life, his battle with the creatures who tried to eat his food, a chain that had broken on his bicycle. Halfway down the first page, possibly in response to something Mother had written him, he started to rant: *The California that you and Father claimed to believe in has been largely destroyed by its avaricious embrace of technology at the expense of its people and its environment.*

Then he dropped any pretense of a mother on the receiving end of his letter.

Modern society fueled by ever more rapid developing technology is killing the human race along with the planet we inhabit. While the actual demise of humankind is in the future, the psychological damage is already upon us. Technology does not serve us. It is our master.

There was so much in this vein that it was hard to keep going. *In a so-called classless society like America, socialization—following the orders of parents, teachers, bosses, and the like—is more insidious than in stratified societies. If you can't make it in America or its apotheosis, California, the problem must be yours. You need a shrink, medication that dumbs you down to living on the street.*

In places, Bobby's handwriting was impossible to read. He left out commas, any intimation of hope. He disdained politicians, the left and the right. He favored anything that made the world economy more fragile, more susceptible to meltdown.

He wrote that the entertainment industry was an arm of the power structure serving to keep modern man *in a mindless stupor of television, movies, and video/computer games more numbing than drugs.* He was convinced that the newest products of consumer technology were the most insidious—that home computers, the Internet, even car phones were poisoning our innermost lives.

I read and reread paragraphs that hovered on the edge of coherence. His words sounded right for a political treatise. Maybe I might even have agreed with some of them. But I wasn't interested in reading a discourse. What I wanted was Bobby.

My brother lived in the wilderness, liberated from the technology he hated, but he didn't sound free.

I rubbed my breast, still aching from the mammogram. I had to get to work. My students would be getting antsy. Even a half day with a sub stretched their tolerance for change in their routine.

I replaced my brother's letter in its envelope, stacked it with last year's cards, and put the whole heartbreaking mess away.

* * *

On the twenty-second of December, Julia got her SAT scores in the mail. I hadn't wanted her to take the test this early. She was only a sophomore. "Let up on yourself," I'd said.

"Mother, this isn't the seventies," she'd answered, pale with disgust, "when any idiot could get into college."

She opened the envelope in front of me, staring at her scores, her face unsmiling.

"It's only the first time you've taken the test," I said. Julia was always so hard on herself.

She thrust the report into my hand. "Thanks for your high opinion of me," she snorted. I saw the 800, and the 790. I should have yelped with joy, scooped her into my arms, but I was suddenly furious. I handed her back her scores. "Don't *ever* use that tone of voice with me again," I said.

Her eyes were huge, uncomprehending, filling with tears. "I'm sorry," she said.

I dropped into a chair at the dining table that was covered with the mess of Christmas wrap, red rolls, green.

"Mommy, please don't cry," Julia said at my side.

All I could get out was that I was sorry.

I was nine when the letter came for Bobby. It sat atop the mail on the kitchen table, where I was downing a peanut butter sandwich with milk. My mother kept glancing from the clock on the stove to the door.

"It looks like your scores came," she said when Bobby came through the kitchen door. He was fifteen with schoolbooks under his arm. I had no idea what scores she meant, only that my mother seemed to be restraining some excitement, or fear. Bobby dropped his books, took a swig from my glass, and tousled my hair. I didn't know if his casualness was real or if it had to do with the way our mother was trying not to behave.

He was center stage in a drama I didn't understand, but I studied him so I'd know how to act when my scores came. He opened the envelope, read what was inside without expression.

"About what I expected," he said.

"May I see?" my mother asked.

"Suit yourself." He tossed the letter on the table and left with his books. My mother looked at it, and then went after him. When she returned, I watched her do something I'd never seen her or anyone do before. She Scotch-taped Bobby's scores smack on the refrigerator door. His perfect, flawless scores.

chapter seven

As usual, my students returned from Christmas break apparently having forgotten everything they'd ever learned in my class. After four days of this, I could barely stand my own two kids. On the ride home from school, Julia sat up front slumping and complaining while Lilly whined in the backseat. I told them if they wanted dinner, they'd have to put up with a stop at the store, because there was no way we were having pizza. To underscore that I meant business, I took back control of the radio dial from Julia, and hit the preset for the news.

We all heard the report: Another bomb. Another professor dead.

He'd been the chairman of the department of chemical engineering at UCLA.

Earlier that afternoon, he'd opened a package addressed to him and been blown apart at his desk.

"Who would do something like that?" Julia's tone was angry, directed at me, as if I somehow had inside knowledge.

"Does *professor* mean the same thing as *teacher*?" Lilly asked from the backseat.

"No, they're different," I said, my look telling Julia not to contradict me. I drove past the grocery parking lot, suddenly too tired to face shopping and making dinner. "Let's skip the store," I said.

Eric was out of town and would be for another week. I ordered pizza and let the kids eat in front of television. I went upstairs and turned on the set at the foot of my bed.

Channel 4 had footage of the bombing at UCLA and a photo of the victim: a sandy-haired man with a trimmed beard, and a good-natured face too young for his fifty years.

There was a live news conference with the FBI agent heading the Cal Bomber task force. Although it was too early to definitively pronounce this new attack the work of the Cal Bomber, the agent said it appeared likely. Today's bomb was of the same type as past bombs connected to that individual. Both this bomb and the one at Stanford in November were sent through the mail.

"They both bore Sacramento postmarks," he said. It was if he'd said my name. Blood rushed in my ears. My throat closed.

It wasn't a conscious reaction, but I knew this sensation. Odorless and colorless, it bit my fingers and choked off my breath. But for every time my panic told the truth, it lied a thousand more. The nights Eric was late and I was sure he was dead; the moments I was certain someone had snatched one of the kids. But Eric always came home. The kids turned up, the tests came back negative, and every day thousands of people mailed packages from Sacramento. I tried to steady myself, longing for Eric to stride through the door. But he wasn't even reachable by phone right now. I turned off the set and dialed my sister.

"The holidays are over and it's not my birthday," Sara said when she heard my voice. "So what's up?"

"Did you hear? Are you watching the news?" I was speaking as if men with earphones were parked in a van outside the house.

Sara's voice carried genuine concern. "No. What's happened? Are you all right?"

I told her about the latest bombing. About the UCLA professor who'd been killed. How both this bomb and the one at Stanford had been mailed from Sacramento. "All of a sudden I had this terrifying thought that someone might think it was Bobby," I said.

Sara could dominate a conversation with her silence. I waited anxiously for her to tell me what I needed to hear. What she did was laugh.

"I think you've finally lost your mind," she said.

I considered the possibility that I'd gone overboard, feeling suddenly silly that I might have.

"I can't imagine anyone accusing Bobby of anything other than bad grooming," Sara said. "He hardly ever leaves his little lean-to. If Mom didn't send him money for shoes, he'd be going around barefoot."

"I know," I said. "I can go ages without thinking about Bobby, but a part of me is always afraid for him."

"Like a severed limb," Sara said. "Your body always knows it's missing."

I told her about finally reading Bobby's letter. "He's obsessed with technology, as if microwave ovens and cordless phones were a plot against mankind. It's like he's become one of those people who wear tinfoil on their head." I stopped for breath. "Then there's all this terrible news about the Cal Bomber blowing people up because *he's* against technology."

"Antitechnology is a movement, Natalie. It's tied up with ecoterrorism. You might not have heard about it, most people probably haven't, but it's out there." My sister spoke knowingly, but without condescension. "You can buy the Cal Bomber's manifesto at a bookstore. I read it when it was published in the newspaper last year. Some of it makes a lot of sense."

I didn't know why I was so surprised. Maybe it was because until the Stanford bombing, I'd paid zero attention to the Cal Bomber.

"The manifesto reads like it was written by more than one person, some fringe group of the environmental movement," Sara said. "Bobby might agree with them in principle. He might read their literature. Maybe he goes to the library and reads their Internet postings. But anyone who spends two seconds with Bobby would know he's not capable of joining any group. The most he is ever going to do is rant and rave in a letter to his mommy. It's sad, but true."

My sister and I shared little but this sadness that bound us. "It's not like he has a phone and we can call him," I said. "We don't even know where he lives."

"That's the way he wants it. He's dug his hole and he's living in it."

"He needs help, Sara."

"I know that," Sara said. "But he doesn't want our help. He's made that clear."

"Maybe we should make one more push. We could fly out there, rent a car, and try to find him," I said. "Show him how much we care."

"Sure, like he has friends in town who'd point the way? Or maybe we could just hang around the post office all day, every day for a month or so until he collected his mail and then pounce on him."

I didn't answer. There was no need. It was always like this with Bobby, the same circular impossibility. He did not respond to the only way we had of reaching him, a postal box. He had long ago let go of us, and yet we still clung to him.

HAD ERIC been home, instead of away on yet another business trip, I would have fallen asleep, resting my hand over the rise of his shoulder, my fingers warmed by the T-shirt he wore to bed in winter. I would not have gotten out of bed, not drunk a glass of wine. I would not have written to Bobby.

I pictured my brother as he looked when I last saw him six years ago, thin, wild-haired, and broken. I would write nothing personal, nothing sentimental, and make no demands. I would reach out to him on his own fragile terms and give him no reason to stop reading.

I wrote that I'd been thinking about the letter he'd sent our mother, the one about the impact of technology on mankind and the environment. I said that I'd like to start a written conversation about it, to deepen my own thinking. I enclosed a fifty-dollar check for postage and whatever else he might need. I ended with *love, Natalie.*

I mailed the letter in the morning, but I knew Bobby would never answer it. I doubted he'd even open it.

chapter eight

I NEVER WANTED to have the smartest baby in the nursery. I'd seen what the burden of a gifted mind had done to my brother. Julia talked in sentences at a year old. At eighteen months, she awoke shrieking every night, pleading with me not to hurt her. Eric was away on a trial that wouldn't end. I took Julia to the pediatrician.

"She's a brilliant child with nightmares to match," she said as if it were no big deal.

Bobby was living in Oregon at the time, working as a janitor. He didn't have a phone but we exchanged letters. Mine were humdrum and tinged with self-pity. I was a new mother with a toddler who never slept and a husband who worked all the time. Bobby wrote diatribes. He ranted for pages about a mechanistic civilization that robbed even the earth we trod on of dignity and the educational system that made this outrage possible. I thought it was my fault that I couldn't grasp what he was saying.

Once, he confided that he was lonely, that he'd seen even morons and the grossly obese with girlfriends, and didn't understand why it was so hard for him. At least this was something I understood, something I could offer in return. I wrote back that it was hard for everyone and to give it time.

Then mysteriously, he was back in California, staying at our family's cabin in Gold Run. He was so much closer, yet he wouldn't connect the phone or answer my letters.

"He's exhausted," my mother said. "He needs time to rest."

My father shrugged. "It's his business if he wants to act like a weirdo." It was the first time I'd ever heard anyone in my family suggest Bobby was strange. I didn't like it. It made me side with my mother.

"He has no patience for your bourgeois life," Sara said as if she couldn't blame him. He wasn't contacting her either, but she took it in stride.

I bought him a book for his birthday, Schopenhauer, *The World as Will and Idea*. He'd mentioned once in a letter wanting a copy.

It came back in the mail, *return to sender* scrawled on it. I felt as if the wind had been knocked out of me. I couldn't let that go. I put Julia in her car seat and drove two hours to Gold Run.

The cabin looked uninhabited, the curtains drawn. I knocked, not knowing what I'd say when, or if, he answered. When there was no response, I tried my key. The door was bolted from the inside. I pounded on it, yelling that it was me. Julia in my arms, I walked through foliage and weeds, rapping on the windows, pleading with him to let me in.

I panicked. What if he was hurt? "I'm calling the fire department," I yelled.

A curtain at the window moved. I caught a glimpse of a face, gaunt and unshaven. I jumped.

"Bobby," I said, my heart making a racket in my chest.

The door opened a crack. An eye squinted against the light. "Bobby," I repeated. I shifted Julia into my other arm. His gaze dropped to her, stayed there.

"Go away," he said. "Now."

I didn't know his voice. I was already stepping back, my baby in my arms. He slammed the door in my face. I put Julia in the car and drove away.

I wrote to him again. *What have I done? I'll leave you alone if you tell me what I've done.*

He wrote back immediately. I was so frightened when the letter arrived that I let it sit an hour before I opened it. I sensed it was reckless of me to read it, alone in the house with a sleepless child, but I could not wait until Eric returned from his trip.

There were two pages scrawled in red ink. The letter did not begin *Dear Natalie.* It just started, as if in midthought. He said that there was nothing between us. That he'd felt a fond protectiveness for me when I was small, but that, too, had been a burden. His own childhood was miserable, he admitted, but at least he'd been wanted. By contrast, I was an afterthought to the family, an accident like dust blowing into a window left open, an unloved girl with a crush on her big brother. There was a time when he'd had hopes for me. I was smarter than Sara. More caring, more truthful than our parents. He had been proud of me when I went to Paris, when I lived in a little room with no water and read Camus and Sartre, cleaning houses to support myself. But I did less than nothing with all that. I'd come home, married a lawyer, and become a breeder.

He wrote that if he'd had any inkling of who Eric was, he never would've consented to come to Julia's christening. He said I'd remade myself into the servant of a man whose job was to defend the corporations that pillaged the poor. I had become the Frau who irons the brown shirt, polishes the black boot.

My hands shook, and for a moment that was all that interested me, a pair of shaking hands, clutching rustling paper. I dropped the pages on the floor.

I wanted to tear them up, throw them away, but I forced myself to keep them because I was sure they couldn't have said what I thought they said. I picked the pages off the floor, shoved them in the envelope, and placed it far back in a drawer in the dining room buffet.

When Eric returned, I didn't tell him about Bobby's letter or going to the family cabin. The first day he was back, we went shopping and bought an expensive stroller for Julia. I'd wanted these things. A safe car, a sturdy stroller, a pretty crib, a perfect nursery for my baby girl, her outfits folded lovingly in her white bureau, the little dresses hung on tiny hangers.

I never told anyone about Bobby's letter. Not even my parents. Telling the story would have made it real. Eventually I threw the letter away without ever looking at it again.

We were a young American family. When we took Julia for a walk, people smiling and fussing over her, I felt there was nothing wrong with me or the stroller we had bought.

chapter nine

BOBBY ONCE TOLD ME that when he was working trying to solve a math problem, he could not stop thinking about it. He analyzed it day and night, took it apart in his head, and started over. I was different. I could lose myself in the everyday. I could push things out of my mind.

The first morning in March, Lilly bounded into my bedroom in her flannel nightgown. "Rabbit, rabbit," she shouted. She climbed into bed with me, the only brown-eyed one of the four of us. "Now you have to say it," she said.

I put my arms around her, and said it. Rabbit, rabbit.

At work, I had an easy morning. Once my students were safely in art class, I headed for the teachers' lounge. Our lounge wasn't much, just a small room in the back of the office with a couch we had to share with sick kids, a small Formica table, a sink, a coffeepot, and—on a good day—a box of Girl Scout cookies in the refrigerator.

The outer office was so oddly quiet that I bypassed the lounge to peek into Claire's office. She was our principal, as well as my good friend. The secretary was inside with Claire and the gym teacher. Heads down, arms identically crossed, they were gathered around a radio in alarming stillness. Whatever this news was, I didn't want to hear it. I had the crazy thought that I could just back away unnoticed and return to some previous point where everything was fine.

Claire looked up, saw me, and reached out an arm. "It's terrible," she said, leaving me no choice but to go forward. "There's been an explosion on Hearst. They think there might have been a bomb."

"That's not possible," I said absurdly, the pounding of my heart telling me that it was, the sound of it as loud as the news. An off-campus office of the university completely destroyed. Less than a mile from where we stood. Three people dead. Almost certainly a bomb. The earmark of the Cal Bomber.

I knew I wasn't well. I saw it in Claire's face. She pushed me into a chair, holding my shoulder to keep me from falling, but I'd already fallen. Everything else was just senseless movement.

I heard my voice, high, false, and lying. I had the flu but I could drive myself home. Someone turned off the news. The drama was all mine now. The secretary brought me a cold cloth. Claire said she'd take my class, and find a ride home for Lilly.

I left without my jacket. The weather was brisk, on the verge of rain, and the bite in the air steadied me. I had become a person who panicked at every disaster. I'd go home, drink a glass of juice, and lie down.

Instead I drove to the library on Shattuck and parked in the lot. When I got out of the car, I smelled smoke from the explosion. I was no more than a ten-minute walk from the site.

This time I wouldn't phone my sister. I'd find what I needed to free my mind on my own. I copied articles from the *Chronicle*, the *Los Angeles Times*, the *New York Times*, the *Sacramento Bee*, *Newsweek*, and *Time*. I printed the Cal Bomber's manifesto.

At home, I shoved the mail off the dining room table onto the floor. I laid out the manifesto, forty pages, single spaced, and started to read it word by word.

It began with a simple thesis. *The past two centuries have been a catastrophe for mankind.* I could, at least partly, agree with that—world wars, genocide, terrorism, environmental damage to the planet. But I soon grasped that the Cal Bomber was focused elsewhere: *Technology has taken man off the land, crowded him into urban areas, separated him from the products of his own labor, left him at the whims of an econ-*

omy run by and for the elites who manipulate the forces of technology for their own ends.

It was all so nightmarishly familiar. I thought of getting up for water, turning on the news, but I refused to stop reading. When my eyes glanced past a sentence, I brought them back, made myself absorb what I had to absorb, forced myself to look. I took notes.

As hard as life was for primitive man, he was not helpless. He could fight for his self-defense, his food, his mate. He was not alone.

Not alone the way my brother was.

I felt shaky when I rose from the table to retrieve Bobby's year-old letter. When I sat back down, I laid the letter beside the manifesto, the pages touching.

Modern man lives in a world in which relatively few people make the decisions for everyone. To put up with this, he must be "socialized." He must be conditioned to follow the rules of authority figures who themselves have been socialized to follow the rules.

Socialization. Technology. I had to be imagining that words seemed to leap from the manifesto to Bobby's letter and back.

Modern man has no dignity, no autonomy. His life is filled with work that has no meaning. His mind is pulverized by the entertainment industry that is the handmaiden of technological society.

I ran my finger from the manifesto to the nearly identical sentence in Bobby's letter: *Now we have an entertainment industry that is an arm of the technological, political system.*

I could barely breathe but I didn't stop reading.

The light pollution produced by massive urbanization does more than blind us to the stars, it takes away humanity's compass. The noise of civilization makes us deaf to the sound of nature and the call of our own souls.

I remembered a hike. I was about nine years old, Bobby fifteen. The two of us must have trekked three miles to a still spot in the Yuba. I was hot and tired but what struck me was the silence. The only sounds came from birds, insects, and the rustling trees. We stood listening for I don't know how long, no words passing between us. "Now you know all that is being lost to the noise of the world," my brother said.

Contrary to accepted theory, people do not come to accept repeated lies as the truth. Rather, the endless repetition of official lies produces indifference. People still know truth from lies, but they are too numb to do anything about it, or even care.

I had tried to imagine my brother's cabin many times. But now I saw it as it must have been, a miner's shack for a man who was not a miner but a PhD. No bathroom, no kitchen, dirt floor, walls of rough planks, a kerosene lamp overhead, maybe one on the small table where he might have written those words.

The phone rang but I didn't answer it. It was nearly three o'clock when I rose from the heavy oak table where Bobby, Sara, and I had eaten dinner all the years of our childhood. I felt dazed as I put the bomber's manifesto and my brother's letter in a manila folder, together. As I was unlocking my car in the front of the house, a strange van pulled up and Lilly got out. "Where are you going?" she demanded. She looked suspicious, and I knew she knew I'd forgotten about her.

The mother who'd driven Lilly home called out to me from the window of her Suburban. "Are you feeling better?" I nodded, trying to smile as she drove off.

"I'm not going anywhere," I said to Lilly despite the fact that I wore a coat and my keys hung from the door lock of my car.

We climbed the stairs, Lilly looking grim. I removed my coat and tried to pretend it was any of the Wednesdays of our old life. I asked about her day while I threw together a salad, but Lilly would have none it.

I sat down next to her. "Where were you going?" she asked. Her hair curled gently around her face but her voice was hard.

"Nowhere," I lied. "I was just getting something from the car. But I do have to go out when Julia comes home."

"Can I come with you?" She wasn't asking. She was confirming her suspicions.

"Not this time," I said, trying to keep my voice light.

"I didn't think so," she said. I reached to pull her close, but she turned away, jumping up to leave me alone in the kitchen.

When Julia got home a half hour later, I gave her money for pizza, and put my coat back on. "Watch your sister," I said, picking up the manila folder. "I have to run an errand in the city."

I took the BART train to San Francisco. In the Montgomery station, I picked up the afternoon *Examiner* with its grisly headline, THREE DEAD IN BERKELEY BOMBING, and tucked it into my coat with the manila folder. I surfaced without an umbrella into a cold, hard rain. Ahead of me, two blocks up Montgomery, was the glass tower that held the law firm of Sterling, Talbot. The rain was drenching my hair and neck, but I barely noticed.

chapter ten

I HAD NEVER shown up unexpected at Eric's office during business hours, though the girls and I occasionally dropped by on weekends when we were in the city. The guard in the lobby would wave us past, and we'd breeze up fourteen floors, through mahogany double doors, past floral displays the Ritz would envy, strolling down the plush corridors as if we owned the place. Now, as I tried to skirt around the firm's circular reception desk, a woman stepped out from behind it.

"May I help you?" Her words were right but her look said a woman with sopping hair and a file folder hidden under her coat had to be stopped, possibly escorted out the door. I explained that I was Eric's wife, and saw the flicker of surprise in her eyes.

The door to his office was open. He sat at his desk, a mess of papers spread in front of him, speaking to but not looking at the young woman who stood above him. She had long straight hair and wore a sleek, short skirt. The two of them could have been having an affair for all I knew. All those weekends and late hours. But even as I thought it, I knew it wasn't true. Eric wasn't the one in our marriage who kept secrets.

In his surprise, Eric seemed first pleased to see me, then concerned. He remembered to introduce me to the young associate at his side, an engagement ring weighted with diamonds on her finger.

When she left, Eric shut the door behind her. "What's wrong?" he asked.

"You didn't hear the news?"

"What news?" Eric's voice rose in alarm. "I've been holed up in here all day."

I handed him the newspaper. "I'm terrified my brother did it," I said, sounding absurd even to myself. "That he's the Cal Bomber, or that he's involved in it in some way." I took the folder out of my coat. "It's all in here."

Eric seemed to be containing his skepticism for my benefit. "Let's see what you've got," he said as if he were a physician about to examine an X-ray. He carried my folder to the small conference table in the corner.

Eric brought material home from work that looked like the phone book. He read it the way I did novels, shutting out the world. Now he read what was in the folder the same way.

I sat next to him at the table, my hand lightly on his thigh, but he could have been alone. I looked out the window. On the street below, people emerged from buildings, pushed up umbrellas, and hurried to wherever they had to go. I didn't remember walking on the street, how I'd arrived at this building.

I've always been prone to exaggeration: a pimple becomes melanoma, a forgotten anniversary is the end of our marriage. Yet as I waited for him to finish, his mouth growing tight, I knew my husband wasn't going to tell me what I so desperately wanted to hear.

Eric didn't answer the phone when it buzzed. Still in my coat, I circled his office, looking at the framed photos of the kids, the little knickknacks they'd constructed from clay and cardboard. *I made it for your paper clips, Daddy.* There was a photo I hadn't seen before. Eric glancing adoringly at a tall, good-looking redhead in a gold-colored dress. It took me a moment to recognize that the woman was me. The picture had been taken at the firm Christmas party, just three months before.

Eric took off his half glasses, and pinched his nose. "I don't like this," he said. "Not at all."

I couldn't move. This wasn't right. Eric was supposed to argue against overreacting. If he wasn't going to, I'd say it for him. "In his letter, he told Mom to read some antitechnology book. We know he goes to the library. He's probably using the Internet, lifting ideas, maybe posting his own. Sara thinks . . ."

I stopped. Eric's eyes were astonished. I saw the hurt in them, and then dawning anger.

"You've talked to Sara about this?"

Suddenly I was floundering. "I heard something on the news about there being a Sacramento postmark on a couple of the mail bombs. I called Sara."

"When? When did you talk to her?"

Everything was all wrong. Eric was here to tell me that my latest drama was baseless, that this was not what I thought it was, that it could wait until tomorrow or next week. I wanted this so much that it didn't occur to me to shade the truth.

"It was a while ago," I said.

"A *while* ago?"

I should have taken a moment to think, but I was so frantic for absolution I told him straight out. "After that UCLA professor got killed in January."

Eric looked as if he didn't recognize me. "You had suspicions your brother could be the bomber two months ago? You've kept this from me all this time?"

"No, no," I protested, "I didn't keep it from you." But anyone could see I had. "It wasn't like that." I was flailing, desperate to make my betrayal understandable. "I never *believed* my brother was the bomber. I was afraid that someone might think he was because of his philosophy. I wanted to reach out to him again even though I knew it was hopeless. I wrote him. I thought maybe if I showed him that I cared about his ideas . . ."

"Oh, Jesus," Eric said, dropping his head into his hands. "You've been in touch with your brother about this." When he looked up, I saw darkness in his eyes. "If Bobby turns out to be this guy, the fact that you wrote him now could look like you were tipping him off, trying to help him avoid suspicion." Eric rubbed his face. "That could mean criminal charges."

"But that's ludicrous. I never heard back from him. And I didn't say that people might think he was the bomber, just that I was interested in his ideas about technology and the environment. He probably threw the letter away."

Eric held up his hands. "I need to know when you first suspected." He spoke as if we were in court. "The first time you made any sort of link between the Cal Bomber and your brother."

I stammered about coming across Bobby's letter when I was going to write Christmas cards, the same day I'd read about the Cal Bomber in a magazine. That I'd read his letter, but that I hadn't made any connection.

He stood, his back to the table, his voice so quiet, so impersonal it made me want to cry. "So that was December."

He faced away from me. Neither of us moved in the long silence. "I think we should talk to Stu," he said finally.

Stu was our friend, one of the few of my husband's partners that I actually liked. I told myself that he was going to come down the corridor on his small feet, a short, fat man with a skewed sense of the world, and convince us all we needed was some Italian food.

He came in smiling, and I had to bend for his kiss. I'd always enjoyed his friendly attraction to me, liked it when he sat with me at firm parties, listening to my stories and laughing at my jokes.

When he saw Eric, he stopped smiling. Until that moment, I'd held on to the hope that someone bigger, taller, shorter, fatter would take my clammy hand in his dry one and say, *Natalie, you've let your imagination run away with you.* Now I understood. Eric hadn't asked Stu to come here because he was our *friend*. Stu headed the firm's white-collar crime practice. This was not just about my brother. This was about me knowing or not knowing that my brother might be part of something that had led to the death of three people this morning.

Eric had gotten me a lawyer.

Stu sat at the conference table, reading the manifesto and the letter that seemed to link Bobby to it. At his desk, Eric looked down at his work, but I doubted he saw anything. I crossed and uncrossed my legs on the brown leather couch I'd helped Eric pick out when he first became a partner at the firm. When Stu finished, he and Eric spoke to each other as if I weren't there. They spoke in the same way the doctors did as my father lay dying, as if their language shielded them from the pain of that room and the sight of me. They were discussing how best to get this information to federal authorities.

"I understand that you want to protect me," I interrupted, looking first to Stu then Eric. "But I'm not turning my only brother over to the FBI on the basis of a single letter containing ideas he copied from the library." I folded my arms. "I'm sorry, but I won't do it, not today. I need to think this through, to talk it over with my mother and Sara. Maybe they know something that can help explain it all away. I owe it to my family to give them a chance."

Eric turned to Stu. "Can we wait?" he said.

I was grateful he had not said what he could have. Instead, Stu said it, softly, without accusation. I *had* waited and now three more people were dead. If I'd come forward sooner, would those people still be alive? I couldn't bear the thought, any more than I could accept that Bobby had anything to do with their deaths.

"Natalie," Stu said gently, his eyes on mine. "I understand how hard this must be for you. But in light of the fact that you were concerned enough that someone might think your brother was the Cal Bomber to talk to your sister and then to write your brother for the first time in years, a letter that could still be in his house, that could be construed as trying to tip him off . . ." He paused, as if to let this settle in. "I'm advising you, as an attorney, and as your friend, to go forward with your information now."

His meaning was clear. In reaching out to my brother, I had damned him.

I stared at my lap. Stu and Eric understood my silence for the capitulation it was. Stu made his phone calls from the club chair in front of Eric's desk. Eric looked down at his desk, at Stu, anywhere but at me.

At the same time, I understood that I wasn't just any person in trouble. I was in my husband's office on the fourteenth floor of the oldest and most prestigious law firm in San Francisco with a former assistant U.S. attorney at my side. Once the FBI knocked on his door, who would Bobby have?

Eric phoned home to check on the girls while Stu coached me on how to answer the agents' questions. The FBI arrived within the hour, two men in nice suits; they could have been on television. I looked at my watch. It was seven thirty.

We sat in the gilded conference room of the law firm whose clients included the university where that morning a bomb had blown three people apart. We had clear demands: My name must be kept from the public. I insisted they guarantee that the government would not seek the death penalty if it turned out Bobby was guilty. They all but swore to the first, and led us to believe they could do the second.

I answered their questions as narrowly as Stu had coached me. I did not mention my conversation with Sara or my correspondence with Bobby. I assured the agents that my brother would never do such a thing, that I was certain he was innocent, and that his mental health was fragile. I had come to them because three people had died this morning. I had to do whatever I could to make sure the real people responsible were found.

"Bobby is the most gentle soul I've ever known," I said, my eyes pleading. "If he ever learned I'd talked to you, he'd be devastated." I didn't want to cry, but I couldn't help it.

They said it was unlikely that my brother was the man they were looking for. But no matter what, he would never know I talked to them. They gave us their word.

IT WAS after nine when Eric and I got in his car and headed home. We drove in silence. I glanced at him a few times, but he never looked back. How many parties had we driven home from deconstructing the evening down to the canapés? Now he had nothing to say to me, and I had said enough around that conference table to last a lifetime.

He dropped me at my car at the BART station. "I'm going to the store," he said. "We need a few things."

I nodded. It was his way of saying that he didn't want to go home right now.

"Where have you been?" Julia demanded when I got back to the house, her arms folded sternly against her chest.

It was ten o'clock. My seven-year-old was still in her clothes watching television. My teenager looked as if she wanted to send me to my room. My husband hadn't come home with me.

"You were gone like six hours," Julia said. She was so exasperated with me, so frightened, she seemed ready to cry.

I said I was sorry, that it couldn't have been helped.

"There was a bomb in Berkeley," Lilly said.

"I know, honey," I said. "But it can't hurt us." I shut off the television, and told the girls to get ready for bed. The next day either Eric or I would have to drive them to school. Eric and I would have to go back to our jobs, pretending that nothing was wrong. As sure as I was that they'd realize he was innocent, I couldn't bear the thought that my mother and Sara—and oh God, Bobby—might learn that I'd gone to the FBI about him.

I went to Lilly's room. She wanted a bedtime story, and I told her a lie, a story in which everything turned out all right in the end.

I SAT ON the edge of my bed, still unmade from this morning, and rewound the day. If only I'd stayed in the classroom, I might not have heard the news. I might never have gone to Eric's office. What had I done?

I went downstairs and filled a glass with red wine from an open bottle in the refrigerator. The glass slipped from my hand and shattered against the floor. I got on my knees to pick up the shards, and cut my finger. I bandaged it, mopped the entire floor. Then I sat at the pine table and waited for Eric.

He came home at twelve thirty carrying a single plastic grocery bag from Safeway.

"It smells like a winery in here," he said. I watched him unpack his groceries, a gallon of milk we didn't need, a box of wheat crackers, a twelve-pack of double-A batteries, and a bag of apples.

"Please don't ignore me," I said.

"I've been driving," he said, still not looking at me. "Just driving." He slumped into a chair. Years of bending toward others had made him slightly stooped. He didn't look like the same man I'd interrupted at work this afternoon.

"What I can't understand," he said, "is why, in all this time, you never mentioned any of this to me." He spread his hands to show his incomprehension in the face of my betrayal. "I know the life story of every kid in your class, Natalie."

"It was too preposterous," I said. "It still is."

He shook his head. "You deliberately kept this from me for weeks. Omitted it from every conversation we had at this table, on the couch, in our bed. You talked to your sister but not to me." His fist came down on the pine table. "My God, Natalie, half my work comes from the University of California, and you never thought to mention any of this to me until you showed up at my office today?"

I had no defense, only this insight: "I suppose, down deep, I was afraid that if I told you, it might make it more than just wild paranoia. It might make it real."

Eric had always been there for me, been on my side in every argument with the world. I waited for a signal that he understood, but he didn't speak.

"Please try to understand," I said, touching his knee. "Bobby's not some abstract person. He's my big brother. He held Julia in his arms at her christening."

I tried to find the man who adored me in Eric's eyes but he looked away. "I've got to get some sleep," he said, rising from his chair.

chapter eleven

THE CHRISTENING had been something Eric's mother wanted, and Eric, too, on some level. I went along. It was a chance to get dressed up, unite my family, and show off my new baby.

Bobby was back from Guatemala, working as a janitor. He hadn't wanted anything to do with the christening. "Those rituals have the blood of millions of innocent people on them," he said.

"The ceremony means nothing to me," I pleaded. "But you being my baby's godfather means everything."

He caved, as I knew he would. I didn't ask him for much, but when I did back then, I knew he'd never let me down.

They all came. My dashing father, still solid in build, imposing in his height—the cancer that would kill him a barely mutating cell—told me how proud he was. My mother feigned interest in my mother-in-law's windy history of the christening gown. Sara had resisted showing up at what she called the Macy's Day Charade, but she eventually did, stoned and wearing an overstated hat with flowers on the band.

Bobby looked gaunt in a suit my mother had bought him, his dark hair brushing his collar. With my whole family in the same place, my big brother at my side, I was ridiculously happy. My baby who kept me up all night, who made me frantic with self-doubt, had brought us all together.

My father, who could deliver a sermon with a baritone that would put the minister to shame, sat in the second row, believing not in God but in the power of churches to deliver votes. My mother sat next to him, her face beaming, her family together for what I now know would be the last time.

Bobby stood beside me at the font, surrounded by symbols that pained him, holding Julia with heartbreaking gentleness. He was doing it for me. It was the last thing he would ever do for me.

I AWOKE in tangled sheets. For a moment, still half asleep, I couldn't remember what was wrong. A second later, fully awake, I knew.

Eric had already left for work. I heard Julia in the shower. I sat up. Nothing in my bedroom had changed. There was no hole blown out of the wall, no blood on the floor.

I cannot do it, I thought. I cannot get up, dress, make breakfast, and go back to work. But I did. Eric had left the *Chronicle*, still in its rubber band, on the kitchen table. I made myself open it. The victims of the Cal Bomber's latest rampage stared at me. The oldest was twenty-eight. The luminous-faced girl was four years older than Julia.

I turned the newspaper facedown. Upstairs, Julia ran for the ringing phone. I couldn't hear what she saying, just the excited tone reserved for friends. I had the crazy thought that if I flipped the newspaper back over, it might have another front page with news of a different yesterday. A yesterday in which those three young people were alive, and I had not betrayed my brother to the FBI.

On the drive to school, I had to slam on my brakes to avoid rear-ending a car.

"What are you trying to do, kill us?" Julia cried.

When I pulled up to her school, she ran off from us in her usual manner, unaware of anything outside her own head. But Lilly was uncommonly silent. She took my hand when we got out of the car at Mountaintop.

"Mommy, are you all right?" she asked.

"Yes," I said, wondering how much longer I could lie to her. I didn't know if she even believed me.

"I've been worried about you," Claire said when I checked in at the office. My closest friend, the one to whom I could confide almost anything. "You looked so pale yesterday. I tried calling you."

I had to answer her, to come up with some sort of decision. Was I sick, or well? Just dropping Lilly off, or working?

"Natalie? Are you feeling okay?"

I said I was, but I couldn't look at her. Claire and I told each other all sorts of things. We didn't sugarcoat our feelings about thoughtless friends, thankless children, and the young school parents who thought they knew more than we did. We weren't afraid to joke about our own shortcomings. We'd never pretended our families were perfect, but I couldn't tell her this.

MY SENSES were so acute that I could barely tolerate the brilliance of fluorescent lighting in my classroom, the buzz of it in my ears, but I was a person who knew how to do a job. Although they try to convince you otherwise, children require order—circle time, math, break. I, too, clung to that order.

At the store with Lilly after school, I leaned over the meat cooler, staring at the flesh in plastic wrap, telling myself that the FBI would find that the only crime Bobby had committed was plagiarism. When I turned around, Lilly was lying on the floor, tears streaming.

"What's wrong?" She didn't look as if she'd been hurt.

"You don't listen to me," she said.

I got her off the grocery-store linoleum, and coaxed her to tell me what I hadn't heard before: her friends had moved up to the next reader and she'd had to stay behind.

"I'm sorry, Mommy, I'm not smart," she said.

I moved us out of the cart traffic. Learning to read was complicated, there was so much to it. "I'm a teacher and I know who's smart and who isn't, and you're smart," I told her. "You're every bit as smart as I was at your age, as smart as your dad."

I didn't say as smart as Julia. None of us was even close to her. Except Bobby.

When we got home, I left the groceries in sacks on the kitchen floor and opened a bottle of beer. The more I swallowed, the longer I left the groceries, the better I began to feel about yesterday's meeting with the FBI. They hadn't behaved as if we'd solved their case, as if our information was as devastating as we imagined. Bobby might never even learn he was under suspicion.

I watched the local news at five. Channel 7 was airing an interview with the wife of the young Indian professor killed in the Berkeley blast. She sat with a child in her lap, another clinging to her side. "The children want to know why their father isn't coming home," she said.

My throat closed and tears burned my eyes. I turned channels, searching for footage of federal agents in flak jackets breaking down my brother's cabin door. I flipped from one news show to the next.

"What's with you?" Julia asked. "You're watching TV all bug-eyed."

I clicked off the set as if I'd been caught viewing porno. Julia picked up the remote and changed the channel to one of her shows. Suddenly I felt grateful for the way kid life blotted out everything else. I finished making dinner, and fed the girls. I jumped when the phone rang, but it was just one of Julia's friends. I gave Lilly a bath, put her to bed, and then lay beside her when she asked.

Eric came home at ten to nine. "It smells good," he said. He walked to the stove, peering into the copper pot. "You didn't have to do this, Nat."

"I wanted to."

He slumped into a chair. "Where are the girls?"

"Lilly's in bed," I said, handing him a glass of the good wine I'd opened. I dropped into a chair beside him. "Julia's holed up in her room."

For a ludicrous moment, I thought one or the other of us might say, *So how was your day?*

Eric gazed into his glass. "Stu talked to his buddy at the Bureau."

One of the things I'd always admired about Eric was that, given half a chance, he went straight to the point.

He looked up. "They don't think Bobby's their man."

This is what I'd been waiting to hear, praying to hear. Now I was certain I'd known it all along. I felt the lifting of weight, the glimmer of normal life ahead. But Eric's expression, still quietly grim, made me cautious.

"He doesn't fit their profile," he said. "They're looking for a younger man, someone of average intelligence without a college education. They're going to investigate, but they're not on fire. Over the past twelve years, they've had four thousand leads on this case that have gone nowhere."

Four thousand false leads, each one of them given by someone as sure and as terrified as I had been. "I knew it," I said. "I knew it couldn't be Bobby."

I was so desperate to have everything be all right that it clouded my head. I was expecting Eric to apologize for railroading us into talking to the FBI.

"I'm not saying this isn't good news," Eric said, sounding like it wasn't.

I stiffened. "But?"

"At this point, I think you and I have to assume that it *is* Bobby."

"I don't get it," I said, my voice rising. "You just said it's not him."

"If there's a one-in-a-thousand chance that he's the guy . . ." he said. "Or if he knows that guy, then for safety's sake, we have to make sure he never finds out we talked to the FBI."

Instantly I was on my feet. "Bobby would never hurt me or my children," I said, hitting the *my* hard in anger. "He'd never hurt anyone. That's how I know it's not him." Then I was crying, wiping my eyes with the back of my hands. I turned away from Eric. He came up behind me, held my shoulders.

"Bobby can't ever know I'd accuse him like that," I said. "It would destroy him. They'd never tell him, would they, the FBI? They promised not to reveal our identity. They'll just investigate, clear him, and move on without giving him any details, right?"

"I'm talking about us." He said us but I knew he meant me. "Don't say anything to your mother or Sara."

I turned around. "You think I want them to know what we've done to Bobby?" I held my gaze on Eric, made him look away.

That night I saw my father in a dream. He stood in the hall of our old house. He wore his tortoiseshell glasses, his gray summer suit with the vest, his hair still dark. I threw my arms around him, felt the light wool of his jacket on my cheek. He smelled of Mennen Skin Bracer in the green bottle, but he did not speak to me. He would not tell me what I needed to hear: that everything was going to turn out all right.

I awoke crying. Although it was cool in the bedroom, my nightgown was damp and sticking to me. Eric was on the other side of the bed, and either he or I, in our sleep, had put a pillow between us.

chapter twelve

WHEN WE FIRST MET, our senior year of college, Eric was a football player, and the only sport that interested me was conversation. All we had in common was an evening class and the rides home he offered me. He drove a boxy Toyota with a stick shift rising from the floor. I'd never seen anyone drive like him—as if his hands and feet were part of the mechanism of the car. I told him as much because it was true. But I wasn't flirting. I had a boyfriend.

There was an out-of-fashion directness to Eric's good looks. Cut off his shaggy blond hair, and I could see him going off to World War I. I enjoyed looking at him, studying him the way a child might.

Our class ended on a cold night in spring. On the ride home we were more serious than usual—we had the specter of graduation hanging over us. Neither of us had any idea what we wanted to do. Eric had Vietnam and the draft to worry about.

He parked the car on the curb opposite the house on Dana Street where my boyfriend and I shared an apartment on the first floor. The lights were on in our place and I could see into the living room. Ron would be inside waiting for me, our dishes from the past week piled high in the sink, a pot with burned brown rice on the stove.

"Have you ever thrown out a perfectly good pot just because you didn't want to wash it?" I asked.

"Sure," Eric said easily. "Everybody has."

His arms and legs were long and solid. He wore a corduroy jacket over a blue work shirt tucked into jeans. I was twenty-two and thought it seemed like a grown-up outfit, as if he were already halfway out in the world. I huddled in a pea coat, jeans, and a sweater. He reached his arm across the back of the seat, and I had the crazy idea that he was thinking of kissing me. I looked over his shoulder and saw Ron walking through our living room. I hadn't realized how easy it was to see inside our house from the street.

Eric asked about the paper I'd written for our class. As he listened, he absently fingered a wayward strand of my hair. Then his lips were softly on mine, and I was kissing him back. He unbuttoned my coat, and I slipped out of it because I was warm and there was nothing wrong with taking off a coat. His hand went under my sweater, and I thought, this is why I stopped wearing a bra. Not because everyone else was doing it, but for this moment. So that a hand under my sweater caressing my breast would be as easy, as casual, as a kiss.

Could Ron see us? No, we'd just be shadows in a car parked across the street.

I could kiss this guy and it would be okay because I wasn't ever going to see him again. I knew I should stop, but I thought, what's the harm in a few more minutes?

His hands were against my bare back, pulling me into him. Mine pressed into the corduroy of his jacket. I wanted to lose myself, to forget, just for a little while longer, but I couldn't. "We have to stop," I said. "I have a boyfriend." What I did not say was that I had a boyfriend I lived with and that he was just behind the window across the street.

"Too bad," he said.

I thanked him for the ride.

"Good-bye," he said, reaching to kiss me once again. I kissed him as if I never expected to see him again, which I didn't. Then I ran from the car.

I had learned something new about myself that night. I was the kind of girl who could kiss another guy practically under her boyfriend's nose, and do it easily.

I hesitated on the porch, knowing that Eric was watching me, and then I stepped inside. Ron was lying on the couch with a book. I looked out the window. With the lights on, all I could see was a large pane of darkness.

* * *

FIVE YEARS LATER, Eric and I happened to stand in line together for the same plane out of Oakland. We hadn't seen each other since that night in the car. Ron was long gone. I'd just spent four years in a European adventure of housecleaning, babysitting, and hitchhiking that had landed me penniless and back at my parents' house.

Eric had grown sideburns and a drooping mustache. He looked like a revolutionary, except he was carrying golf clubs. I'd never known anyone who golfed, at least not anyone under sixty. He recognized me right away, but I pretended I didn't quite remember him. We sat together on the plane, not talking about the kiss in the car. He said he was coaching high school football and giving golf lessons, but his parents had browbeaten him into applying to law school. I said mine had cowed me into going back to school for a teaching credential. He bought me a drink on the plane, and took my phone number.

Eric was different from me. He had a clear way of thinking. If he liked you, he showed you. He thought I was glamorous and edgy because I'd lived in Europe. He told me I was beautiful. He didn't keep secrets, or waste time with needless debate. We were married two years later. I had been flailing and he reached his solid arms out to steady me.

chapter thirteen

As soon as I heard the male voice on the phone asking for me, I knew it was the FBI. It had been two weeks since we'd met with them, two weeks in which Eric and I had monitored every word we spoke. Sharing this secret hadn't brought us closer, it had only made us careful with each other.

Agent Miller's voice still carried the slight tentativeness of youth, although he must have been forty. I held my breath waiting to hear what he had to tell me.

"We'd like to talk to your mother," he said. "With you there, of course."

They wanted letters from Bobby, as well as a record of the dates my mother had seen him and any money she'd given him. "Then maybe we can clear all this up," he said. He spoke like a doctor who'd seen cases far worse than ours, and I clung to his reassurance.

When Eric came home, I told him about Miller's call. The kids were upstairs, but I wondered if they'd noticed how often their parents spoke in whispers now. "If the FBI wants to interview your mother, they're going to do it, whether you set it up or not," he said.

I waited until the girls had gone to bed before I went into my bedroom and shut the door. I dialed the phone, my mouth dry.

It was after ten. I never phoned my mother this late, but when she answered, her voice carried no trace of apprehension. "Is it raining there?" she asked. I sat on the edge of my bed as she chattered on about the weather. She must have sensed something was wrong.

I didn't know how to begin. I hadn't rehearsed what I would say. If I had, I knew I couldn't have made the call. When I finally began, I rushed the words. The bombing two weeks before. The three people killed. Bobby's letter to her—the one she'd photocopied and sent to Sara and me. How I read the bomber's manifesto and compared it to the letter. My trip to Eric's office. The FBI.

"Natalie, I don't understand a word you're saying." Here at least was the mother I knew, a woman who did not prattle about the weather but gave the impression she controlled it. I took a deep breath and went back over the same territory more coherently, this time trying to make her understand what I'd done, and why.

She was silent when I finished. I stared at my bedside table, my half-empty water glass from the night before still sitting beside the novel I'd hadn't been able to concentrate on for weeks.

"You think I don't know my own children," she said in a way that made me feel I was no longer one of them. "Your brother's not capable of such vile acts, and you'd never accuse him of such awful things."

I felt as if I were five years old, awaking in darkness. But there was no one I could cry out to. "Mother," I said.

"This all came from Eric," she said.

Was that true? He'd given me no time to find another way, but then I'd given him no choice.

"There's something wrong with him," she said.

"Bobby?" I asked foolishly.

"Eric," she said, her voice biting with a cold rage that I feared might be turned on me next.

"I think Eric was trying to protect us," I said. "All of us. There were too many similarities between Bobby's letter and that manifesto for us to keep quiet."

"Why would you even read some ridiculous manifesto?"

When I tried to answer, she interrupted.

"Your brother's letter belonged to me. He wrote it to *me*. It wasn't yours to give to anyone, much less the FBI." I heard my mother's strangled cry. "How could you have done this?"

My rationale didn't matter. The lives at stake didn't matter. That

I loved Bobby, too, didn't matter. "Mom, it's not as bad as you think. It looks like there's real hope this can all go away, that they'll find the people responsible and Bobby will never even know." My voice was shaking but I sensed her listening. I told her what Agent Miller had said about clearing this all up, what the FBI wanted from her. I felt her silence when I mentioned the money she might have given Bobby.

"You don't have to meet with them," I said finally.

"I'll talk to the ghost of J. Edgar Hoover in a dress if that's what it takes to get them to leave us alone."

I didn't ask Eric to come with me to my mother's that weekend. Nor did he offer. But he insisted I take Stu. "If there's one thing I need to impress on you, it's never to talk to the law without your lawyer present," he said.

STU DROVE ME to Sacramento in his leather-upholstered car, driver's seat pulled close to the dash for his short legs. He patted my hand as he tried to reassure me that this meeting with the FBI was no big deal. Agent Miller, dressed in a tan suit with an American-flag pin in his lapel, met us outside my mother's condo.

Mother answered the door dressed as if she were a country-club woman and we'd just dropped by after a round of golf. She couldn't have been happy inviting the FBI into her house, but she gave no hint of it. She greeted Stu and Agent Miller as if they were on a social call. "I thought we'd have coffee and rolls," she said. "Shall we sit at the dining room table?"

I stared at my mother, who could not stand meaningless socializing, behaving as if she lived for it. I didn't know what I was expecting, but it wasn't this chilling performance. She poured the coffee, stirred in the cream and sugar for Stu, wiped up drips with a cloth napkin. She served cinnamon buns. When I refused one, she served me anyway, saying, "Don't be shy, darling. I bought these for you." I gave her a look. She knew I couldn't stand cinnamon buns.

"Agent Miller has assured us that all of your identities will be protected," Stu said to my mother, a bun on the plate in front of him.

"You have my word, absolutely," Miller said. My mother looked from his lapel pin to me. I knew what she was thinking. It wasn't just the flag pin she distrusted. It was his use of the word *absolutely*.

I was afraid Miller might see the contempt in my mother's eyes. I wanted him to like us, to see what decent, pleasant people we were. To close the file on us and move on. Though really what I wanted was to have it all taken back. Every step, every breath since I'd heard that radio playing in Claire's office three weeks before.

My mother was seventy-nine but she could have been thirty-nine, the way she answered Miller's questions. She never flinched, never struggled to recall a name or a date. Her eyes never darted. She handed Miller a slender packet of letters. "My children aren't writers," she said, the point so soft I wondered if Miller got it. No writers, no manifestos.

I glanced at Stu. The cinnamon bun he'd eaten had left crumbs on his shirt. He looked rumpled even when he was pressed, but there was nothing messy about his mind. I realized that, in all of this, he'd never told me what he really believed about Bobby.

My mother gave Miller dates for money she'd sent Bobby over the years, a thousand dollars here and there, always for a purpose, the filtration pump he needed, a chain saw to help with the wood.

I stared at my plate, my legs shaking. In a calm, steady voice, my mother was lying. She'd given Bobby far more than that. She'd given him her grandmother's silver to sell.

chapter fourteen

We heard no more from the FBI. I told myself it was a good sign. By the start of the second month after meeting in Eric's office, our pretending to be normal seemed almost normal. There were times I forgot, stretches when there was only the blankness of anxiety, the demands of work and children, when the refrain faded into background noise: *It's not Bobby. Even the FBI doesn't think it is.*

I never tired of concocting scenarios in which everything turned out fine in the end. I imagined my now-gray-haired brother riding the bike he'd built from spare parts, parking it at the rack in front of the library in town. He'd sit at a table with the other unwashed guys—they might even greet one another—and read a newspaper on a wooden pole. He'd skip right past the story about the Cal Bomber being caught because it meant nothing to him. I pictured Eric and me, delirious with relief, the stress of these last weeks erased.

Eric's brother phoned to invite us to a birthday party for their father. "I wish it wasn't going to be such a big deal," I said to Eric.

"Turning eighty is a big deal," he said.

But he knew what I meant. The lavish affair his brother was hosting, all the people, the hours of acting as if we didn't worry that the FBI would be on the other end of every phone call.

I put on my black party slacks. They were tighter around the waist than when I'd last worn them in December. I hadn't been aware I was eating more, just that I craved the comfort of fluffy potatoes and pudding in plastic cups. I slipped on a beaded top—there was no way to be too dressed up for one of my sister-in-law's parties.

It had been months since I'd worn makeup. Julia once asked me if I'd always been so low maintenance, and except for a heavy eyeliner period in college, I had. The pale skin and red hair I'd hated as a girl had seemed attractive as an adult, and these—and lipstick—had been enough.

"You look beautiful," Eric said. His eyes showed that he meant it. In the glow of his compliment, I started to think something good might come from this party.

Lilly appeared in a polished-cotton flower-print dress I'd paid too much for. I was so grateful to see her looking like a perfect, and perfectly normal, little girl that I knew it had been worth it. When Eric, Lilly, and I were gathered at the front door, I called Julia for the third time. She came downstairs wearing a secondhand, lime-green pencil-straight skirt with a small rip in the back seam, a thrift-shop blouse safety-pinned where the buttons were missing, a tiny black cardigan, and high heels from the Goodwill store.

"No," I said.

"What's wrong with this?"

"Nothing," I said carefully. "I just want you to wear something else. How about the pink-and-gray dress?"

"How about I put on one of Lilly's dresses and look like a real dweeb?" Julia glared at me. "That's what you want, isn't it? To infantilize me."

I glanced at Lilly, who looked crestfallen. I wanted to smack Julia. No, what I wanted was to get through this party with no sign in word, deed, or dress that our family might be hiding something.

"You'll do as your mother tells you," Eric told Julia, angry blotches rising to his cheeks.

I tried to calm Eric with a look. This battle wasn't worth it. We hadn't even made it out the door. "Wear what you want, but not another word out of you," I said to Julia, my hand on Eric's sleeve.

I touched Lilly's shoulder in her pretty dress, but she jerked away from me as if I, too, had betrayed her. In the car, the kids turned away from each other. Eric and I were quiet, the gossamer web of desire and possibility we'd shared ten minutes before swept away.

Richard and Kelley lived in Woodside, in a spectacular house with views in every direction—ocean, bay, rolling hills. When I first met them, they were renting a two-bedroom bungalow, but even then, Kelley looked rich to me. She was a young mother with sleek blond hair and framed museum prints on her walls. By the time I got my own chrome-framed prints, Kelley was hanging original art.

"There are parking attendants," I said as we pulled up.

"Oh, brother," Eric said under his breath.

"It's all so perfect," I told Kelley. I meant it. The food, the flowers, the musicians. She smiled. "The party's for Richard. His father would've been fine with the grandkids and a cake."

Lilly ran to be with her grandparents, but Julia was glued to my side. I suggested she join her cousin, home from college for the party. It made her frantic. "Must you talk so loudly," she hissed.

I got a glass of wine, then looked for a place to sit. Julia shadowed me. I found an aunt of Eric's I liked and asked after her family, happy to be able to keep the focus off me.

Eric's father came into the crowded living room carrying Lilly. At eighty he was still strong enough to ferry her in his arms. He motioned for Julia to follow them.

"Is your mother here?" Eric's aunt asked.

I pictured my mother getting the invitation, wasting no time declining. It was too far for her to come, I said. But, of course, it wasn't. Last year, my mother had posed with a camel in Egypt. I excused myself to get some food.

Eric, in his best sport coat, stood with a group of men near the bar, a drink in his hand. I knew he needed it. We were both drinking more these days. My wineglass was already drained. I got a refill, and stood beside him. They were talking cars. I left for the buffet table, piled up my plate, and looked for somewhere to eat.

The den, really a smaller living room and just as elegant, was a step down from the dining room. I don't know how I missed it. My plate went flying. I saw the wine shoot from my glass. Someone asked if I was all right. I got up carefully, afraid that I wasn't, then saw the dark stains on the overstuffed white chair, the splattered food. Guests were already springing from their seats to perform triage.

I knelt to pick up my plate, and tried to wipe the seafood curry off the Persian rug with my hand. When I stood, I saw Julia staring at me from a corner of the room. I opened my mouth to say something to her, I wasn't sure what, but she bolted, a hand over her face.

I found Kelley as I carried the mess of my plate into the kitchen. I was in anguish as I apologized for the ruined chair, the carpet. Kelley just laughed, her eyes sympathetic. "Get yourself some more wine," she said. "I'll fix you another plate."

More guests arrived. There must have been a hundred people in the house. This was an old man's birthday? Sara and I had been enough for my mother, who may not have even wanted us with her.

There was an elaborate cake, toasts, speeches. I switched to champagne, and tried hard to chat.

Eric caught my eye and tilted his head toward the door. I was more than ready to go. He had Lilly with him, her dress stained with chocolate ice cream.

"Where's Julia?" he asked.

I looked around and shrugged. Eric sighed. "I'll find her," I said. I walked through the living room asking if anyone had seen her, went out on the terrace. When I passed through the den, unable to avoid the site of my ignominy, I was suddenly certain she was hiding in a bedroom, humiliated.

We had an upstairs. Kelley and Richard had a second wing. I went through each room, every picture perfectly hung, every accent pillow in place, orchids in the bathroom, expecting to find Julia behind each door.

I met up with Eric in the foyer. "She's not in the house," I told him. Our annoyance was shading into alarm. We questioned Kelley and her kids. Eric went outside, circling the house calling her name. People offered to help.

I retraced my steps, this time opening closet doors. This is insane, I thought. Julia hasn't been kidnapped. She's not a baby. She's punishing me. It will turn out to be nothing, just like this thing with Bobby will turn out to be nothing.

Kelley came up behind me, put her hand on my back. "Eric's found her," she said. "She got the keys from the attendants and found your car. Guess my party was pretty dull."

I turned. She put her arms around me, and I held on to her. "Kids," she said, patting my back.

"Kids," I repeated, my face still buried in her shoulder, wishing that was all it was.

AT HOME, I put Lilly to bed and then went to Julia's room. She sat on the floor, her back against her bed, still in her party outfit—if I hadn't criticized it, would the evening have gone differently? Her face was streaked with mascara. Before tonight, I'd never even seen her wear any.

"I'm not talking to you," she said.

I sat on her bed, and patted the space next to me. She shook her head. I waited. She finally got up and sat next to me, her eyes downcast.

"I'm sorry," I said, surprising myself. I hadn't meant to say this. "I'm sorry I gave you a hard time about your outfit. I'm sorry I fell and splattered all that food."

She looked up at me, astonished and wary. Without warning, I started to cry. She told me it didn't matter, that it was just a spill. Then she put her arms around me, as if we'd traded places and she was the grown-up now.

chapter fifteen

ELEVEN LITTLE GIRLS in sleeping bags were packed on the floor of my family room. Smack in the middle was my own little girl, my baby, eight years old today. The slumber partiers all seemed to be asleep, each one clutching her doll. I'd already checked on them more times than necessary, but I wasn't ready to go back upstairs. I just stood there in the low light, taking in these girls and their dolls.

On the Thursday after the sleepover, Lilly and I were still reveling in the party's success. I made meat loaf for dinner, Eric's favorite. It was one of the things that endeared him to me, the way I could count on ground beef to make him happy.

Lilly wanted to help and I said sure. She washed her hands proudly at the sink, and shoved them into the bowl next to mine. When Julia came downstairs for a snack, she ate her apple leaning next to us at the counter. I was happy, my girls and I in our sunny kitchen, the breeze through the windows carrying the scent of spring.

I put the meat loaf in the oven with four potatoes. The kids went upstairs. I made a salad, opened a bottle of Cabernet, poured myself a glass, and took it to the family room. I flipped on the national news, and sank onto the couch, my reward for being so far ahead of the game. A commercial aired for Australian tourism. We could go there sometime, the four of us.

I got up to shut the patio door against the cooling air. There was a hummingbird at the feeder Eric had hung. I watched it suspended in space. All that work to stay in one place. Did it ever think it wasn't worth it? I heard the words *federal agents apprehended*, jerked my head around. I'd never seen my brother's cabin, yet I knew it was his.

Then I heard my brother's name broadcast to the nation.

I fell into a chair. I recognized the anchor's voice but not the roar of his words. There was footage of a slight man, hair wild and matted, dwarfed on either side by federal agents in Kevlar vests. His head was down, resting on his filthy clothes. Absent the shackles and federal agents, he could have been any of the down-and-out men I passed by every day in Berkeley.

I wanted to see his face, to know that he hadn't been hurt. Yet I feared him lifting his head, having to see the look in my brother's eyes.

Suddenly I heard my own name. The name I was born with, the name I'd kept when I married barefoot on my parents' lawn, the name I still used: Natalie Askedahl. The only name I'd ever had. Agents acting on a tip provided by the suspect's sister. Me.

The shower came on upstairs. Julia in her safe world, primping unaware. The phone rang. I could not move to answer it. I flipped through the channels and saw more shots of the same rude shack, surrounded by FBI sharpshooters, rifles held high. So many guns for such a small, grubby captive, a caravan of vehicles in the woods. My brother.

Lilly, carrying her American Girl doll, found me. "Can I watch?"

"Absolutely not," I said, switching off the set. "Go play in your room."

She looked at me suspiciously, but she did as she was told. I wanted Julia to never turn off the shower.

I'd have to call Mother, call Sara. I got up slowly, locked the patio door, and gave it a tug to be sure. As if that was going to keep us safe.

I looked up. Eric was coming in the door, his face bloodless, his briefcase sagging in his hand. "I heard," he said. "On the radio in the car." He brought his fist down on the back of the couch. "Those sons of bitches."

The shower went off upstairs. "Maybe the arrest doesn't mean what we think it does." I sounded frantic. "Maybe they're not that sure about Bobby?"

"Natalie," Eric said, the pain in his voice pleading with me not to go there.

He collapsed onto the couch. I sat beside him. "What are we going to tell the girls?"

"Oh, Jesus," he said, dropping his head into his hands.

"What's wrong with Daddy?" Lilly had reappeared like a cat at our sides.

Eric lifted his head. "Get your sister so we can talk to you both."

"I think maybe you should take the kids and go somewhere until this blows over," he said when she left.

"Blows over?" It was the first feeling of anger I'd had, but it was directed at the wrong person. "This is *never* going to blow over."

"What's the big deal?" Julia asked when she came back with Lilly. She was barefoot in big jeans and a tiny top, her hair wrapped in a pink towel. With her head covered and a dust of freckles on her nose, she looked twelve instead of fifteen.

"Sit down," Eric said. The phone rang, and Julia bolted to answer it. "Let it ring," Eric said. "Come back here."

"Oh, great," Julia said, her arms folded protectively across her small chest. "What have I done now?"

"Do as you're told," I said.

She sat scowling in the rocking chair. "Does she have to be here?" Julia pointed at Lilly. But Lilly, her breath shallow, had already gotten it. This wasn't about Julia. This wasn't about anything usual.

"Your uncle Bobby has been arrested," Eric said in a voice that was even and soft, and to me utterly false. "The police think he may have made bombs that killed people. If he did, and we don't know that he did, it's because he's not well, his brain is sick. Mom and I helped the FBI find him."

I felt Lilly shrink, but I couldn't look away from Julia.

"You're kidding, right?" Her eyes were enormous in her small face, pleading for me to take it all back. "Are you seriously trying to tell us that *your* brother sent those bombs to Berkeley and UCLA? That *he* killed those people?"

"We don't know that for sure," I said, my voice breaking.

"You don't know for sure?" Julia threw up her hands. "They've *arrested* him."

"Will my uncle make a bomb and kill us?" Lilly asked.

"No," Eric and I answered together, too quickly. I couldn't bear the thought of my children frightened of Bobby. I still couldn't believe they had a right to be.

Eric laid down the law. The girls were not to answer the phone. Julia was not to call her friends. We'd eat dinner. They'd do their homework and get into bed.

"I can't believe this," Julia said, red-faced and crying, jumping to her feet. "My uncle could be a mass murderer. You turned him over to the FBI, and you *never* told me. Our dysfunctional family's going to be all over the news, and I'm supposed to what? Just live my life? My life is ruined."

I grabbed her, the way I did my out-of-control third graders, and held her against me, trying to absorb her wild confusion. Finally, she broke away and ran to her room.

I don't know how we managed it, but we sat down to dinner. Julia ate silently and quickly. Lilly talked about school as if nothing were wrong. Eric and I gulped our wine and poured more.

After dinner Eric spent an hour on the phone with Stu, at first furious, then sounding as if this were just another legal battle to be fought and won.

I put Lilly to bed, lying next to her until she was asleep.

"I'm not going to school tomorrow," Julia said when I went to check on her.

"You don't have to."

"But I can't miss school."

"Okay," I said. It was all so familiar, the circular argument, her clothes all over the floor, my wanting to go to bed. It could have been any night.

I sat beside her. "We can talk about this," I said.

"How? You can't even grasp the implications of this for yourself, much less for me." I couldn't bring myself to reprimand her for speaking to me that way. She was right.

"How long have you thought Uncle Bobby might be the Cal Bomber? Since he came to Grandma's when I was nine?"

"Of course not," I snapped. We were a breath away from fighting. It would've been the easier route to take.

"But we never talked about him," Julia said. "You brushed me off when I tried to ask. I had this mythical uncle, who was supposed to be a genius, and was great to you when you were a kid. But the only time I met him he looked like this scary homeless person, and you just expected me to normalize it."

Had I really given her that message? I put a hand to my mouth, too overwhelmed to even consider the possibility.

"All I can tell you is that we're going to get through this." I looked away, determined not to cry.

I felt Julia's hand on mine. "He's your brother, Mom. I can't even imagine how you must be feeling."

I took her in my arms, kissed her good night. She hugged me back. Then I turned out her light, every question, even about school in the morning, unresolved.

I downed two Tylenol PMs, before phoning my mother from the edge of my bed. She refused to answer. "Mom, please call me," I pleaded on her tape. I put the receiver down. I didn't have the stomach to call Sara.

Eric came in and slumped onto the bed next to me. "I should've known better than to trust the FBI," he said. "I should have kept us out of this."

I put my arm around him. "This isn't your fault," I said, my voice soothing. This, too, was everyday life, my role as wife and comforter. But neither of us really had any idea what was happening.

chapter sixteen

I'm running for the swing, pink sandals on my chubby feet. A boy shoves me out of his way. I hit the ground hard, tasting blood. I am alone in the world, sobbing in the dirt, but then suddenly I am scooped up. The boy who pushed me cowers in the face of my big brother's anger. When Bobby carries me home, his shirt against my damp face smells like the clothesline.

I wasn't sure whether I had been dreaming or remembering. I got out of bed, went to the bathroom, and sat on the toilet lid, crying as I had not since the night my father died. There was an old prescription vial in the medicine cabinet with a single Vicodin inside. I swallowed it and went back to bed.

I dreamed that Julia was calling me but that I couldn't wake up to go to her, and then she was at my side shaking my shoulder. "There are people sneaking around in the yard," she said, her voice urgent.

"No they're not." My tongue felt enormous. "Go back to sleep." I couldn't stay awake. A loud noise came from downstairs. I thought it was Julia, but she still had her hand on my shoulder. Someone was pounding on our front door. Eric raised his head from the pillow.

"It's the police," I said to him. Only the police rapped on a door that way. Our alarm sounded. It was six thirty. Eric got up and pulled on a pair of pants and a sweatshirt. "Stay here," he said. At least he was home, not away on a business trip.

Julia climbed into his spot in bed, grabbing on to me. "I'm scared," she said.

Downstairs there was yelling. I heard Eric shouting, "Get the fuck off my porch," the door slamming, and then my husband's furious steps on the stairs.

Julia and I huddled together like small children.

"Get dressed," Eric said when he came back. His face was pale but his voice was calm. "Now," he said to Julia. "And close your blinds."

"What's going on?" I asked. It was too noisy outside.

"It's news slime. Get dressed. You have to see this."

As I followed Eric down the stairs, I saw he had drawn the curtains to the front windows that we almost always left open. We peered between the drapes.

Satellite vans were parked in front of the house. Clusters of what I presumed were newspeople stood on the sidewalk with their gear. Beyond them our neighbors in their robes and jogging outfits chatted in small groups, their dogs on leashes, all of them looking up at our house. I had my hand over my mouth. There was no reason to laugh, but once I started, I couldn't stop.

"Jesus, Natalie, will you get hold of yourself?" Eric said.

I could see how angry he was, how frightened, and I tried to look serious, but the effort just kept me laughing. Couldn't I just go back to sleep and deal with this in the morning? Except that it was morning.

"There's a man looking in the kitchen window," Lilly said, coming toward us in her flannel nightgown, her hair a tangle of dark curls, her teddy bear under her arm.

Eric pulled her into his lap, staring at me fiercely, as if to say, *Get it?* This is real.

It had the intended effect.

"What are we going to do?" I asked, suddenly sober.

"We can't stay prisoners in here," he said.

"I have to go to work and the kids have school." But as I said it, I thought, we really don't have to do anything. Our old life is gone.

As if he were a lieutenant commanding us, Eric snapped into control. "I want everyone packed with an overnight bag and ready to leave in ten minutes."

I didn't even think to ask where we were going. I threw a nightgown and some work clothes in a duffel bag. I got Lilly dressed and packed. I checked on Julia. She was still in her nightgown, on the floor of her room, crying on the telephone.

"Hang up," I said.

"Everyone knows," she said.

"Get dressed," I said. "Put your nightgown and a change of clothes in a bag. Now."

Like escaped convicts, the four of us dashed across our own back lawn to the garage. The girls and I slumped in Eric's car with our heads down. A news van blocked the end of the driveway. Eric cut across our neighbor's lawn and over their curb. The newspeople shoved cameras at the windows of the car, yelled questions at us. Eric gunned past them. This too-familiar picture would be on the news tonight, except it would be *us* running away, not some anonymous others. Us. People I hadn't seen since junior high, old boyfriends, acquaintances I couldn't stand, would see us on the news and say, "I know her." They'd have a story for their friends. Maybe I shouldn't have cared, not in the face of what Bobby was going through right then, but I did. I tore the address labels from magazines I discarded because I was afraid of strangers knowing too much. I wondered how upset the neighbors would be about the tire marks we were leaving on their lawn.

"You and the girls stay out of school today," Eric said when we were safely on Marin. We didn't argue, not even Julia. I used Eric's cell phone to call work.

"Oh my God, Natalie," Claire said.

"I'm sorry I couldn't tell you before. And that I can't talk now."

"Whatever I can do," Claire said. I thanked her. I felt so far from her and the world outside our car that it was a relief to say good-bye.

"Could we at least listen to the radio?" Julia asked from the backseat.

"No," Eric and I said in unison.

We got on the freeway heading south. The sun was breaking through the clouds over the San Francisco Bay. I cracked open the window to smell the water. The dread-thickened air of the past weeks had given way to the in-the-moment specificity of disaster.

I felt suddenly liberated, giddy, on the lam.

"Where will we go?" I asked Eric.

"I have to go in to work," he said.

I stiffened. I didn't even know why I was so angry. "Why?" I asked, but I sensed the answer in the tense grip of his hand on the steering wheel. I pictured the partners' meeting, the grim discussion of damage control.

"Don't give me a hard time on this," he said.

"We can't just hang around your office all day."

"I know," he said, sidestepping the anger in my tone. "I think you should go down to my folks'."

I wanted to say, *because of what my family's done, I have to be taken in by yours?* But I thought better of it, the kids too quiet in the backseat. I glanced over my shoulder. Lilly was clutching Julia's hand. "The girls and I are going to spend the day in the city," I said. "We'll meet up with you after work."

I was stalling, improvising, but Eric didn't argue. We parked in the garage beneath his office. When we said good-bye, I felt lighter, then lighter still walking away from the reflecting glass of his tall building. The sky had become an unambiguous blue. The girls and I turned on Sutter toward Union Square, grateful to be anonymous. I told them we'd have breakfast at Sears Famous Pancakes. They were quiet, Lilly hanging on to Julia rather than me, neither one complaining about having to stand in line for a table.

"This is so bizarre," Julia said, staring at her plate. "What are we supposed to do all day?"

"I thought we'd do some shopping."

"At the Gap?" she asked, brightening for the first time.

I pretended to think it over before saying yes. I'd give them anything they asked for.

It didn't take them long to catch on. When we'd worn ourselves out shopping, we went to the movies. I let them buy candy and ice cream. I got cash out of the bank machine to give them money to play video games.

I reserved a room under my married name for all of us at a hotel in

Half Moon Bay. I'd stayed there before. It had a heated pool; the girls could go swimming in their brand-new suits. It made as much sense as anything else. When we met up with Eric after work, he quietly went along with the plan.

Our room had a rose-colored carpet, queen beds with floral-print spreads, and overdone window treatments. I found it oddly comforting. The girls put their things in dresser drawers. Even Eric unpacked. I was the only one who never unpacked no matter where we were.

"How much is this place?" he asked after the girls had run off to the pool.

"Does it matter?"

He let it drop but I understood. On top of everything else, he was worried about his job. "Tell me what happened at work," I said.

"Damage control." He described the meetings, the phone calls. "They want me to hand off my UC work for now."

I nodded. "A bit awkward, I guess, having the brother-in-law bombing the client." Eric actually laughed, and I loved him for it.

"Agent Miller called," he said. "He said he didn't know how your name got out to the press. He said he felt personally betrayed. I told him his was the last call we'd ever take from the FBI."

"Good," I said.

Eric took my hands. "Bobby was arraigned in Boise this afternoon on a charge of possessing bomb components."

"They found bomb parts at his place?" I asked as if there were a different answer to be had.

Eric nodded.

"He really did it?" I was no longer Bonnie on the lam with the Barrow gang. I was me again, my eyes flooding, my head thick.

"What we know," Eric said carefully, "is that he's guilty of something."

I had tried to run, but I'd gotten no farther than a hotel room in Half Moon Bay. Maybe it was as far as I would ever get. I was shaking, sobbing, out of control. Eric put his arms around me while I struggled to compose myself.

"I can't let the girls find me this way," I said.

"They'll take their cues from us," he said. I let him talk. He was trying to make me feel better, make himself feel better, but there was fear in his voice. As I was grieving for what I'd lost, he was terrified by all we stood to lose.

"I have to try to get through to my mother," I said as soon as I could speak again.

I pleaded with my mother on the answering machine to pick up until finally she did. Her voice was thick with tears but her words were steely. "You girls made fun of me when I moved into a gated complex, and now thank God I did. Otherwise I'd have those damned reporters at my front door. I couldn't call you back because I had to find a lawyer for Bobby."

"I could stay with you," I said. "Leave the kids with Eric. Help however."

"I don't need any help."

We hung up. There was nothing more to say. "I don't know if she's punishing me or trying to protect me," I said to Eric. "Or both."

We ordered pizza when the girls came back. Julia and Lilly exchanged their swimsuits for pajamas. We watched pay-per-view movies and let the kids eat candy from the minibar, the four of us clinging to one another until it was time for bed.

By Saturday afternoon, we'd decided: Eric and I would go home, but we weren't going to put the girls through that kind of exposure. Lilly, who could miss the last week of school before spring break, would go to Eric's parents. Julia, who could not, would stay at her friend Donna's. I trusted Donna's mother.

We were quiet in the car on Sunday, me dreading facing Eric's parents. "I don't want to stay at Grandma and Grandpa's," Lilly said as if she could read my thoughts from the backseat. I wondered how long she'd been mulling this over, and calmly explained, again, that it was just for a week until the reporters stopped bothering us.

"Okay," Lilly said, my sweetly reasonable child. "I'll stay there if Julia does, too."

"I'm staying at Donna's," Julia said. She wasn't being bratty, just thoughtlessly matter-of-fact.

"Then I'm staying at . . ." Lilly considered her options. "At Brittany's." I tried not to laugh. Brittany's mother was notorious for always being too exhausted from her own self-importance to have other kids over.

"I thought Tessa was your best friend now."

"Okay, Tessa's house."

"Another time. This week you're going to see your grandparents."

"You can't make me," she said, kicking the back of my seat hard.

"Stop it," I said, craning my neck to look her in the eye. She let loose, slipping down in the seat, screaming and thrashing, a full-on tantrum. I couldn't remember the last time she'd thrown one.

Julia yelled at her to shut up. Eric looked over his shoulder and yelled at both of them. Lilly kept on kicking my seat. Eric reached his arm out to stop her. I cradled my head, feeling sorry for myself. I glanced up just in time to see brake lights flash in front of us.

"Eric," I screamed. I braced myself. I don't know how he did it. There wasn't enough time. He swerved into the next lane, cut off a car, the driver honking, my heart pounding, the girls silenced. The miss was so close that my eyes welled. Eric maneuvered the car two lanes to the right and stopped on the shoulder. He got out and walked around the back to where Lilly sat. I jumped out after him. I thought he was going to hit her. Instead he stepped over the metal barrier into a patch of bright wildflowers. I followed him across.

"Are you all right?"

"I might throw up."

I patted his arm. "Thank you for getting us out of that. You were amazing."

"It was too close," he said under his breath.

I didn't know how to comfort him. Where I saw escape from a near miss, he saw something much darker. He headed back without looking at me, the girls watching from the car. I stopped him, the traffic blowing our clothes. "Maybe Lilly would be better off coming home with us."

"That's a laugh," he said.

Lilly's tantrum had given way to a quiet sobbing she kept up all the way to Los Gatos. When we got to Eric's parents, she refused to get out of the car. I went to her door, just wanting to hold her, but she locked it on me. We had to go inside without her.

Eric's parents looked strained but greeted us as if this were any normal visit. "I've made tuna sandwiches with homemade pickle relish," his mother said. Eric said he'd just like a beer, and I said that's all I wanted, too.

"*I'd* like a sandwich, Grandma," Julia said.

Eric and his father went to the den and shut the door. "Where's Lilly?" my mother-in-law asked. When I explained, she said, "I'll get her."

"You could have at least shown some appreciation for her sandwiches," Julia said in the kitchen after Eric's mother left.

"I hate pickle relish," I said. Julia sat with her back to me and wolfed down her sandwich. She couldn't have possibly been that hungry.

Eric's mother led Lilly into the kitchen by the hand, my daughter's face red and snot smeared. My mother-in-law sat, pulling Lilly into her lap, and told her all the fun things they were going to do: make cookies, dye Easter eggs. Uncharacteristically, Eric's mother didn't make a fuss about our not staying long. Lilly clung to her grandmother's waist, wearing the same look of resigned betrayal she had given me when I left her at the kindergarten door.

BY THE TIME we dropped off Julia, it was dark. Eric and I approached our own house as furtively as robbers. Our neighbor had collected our newspapers and stacked them in front of the door. He did this whenever we were away, and we did it for him, except this time the newspapers had my brother's picture on the front page.

Inside, the drapes we always left open were drawn tightly, giving the place a dark, unhappy air. The belongings scattered about—a pair of shoes by the door, a sweater tossed casually over a chair, a magazine lying open on the floor—seemed to have been left behind by some other family.

Eric carried our bags upstairs, and I wandered into the kitchen. When the phone rang, I jumped, answering it to stop the ringing. It was Sara.

"What did you think, Natalie?" she said without greeting. "That I didn't merit being told that you'd turned *my* brother over to the FBI?"

I was so afraid of this conversation that the fierce beating of my heart hurt my chest.

"It wasn't like that," I said. "It was the day of the Berkeley bombing. I felt I had no choice but to talk to the FBI. Once I did, I couldn't tell anyone else. I really believed that Bobby would be eliminated as a suspect and I could tell you everything."

The sound of her breath through her silence was worse than anything she could say.

"You went ahead and made the biggest decision of *our* family's life without even talking to me? Without giving me even the courtesy of a heads-up? Did you even talk to Mother? Or did you let her hear like I did?"

"I can explain," I said.

"Natalie, you are piece of work. I have just one last question." She hit the *last* hard, and I had no doubt she meant it. "Did you turn me in, too?"

"What are you talking about? Turn you in for what?"

"Oh, I don't know." Sara was shouting at me now. "Pot smoking. Income tax evasion. Not wanting to see my brother dead."

"They aren't going to go after the death penalty," I said desperately. "The FBI assured us of that."

"And you believed them?" She didn't wait for my answer. "Fuck you," she said quietly. She hung up on me. I collapsed into a chair, still clutching the receiver, an awful tightness in my throat. I don't know how long I'd been sitting like that when Eric came into the room with an armload of blankets and towels. I got up, and together we strung them across the kitchen windows.

chapter seventeen

SHOUTS PIERCED my troubled sleep. I heard the furious slam of the front door, footsteps on the stairs. Then Eric was in the bedroom. He was dressed for his morning run, but I could tell by his dry T-shirt that he hadn't taken it.

"They're vultures," he said. "They won't be happy until they pick us dry."

I raised my head from the pillow and squinted at the clock. Six forty-five. "I opened the front door and they dive-bombed." He sat on the edge of the bed, his head in hands. "And people think *lawyers* are scum."

He turned to me. "I think you should consider staying home today," he said.

The prospect of having to get past the news crews camped outside terrified me, but I wasn't staying home. If I had learned one thing from my parents, it was that no matter what, you get up in the morning, put one foot in front of the other, and go to work. Even Bobby, I imagined, got up every morning, got dressed, and went to work doing his research, tending his garden, and I didn't want to think what else.

As I left the house, what I dreaded facing, almost as much as the reporters, were our neighbors. I dashed out the kitchen door to the car and backed down the driveway as quickly as I dared. I sensed commotion, cameras coming toward me, but I didn't divert my focus as I turned sharply into the street. I drove away before I could see what was going on in front of my own house.

At Mountaintop, I parked in the lot and overdid a wave to a passing parent. The sun was already brilliant, and when I entered the office, it took a moment for my eyes to focus on the group huddled in front of the secretary's desk. I was as much an insider at this school as insiders got. The people in the tight circle, talking about me, were my friends.

Claire saw me first. "You've come in," she said, too evenly. The others, trying to behave as if this were any other awkward moment, made sympathetic faces. Claire motioned me toward her office. "I've been so worried about you," she said when we were behind her door. "This whole thing is unbelievable."

We sat on her couch. I looked down at the familiar fabric.

"We went to the FBI because we felt we had to," I said, my eyes glistening. "They weren't supposed to swoop down on him like that on the basis of our puny tip. They were never supposed to reveal my name. We've got news vans outside our house."

"Oh my God, what you're going through," Claire said, enclosing my clenched hands in hers.

"I can't believe my brother would hurt anyone," I said. "I can't believe any of this. I'm sure they'll find him innocent somehow."

Claire didn't seem to know what to say. I imagined she couldn't believe it either.

When my students filed in, I was frozen in front of the board, unable to wipe away the assignments I'd put there just the week before. The children seemed unusually orderly. They looked up at me, waiting, I supposed, for me to make everything all right.

The first thing in the morning, we generally had circle, the third-grade version of sharing time. The kids seemed relieved when I directed them to our usual spot on the floor. Despite everything that had happened, I remembered that it was Benjamin's turn to start.

"I saw your brother get arrested on TV," he said.

"I saw it, too," I said, my legs folded on the rug under my big skirt. I told them I'd take questions. To make them feel safe, I reminded them of the rules they knew by heart—no talking out of turn and to raise their hands if they wanted to speak. Hands shot up.

Would my brother bomb the school?

No.

Was he Lilly's uncle, too?

Yes.

Could they meet him?

No.

Was he mean to me when we were little?

Not even one time.

Did I know how to blow things up?

No.

Would Lilly be coming back to school?

Yes.

Was I still going to be their teacher?

It was the first question that made me wince. "I would like to," I said.

At lunch Claire came in to tell me there were satellite vans outside. "I don't think we dare dash out for food," she said.

"I don't know what I was thinking coming in today," I said. But I did. I couldn't bear the alternative.

"You belong here," she said. "We're your family."

But I wasn't Claire's family in this, and she wasn't mine. Maybe for the rest of my life everything would come down to that, a line the color of blood between family and not.

She came back just before afternoon break. It was my day for playground duty, but Claire had asked another teacher to take over for me. "I wish I knew how to handle all this," she said after the kids went outside. She seemed so nervous I wondered what she was holding back. I'd already heard the nonstop ringing of the school phones all day. Now I pictured telephoto lenses peeking over the playground fence.

"Maybe you should take the rest of the week off?" she said as if she were not sure how I'd take the suggestion. "By the time we come back from spring break, all this will have blown over."

"We don't know that," I said. I couldn't bear to think about how long it might go on. I didn't want to leave my job. The kids needed me. I needed them. But my presence here was disrupting the whole school.

"I think it's best," I said, "better for the school, fairer to the children, if you find someone to take my class until June."

Claire tried to argue, but she knew I was right.

At dismissal time, I lined up the kids and hugged each one good-bye. Claire escorted them out. When they left, I sat at my desk and began working on notes for whoever would take over my class: *Annie is afraid to read aloud. Benjamin reads at the adult level. All the boys look up to Tom.*

I stayed until the notes were finished, waiting out the news vans.

Then I cleared out my desk and erased the board.

I WAS SO out of it when the phone beside the bed woke me Tuesday morning that I thought the man from *Newsweek* was trying to sell me a subscription.

"I can't talk to you," I said, when I grasped what he wanted. "I'm sure you can understand," I added politely, before I hung up on him.

I unplugged the phone next to the bed and slid back under the covers. Eric came in naked and glistening from the shower. His body had softened with middle age but he was still a powerful man. I lay quietly watching him. He dressed quietly, slowly transforming himself with each article of clothing into a man who made money. He stood at the dresser without moving, staring at nothing. Then he put his wallet and keys in his pockets and clasped on his watch.

I'd given him that watch with my first paycheck as a teacher, before he was even a lawyer. He'd exchanged his canvas briefcase for a leather one, his Toyota for a Lexus, but he'd kept the watch. Years ago, when he was an athlete and I had never dated a man so quiet and steady, he'd made me feel graceful. I wanted to tell him that now. But I felt too unsure to even let him know I was awake when he kissed me on top of the head.

I lay still as I listened to him leave, the pillow damp beneath my face, waiting for something to pull me back from where I had drifted and make me normal again. But the house was enormous in its silence.

I forced myself out of bed, wandered down the hall. I stepped into Julia's room and stood in front of her empty bed. Her wall was covered with pages torn from magazines, sexy photos of young men with tousled hair and long-legged young women in stiletto heels. I'd never really looked at the pictures before, and now I didn't know what I was seeing except that she was leaving us, that every year I would know her less, and it was possible one day I wouldn't know her at all.

The alarm, still set for work, went off down the hall in my bedroom. It felt like I'd been up for hours, days, weeks, but it was only seven fifteen.

Blankets and drapes still covered the windows, shutting out the light, but it would be worse to remove them. I didn't know how I was going to live like this: sealed up, dodging the phone, afraid of the doorbell, the day endless.

The house unbearably stuffy, I felt like I was in prison. But Bobby was the one locked in a cell. He hated not having fresh air. Even on the coolest of nights, he had always slept with his windows open. He couldn't tolerate noise. Fluorescent lighting agitated him to the point of illness. He said fluorescent lighting was one of the factors that made school agonizing for sensitive children, and as a teacher, I knew that to be true. I couldn't bear thinking about how frightened my brother might be in jail—or how furious at me. No matter how hard I tried to imagine otherwise, Bobby had to know what I'd done to him by now.

THAT EVENING, Eric presented me with a cell phone of my own. "I don't want an argument," he said as I was about to protest the unnecessary expense. "Just keep it with you."

"You make it sound like a gun," I said. Neither of us cracked a smile.

On Wednesday, I slept through Eric's leaving for work. I felt as if I'd been drugged when I finally woke up groggy at ten thirty. I went downstairs in my robe and finished a full carafe of coffee, surprised I could hold so much. Finally, I slipped the *Chronicle* out of its rubber band. There was a first-page story on the case against my brother. Defiantly, I started reading: show me what you've got. What they had were bomb components and a completed bomb ready for mailing.

Inside the paper was a photo: an emaciated, hollow-eyed man against a height marker that made him seem too short. Bobby had been bedraggled when I'd last seen him, but I didn't even recognize this person.

You didn't know him before, I'd said to Eric so many times over the years. You didn't know him when he was like a young Jesuit, narrow-shouldered, fine-featured, head bent in quiet contemplation, his hair falling onto his brow. You didn't know him when he showed me how to find Orion in the night sky, naming the stars in his belt, in his sword, how protected I felt, how I get a little of that back each fall when I see Orion return to the sky. You didn't know him when he made me feel I mattered in a house of giants.

When the kitchen phone rang, I answered. I shouldn't have, but I thought it might be one of the girls. The woman's voice on the other end was so warm, so natural, I listened for longer than I should have. She was a reporter from *Time.* She'd tracked down former colleagues of Bobby's, read me quotes testifying to his gentleness and his genius. She made me believe the story she was after was not about a terrorist captured, but an understanding of my gifted brother's descent, his transformation from a professor of mathematics at Columbia into the man arrested on TV. I was talking when I should have been silent, charged by her premise. She said she wasn't far away. When she asked if she could come by, I heard myself saying yes.

I phoned Eric, and pleaded "call me" on his voice mail, an idea forming in my head so big I feared it was crazy: this interview could help change the public perception of Bobby, make people understand the truth of who my brother really was.

I jumped in the shower, dressed, made fresh coffee, dug up an unopened box of cookies, and pulled the blanket down from the kitchen window. I hid the mess of our lives behind closet doors, and waited for the call from Eric that would bring me to my senses. But it never came.

The reporter was at my door in less than an hour. She hadn't given me time to change my mind. Maybe that had been her plan. Maybe it was mine. She'd had to work her way through the television people, a pair of them following her to the door.

"My goodness," she said, after I'd gotten her in and shut them out.

"Yes," I said simply. I didn't embellish. She'd seen it for herself.

She was older than I expected, at least my age, with an ordinary name, Maureen. Her hair was cut simply, dyed dark, her roots showing gray. She wore slacks, a sweater, and an ordinary chain necklace. I didn't know whether it was her gray roots or the necklace, but I was seized with a wobbly hope that I could trust her.

She went straight to the rocking chair in the living room. "Is this an original Stickley?" she asked, rubbing her hands across the grain.

I nodded. "It was my grandfather's." She looked around. I saw her picking out the good things, calculating fair market value. "The old pieces belonged to my grandparents, then my parents," I said. "You don't want to know about the Craftsman furniture my sister and I decoupaged when we were teenagers."

She laughed, and I thought, Good.

I offered coffee and a small plate of cookies. "I never turn down a cookie," she said, taking one. I sensed she was playing at being a regular gal, that she had the act down pat, yet I bought it anyway.

She reached into a leather bag that seemed half purse, half briefcase, and took out a notebook, a small tape recorder, and a pair of glasses. She sat back against the couch pillows as if we'd known each other since high school. She asked about my childhood. Anxiety chilling my fingers, what came to me in memory was heat. Heat so thick, you could see it rising from the sidewalk. "It was hot in the Sacramento Valley where we grew up," I said. "My father was in politics, but his parents were farmers."

She already knew about my father, probably my grandfathers. Certainly, this woman, this successful journalist, was not interested in a weather report. She wanted the same thing as the government. She wanted Bobby. But I wanted him, too.

I was trying to make her understand that Bobby came from a real place, a valley that was hot, where people farmed and bought solid furniture they passed down to their grandchildren. Four generations of my family had helped build this state.

I took a framed photo from the circular table that had once stood in my father's study and gave it to Maureen. It showed my father in his office in Sacramento, papers covering his desk, leaning back in his chair. I always thought he looked like Gregory Peck. You can see it in the photo, the dark hair and eyebrows, the square jaw. My father is laughing, enjoying a joke with the man standing over him. That man is the governor of California.

"In my family, politics wasn't this thing separate from life," I said. "It *was* life. My father was one of the architects of the California Master Plan for Education. He helped get it through the legislature. Higher education accessible to every Californian. That plan became a model for the nation."

I told Maureen about our house on Forty-Sixth Street, the noise of three children running on hardwood floors, how Bobby as a teenager held his own with the senators and journalists and scientists who came to dinner. I described how my mother served our guests the same meat loaves and stews she served the family. Once I started talking about the past, I couldn't stop.

"Bobby taught me to ride a bike by drawing a diagram," I said. "He told me that if I kept the picture in my head, I'd never fall, and I didn't." She wrote this down, and I pretended not to notice, not to be pleased.

I told her about Princeton, how Bobby had come home early.

"You're saying he had some sort of breakdown?"

"I'm not sure. I was only ten at the time."

"Your parents, what did they think?"

"They thought it was a mistake that he'd gone to Princeton so young. That it was too much for him being so far away. That all he needed was rest." *They thought that barely leaving his room for ten months was normal behavior for a seventeen-year-old boy.*

Maureen shifted on the sofa, and for the first time, I sensed impatience with what I was giving her. I wanted off the subject of my parents, and what they did and did not do for Bobby. I glanced at the clock. I'd been talking for nearly an hour, and we still had thirty-seven years to cover.

"Bobby went to Berkeley the following year," I said.

"Did you ever visit him there?"

Suddenly there was an image in my head. Before I could bury it, Maureen was on the trail, probing for what I wanted to hide.

"He was living alone in a room. There were dirty dishes everywhere, layers of stuff on the floor." I held back the full picture, Bobby at his desk hunched over, barely speaking, certainly not to me, or to my father, who was grim-faced and disgusted with him. There was my mother, bustling around, collecting dirty plates, carting them off with a stubborn cheerfulness.

I looked away. I didn't want these memories showing on my face. This was no therapy session. Maureen wanted something from me, and I from her. I returned to Bobby's biography. His dissertation won a prize. Columbia hired him as an assistant professor of mathematics. The chairman of the department said Bobby was among the top twenty of the new PhDs in the nation that year. But Bobby quit after three years, telling my parents he was giving up mathematics. I told her that he moved to Guatemala for six years before coming home to work as a janitor.

"He wrote me anguished letters from Guatemala about the Indians, how their way of life was being destroyed."

I got up again, to show Maureen the framed photo from Julia's christening. In it, Bobby is holding Julia in her christening gown, and I am clutching his arm. Eric stands slightly apart from us, his hair longish, his face shockingly young.

"Can I borrow these?" she asked. I nodded, handing her the photographs that portrayed the brother I wanted people to know, the man who held my baby in his arms.

"My father died four years after the christening," I said. "Bobby refused to come to the funeral. My mother told everyone he had the flu."

I didn't need to expose my mother like that, and I regretted it immediately. But Maureen wanted to know why Bobby didn't come to the funeral.

"He'd pulled away from the family by then, not wanting to see any of us, returning our letters. I don't know why," I said truthfully. "We were like a lot of families, I suppose. We didn't talk about it."

I told Maureen about the money my father had left us, how Bobby had bought his land in Idaho with his share.

"What did you do with yours?"

"We put it into savings for the girls' education," I said, not knowing why I was lying. I'd used my inheritance to remodel the kitchen.

Then Maureen asked about me, a series of ordinary questions leading up to the big one: why I'd turned Bobby in.

"Because I was scared," I said. "I never wanted to do anything that would hurt my brother. But I was afraid that if he really was the bomber, and I didn't say anything, more people could die. The FBI promised that my identity would be kept absolutely anonymous, that my brother would never know. Now he does."

Maureen nodded sympathetically. "The government seems pretty certain that they have their man," she said gently, as if I were some poor soul who couldn't handle the truth.

I didn't wait for whatever question she might be forming.

"I'm not in a position to know," I said coolly, "but what I do know is that my brother is mentally ill."

I watched her write this down. I'd planned to say this. It was the point I had to get across. If Bobby had truly murdered these people in cold blood, this was the only possible explanation for it. Yet, I was telling the world something that had never even been spoken in my family. I knew the characterization would do more than wound my brother. It would infuriate him.

Maureen said she'd had just one more thing to ask. "Did your brother's brilliance have an impact on you when you were young?"

The question surprised me. No one had ever asked me that before. "He deconstructed things in his head," I said slowly. "Then he put them back together in a way I could understand. Brilliance is seeing what others can't and rendering it simple. My brother never spoke down to me."

There was another memory, my earliest, but I did not tell the reporter. My brother's face over my crib, his arms reaching toward me, lifting me over the bars and out into the world.

I looked away, toward the clock. It was nearly three, the time the girls and I normally would be getting out of school. Maureen had seen the horde of reporters outside. I told her that they'd been also been at my school and that we'd sent the kids to stay with friends and family. She looked the faintest bit abashed, and then she thanked me. She removed my photos from their frames, and put them in her bag along with her tape recorder and notebook. I walked her to the door, locking it behind her.

I had thought I'd feel better after talking to her, that it was the right, the moral thing to do what I could to save my brother's life. Instead, I sank back onto the couch, overwhelmed by the sense that I'd just betrayed everyone I had ever loved.

chapter eighteen

I HAD DONE this thing without talking to Eric first, and now I'd have to make him understand. No matter what Bobby might have done or not done, if we hadn't gone to the FBI, he'd still be safe in his shack. More than anything, I wanted him to be innocent. But even if he'd killed a thousand people, he was still my brother. I needed Eric to see that when the opportunity to defend him came to my door, I had no choice but to open it.

It was just four o'clock. If the kids had been home, I wouldn't have been able to think for the noise. Now I couldn't think for the silence. The package of cookies I'd opened for Maureen sat on the kitchen counter. I took one without thinking, and then ate another and another. I could have eaten cardboard. I wanted my girls home.

Despite my queasiness, I started planning dinner. If I cooked for Eric, a real meal with salad and vegetables, then we might feel as if we still had our old life. He might even agree that talking to Maureen had been the right thing to do. Besides, dinner meant shopping, preparation, forcing shape and discipline onto the hours of waiting. The thought made me willing to make another run past the reporters camped outside.

I felt like I'd accomplished something when I found a parking space right in front of the store after my getaway from the house. I didn't much like this market but it was close to home. I knew the checkers, where everything was. But, as I reached to unbuckle my seat belt, I realized the obvious: people recognized me in there.

I threw the car in reverse, felt a thud. When I looked behind me all I could see was the shiny green of the car I'd just hit. It took me a moment to understand that I'd backed up while staring straight ahead. A small crowd was forming. The other driver was a woman, a trim blonde in office clothes, upset but clearly not going to yell.

"I'm so sorry," I said. I'd bashed in the passenger door of her new car. I felt terrible, but my continued apologizing only seemed to annoy her more. We exchanged information. A man came forward to vouch that the accident was entirely my fault. "She wasn't even looking," he said. The blonde took his card and drove away. I followed her out of the lot with my dented bumper, making a show of cautious driving, wishing I could disappear.

I drove aimlessly down San Pablo and pulled into a car wash. I felt like people were staring at me. I wanted to be invisible, yet I'd just given a private photo of my family to *Time* magazine.

A small white-haired man, too old to be working at a car wash, hand-finished my car with a diligence the task did not deserve. "Stop," I said, crossing the damp pavement toward him. He pointed to the opposite side of my car still covered with droplets. "It doesn't matter," I said, pressing some folded bills into his palm. He did something odd. He clutched my hand. Like a child, I gripped his in return, holding on without thought or shame. When I got back into my car, I understood that I wasn't going to phone my insurance company. I wasn't going to make dinner. I wasn't even going home.

I pulled onto I-80 because the on-ramp appeared in front of me. I sat in traffic with everyone else, and phoned Eric from the car. He apologized for not getting back to me. I said I understood. I told him I was going to my mother's because it seemed a logical thing to say. "It's a good idea," he said. "Take some time, relax." I'll give you anything you want; he'd said when he asked me to marry him. I hadn't believed him, but I liked the way it sounded. Now I just wanted for one night not to have to confront him—or what I'd done behind his back.

I drove to my mother's, so at least that part of what I'd told Eric would be the truth. Instead of waving me past this time, though, the guard at the gatehouse picked up his phone. "You can go through," he said as gravely as if we were at the entrance to the White House.

I hesitated when I saw Sara's Volvo parked outside my mother's condo. I didn't want to have to face her. I doubted she'd softened her judgment about what I'd done. I tried not to dwell on the fact my mother had wanted Sara here and not me.

Mother's door was locked. I rang the bell.

"What are you doing here?" my mother asked. I studied her face for a moment. It gave no clue to what she was going through. I didn't offer any answer—maybe she didn't expect one. I kissed her on the cheek and followed her inside. The kitchen table was set for two. "Sara's here?" I tried to sound nonchalant.

"We're flying to Washington, DC, tomorrow to interview federal public defenders." My mother's voice cracked. She looked away from me. "Ones with experience in death penalty cases."

I wanted to argue, to set her straight, to say: *We don't know that he's even guilty!* But all I could do was stare at my lap.

"Your sister's out jogging," my mother said, in control of herself once again. "You know how athletic she is."

Yes, I thought. She's in great shape, and she didn't turn Bobby in.

"How about a beer?" she said, opening her shiny black refrigerator. She must have known I'd say yes.

All her appliances matched. Her kitchen was as clean and uncluttered as a picture in a brochure. I couldn't help thinking of the old house. My mother'd had the same cleaning woman there for thirty years, a Japanese American who wore her pearls to mop floors, and, although she never spoke of it, had been interned at Manzanar. Despite her efforts, the dark wood of our old house was perpetually layered in dust.

I wanted to talk about anything other than where my mother was going tomorrow and why. I wanted to reminisce about our old kitchen, how much I'd loved the massive O'Keefe & Merritt range with the griddle in the middle, the books and papers piled on the green tile counters, and my mother's work spread across the table. But Sara was coming through the door.

"Well" was all she said when she saw me. She had on a faded, baggy T-shirt, worn gym shorts, and running shoes. Her wavy salt-and-pepper hair was pulled into a braid down her back, an old sweatband across her forehead. She had the weathered face of a pioneer woman, but her legs were still those of the high school cheerleader she once had been. She looked old. She looked young. I was suddenly afraid of her.

Sara went to the cupboard, took a tall glass, and filled it with water from the tap while Mother left to pack. Maybe she really did have things to get done, I thought, maybe she just didn't want to hear what Sara and I had to say to each other. Sara drank with her back to me, staring at the sky, now dark outside the kitchen window.

"How long have you been here?" I tried to make the question conversational, my fingers busy peeling the beer label from the bottle.

"Do us both a favor," she said. She turned to face me. "Don't make this into some who-does-Mommy-love-best ordeal." She refilled her glass and sat at the table. "Mother doesn't want me here any more than she wants you. But she's almost eighty. She needs help getting around DC." Sara removed the sweatband from her head and wrapped it around her wrist. "And I want to see what I can do to keep them from killing Bobby."

"They're not going to kill him," I said.

"Yeah, yeah, I know," Sara said. "The FBI promised you."

"This isn't my fault," I said, too frantically.

"Spare me," Sara said. "Without you and Eric doing what you did, I can't see that any of us would be where we are tonight."

"You're acting like I'm the one who fucked up your life by talking to the FBI," I said. "Not Bobby, who might have been killing people."

Sara's look was hard. "Tell me something, Natalie. Did you spend even one minute thinking about Mom? About what this would do to her?"

"That's not fair," I said, my voice high and desperate. "Two college kids and a professor were blown to bits in Berkeley."

"Bobby didn't do that."

"I hope to God he didn't," I said. "But if he was involved, I couldn't sit back and take the chance more people might die." I stopped myself from saying that even Julia could have been a victim.

"You mean Eric couldn't take any chances with his career in the corridors of power at Sterling fucking Tea Service," she said. "What did you two think? That you could hire an FBI agent the way you hire a plumber, and have him clear up the problem for you?"

We'd been trying to keep our voices low, conscious of Mother in the other room, but now, in our anger, we forgot about her. "You handed them Bobby," Sara said, her voice raised. "It doesn't matter that he's not their man. They'll make him their man."

"They found a bomb and explosive parts at his cabin."

"Or so they say."

"Why would they lie?" I shot back. But even as I said it, I realized: they *had* lied. They'd told the world my name. Now they might be planning to celebrate Bobby's death, just as they'd celebrated his arrest.

"You could have at least talked to me before going to the FBI." Sara slammed her fist against her thigh. "Given me that consideration. He's my brother, too."

"Telling you would have been the same as not doing it. You would have talked me out of it and I would have been grateful."

"Right," Sara said, rolling her eyes.

"You think this hasn't torn me apart?"

Sara didn't answer. We sat without speaking, my sister with her defiant glass of tap water, me with my empty beer bottle, its label now torn to shreds. Sara was comfortable with silence. It was one of her great strengths, greater even than the moral certainty she was using to damn me.

"I shouldn't have come," I said. "I'm leaving." Sara didn't try to stop me.

I went to my mother's room to say good-bye. She was zipping her small, wheeled bag on top of the bed. My mother loved to pack and she'd taught me to love it, too—just enough clothes carefully folded, the one change of shoes in a plastic bag, the travel-size toiletries, the miniature sewing kit, every contingency planned for, your life under control.

"I'm not going to stay," I said.

"I wish you and your sister would try to get along." She turned from me and sat on the bed, covering her face.

I felt helpless, wanting to plead, *Please don't cry.* I touched my mother's shoulder, felt her stiffen. When she looked up, her eyes had dried. "Drive carefully," she said.

Sara caught up with me outside my car. Wildly, I hoped she was going to make everything all right between us.

"I'm giving you a gift," she said. I couldn't help it, I looked to her empty hands.

For the first time, she smiled. "I'm taking responsibility for Mother, for whatever we have to do to defend Bobby. You're free to live your life."

"Bullshit," I said. "You don't want me around because you blame me for everything."

She shrugged. "If that's how you want to see it," she said.

I got in the car and drove away without looking back. I passed the entrance to the freeway and kept driving.

I TRAVELED MILES along Folsom Boulevard, before turning right onto Forty-Sixth Street. I should have been going home, and in a sense I was. There were no lights on when I parked at the curb. I waited in the dark, staring at the house I grew up in, wanting what I could not have: someone to open the door and call me inside.

When we were kids, our friends wished they had our lives in this big house with an upstairs and down, cookies in the kitchen, plays in the backyard, trees you could climb, parents benignly indifferent to kids and noise. My friends and I could dismantle the furniture over my mother's head and she'd never come up to check. "I don't want to know unless there's blood," she said.

"We had the best and the worst kind of childhood," Sara once said to me. "Parents who paid no attention to us."

The old oak tree still stood beside the house. Sara used to crawl out her window and down the tree to sneak out of the house at night. She wasn't like me, or even Bobby. She wasn't afraid of getting into trouble. She was agile, physically fearless, and she had places to go after midnight.

When I was five she took me under the oak to tell me how babies were made. She spared me nothing. "They call it fucking," she said. I cried and called her a liar. But when I ran inside to my mother, I couldn't tell her what the matter was. It was too terrible to say and I knew it was true.

Sara would never sit outside this house in a car with the window rolled down, shivering in the juniper-scented air, longing for what she could not have. She would never have allowed any husband of hers to hand Bobby over to the FBI.

I CRAWLED INTO bed beside Eric, who did not wake up when I whispered, "I'm home."

I'd been so tired driving back from Sacramento that I'd feared I might fall asleep. Now in my own bed, sleep seemed impossible. I lay still, trying not to think, not to imagine tomorrow or the days after that. It was two o'clock, then three. I thought I heard Lilly calling *mommy*. "Everything's okay," I said aloud before I remembered that she wasn't even home.

When I was Lilly's age, the girls drew pictures of houses and the boys drew pictures of bombs falling from airplanes. The teacher hung them around the room, the airplanes, then the houses, side by side. When we played dolls, the husbands were always away at war. We didn't need those husbands. War was a good place for them. We got tired of the dolls, too, left them outside, our babies, where they could drown in the rain, asphyxiate in the heat, get chewed by dogs. We wore dresses to school with bows in the back and the bows became untied and trailed behind us as we ran for the swings and the hanging bars. I was good at the bars. We toughened our hands for them, delighted when our blisters oozed blood.

In the dark, I felt for calluses on my hands. I had only one now, under my wedding ring.

* * *

I DIDN'T KNOW how late I'd slept, or even what time I'd fallen asleep. The sunlight behind the curtains was bright. The clock radio by the bed said twelve thirty. When I went downstairs, I saw that Eric had rehung the blanket I'd taken down from the kitchen window the day before. Just before the reporter came over.

I had to find a way to tell Eric. I sat in a kitchen chair and phoned him at his office. He answered on the first ring with his name, the ordinary last name he shared with thousands. For the first time in twenty years, I wished I'd taken it.

He sounded impatient. He was in the middle of something. I'll tell him about the interview tonight, I thought. I was brief. I let him know that Sara and my mother were on their way to DC and that I was going to pick up Lilly. I said I didn't care about the television crews.

"I'm not sure that's such a good idea," he said.

"I am," I said. I wanted my daughters back. I telephoned Eric's mother, and left a message for Julia at Donna's house.

It was four o'clock by the time I reached Los Gatos. When Eric and I first began dating, my in-laws had just moved into their house fronting the endless green of their country club. What should I wear? I asked Eric when I was going to meet them for the first time. I was twenty-eight but my wardrobe ran only to jeans and little teaching dresses. I don't remember what he said or what I wore. Only that I was either too dressed up or dressed down for Eric's mother in her culottes and sleeveless polo shirt, with her Nancy Reagan hairdo.

Now I went around back to the sliding door of the huge room that served as a combination kitchen, dining, and family room. Their family portraits hung on the wall: Mom and Dad, suntanned and self-satisfied; Eric and Richard as they progressed from babyhood to law school without so much as a hint of irony in their eyes. There was no Sara in their family, no in-your-face, pot-smoking, aging hippie. God knows, there was no Bobby, not even a me, tainted by the two of them. Politics was an unimaginable pastime in their spotless house. No little men with cigars pictured on that wall. No gals who swore. My in-laws were old but their politics belonged to the present. My parents' New Deal–style liberalism had fallen out of fashion long before Bobby made us outcasts.

My father-in-law, reading the *Wall Street Journal* in his easy chair, looked up and waved at me through the glass. I realized I'd just been standing there.

I slipped in the door. My mother-in-law stood at the counter arranging slivers of celery on a vegetable tray. They expected me, but total surprise would have played no differently in this kitchen.

Lilly lay on the floor coloring in the kind of flowers-and-baby-animals book she'd outgrown in kindergarten. "Oh, hi," she said icily before turning back to the coloring book my mother-in law had bought her. I dropped to my knees, kissed her on the head, but she just kept looking at the page she was working on. An Easter bunny. I'd forgotten Easter was this Sunday.

I sent Lilly to get her things. She was sullen but did as she was told. Eric's mother picked up a knife and began cutting radishes to look like roses. She asked how my mother was. "I feel so terrible for her," she said. "I just can't imagine."

"Yes," I said, the politeness in my tone a lie, my anger unexpected. My parents had devoted their lives to the vision of California that my country-club in-laws had proudly voted to undo. I doubted my mother could tolerate the pity of this woman who couldn't even imagine having a son like Bobby.

Lilly came back dragging her small duffel and the huge Easter bunny Eric's mother had bought her. She played out an elaborate and prolonged good-bye scene for my benefit. Eric's mother gave her a baggie of radish roses, Lilly accepting as if they were chocolate bunnies.

"I didn't know you liked radishes," I said when we were out the door.

"There's a lot you don't know about me," she said.

I wanted to kneel right there, go eye to eye with her, find out what it was I didn't know, but I recognized the person heading up the drive toward us. No, I thought. I didn't want to have to face my sister-in-law. Kelley threw her arms around me. "I've been trying to reach you," she said.

I knew. I hadn't returned her calls. Another person I'd let down. "I haven't been able to talk to anyone," I said. It wasn't an apology. It was a confession. I meant my own husband. I sent Lilly to the car.

"I don't blame Eric for not talking to Richard about any of this," Kelley said. "My husband doesn't know how to deal with anything that's beyond his control."

I looked down at the driveway. I didn't like thinking that Eric might be ashamed to talk to his own brother.

"What I wanted to say is that I'm here if you want to talk, and that I understand if you don't," she said.

My knees went weak from the desire to fall against her, to tell her about *Time* magazine, to tell her everything, to never stop talking. But I was hiding too much, and she was Eric's brother's wife.

Instead, I looked toward Lilly, waiting in the car, letting Kelley be the one to say, "Of course, you need to go."

chapter nineteen

When I was a girl, I had a way with words. Vaccinated with a Victrola needle, my mother said. A born pol, my father said proudly. A liar and a tattletale, Sara said. I still had a talent for explaining, for convincing myself as well as my listener. I was a salesman's mark, Eric said, because I was a salesman myself. Lilly didn't make it as far as the first McDonald's out of Los Gatos before I'd won her back, but then she was only eight.

It was late when we turned up our driveway. The light was out on the kitchen porch, the house completely dark. I fumbled for the right key on my chain.

"You go in first," Lilly said.

This isn't my house, I thought, when I turned on the lights inside. Blankets and towels strung across the windows. Who would live like this? The warm, sunny kitchen, the room we'd so lovingly remodeled now reeked of stale air. The kitchen table where no one had sat in days was covered with unopened mail.

I tugged hard at a blanket on the window to bring it down, but it didn't budge. I looked up and saw that Eric had nailed it in place.

I'd brought my little girl home to this.

"Tell me again," Lilly said. "Why did we put these blankets up?"

"For privacy," I explained. "But, we'll take them down tomorrow because everything's back to normal now."

Julia phoned to say she couldn't come home before Friday evening.

She had too many plans. I looked to the blanket-covered window and said I understood.

I put Lilly in the bathtub, aired out her room, tucked in her sheets, and pulled a flannel nightgown from her dresser. We read stories in her bed, one after another. The whole time, I dreaded the sound of Eric's key in the door and having to tell him about my interview. At ten o'clock, I finally turned out her light. Lie down beside me, she asked. "Just for a minute," I said. I wrapped my arms around her, breathing in her shampooed hair. I'll get up in a minute, I thought.

I TRIED TO grasp where I was. Eric, in shorts, his T-shirt damp from running, stood in the doorway, smiling. He seemed so glad to see me there in our daughter's bed that I flushed with guilt. I got up and glanced at my jeans. "I just lay down for a minute."

"I tried to wake you," Eric said, "but you were completely out."

Lilly looked up. "Mommy slept with me all night," she said triumphantly before scrambling to Eric. He held her with one arm and me with the other. "I have my Lilly back," he said.

"I'll just take a quick shower," I said, backing away from his grip.

"Later," he said. "I've got breakfast."

I started to gather the mail on the kitchen table, picking up a bright FedEx envelope. It was from ABC in New York. All I could think to do was bury it inside the stack I was transferring to the dining room table.

Eric sliced bagels from a brown bag and put them on the table with cream cheese. We didn't talk. Lilly did it for us. She spoke as if she'd just been released from a vow of silence, one thought tumbling joyously into the next. I wanted to cry from the realization of all she'd been holding inside.

"Mom and I are taking down the blankets today because everything's back to normal," she said. Eric smiled indulgently but said nothing.

"I think she's glad to be home," I said after she ran off. I took a breath. "We need to talk."

He nodded. "Not a good idea taking the blankets down," he said, pointing to the window. "People have been driving by, getting out of their cars to stare."

"Oh God," I said. I hadn't noticed, but then I hadn't been looking. I wanted to make sure Lilly was all right, but she'd just left the room.

"I've gone through the phone messages," he said. "We've gotten some really nasty ones. I've applied for a new, unlisted phone number. Until it's installed, let's keep the phones unplugged." I nodded. "Then there's the mail," he said. It was starting to dawn on me: we were suddenly getting a lot of mail, even for us. "Don't open anything from people you don't know."

I stared at my lap, groping for words to tell him what I had to confess.

"I'm sorry to have to leave you with all this," Eric said. "That I can't be around."

For the first time in days, I looked straight at him. His face was etched with exhaustion. I didn't have to listen carefully to hear what he was telling me—the Monday deadline, all the hours, the late nights he had to work between now and then. He sounded beaten.

I squeezed his hand. There was time. The article wouldn't come out until the middle of next week. My confession could wait until Monday. I told myself that I'd made the decision out of kindness.

Lilly and I picked up Julia on the way to dinner, Julia making it clear she wanted no greeting fuss from me. Eric met us at an Indian restaurant near the campus. Julia, unable to decide on her order, kept the server waiting. Lilly wasn't happy with her chair. Julia sulked because the waiter brought her the wrong soda, but she refused to ask him to change it. Lilly whined and leaned too close to her sister even though she knew Julia hated being crowded.

"It looks like everything's back to normal," Eric said. I laughed but I couldn't look at him.

Eric rode the BART back to work, and I took the girls to a movie. This was family life in full throttle. The napkin is dropped, the bill is paid, the popcorn is bought. She said, you said. I want, I need, I love, I hate. Children take up all your time and attention, and I was grateful.

At home, I put Lilly to bed, and then went into Julia's room. She was already under the covers. I sat beside her. "How's it been for you at school?" I left the rest of the sentence unspoken, *since Bobby's arrest*.

"The teachers acted weird around me, like they were trying too hard to be normal. But the kids were cool. I got popular." If you asked Julia a direct question, you got a direct answer.

"Well, the popular part sounds nice," I said cautiously.

"I just want the whole thing over and never have to talk about it again," she said quietly.

"Me, too," I said, sensing there was more.

"Mom, I know you're worried about how this thing with your brother is affecting me." She hesitated and I braced myself. "But, I just want to feel normal, and your anxiety about me makes me feel that I'm not."

I tried to take this in. "I *am* worried about how all this is affecting you and Lilly," I said. "Especially you, because you're older."

"Well, it's not helping me," she said.

I said I'd try to do better, not knowing if I could.

Eric came home at eleven. By the time I joined him for bed, he was already asleep, his arm across his eyes. I got in beside him, touching his T-shirt where it fell against the sheet. My eyes wide open, I waited for nothingness.

ERIC WORKED all day Saturday and from morning until late into the night on Easter. Julia took off to be with Donna. Lilly and I made a picnic at the park with candy from her Easter basket for dessert. By the time the kids and I woke up on Monday, Eric had already been at the office for three hours. The girls pulled me out of bed. It was the first day of their spring break. We'd disconnected the cable and the Internet. They needed me for entertainment.

I involved them in an elaborate breakfast which was really lunch, and then we moved to the family room couch, the three of us still in our pajamas at two o'clock. I could hear the birds chirping in the backyard, but I didn't look between the drawn drapes to see what the day was like outside. We put on another video, *My Fair Lady*, and watched it as if we'd never seen it before.

Halfway into the movie, Eric came through the door. My heart jolted. He was far too early. It wasn't even four o'clock.

"Why's *he* home?" Julia asked in a tone that would ordinarily have gotten her a reprimand.

"I just wanted to come home to my family," he said evenly. He was lying. He looked ghastly, his face off-color, his suit wrinkled with his shirt sticking to him. The weight of his briefcase seemed too much for him to bear.

I forced a smile and he looked away. "You girls take the movie and watch it upstairs," he said. His voice was so eerily quiet, they did as they were told. I hadn't moved since I'd heard him at the door. He opened his briefcase and hurled a pair of magazines into my lap with a violence I'd never seen in him. The magazines had bright liquor ads on the back, and I could see where the sweat of his hands had bleached the color.

I turned the magazines over. *Newsweek*'s cover was a photograph of Bobby, vacant eyed, his hair matted and filthy. His hands were cuffed and his feet were chained.

"No," I gasped when I saw *Time*, the photo on the cover so shockingly familiar, because I'd given it to them. Bobby in the center, Julia in his arms, Eric and me on either side, the day of Julia's christening.

Eric's fist came down on the high back of the easy chair. "You put us on the cover of fucking *Time* magazine," he said, "and you never even bothered to tell me."

"I can explain," I said, although suddenly I didn't think I could.

"What were you thinking?" he asked. "That I wouldn't notice a *Time* with our picture on the cover? That people wouldn't be asking me about it all the goddamned day? Or did you just not feel like telling me?"

"No, no, no," I said. "You were working so hard. You had the court filing today. I was going to tell you tonight. I was so sure there was time."

Eric's face was so incredulous, so angry, that I wondered if it was worth going on. "The reporter called on Wednesday. When she described the story she was working on, I thought I could use the interview to help Bobby, that it would be wrong not to. I tried to reach you."

Eric looked as if couldn't comprehend my idiocy.

"I never dreamed the magazine would be out in so few days, that they'd put that picture on the cover."

My husband swore, and then held his mouth as if to stop himself from saying more.

I felt frantic. "I never meant to hurt you. Please, just sit down and let's talk this through."

"I'm going out," he said.

"Where?"

"I don't know."

"You don't know? Don't be crazy."

"Don't talk to me about crazy," he said.

"Please, don't go," I said, watching him leave. My chest heaving, I told myself he'd calm down and we'd work things out. Then, because I couldn't not do it, I opened the *Time.* The magazine had Bobby on the couch, the center of a family melodrama, because that's what I'd given them. Their story made a point of our family's political connections and my father's role in expanding California's universities. I'd provided the dots, but they'd connected them: a messed-up son out to destroy his father's lifework.

Time also had the photos showing that Bobby was once someone else, my stories of our childhood, and me as the *sister*. I came across as anguished, conflicted, self-deluding, but essentially decent, married to a man who was the anti-Bobby, an attorney in San Francisco's oldest and most prestigious firm, defending the sort of clients my brother might have wanted to bomb out of existence.

"What's up with Daddy?" Julia, small in her oversize pajamas, was suddenly next to me.

I handed her the *Newsweek*. She stared at the cover. "So much for the unbiased press," she said. "You need glasses to read the word *suspect* below all those capital letters above Uncle's Bobby head. I feel sorry for him." She moved to get up, giving me back the magazine.

"Wait." I handed her the *Time*. "Your friends might ask you about this."

She stared openmouthed at the cover. "This is us," she said. She glanced to the shelf where the photo had always been. "How'd they get this?"

I took a breath. "I gave it to them."

She hit her index finger smack on her infant self in Bobby's arms. "Why would you give them a picture of me? What do I have to do with any of this?" Her face was flushed. "How could you betray my privacy like this?"

"I had no idea they were going to put that picture on the cover," I said.

"I don't believe you," she said, jumping up. I could feel the outrage in her breathing. "I'm plugging in the phone. I don't care what you say. I'm calling Donna."

"Go ahead," I said. I didn't blame her for wanting to talk to someone outside this house. As soon as Julia disappeared upstairs, Lilly was at my side, pulling on my sleeve. Sometimes, the kids pulled on me so hard they left bruises. "There's nothing to eat and I'm hungry," she said.

I HEARD THE squeak of pipes in the morning, the shower turning off, followed by Eric's heavy footsteps. Thank God, I thought. I looked toward the space that should have been mussed from his sleeping there. The sheets and blankets were undisturbed.

He came into the bedroom, moving slowly, quietly, dressing for work. I could tell by the light that it was early.

I sat upright. Our king-size bed felt enormous.

"Where were you last night?"

"I went back to the office," he said.

Maybe I shouldn't have been, but I was relieved.

He clipped on his watch. "I've got a long day today. Don't wait up." He did not kiss me or even say the word *good-bye*.

chapter twenty

I LISTENED TO the front door shut, the slap of Eric's wordless departure. Going back to sleep seemed impossible. Cold beyond the chill of morning, I put on hiking socks with my slippers and a sweater over my robe. It was barely six o'clock. I tried not to think how long the day would be. Eric had made coffee—he'd made the coffee all the years of our marriage. I poured a cup, carried it to the family room, and opened the *Newsweek* I'd shoved under the couch the day before. They wanted to know what had turned this "shy, gentle genius into a diabolic killer," and they had an answer from a criminal psychologist: family pathology. Only two words, but they held my eyes until they burned. How dare he smear my parents like that, this Freudian know-it-all, who'd never even met us? I wanted to pay him back with such intensity it actually made me wonder if he was right. If my brother could do what he was accused of doing, what was I capable of?

The magazines made a big deal of Bobby never having had a girlfriend, as if he blew things up because he couldn't get a date. They said his loneliness turned to rage at the world, that he developed his philosophy to rationalize his acts.

They had everything backward.

It wasn't his loneliness that drove his thinking. It was his thinking that made him lonely. When he was teaching at Columbia, he told me that there were only a hundred mathematicians in the world who understood his work and half of them were in Israel, and that if he kept pushing ahead there would be none.

* * *

"WHAT ARE you reading?" Julia asked cautiously, Lilly padding along behind her. It was past ten a.m., the kids were finally up, and I was thrilled not to be alone any longer. A box from the attic lay at my feet.

"It's a commemorative copy of Governor Brown's first inaugural address," I said, showing too much enthusiasm. I ignored the look that said Julia was sorry she'd asked. "Listen to this: 'The essence of liberalism is a genuine concern and deep respect for all people.'"

"Uh-huh," she said. "Please don't read me any more."

I handed her a photo from the box. "This is me when I was your age."

"Maybe you'd like me to put it on the cover of *Time* magazine," she said drily.

What had I been thinking? That Julia would be interested in my past? My past was strangling her.

But Lilly wanted to see the picture. "You looked pretty," she said. I replaced the photo and the speech I'd read too many times this morning, closed the box. Julia put *My Fair Lady* back on the video player. I didn't stop her.

Halfway through the video, our doorbell rang. "Don't answer it," I said.

Julia rolled her eyes. "Are you going to act this scary forever?"

The ringer was persistent, one long bell followed by another. My breathing went shallow. Last year a couple from Los Angeles had bought an Italianate house at the end of our street and put in a security fence. The neighborhood was appalled. Now I wished I had one.

I looked behind the blanket covering the window, and saw the mailman patiently waiting. Cowed, I opened the door.

"You've got a registered letter," he said as if I'd answered the door like a normal person. It was from our auto insurance company. I'd never reported bashing into the side of another car.

I filled out the insurance form. Percentage my fault: one hundred. I wasn't even looking.

An hour later, the bell rang a second time. "Here we go again," Lilly said. I waited, then checked the porch from behind the blanket. An enormous spray of flowers sat in front of the door. Eric had sent flowers, at least a hundred dollars' worth, I thought, bringing the display inside. He was sorry. He'd forgiven me. I felt like a girl with a new boyfriend.

There was a letter attached to the bouquet, but it wasn't from Eric. It was from the *Today* show. They wanted me to appear on their program to tell my story. They'd make all the arrangements, fly me first class, and put me up in New York.

The phone rang upstairs. I heard Julia's footsteps bolting for it, even though I'd told her not to answer, to unplug it after she used it. I ran upstairs, got to her room as she hung up. I clutched the doorframe, trying to control my anger.

"I'm sorry," she said, moving quickly to unplug it. "I forgot. It was just Cindy. Don't be so mad."

"This is the last time," I said, as if that made any sense.

Julia followed me at a distance back downstairs.

"Can I spend the night at Cindy's house? It's okay with her mom."

I couldn't think. I didn't know what to do about the flowers, whether Eric was even coming home.

Julia looked at me. "I love you, Mom, but I have to get out of here."

"Go," I said.

She was out the door in less than five minutes. I watched her go. I wanted to run like that, out the door, down the street, my back to this house.

Instead, I grabbed a thirty-gallon trash bag and started sorting mail, tossing the easy stuff. There was a letter addressed to me in a child's penmanship, my name misspelled, with no return address. I opened it. No salutation, just a note on a small piece of paper. *You bich. I hope you get whats coming to you. Only scum sells out their own.*

I laughed, probably too hard, before throwing it away. I opened the FedEx from ABC. They wanted to give me a full hour to tell my story. They'd help me with hair, makeup, clothes, even provide medication for stage fright if I wanted. I needed only to fly out first class, and if I couldn't do that, they'd come to me.

I saw myself quietly glamorous, medically calm, making everything all right with the power of my words, what had been nightmare transformed into advantage—Bobby saved from death, my mother and Sara appeased, forgiveness from Eric, my girls proud. But even as fantasy, I couldn't buy it. All I had to do was look at what the last interview I'd given had done.

The scent of the bouquet perched amid the mail on the table was overly sweet, the roses, tiger lilies, and baby's breath mingling into a single funereal scent. I didn't want Eric to see them. I considered throwing out the bouquet, vase and all, but the flowers in the overwrought display were lovely. I heard Bobby's voice in my head: *It's not the flowers' fault.*

For the first time that day, I had a clear idea. I called Lilly from her endless video watching to help me. We got out all the vases in the house, washed and dried them. Then we took the arrangement apart, flower by flower.

"Yell at me," I said when Eric and I were finally alone on Tuesday night. "Swear, anything."

"I'm too defeated," he said.

He lay on our bed, staring at the ceiling. I touched his shoulder. "We could be defeated together," I said. He rolled onto his side, his back to me. "I have to get some sleep," he said.

The next evening, I finally reached my mother. It had been a week since I'd fled her house, a week without a word. "Why haven't you called?" I asked. I knew better than to lead with my chin but I'd done just that.

"I saw your interview in *Time*," she said. "Not that I could have missed it."

I sucked in my breath, and like a child, waited to hear how much trouble I was in.

"Did Eric put you up to it?"

"Eric?"

"To justify what the two of you did?"

I sighed. There would always be that. What the two of us had done.

"Eric had nothing to do with it," I said. "I wanted people to know the real Bobby."

"The real Bobby? Or the real you?"

Was that true? Was the understanding I'd sought less for Bobby than for me? Did everyone understand me better than I understood myself?

Her tone softened. "We've got two of the best federal public defenders in the country for your brother." She described them, a man and a woman, each with a string of victories behind them, dedicated public servants courageously opposed to the death penalty.

The phone carried my mother's sigh. "Even with public defenders, a good defense doesn't come cheap," she said. "I hope you weren't expecting an inheritance."

I have an inheritance, I thought without emotion. This.

NIGHT AFTER NIGHT of that somber spring break, I sat downstairs alone in the dark, an afghan around my shoulders, breathing the eucalyptus-scented air. The clutter of rooms reduced to lines, I sifted through my memory, my own kind of anthropologist, determined to find the place where the old Bobby ended and a new one began.

I was just out of college when Bobby invited me to visit him in Guatemala. It was my first big solo trip. I pretended to be fearless, struggling to find the bus in Flores, on the hours-long ride on impossible roads, arriving at the hotel, which was just a room in the back of a four-table café. I waited a day for my brother to collect me, the local men eyeing me. I never thought to complain. It was a rite of passage, living up to Bobby.

He took me to a village at sunset. We watched the candlelight procession, a plaster Virgin Mary held aloft at the lead. They carried placards with photos of their children—a village of them dying from the measles. I remember the fury in his voice when he said, "They're praying to the Virgin Mary when they should be praying to Eli Lilly to donate their vaccine."

We traveled to the Mayan ruins at Tikal. I would have never seen them without Bobby. At least, not like that, with no other people around and howler monkeys swinging above us. "In ten years, there'll be tour buses here," he said. "There'll be McDonald's in the rain forest." I looked to see if he was kidding but his expression was grim under the straw hat he wore.

During my entire visit, I never saw where my brother lived. He didn't show me his room or his neighborhood. I never met any friends he might have made, or even someone who knew him. When he said good-bye to me at the bus, I clung to him, as if to assure myself that he was still there, that nothing had changed.

chapter twenty-one

I WAS TEN and Bobby sixteen that last good summer at our family's cabin in Gold Run. Sara was queen of the teens at the WPA pool. Bobby and I were on strike from swimming, from even venturing outside. Deathly bored, I was reduced to slapping the couch around Bobby with a flyswatter, squinting and saying, "I missed." It must have taken ten swats to get a reaction. "Knock it off," he yelled over his book.

"Go outside, both of you, and stay out," Mother ordered.

Bobby asked for the car to go to the library in Auburn. Mother said only if he took me. I was drunk with happiness, high on my own power to make things go my way.

My parents didn't care about having new cars. My mother's was ancient, with upholstery on the ceiling, a stick shift topped by a two-tone knob on the floor, and windows that took all your strength to crank. I hated my usual seat in the back, but now I was up front, windows down, hot air blowing through my sleeveless blouse, our channel, not my mother's, on the radio.

"I don't want to go the library," I said.

Bobby shrugged. "Got any money?"

I didn't but I scooted forward, opened the glove box, and came up with forty-six cents and grit under my nails. Bobby seemed pleased. "We can get a couple of Cokes," he said. He asked me what I had against the library in Auburn. I relayed a long story about being upbraided for reading a book from the adult shelf without a note from my mother, telling my brother how I'd defended myself to the librarian.

"You were thinking outside your head," he said of my defense. "That's how I try to operate." He must have realized that I didn't understand, because he elaborated. "Physical stuff like fear, self-consciousness, even hunger inhibits thinking," he said. "Pure thought happens outside your physical self. I train myself to think that way. You just did it naturally."

I wasn't sure that I had. I'd embellished the librarian story. Still, the moment was so large all I could think to do was make it bigger.

"Teach me to drive," I said.

I never thought he'd agree, but when he did, I knew I couldn't back down. He turned off the highway onto a country road, pulled over, and told me to put my hands up as if we were playing patty cake. He demonstrated how to use the foot pedals by having me push against his hands. He said he'd push the stick. I'd steer and do the foot thing. We traded places. Bobby didn't get angry when I stalled the car. He told me to think outside my head, and I must have because the car lurched forward.

"Turn left," Bobby said, and I did, immediately. It took a moment to grasp that we were airborne. "Oh, Jesus," Bobby hooted as we hit the ground, tearing through a field of foxtails, his hand slapping his thigh, mine glued to the steering wheel.

"I meant turn left at the corner," Bobby said, holding his stomach. I'd never seen him laugh so long or so hard.

He had to flag down a pickup truck to tow us out of the field. "I was teaching my kid sister to drive," Bobby said to the guy who helped us.

"You could have been hurt," the man said.

"I almost bust a gut laughing," Bobby said.

I wanted to keep on laughing like that forever but Bobby said we had to keep our cool to avoid suspicion. My mother didn't notice the new scratches on the car. A few days later we went home to Sacramento. And a week after that Bobby left for Princeton.

chapter twenty-two

I'D WITNESSED the suffering of friends, wondered how they could endure. I'd held my children tight and counted myself lucky.

Now that the life upended was mine, I lacked the specificity of grief, the focus of terror. In their place was the dull, unending sense that I was dreaming.

On Sunday, I drove into Oakland to shop at a grocery store where I wouldn't bump into anyone I knew. In the cereal aisle, a woman called my name. It was Jane from my book group. "What are you doing shopping clear over here?" she asked as her squeaky-wheeled cart trapped me against the Raisin Bran.

My eyelid pulsed and I put a finger on it to make it stop.

"I feel so terrible for everything you must be going through." She hesitated. "I thought what you did was very brave."

Brave? The sympathy in her eyes seemed genuine. Something was being asked of me, and I didn't know how to deliver it. This was how it must have always been for Bobby, I thought, the strain to fake behavior that comes naturally to everyone else.

"Thank you for thinking of me," I said. It sounded right but I didn't mean it. I didn't want her thinking of me. It seemed like a kind of invasion. The only thing she and I had ever shared was a dislike of *The English Patient*. My heart was off its rhythm, stuttering. I was afraid of never getting out from behind her basket, or worse, bumping into her in aisle after aisle, and then in the parking lot. When we finally parted, I went straight to the checkout stand, my shopping less than half done.

Eric was in the side yard clipping dead hydrangeas when I got home. He hadn't shaved all weekend, and the white in his stubble gave him a grizzled look.

"What's with the gardening?" I asked, sounding more sarcastic than I meant. Except for the occasional sweeping of leaves, I'd never seen him do yard work.

"It needed to be done," he said, keeping his back to me.

I shifted the grocery bags in my arms. "I can't face walking Lilly into school tomorrow."

He stopped clipping, his hand taut on the shears. "What *can* you do?" he asked.

I was thankful that he left unsaid *besides putting our family on the cover of* Time *magazine.*

He waited for my answer. It was the first time we'd looked eye to eye in days. He'd been blond when we met. Now his hair was white in the sunlight. In his bleached-stained sweatshirt and old jeans, he looked like a guy who drove a beat-up van and fixed things. I pictured us in an alternative life, one where we worked for cash and didn't wait until five o'clock to start drinking, a life where the waste was right out in the open. I wanted to touch his face, to feel the sting of bristle against the inside of my wrists.

"I can take the groceries inside," I said.

He turned back to his reckless cutting.

I put the bags on the kitchen floor. There wasn't much in them. Upstairs, the girls were fighting. They were like inmates now, nothing passed unchallenged. I stood at the kitchen table staring at a slender crack snaking down the wall. I didn't know whether I was dreading or craving the moment when they'd call out for me.

The noise I anticipated came not from upstairs but from Eric. A sharp yelp followed by the sound of the garden hose. He'd cut himself.

It wasn't blood that bothered me so much as bleeding, the idea of what was supposed to be inside of you coming out. Eric came in the house through the kitchen and turned on the water at the sink. He didn't react when I walked up behind him, his hand under the faucet, water running red down the drain.

"What possessed you to start gardening today?" I said, furious with fear.

"I couldn't stand looking at those dead hydrangeas," he said.

I suppose I should have been grateful that he was raging at hydrangeas instead of me, but I was afraid. I watched the blood pour from his hand, and change hue under the water. I wanted to call him an idiot. Instead, I said, "Let me see." My voice was at odds with my pounding heart, but I recognized the tone. It was my calm teacher's voice, the quietly certain mother's voice that I feared my children no longer trusted.

Eric let me examine his hand. The cut went deep into the flesh above his thumb. I could see the tendon.

"I'll drive you to the emergency room," I said.

"I can go myself."

"I said I'd drive you."

Eric yanked open the dish-towel drawer, searching through the pile for one of the older towels. Even bleeding, he was unfailingly considerate.

In the car, aware of my panic, and wishing I was steadier in an emergency, I looked over at Eric. His skin was gray against the white of his unshaved stubble. The dish towel around his hand was soaked red. He stared ahead, not returning my glance.

I dropped him in front of the emergency room and found a place to park. In the waiting room, Eric was attempting to fill out a hospital form on a clipboard in his lap. I finished it for him, my leg touching his for the first time in days. "A person could bleed to death in a place like this," I said. Eric laughed a little.

Finally a tall woman in blue scrubs called his name. As if Eric were one of the kids, I went with him. The nurse put us in a small room with metal chairs, a table, and too much light. She sat Eric at the table and made a lot of noise putting on latex gloves. Then she unwrapped his hand. "Oh," she said with a sharp intake of air. I looked past her at the jars of cotton swabs and tongue depressors. Say "ah," my grandfather used to say when we were small. He pressed our tongues with a stick he unwrapped from his black bag. Sara said the stick made her gag. But

I liked it, the taste of smooth wood against my tongue, the sense that I was holding my mouth open just right.

The emergency room doctor was too fat for his white coat. He had a German accent and he winked at me in my metal chair by the door. He seemed to belong to some other era, to some jollier world. He took a long time with Eric's hand, then told us that a surgeon should look at it, too.

I could leave this room. I wasn't the patient. Eric was angry with me. He wasn't dying. "I think we need to take care of you," the nurse said, standing over me. She stared at my hand. I did, too. It shook all by itself, my rings rattling against the metal arm of my chair. She took me out of the room to a gurney in the hall, and strapped on a blood pressure cuff. She squeezed it too hard, shaking her head.

"Calm down," she said. "We can't let you leave until you do."

"I'm perfectly calm," I said.

"Who's your doctor?" The way she asked the question made it sound like an accusation.

Doctor? I couldn't think.

When I didn't answer her, she said. "Wait here."

As soon as she disappeared, I climbed down from the gurney. I slipped out through a side door and found a bench outside. An ambulance pulled up and I looked away. Eric found me fifteen minutes later, his arm in a sling. "Are you okay?"

My face was damp with tears. I did not look up. He sat beside me.

"Are you going to leave me?" I asked.

"I could ask you the same thing," he said.

I clutched the inside of his thigh, sliding my icy fingers upward. "I was so scared when I saw your hand."

He nodded, growing hard against my touch. I felt the worn denim of his jeans, the metal track of his zipper, his firm outline. We kissed. I knew he hadn't forgiven me, but it was something.

"Look what I got," he said when we broke apart. He shook a pill vial in his good hand. "Vicodin."

"You'll have to share," I said, only half kidding.

* * *

MONDAY, the alarm woke me but Eric slept as if unconscious, his face in the pillow, his bandaged hand above his head. He wasn't driving anyone to school. I got up feeling as if I'd taken the Vicodin instead of him.

At breakfast, Lilly moved so slowly, ate so little, I put my hand on her forehead. She pushed it away. "I can't miss any more school," she said. She'd understood my wish before I did, my desire to keep her with me, to avoid walking her into the school where I no longer had a job.

Julia asked to be dropped two blocks from her campus. "I need the exercise," she said.

At Mountaintop, I signaled to turn into the teachers' parking lot. "Don't park," Lilly said, her voice too even. "Just drop me off like everyone else." I'd told Eric I couldn't do it, walk Lilly into school, face everyone. Now I grieved the end of that walk.

Eric was up when I got back, dressed for work. He had an appointment at ten with a doctor to treat his hand. "I can take you," I said. "I don't have anything else to do."

"Ease up on the self-pity," he said.

I didn't argue. Eric didn't hang around the watercooler complaining like the rest of us. He just kept on working quietly at his desk.

THE WAITING ROOM of the surgeon's office was cushy with new magazines, a large aquarium, and a closed-caption television hanging from struts, tuned to CNN. An older, softly gray-haired woman, trim in jeans and tennis shoes, sat a few seats down watching the silent television. Eric talked with clients on his cell phone, one call after another. When the nurse called him, he went in still talking on the phone. I rolled my eyes. The woman seated near me caught my expression and we traded smiles.

I picked up a shiny *Architectural Digest*. I'd always liked trying to imagine our house perfectly done, the next house we'd have, but now these pictures led me nowhere. I closed the magazine and stared at the television.

Suddenly my brother was on the screen in an orange prison jumpsuit, his hands and feet shackled, his glance downward. The magazine slipped from my lap. I walked over to the set, and stood right in front of it so that I could see everything. A federal grand jury in Idaho had indicted Bobby in five Cal Bomber explosions.

The woman sitting behind me cleared her throat. I was blocking her view of the set. For once I didn't care about people knowing who I was. "He's my brother," I said. "I'm the sister who turned him in."

"I thought you looked familiar," she said cautiously, as though I might be dangerous myself.

I returned to my chair, my eyes fixed on the television as if this were a disaster and I needed to be told where to go. The governor of California, resolute and unsmiling, was on the screen speaking to the press. I couldn't hear his tone of controlled anger but I read it in his captioned words: "The Cal Bomber chose Californians as targets of his heinous crimes. If federal officials don't think they have a case that warrants the death penalty, the state of California does." Underneath him a crawling headline read: GOVERNOR OF CALIFORNIA SEEKS TO HAVE CAL BOMBER EXECUTED.

My brother hadn't even been tried and already they were fighting over the chance to kill him. The gray-haired woman looked at me, then glanced away. I grabbed my purse, and left. Sitting in the car, I scanned stations on the radio, hearing the same news over and over, when what I wanted was to be told something else entirely.

I shut off the radio and stared into the sunlight, remembering myself as a child on our front steps, waiting for Bobby to come home. He'd come up the walkway smiling, a package of Bazooka in his pocket. He'd sit and read the comic to me, give me the paper to smell. Then he'd split the pink gum down the line in the middle and teach me how to blow bubbles.

"YOU'VE BEEN CRYING," Eric said when he got in the car.

"Bobby's been indicted," I said.

Eric was quiet in a way that meant he was thinking. "It's not hopeless," he said finally. "There's his mental state. We don't know that the government's evidence means what they say it does. Despite what they're claiming, it's not a slam dunk."

I looked at Eric in his striped, button-down shirt, his bandaged hand in a sling. For all he'd been through in the past weeks, the last twenty-four hours, he looked better. Rested. Resolved. This was the Eric his clients saw, and I clung to his words.

"There's more." I told him what the governor had said.

Eric's laugh was short and sarcastic. "Guess he's decided to run for president." He took my hand. "Bobby's got good lawyers. They know how to use pretrial prejudice to their advantage."

I nodded, willing our marriage back to the way it had been before, the two of us on the same side of every significant thing.

"Look, the pretrial motions can go on for months," he said. "In the meantime, Bobby's going to be sleeping in a clean bed, getting enough to eat, having medical attention." He paused, looked at me. "And we're going to get back to a normal life."

I understood his words as a command. "Yes," I said. Until that moment I hadn't realized how badly I'd wanted someone to tell me what to do.

He seemed surprised at the passion in my kiss in the car outside the BART station. "You don't need to go in today," I said.

"I'm a lawyer," he said. "I don't need a left hand."

I watched him leave. I hadn't been looking out for his health. I was picturing us back in bed. But I didn't mind that he hadn't picked up on the possibility. That it had entered my imagination was enough.

WHEN I GOT HOME, I phoned my mother. She answered on the first ring.

"You heard," she said at the sound of my voice.

"On CNN."

"There's so much wrong with their case," she said. "The FBI never told the judge who issued the warrant that they had other suspects."

"Good," I said. "I mean for Bobby's defense."

"He's coming home," she said.

"To your house? There's bail?"

She sighed as if my idiocy were too much to bear. "To the Sacramento County Jail to wait for his trial."

My neck pulsed. Idaho was far away. It wasn't real. But I knew just where the Sacramento County Jail was. It was two blocks from my father's old office.

THAT EVENING, we sat down to an actual dinner, Eric and the girls overpraising my pot roast. Once again, he and I had gotten it backward. We weren't imposing structure on the girls as much as they were imposing structure on us. Julia had already given our new, unlisted phone number to all her friends, and we were in the business of playing secretary to her again. Lilly's best friend had found a new best friend in the time Lilly was absent. Lilly and I schemed to get her back. The old arguments about homework, dishes, and bedtime returned as if we'd never been on the cover of *Time*.

Eric resumed his position as the parent-in-charge in the morning, making breakfast, hurrying the girls, and driving them to school. In their early-morning noise, the stomping down the hall, the running of water, the banging of doors, they asserted their membership in the real world, the world of people who had somewhere to be in the morning. But now in the sounds of their departure from the house, I heard their eagerness to leave.

It had barely been three weeks since my brother's arrest. The world was continuing on but I'd been cut adrift.

"Do you have time to go over some things this evening?" Eric asked on Friday. His anger at me had been replaced by resignation. The anger had been easier to bear. "Can you get together what we owe on everything so we can look at where we stand?"

Eric worried about his job in normal times, the finicky blue-chip clients, the prestige firm whose plush carpets and stunning floral arrangements hid a relentless demand for billable hours. I rubbed the shirtsleeve that smelled of his anxiety. "Tell me what's going on," I said, bracing myself. He explained how the department head had come into his office and shut the door.

"How did he put it?" Eric asked sarcastically. "The client has some understandable concern that you might not be as focused as you need to be right now, and they'd like Carl to take over."

I was outraged. "How can they treat you like that after all the cases you've won for them?"

"They're the client," Eric said. "They can treat me any way they want."

I wanted to reassure him that this was only a bump in the road, but we both knew better. Instead I gathered the bank statements, bills, and loan notices, and brought them to the kitchen table. I gave Eric figures and he wrote them down on his yellow legal pad. We were like most everyone we knew. We lived a sliver beyond our means. Two kids in private schools, an old house that endlessly needed repairs, vacations that maybe we shouldn't have taken, but the kids were only young once. We'd believed in a future of rising salaries and appreciating homes.

"Do you blame me?" I asked.

"For what?"

"This thing with Bobby. Not fighting to keep my job."

"It's not your job I'm worried about," he said.

"But without this . . ." I flipped my hand so that I wouldn't have to say my brother's name again.

He shrugged. "I'm smart, I work hard, but I'll never be more than a midlevel partner at Sterling, Talbot. I'm one of the fungibles not one of the indispensables, and that's got nothing to do with you or your brother."

"We'll tighten our belts," I said. It was our joke, the line that always closed our let's-look-at-the-bills meetings, the line that led to one of us suggesting dinner out, the line that made us laugh, that reassured us we were still young and foolhardy.

But this time, we didn't laugh.

chapter twenty-three

OUTSIDE, the May breeze carried the scent of geraniums and rosemary. Inside, I slept with my head under my pillow to keep out the light, my dreams hot and jumbled. When the phone rang, I reached for it, clearing my throat. I didn't want anyone to know I was sleeping the morning away. I said hello, trying to approximate the tone of someone who'd been up for hours doing meaningful things. No one answered. Before I hung up, I heard what sounded like squealing.

Downstairs, in my flannel nightgown, so wrong for the hour, wrong even for the season, I poured a cup of not-quite-hot coffee from the carafe, and watched the digital clock on the stove turn eleven. When the phone rang, I answered with a hint of furtiveness, as if the caller could see what I was wearing.

There was the same squealing sound as before but louder. Then a man spoke, his voice adult and hard. "You know what happens to little piggies who squeal, don't you Natalie Askedahl?"

I slammed the receiver into its cradle. There had been threatening messages before, but we had an unlisted number now. My hand was still on the phone when it rang again. I pulled it from its metal plate on the wall, heard our other phones ringing. I used my cell to call the police, my voice shaking from the sense that I was the one who'd done something wrong. They said they'd send an officer. To take the squealer's report.

* * *

WHEN THE doorbell rang, I was still in my nightgown. I hadn't expected the police to come so quickly. I threw on yesterday's clothes and answered the door barefoot.

My sister stood in front of me, her gray, curly hair loose on her back, her body fit in shorts and a T-shirt. She had a sweater tied around her waist, a worn canvas grocery bag on her shoulder, and rubber flip-flops on her feet. Sara hadn't been to our place in years. We hadn't spoken since she'd all but banished me from Mother's house six weeks before.

I couldn't read her expression, her eyes behind dark glasses in outdated aviator frames. Something's happened to Mother, I thought.

"I've got to pee," Sara said, pushing past me. She took off her sunglasses and squinted, trying to remember where the bathroom was.

She was back quickly. Sara never lingered. She gave me an appraising look.

"Been out of the house lately?" she asked with more good humor than not. "You seem a bit"—she wiggled her fingers—"musty."

I glanced down, and saw a spot on my shirt, but of course that wasn't what she meant. She looked around as if trying to square the room with her memory. "You got a new couch?"

"Four years ago."

She tilted her head as if making a calculation.

"Has something happened to Mom?" I asked.

She looked confused, then laughed as one does at a small child who's gotten everything wrong. "She's fine as of an hour ago. I tried phoning you."

A part of me wanted to laugh, every phone in our house unplugged. I wasn't ready to forgive her but I was glad she was here, and I wasn't alone. Sara perched on the ottoman, her canvas bag on the floor, her keys in her lap as if she could only stay a minute. I sat on the couch.

"Looks like you're hiding from the law," she said, pointing at the drawn drapes and the blanket that still covered the porch window.

"People drive by," I said. "They call. Reporters hang out. I'm famous. Or haven't you heard?"

"Self-pity doesn't suit you, Natalie."

"I'm trying to be polite," I said. "Which is more than you were to me the last time we saw each other."

There it was. It had taken all of three minutes for me to spit it out.

"I'm sorry about that," Sara said.

At our house, we tossed around apologies: sorry about the spilt milk, the errand forgotten, the tantrum, the grumpy mood. But Sara wasn't like Eric, the kids, and me. She didn't explain herself. She didn't traffic in apologies. In surprise, I dropped the arms I'd folded across my chest.

Sara reached into her canvas bag with its faded store logo and pulled out a plastic bag of dried figs and a jar of peanut butter. I watched her dip a fig into the peanut butter. "Want one?" she asked.

"We have food here," I said. "I can make you a sandwich."

"Your sandwiches are always so overmade," she said. She licked her fingers, then put the figs and peanut butter back in her bag. "You heard what that asshole governor of ours said on television the day Bobby was indicted?"

I said I had.

"I mean why wait for a trial before demanding the death penalty, right?" Sara's voice rose, her arm batted the air. "You know, fuck the Bill of Rights, fuck presumed innocent. Even the president's on the blood wagon." She sighed. "That's what we're up against, Natalie."

I glanced away from her eyes on mine. "I don't know what we can do," I said.

Uncharacteristically, Sara touched me. A pat on the knee. "Yes you do," she said. "We fight back, just like you did with *Time*. We counter the monster they portray with the truth about who Bobby is."

"I'm afraid the only truth I know is who Bobby *was*," I said.

Sara looked as if she wanted to hit me upside the head. But her voice didn't show it. "You know who he is," she said. "He's our brother, a profoundly gifted, gentle soul who has spiraled into mental illness. But the government is treating him as if he is some Middle Eastern terrorist mastermind unworthy of constitutional protection."

I couldn't argue. It was the truth. "Have you seen him?"

Sara shook her head. "I've tried, but he refuses. He won't even see Mom."

Bobby was consuming all of our lives, yet he wanted nothing to do with us. He remained a phantom, an abstraction we could each define in our separate ways. I wondered if Sara or my mother was any closer to understanding him than I was.

Sara talked about Bobby's new lawyers, how I'd like them, what an incredible job they were doing, but how they could only do so much. "Mom's hired a lawyer for the family," she said, "someone with media connections. He's talked to *60 Minutes*. They want us. All of us."

"I can't," I said.

Sara laughed. "You're too busy?"

"I can't drag Eric and the kids into this any more than I already have. I have to put them first."

"We don't have that luxury," Sara said. "It's you *60 Minutes* wants."

"Because I'm the one who turned Bobby in."

"If you want to state the obvious. You and Eric."

"Oh, no," I said. "He won't do it."

"He has to. He can't look like he agrees with the other side."

Sara retied the sweater around her waist and stood. "Don't worry," she said. "The taping won't be for a few weeks. You've got time to work your magic on hubby." She put the canvas bag on her shoulder, a finger through the ring of her key chain.

"We'll talk," she said as if we did it all the time. I watched her as she hurried down my front stairs without a trace of uncertainty in her footing.

"I WISH there were somewhere you and the girls could go," Eric said that evening when I told him about the phone calls and the policeman who'd come to take the report.

I took the opening, rushing onto shaky ground, presenting *60 Minutes* as a family vacation, with free airfare and hotels, tea with the girls at the Plaza, a Broadway show. Eric listened to me with a face that gave nothing away. He must have been an excellent negotiator, never betraying with a slight nod or a raised brow where you stood with him.

"No," he said when I finished. "We're not exposing our kids to that. They need us to be here, being their parents, taking care of them. Bobby's got your mother and sister. You want to have tea with the girls at the Plaza, see a Broadway show? Take a credit card and go."

He drained the bottle of wine, pouring more into my glass than his. That was Eric. He took the burned toast, the smaller cookie, the seat behind the post. After twenty years of marriage, he still opened the car door for me. Maybe that's why I didn't hear his no for what it was.

JULIA WAS SHOWING a sudden interest in the mail, rushing to the mailbox when I brought her home from school. "What have you got?" I asked. She'd pulled out two shiny, stiff-covered publications, then handed me the rest.

"Colleges are sending me catalogs," she said in a way that was both casual and sneaky.

I let it drop. Later, when she stomped down the hall to take a shower, I went to her room. Her bed was unmade, the blankets spilling off. Her nightgown and three days' worth of clothes were scattered across the floor along with the contents of her backpack. The only neat spot was a perfect stack of bright catalogs. I scooped up the pile and sat on the mess of her bed.

Each catalog was more beautiful than the last. Full-color pages of ethnically diverse young people studying in cathedral libraries, under green trees, and beside flowing rivers, walking to class in snow and autumn leaves. There were colleges I'd only vaguely heard of, Bates, Bowdoin, Carleton, Colby, Haverford, Williams, along with the famous ones. None was closer than Minnesota, and not one cost less than thirty thousand dollars a year.

I was so lost in the promise and the horror that I didn't notice Julia at the door of her own room.

"What are you doing? Snooping?" Her pale face was blotched with outrage.

"I was just interested," I said.

"That's a first." Then she corrected herself in acknowledgment of the chasm between before and now: "These days."

"How long have you been collecting these?" She was only a sophomore.

"You're acting like you just discovered I'm on the pill or something," she said. Her body looked tiny wrapped in a pink bath towel. "I'm the only one in my class who hasn't even visited a single college."

I wanted to say, *UC Berkeley's down the street.*

She sat beside me, put her hand on my arm, and spoke in a voice that longed for more than she even understood. "Do you think we could look this summer? Go back east?"

I looked out her window at the shingled roofs nestled in eucalyptus, the evergreen-studded hills leading to the bay. "We'll try," I said, unable to picture it. *The college bomber's family looks at colleges.*

WHEN I WENT to check on Lilly that evening, I found her sitting cross-legged on the floor of Julia's room. She looked guilty. She was going through Julia's catalogs.

"I'm picking out my college," she said as if she were not sure how I'd take this.

"Have you found one?" I asked lightly.

She held one up. "I'm going to Yale."

I wondered if she'd chosen Yale because she could read the name, or if she had inside information from Julia.

I sat on the bed. "Why there?"

"Because it has snow and the buildings look like castles."

I nodded, how nice, but I couldn't leave it at that. "You're years away from going to college."

"You don't have worry," she said, her tone matter-of-fact. "Julia's going to take care of me there."

* * *

THE NEXT DAY, I saw him through the window, one hand still bandaged from his gardening mishap, the other holding his briefcase. Eric was home early again. I opened the door to him.

"How come you're home?" It was barely one o'clock. "Anything wrong?"

"The partners want me to take some time off," he said. "To find another job." His laugh was dry. "Their letting me go is solely a question of the business outlook. If you can believe that."

I sank onto the couch. Eric sat down beside me. He reached into his briefcase and pulled out a legal pad covered with figures. His eyes were brilliant. He had it figured out. How we could tighten our belts. Where he could expect to land. How this was a kind of opportunity if only we could learn to manage on a lot less. Those scrawls on the legal pad represented the dream parcel, the corner lot, the view of the beach that could be ours. "Our problem is the credit cards." He looked at the ceiling. "That and the kids' schools and all we owe on the house."

We both knew I wouldn't be earning money at my old job or anywhere else anytime soon.

chapter twenty-four

I AWOKE to the girls arguing over a hairbrush and Eric dressing for work. It took me a moment to figure out what wasn't right.

"Where are you going?" I asked.

"To take the kids to school and then to work," he said.

I considered how I could have misunderstood what he'd told me the day before. "But you've been fired," I said tentatively.

He sat on the bed next to me. "If only it were that easy." He sounded chipper. "This is supposed to look like my idea. I keep my office until I get an offer, then everyone acts sad to see me go."

"I'll be home early," he said, leaning to kiss me. "I can pick up Lilly." The lines were smoothed from his face, and his eyes were clear. He'd been dreading this for so long that when it finally came, he was relieved.

WHEN THE phone rang, I feared it was Sara calling about *60 Minutes*. I hadn't broached the topic again with Eric. I was so preoccupied with excuses that I wasn't prepared for the male voice, so close to Eric's but not his. It was his brother, a busy man, seeming irritated Eric hadn't been at his office when he called.

I fumbled for a chatty tone, but Richard cut me off. "Dad died this afternoon."

"No," I said as if I had the power to rescind this news.

Eric's father had collapsed tending to his roses. He was dead by the time the ambulance reached the hospital.

When Eric walked in the door with Lilly, he read my face and knew immediately that something was wrong. "What is it?" he asked. I sent Lilly upstairs, then reached for his hand. "I should call," he said when I told him.

Eric's mother wasn't like mine, relentless in her stoicism. His mother needed her children, her friends, the comfort of other people. Eric would go there immediately and I would drive down later with the girls.

I helped him pack. I tried not to think of him going through the next few days on top of having just lost his job. I dreaded telling the girls. When Julia came home, I sat them on the couch.

"This isn't fair," Julia said after I told them. "Hasn't our family been through enough crap?"

"Apparently not," I said.

"Now I don't have a single grandfather," Lilly said.

MY FATHER-IN-LAW and my father were men of the same generation. They fought for their country, drank hard liquor, and smoked cigarettes until their doctors made them quit. They talked like tough guys and kept their emotions to themselves.

I phoned my mother. "I suppose I'll have to come to the funeral," she said. "I suppose they'll make a big production."

No bigger than our family's current production, I thought.

She insisted on taking the train from Sacramento. The girls and I waited for her at the station. Though I'd seen her just six weeks before, it was an old woman that the conductor helped from the train. I had to be imagining this frailness, the loss of height.

Outside the church, someone whispered, "That's her." I turned without thinking and three women averted their eyes.

We took our seats, recorded funeral music on the sound system. Eric, Richard, his son, and three other men carried the coffin to the altar. People dabbed their eyes and I wished for easy tears, to feel something other than anger at the minister's clichés.

My mother had wanted a small private funeral for my father, but my father was a public man with public friends. She'd sent Bobby an overnight letter with directions and a money order for a ticket. She'd acted as if she expected him to show up.

More than five hundred people packed into the Episcopal cathedral a mile from the capitol building where my father had worked. Both Governor Browns were there, along with the president of the University of California, and chancellors from most of the campuses. Willie Brown came. So did Dianne Feinstein, and Clark Kerr. The Bear Flag of California covered my father's coffin.

We did not cry. We wore our public faces under stained-glass windows. The oratory was political, the platitudes were those of the Democratic Party. Eric sat next to me holding my hand, but he couldn't help looking around. I saw in his eyes that he was impressed. My eyes wandered, too, but I was searching for the brother I knew would never come.

KELLEY HAD the mourners over to her house after the service. Everything was impeccable—the flowers, the food. I'd always admired my sister-in-law's perfection, her flawless taste, her ease in what she wore and the way she entertained. All attributes I lacked. But Kelley was impossible to resent; she was far too nice. I complimented her on how lovely everything was.

"When you get down to it," my sister-in-law said, looking weary, "it's just another party."

I brought a plate to my mother, sitting purposely alone in a corner of the living room. "Just eat a little," I said as if she were a child. She put a cold hand on mine. "The last thing I ever wanted was for us to be one of those families weeping on television," she said, her voice so low I had to lean to hear. "But the politicians and the press have left us no choice." She squeezed my hand, her grip intense. "If it weren't a question of Bobby's life"—her voice broke but she did not look away—"I would never ask this of you."

"But there's still the possibility that Bobby's innocent," I whispered.

"You think that makes any difference?" she said.

I had no answer, just a burning in my eyes. I excused myself to dab cold water on my face in the bathroom off Kelley's bedroom. Afterward, I just sat on the edge of her bed. There was a David Hockney on the wall across from me. Any person other than Kelley would have hung it in the living room.

I don't know how long I'd been sitting there when Kelley found me. "So this where you've come to hide," she said.

I jumped up. "Stay," she said, motioning down. She sat beside me. "I want to talk to you."

I took a breath.

"What I want to say is that if you need anything—help with the kids, money, anything—call me. Not Richard. Me."

Kelley's face was far too serious. I suddenly feared she knew something about Eric and me that I didn't.

"Money? I don't understand."

"I have my own is what I'm trying to tell you."

"We're going to be all right."

"I'm talking about you," Kelley said. "Don't think about it now. Just remember that it's there."

Did she mean if Eric left me? I was afraid to ask. I couldn't imagine leaving him any more than I could imagine Kelley socking money away to escape her perfect life. She patted my hand. "I'd better get back to my mourners," she said

When I finally left her room, it was to stand at Eric's side. I greeted people I didn't want to greet, picked up the slack in conversations I didn't want to be having. I stood by him just as I was sure Eric would be at my side on *60 Minutes*.

"You know what people kept saying to me?" Eric asked when we were home alone in our bedroom. I looked at his grief-stricken face and waited for him to tell me. "That I'd been a good son," he said.

I put my arms around him. A good son. A good husband. A team player. And look where it got him.

* * *

"YOUR MOTHER'S lawyer phoned," Eric said two days later. I'd come into the house carrying groceries in my arms, proud of having gone shopping.

I inhaled too quickly. "Do I have to call him back?"

"He called to talk to me." Eric took the bags, absently unpacking them. I didn't move.

"And?" I said.

He shut the refrigerator. "I'm not doing it. Not *60 Minutes*. Not *6 Minutes*." He looked at me. "Not for your brother. Not for your mother. Not even to save all the people on death row who might be innocent."

I'd been the youngest child in my family, powerless except to point fingers. "I went to *you*, not the FBI," I said. "You called the shots. You put us at the center of this."

"I know," Eric said, and I saw from his face he did. "I should've kept us out of it, said you were wrong about Bobby. Carried your manila file to the paper shredder. Not been such a lawyer. We could have gone out to dinner."

I saw us at that dinner as clearly as he must have a thousand times, sitting in a leather booth in one of the old-fashioned places, maybe Jack's, a pair of martinis on a starched white cloth, everything all right, just a false alarm.

"I've been clinging to the hope that Bobby's innocent," I said, trying to put my feelings into words. "Now I see how naive that was. They're going to execute someone for these terrible crimes, and Bobby's who they have."

Eric listened without saying a word. I gripped the tile counter. This time I would plead. "I don't feel I have a choice. It's not just for Bobby. I have to do this for my mother, too. He's her son. But I'm not asking you to do this for them. I'm asking you to do it for me. Please. Just this one thing."

Eric glanced away from my imploring eyes and I dared to feel hope.

"It isn't just this one thing," he said too quietly. "It's the beginning of months and probably years of your brother's case consuming our lives. Look what it has already done to us."

I dropped into a chair, suddenly not sure we were even talking about

Bobby. "Do you mean what *I've* done to us? Put us on the cover of *Time* magazine, helped you lose your job."

"Don't go there," he said. "If it weren't for Bobby, we'd be fine."

I shook my head. "I don't know if Bobby even thinks about me anymore, except in hatred. But I won't be able to live with myself if I don't do what I can to save his life."

"You've clearly made up your mind," he said.

"I have to go," I said

"I can't stop you."

"Eric, please, I need you there with me, whether you agree with me or not."

"I'm sorry," he said.

Until that moment, a part of me believed the old rules still applied, that for better or worse, I could always count on Eric being at my side.

Now, I understood, I could no longer count on anything.

chapter twenty-five

ALTHOUGH it was out of character with her running, her vegetarianism, her organic gardening, not to mention her politics, my sister had never been able to quit smoking. It was as if the smoking connected her to another Sara, not the cheerleader she had been or the hippie she still was, but someone closer to my father and the rooms he worked in.

When our *60 Minutes* interview finished, I felt as if I'd been shut down along with the cameras, that I couldn't rise from my seat. But Sara was on her feet, in motion, itching for a cigarette. I found her on the plaza outside the studio, lighting a Marlboro from the butt of a previous one.

"We got through it," I said.

She exhaled, her smoke rising in the soft breeze. "Our dog and pony show."

I'd been afraid I'd go blank in front of the cameras, that I'd be too nervous, or not nervous enough—that I'd fail to defend Bobby or defend him too much. I looked at Sara. "Did I do all right?"

"You did all right," she said.

She looked like a farmwife in her dirndl skirt, clogs, and a cardigan with shiny buttons that I was sure my mother had given her. Her gray hair was wrapped in braids around her head.

"Last night I had this awful dream that Dad gave me talking points for our interview but they disappeared from the paper they were written on," I said.

"Dad would have never used talking points," Sara said.

My father had only been dead ten years, but he belonged to another age. "What do you think he would've said if he'd been with us?"

"He'd have said that Bobby threw away the gift of a brilliant mind, that he wasted his life." Sara took a deep drag, and for the first time, I envied her smoking, the sensation of smoke warming the emptiness in my chest.

ON SUNDAY, Eric took the kids out to dinner so I could watch *60 Minutes* alone before we watched the tape later in the evening with Julia. I painted this as necessary preparation for her questions. We both agreed that Lilly was better off not watching. Eric and I were like that with each other now, polite, reasonable, distant.

I sat on an ottoman in front of the television the way the girls did, up close, drawn to the image of myself in a way that shut out all else. Despite the enormity of the drama, I was still an American woman who measured her life in desserts eaten and not eaten, and my first thought was: She doesn't look fat. She looks fine.

My mother, sitting between Sara and me on the couch, looked even older than in real life, smaller and more breakable. In a sad, clear voice, her spotted hands quietly folded, she talked about sending Bobby to Princeton too young. "He was so bright that it obscured his social immaturity, and he wanted to go so badly." She took a long, heartrending breath. "When it didn't work out, and he had to come home, we thought it was just his age."

She brightened talking about how Bobby's extraordinary intelligence was recognizable in infancy, how she'd fed him a special diet of spinach and pureed liver to enhance the development of his brain. I'd never heard this story before, and it made me the faintest bit queasy.

Sara buried her rage and sorrow under a flat affect, the lights making her salt-and-pepper hair appear a stark white. I couldn't help noticing that the camera seemed to like me best: on television, Natalie Askedahl seemed more regular than in life. She was someone you'd want for a neighbor, a friend. You even could imagine yourself in her spot.

The show went by so much more quickly than I remembered living it. At the commercial break, I waited, hunched up as if it were thirty degrees inside the house for what was promised next: the story of how Natalie Askedahl could turn her own brother over to the FBI.

The camera shone on the interviewer in all his sonorous celebrity. "If you'd known going to the FBI would lead without question to your brother, that it could result in his execution, would you still have done it?"

Although I was the one who'd given the answer, the hint of rage in the chill of my reply shocked me: "If you mean, had I known the FBI would leak my identity, break their other promises, and the principle of innocent until proven guilty would be tossed aside by public officials and the press, then my answer is no."

My interrogator lifted his brows in a way I'd seen him do on television many times before. "Although you went to the FBI with your husband, he declined our invitation to appear on this program. Does he feel differently about this than you do?"

"My husband stayed with our children," I said, looking him square in the eye. "His father—their grandfather—died just last week."

The interviewer looked the faintest bit abashed, or maybe he just accepted that the line of questioning was over. But instead of triumph, I saw humiliation in my eyes. My husband wasn't at my side for this interview even though I'd pleaded.

AFTER LILLY went to bed, Julia watched the tape with her head against Eric's shoulder. I sat on the other end of the couch, my mind trying to hurry the program along.

"I didn't like seeing Grandma cry," Julia said when it was over. "But you were great."

"Was it that awful watching me?" I asked him after Julia had left us.

"I've never found you awful to watch," Eric said, his tone unexpectedly sad. I lowered my eyes. He was wearing his father's watch. There was no point in pushing Eric to see things my way. He wasn't willing even to share his grief with me.

He climbed the stairs to bed. I followed a few minutes later, but I turned the other way, toward my children. Lilly was sweetly asleep in her room. Julia lay under the covers reading in hers. I sat down beside her. "Everything okay?" I asked.

She hesitated. "Are you and Dad fighting?"

"What makes you ask that?" I said to buy time.

"You and Daddy don't act like you used to together."

"We're not fighting," I said. It might even have been the truth. I feared this was something else entirely. "We're tired, that's all."

She seemed to accept the answer, but she had more on her mind.

"Mom?"

I tried to look as if she could ask me anything.

"Do you really still think that Uncle Bobby's innocent? That he didn't kill those professors or those college kids?"

Not even Eric had asked me this point-blank. "All I know is the brother I knew would never have hurt anybody," I said slowly. "I want to believe that he still wouldn't."

Julia was quiet a moment. "Was Uncle Bobby abused as a child?"

I was aghast. My face must have showed it because Julia looked like she wanted to withdraw the question. Then I understood. "Did you read that somewhere?" I tried to sound collected. "In one of the newsmagazines?"

"Yes," she said. "Do you think Uncle Bobby could be a sociopath?"

"There was no abuse our house," I said.

"Then what do think happened to him? He's hardly normal."

It was such an obvious observation, but I didn't even have an answer for myself. Not one that could explain all of this. "I think the weight of genius was too much for Uncle Bobby," I said. "Everyone expected so much of him. He couldn't handle the pressure."

Julia was quiet, watching me.

"I also think he might have been born with some sort of mental illness like schizophrenia that didn't show up until he was an adult."

"But, no one ever said anything like that before he got arrested."

"Mental illness isn't like the chicken pox," I said. "It can be really hard to see in your own family."

"In AP Biology, we studied genetic markers. You know what they are, right?"

"More or less."

Julia took a breath. "Schizophrenia is hereditary. It runs in families."

I wondered how much of this was coming from AP Biology, and how much from her own reading. How much research had she done without saying a word to anyone?

"The risk increases with high intelligence," she said, her voice breaking.

"It's not going to happen to you," I said too quickly.

"But we don't know, do we?"

I tried to slow down. "What I know is that if you or Lilly ever felt like you couldn't handle something, that you couldn't cope, we would get you help."

"But *you* didn't help Uncle Bobby. You didn't even notice."

"He didn't want my help," I said. "He pushed me away. He didn't want me noticing him. When adults don't want you in their lives, there's not much you can do."

She let me pull her into my arms, the embrace as much for me as for her. "It's going to be all right," I repeated one too many times.

Eric was asleep by the time I slipped into bed. I kept to my own side, staring into the darkness.

When Julia was in kindergarten, another child on the playground told her about the Holocaust. She became so hysterical, the school called for me to pick her up. None of the adults knew what had upset her so. Finally, at home she told me what she'd learned.

"How do you expect me to live with this?" she asked.

I didn't know how to answer her. I still didn't, but I feared my brother had found his way to live both with the horrors of this world and the nightmare inside his mind.

chapter twenty-six

My mother's voice on the phone had a rare tentativeness. She hated asking anyone for anything. "I have to sell the cabin in Gold Run," she said.

I took a painful breath, but I understood. I didn't like thinking about how much Bobby's defense was costing her, where she was getting the money, that Eric and I hadn't contributed a dime.

"The cabin belongs to you children," she said. "It would've been a place Bobby could go, after." She stopped herself.

"That's fine," I said. The land would be worth something. With the money she got for it, I'd be contributing in some small way to Bobby's defense.

"I need you to clean it out," she said. "Soon. Not the furniture. Just the personal stuff. Toss it in the trash."

My great-grandfather had bought the land along the Bear River after the gold was gone. He'd built the cabin with my grandfather. My dad had spent his summers there as a boy. As kids, we had, too. Now I came there with my own family.

I packed clean sheets, a cooler and Julia's CD player, two sets of rubber gloves, rags, and a box of forty-gallon trash bags. This was going to be dirty work. Still, I felt recklessly on vacation as I drove into the Sierras, away from Eric's quiet withdrawal, a faultless sky overhead, the scent of evergreens in dry mountain air.

I drove across the railroad tracks where Bobby and I had once laid pennies. We used to follow the railway to the next town. We were in scenic country but the terrain along the tracks was ugly, crumbling rocks scattered across barren red earth. The scarred landscape sickened Bobby. It was an atrocity, he told me. Hydraulic mining during the Gold Rush had ruined one of the loveliest places on earth.

I parked in front of our cabin, acorns and pine needles cracking under my tires. The place looked the same, a timber rectangle with a screened-in front porch, among the pines above the Bear River. It was a beautiful spot with enough land around it to make a difference in Bobby's defense.

I switched on the power and the water, opened the windows in the big central room to let out the stale air, and went to work in the kitchen. The spices in the cupboard could have been in a museum. No one, including me, had ever thrown anything out. I examined the old pots and pans that I still used. This wasn't what my mother meant by personal stuff.

In the bedroom off the kitchen, the small double bed was made. My daughters slept here now, just as Sara and I had years ago. Once, I wet the bed. "At least we'll be warm for a while," Sara said.

A plaid shirt of my father's hung in the closet. I put the sleeve to my nose, longing for the familiar scent of Parliament cigarettes and newspaper ink, but all I could detect was old wool. Within a week of my father's death, my mother had cleared his closet and sent his clothes to Goodwill. She was the person for this job, not me, clinging to an old shirt like a child with her blanket.

I moved to the next room, and stood in front of the narrow bed with the lumpy mattress. I'd slept here when I was older, Bobby sleeping on the porch on the other side of the open window. We whispered in the dark. Bobby told me there was no God, that it was just an idea people made up to make themselves feel better, that if God were real, people wouldn't need to work so hard to get other people to believe in Him. I accepted what he told me lying there in a dark so perfect you couldn't see at all, smelling the pines, his whispers the only sound I heard.

The room my parents slept in had a quilt-covered bed with an oak headboard. There was a bureau, a closet, and a tall bookcase crammed with books and old issues of the *Atlantic Monthly*. The closet held a few old jackets, the bureau netted nothing more interesting than a hideous rubber bathing cap and a solitary black pawn. I slipped the chess piece into the pocket of my jeans.

I must have been eight, Bobby fifteen, when a summer storm drove me into the house, my shirt wet, goose bumps on my chubby legs. Bobby was at the kitchen table with another boy. They spoke in code, jotting notes on pieces of paper. I asked what they were doing.

"Playing chess," Bobby said. "Don't bother us."

"But there's no board. Where are the pieces?"

"We don't need that stuff," Bobby said.

I saw him play blindfolded once, two games simultaneously, against boys with boards. Everyone seemed surprised when he won, except Bobby. I begged him to teach me how to play. He tried, but gave up. He said I had the aptitude but not the will. "You're too much of a girl," he said. "You're afraid to use your power, if you think someone else might get hurt."

The door open to the back porch, I sat on the quilt, and worked my way through the books. After a while I didn't want to touch them anymore, the paperbacks with yellow pages and torn covers, the musty hardbacks. Still I opened each one, turned it over, and shook it. We were a family of readers. We carried books in pockets, in purses, in cars, on planes. We stacked them next to beds and couches. We tripped over them and we stuck things in them, whatever was at hand to mark our places.

I worked all afternoon throwing away bits of paper, business cards—one so old it had only a four-digit phone number—and envelopes, one from 1935 with a pink, three-cent postage stamp. In a 1942 edition of the *Tales of Edgar Allan Poe*, I found a three-by-five lined card with Bobby's young handwriting. It said, *The weaker repelling force has been identified with the pressure of solar radiation.*

The bookshelf hadn't been moved in so many years that it stuck to the linoleum when I pushed it from the wall to pull out what had fallen behind it: odd bits of paper; blowout cards from magazines; half a study guide to *Finnegan's Wake*; and a pocket-size notebook with a missing cover. I shook the dust from the notebook. Tiny shorthandlike squiggles and barely decipherable symbols crammed the pages edge to edge. Bobby had made up his own chess notation because the standard one took up too much space, but these markings were different. I made out what I thought was the numeral "5" or maybe an *S*, a division sign, possibly an equals sign. There was so much indecipherable meaninglessness, it made me dizzy. I fingered the notebook a moment before tossing it in the black bag with the other trash.

It was almost dark when I headed for dinner in Nevada City, where everything from the past had already been cleaned out of attics and basements and sold in shops. When I returned, I put clean sheets on my parents' bed and crawled in with a copy of *Best American Short Stories 1960* that I'd found on the shelf. We'd never had a television in the cabin. I'd once tried to explain to my children that it was possible to go an entire summer without TV, that I'd done it as a kid. They couldn't conceive of days of doing nothing, not even a radio to listen to, the kind of empty staring you got into, whole tableaus emerging in the grain of knotty pine. They wouldn't be able to fathom the dreamy walks, the aimless destruction of wildflowers, the fevered reading. Parents didn't care what kids read back then—at least, mine didn't—nuclear-fallout horror stories, tales of bad girls who hitchhiked. I read Bobby's discards, the fat novels he tossed off in an afternoon that took me days to forge through, rewarded only by the occasional sex scene and the triumph of reading whatever Bobby did.

ERIC AND I had always planned to fix the cabin up, I thought the next day. Put in a new kitchen and bath, add a fireplace, build a deck. Now someone else would fix it up. Who was I kidding? Whoever bought this land was going to tear this place down.

I had on my rubber gloves as I worked my way through the large main room with its broken-down furniture and shelves holding board games with missing pieces. I found the letter late in the afternoon, stuck to the back of an old *Mother Jones* in a pile of magazines. There was no envelope, no first page, just a badly typed missive that started in midsentence:

"told me that people are beginning to talk about you here and say that man is not right. I let you talk to me because you are so smart and nice, but you took advantage. I told you I did not want what you wanted. I told you if you did not stop bothering me like that I would call your father. You left me no choice. And don't try to scare me again by getting mad."

The signature was merely a penciled *J*.

The letter could only be from a woman, a girl, to Bobby. I'd never known him to have a girlfriend, but then it was growing increasingly clear that there was a lot I didn't know about my brother.

My gentle brother had harassed a woman in this town of a hundred people, and my father must have taken care of it somehow. This was what my mother had meant by personal stuff. Covering up for Bobby. Fifteen years ago, when my parents had said that Bobby was fine, that I shouldn't bother him because he just needed rest, they knew differently. They knew Bobby wasn't right back then. The whole town knew it. I'd known it, too. Just as part of me had known what I was doing when I threw Bobby's coded notebook in the trash.

I came from a long line of dreamers, of storytellers, and the most dangerous stories we told were about ourselves.

chapter twenty-seven

As if we were impersonating some happy, mindless couple, Eric and I stopped arguing after I came home from the cabin. He did his things, I did mine. We didn't talk about my brother or *60 Minutes* or anything that might end in a fight. At night, we read our books, and kept to our own sides of the bed. Another couple could have slept in the distance between us.

Eric invented a new routine. He went to the office for a few hours, made calls, and scribbled calculations on his yellow legal pad. He brought Lilly home from school and then left for the golf course at Tilden Park. In his gait, his suntanned visage, I saw what he'd kept from me all these years. Eric had never confided how it felt to perform flawlessly on a green. He never imagined that I'd understand the art in hitting a ball. He'd never known me to do something just for the grace of the moment. I lived for the retelling—the power of the story and the burnishing of memory.

The girls seemed to prefer the newly present Eric to the distracted me. Lilly sat on his lap instead of mine. Julia assiduously overlooked the obvious, refusing to question why her father was working so much less.

The receptionist at Julia's dentist phoned to remind us of her appointment. "We'll be there," I said, pretending I remembered, determined to be the parent who brought her there. The next afternoon, we took the only empty spot in the overdecorated waiting room, a gingham love seat.

I should've gone for a walk when they called Julia in. I needed the exercise, to connect with pavement and noise outside my head. Instead I picked up a well-thumbed *People* from a stack on the pine table beside me. I liked reading about movie stars, their constantly shifting houses and relationships. I usually skipped the stories about ordinary people, but a black-and-white photo of a pretty nineteen-year-old made my mouth go dry.

The girl had a beautiful name, Olivia, but her Philippine American family called her Kiddie for kid sister. She would always be that—a kid sister—even when she was my age, but she would never be my age, never have daughters of her own. I touched the photo of her round face, her black blunt-cut hair. Her smile was impish, as if she could not hide her sense of fun. She could have been my own daughter.

Olivia had been opening the mail at her five-dollar-an-hour work-study job in Berkeley three months ago when the package bomb from the Cal Bomber blew her apart.

Julia came through the door, a new toothbrush in her hand. She pointed to the receptionist's desk behind the glass window. "We have to make an appointment for six months," she said.

I shook my head. "Not now," I said. I didn't know that I could even get up.

She peered at me. "Are you okay?"

"Yes," I said, although it wasn't even close to being true.

I got up gingerly, leaving the *People* on the floor where it had fallen.

"Let's get a soda," I said when we were on the street.

Julia looked as if I were deranged. "But I've just had my teeth cleaned."

I remembered Bobby the last time I'd seen him, the way it hurt to look at his teeth. "Over there," I said, pointing to a small market. "You can have a water."

"I don't want water," Julia said, but I was pressing the button to cross the street. She complained but she came with me. Inside the grocery, I opened a cooler and felt around for the coldest soda. When I found it, I opened the can right there, and put it to my mouth.

What if everyone was right and Bobby had done this? There had been three months between the time I first reread Bobby's letter and the day Olivia Trinidad was blown to bits, three months of keeping my eyes shut to what I didn't want to see. A season in which I had done nothing that might have saved her.

ERIC WAS HOME early again the next afternoon, a case from the wine store under his arm. He was practically unemployed, but he was buying better wine than ever. I made a shrewish face and counted the bottles, irritated not about the wine but that he was home so early. It wasn't even two o'clock. I said I was going grocery shopping.

I drove past the nearest store and the one after that, then south to Oakland, east on winding streets, greedy for the thoughtlessness that accompanied aimless driving. I passed the cemetery I'd visited with my class on the Day of the Dead. The sky that day a perfect blue, the sun warming our arms, I'd been nearly as delighted as the kids by our escape from school. I recognized that I'd never be that person again.

A few blocks from the cemetery, I saw the statute of the Virgin Mary on the landscaped rise in front of Sacred Heart High School. As if it had been my destination all along, I turned right into the parking lot.

I pretended I knew where I was going, walking inside a building that smelled like wet shoes. There was another Mary in a niche by the entrance and a trophy case beneath a crucifix. The symbols transfixed me. We didn't put up as much as a Christmas wreath at Mountaintop School. I studied the statue as if I hoped she'd speak to me, touching her robe where the blue paint was chipped.

A buzzer sounded so loudly it made me jump. Doors swung open and girls in checkered skirts crowded into the hall. I followed the girls in their heedless rush from the building, surrounded by their noise. A girl with small-framed glasses asked if I was lost. I asked where the yearbooks were and she took me to the library.

Olivia Trinidad was easy to find. Two years ago, she had been a student here, her backpack heavy on one shoulder, her checkered Catholic-girls-school skirt hiked high, her white blouse coming untucked in the back. In her senior portrait, she wore a photographer's drape around her brown shoulders and pearls around her neck. The quote from J. R. R. Tolkien beneath her picture said, *Not all who wander are lost.*

I touched her picture. It was impossible to believe she was dead. She was living at home when she was killed, her school sweaters still folded in her drawers. I didn't want to leave her.

I went into the stacks, the slender yearbook in my arms. I intended to put it back on the shelf. I'd never stolen so much as a pack of gum. Instead I slipped it into my jacket. It felt like a vile thing to do, stealing Olivia away from her school. But what did it matter? I'd taken much more than that from her already.

I KNEW I was in trouble as soon as I walked into the house. Eric and Lilly just sat on the couch, looking at me. Lilly's cheeks were blotchy and she was sucking her thumb, behavior she'd outgrown. She pulled it noisily from her mouth, wiped the spit on her corduroy pants.

"I waited after school and you never came," she said, her eyes wary. "I called and you weren't home." She looked away. "I thought you got killed. I cried so much they made me lie down."

I was confused. "But you have gymnastics," I said.

"That's Wednesday," she said as if she were forty. "This is Tuesday."

I turned to Eric to pass the blame. "But you were here."

"I went jogging. I didn't know."

"I'm sorry, I got mixed up," I said to Lilly.

"Where are the groceries?" Eric asked, his brows arched.

"I thought we'd order pizza," I said, clutching the yearbook under my jacket.

"I think I'll go to the store," Eric said.

"I want to go with you," Lilly said. She looked at me to make sure I got the point.

I watched them leave. In our old lives, Eric might have asked me where I'd been, why my face was pale and my eyes red from crying.

I took the yearbook from under my jacket and pulled the White

Pages from the shelf in the hall. George and Gloria Trinidad, an ampersand between their first names, were right there, easy to find. Out of politeness, out of fear, out of confusion, they would have to let me in.

THE TRINIDADS' house was on a corner of an everyday street, elevated behind a chain-link fence. The windows on the house next door had iron bars. We didn't have chain-link fences or barred windows in the Berkeley neighborhood I lived in, the one I described as ordinary. When I was growing up, my parents worked to improve the lives of wage earners. We sang the union songs, but we lived in a big house in the city's finest district.

I always felt uncomfortable having more. I still had two daughters. Now the Trinidads were down to one.

Their gate was unlocked. The wind blew cold wet air, but I was too warm under my raincoat. Their blinds were pulled, but I could hear the family through an open window. The father was watching *Jeopardy!* silently, not calling out the answers like Eric.

"We can have the chicken adobo," Mrs. Trinidad said, her voice carrying the accent of the Philippines. "Or I can make lamb chops."

"I don't care," he said. How could he? His daughter was dead.

As I stood there on the uncovered porch, it started to rain. I had children at home wanting dinner, needing at least the facade of a mother. I turned to head back down the stairs. All my life I'd hidden my feelings. Now I was sure they were visible to the people in passing cars.

I hadn't rung the bell, but the door opened. I wanted to scurry down the steps. Instead, I turned. Olivia's father was small, slightly built, with a thin mustache and exhausted eyes.

"Can I help you?"

"Mr. Trinidad, I'm Natalie Askedahl."

I saw in his expression that he recognized my name, but he didn't move. I didn't move either. Rain splattered my face, my hair.

For months I'd been traveling in circles, great looping circles that had always led me home. Now I'd gone too far.

"I'd like to come in," I said. "Please."

He didn't answer. He seemed helpless, but even so I waited for him to take care of me, to tell me why I'd come. The door opened wider. He wife stood beside him. She was stronger than he, clear-eyed and unsmiling.

"It's raining," she said. "Come inside."

She led me past the living room with Mr. Trinidad's reclining chair, his television program playing, to a dining room with dark, formal furniture. She showed me in and said she'd be with me shortly. The table was covered with a lace cloth, a cut-glass bowl in the middle. This was where they ate their holiday dinners, celebrated their special occasions, where they would sit down to the first birthday, the first Thanksgiving, the first Christmas without Olivia.

I heard them talking. But I didn't have even a haphazard acquaintance with the language they were now speaking.

Against the wall was a glass-and-gold-framed cabinet lined with photographs. Olivia in her cap and gown, in her yellow prom dress beside a boy in a white jacket, his arm gingerly around her. There was a black-and-white photo of Mr. Trinidad in the military uniform of another country, his name, age, and a date handwritten on the cardboard mounting. He was four years younger than me.

Mrs. Trinidad stepped back into the room. "It's our dinnertime," she said in a way that meant she wanted me gone quickly.

"I'd just like a few minutes." It wasn't true. I wanted much more.

She sighed. "Please sit." She waited for me to begin.

I pulled my gaze from the large, hand-carved wooden crucifix on the wall facing me. The rain hit hard against their roof, and I shivered from the dampness of my clothes.

"I came to say how sorry I am."

Mrs. Trinidad looked at me, her expression unchanged, her hands clasped tightly on the table.

"I have two daughters," I said. "I can only . . ."

"And you're offering to give me one?"

My mouth opened.

"I thought not," she said.

I looked down at the table. I'd brought this on myself, brought it on this no-nonsense woman with the firm, melodious voice. "I'm sorry," I repeated.

"I don't understand," she said. "Did you have some knowledge of what your brother planned? Could you have stopped him?"

"I don't know," I said, running my hands over my thighs to warm them.

I heard the anger in her voice, saw it mingled with astonishment in her eyes. "You don't know?" she repeated.

What was I saying? "Of course I didn't know what he was going to do. I don't even know if he did these terrible things."

Mrs. Trinidad stared at me, her eyes behind her glasses unreadable. I was shivering, but my face was hot. What was I doing here? What had I thought? That this tragedy connected us somehow, that my sorrow might mean something to her?

"I don't understand," she said. She was suddenly like a lawyer with a witness on the stand. She suspected something and she wasn't going to let it go. "You don't think your brother killed my child, but somehow you feel some responsibility, some need to comfort me?"

I had no control. When I started confessing I couldn't stop. The brother I knew could never have done this, but the truth was I didn't know him anymore. Still, had I acted a few months earlier when I first had suspicions instead of being in such denial, everything might have been different.

Mrs. Trinidad's face sagged. Her hands clenched on the table were bloodless at the knuckles. "You've come to the wrong place," she said. She turned to the crucifix above her head, then back to me. "Only God can absolve you." She told me where I could find a priest. Then she asked me to please go. "My husband needs to eat," she said.

I wanted to say that I'd like to help her in any way I could, but I'd already gone too far and said too much.

IT WAS ONLY eight thirty when I got home, but dinner was already over and the dishes done. The house smelled of fabric softener. Eric was folding laundry in the family room. I took off my coat and picked up a towel to fold. Eric stared at me as if he didn't recognize me. "Where have you been?"

On the way home, I'd tried to think of how I was going to explain disappearing from the house while he and Lilly were at the store, gone for four hours with no note, no phone call. Why I'd done what I'd just done. All that came out of my mouth was "Where are the kids?"

"Their rooms," he said. "Well?" His single-syllable words carried anger and fear, masked by control.

"I did something," I said.

Eric expression was wary. He didn't speak, and for a moment I couldn't either.

"I went to see the family of the girl killed in the Berkeley bombing."

He stared at me, his face off-color. "No. You wouldn't."

I picked up one of his laundered T-shirts, absently folded it. Eric grabbed my wrist. "Whatever possessed you?"

My wrist burned but I didn't flinch. "I had this idea," I said, almost casually, as if the idea was something separate and apart from me. "I wanted to tell them how sorry I was for their loss, that I was grieving for Olivia, too."

"Oh, Jesus," Eric said. "You think that matters to them?"

The anger in his voice made me panicky. I wrenched my hand from his grip. "And you wanted these people to what?" he asked. "Make you feel better?"

"Not in the way you're making it sound," I said thoughtfully. "Look, since this whole terrible thing started, it's been all about you and me, my mother, my brother, the kids, what's happened to us, and what we've lost. But there are people who've lost far more than us in this. As stupid as it sounds, I wanted to reach out."

"No," Eric said as if I'd done the truly incomprehensible. "You wanted them to tell you that you didn't do anything wrong." There was violence in his tone. "What if that were our daughter?" With a swipe of his fist, he knocked over the laundry he'd folded. "You could have gotten yourself killed."

chapter twenty-eight

IN MY LIFE as it used to be, I was forever late, in a rush, my foot heavy on the pedal, haunted by something I'd forgotten to do, to pay, to sign. I ate on the run, balanced hot coffee while shifting in traffic, and dreamed of being organized, believing I could be if only I had the right containers.

When Eric left to take the girls to school in the morning, I was in the nightgown I would wear for hours. He was in a suit and tie.

"What's up?" I asked, meaning the suit, uncertain if he'd even answer me.

"Probably nothing," he said. He made a gesture that meant *we'll talk later*.

When he came home in the afternoon, he sat with me at the kitchen table, still in his suit, speaking in his business voice. I tried to behave casually but my mouth tasted of dread.

He'd been thinking, he said. Everything that had happened, Bobby, his grief over his father's death, the firm pushing him out, his anger at me for going to the Trinidads the night before, all of it had led to this one conclusion. We had to act to save us before there was no us left.

I let my breath out. I'd thought he was going say that he was leaving me.

He said he'd been offered a job as an in-house attorney at a company headquartered a few blocks from his old firm. It would mean less money, but he'd have regular hours and weekends off.

"I told them I wouldn't be able to start until mid-August, and they said fine."

It was early June. "Mid-August?"

"We're going to take a vacation on Sterling, Talbot's dime," he said. "Get the hell out of California. We'll camp. Colorado, Montana, it doesn't matter where. Just somewhere away from this." He took my hand, looked at me with an openness, a softness, I hadn't seen in weeks. "Somewhere we can find a way back to being together."

I should have flung myself at him, jumped up to gather maps. But I couldn't move. Eric stared at me, a hint of anger, or maybe it was hurt that reddened his cheeks.

"I can't," I said, the words just coming out.

"You can't what?" The softness was gone from his eyes.

"Travel around the country." My voice was desperate. "Don't you get it? I'm a circus geek. The bomber's sister. I've been on television. It's bad enough in Berkeley, where people are too hip to stare." I flung my arm. "Can you imagine it out there? What that would do to the girls?"

Eric's look was implacable, his words hard edged. "And whose fault is it, that you're so recognizable?"

I stared right back. "Whose fault is it that everyone knows me as the woman who turned in her own brother to the FBI?"

"I get it," Eric said too quietly. "You blame me for turning in Bobby."

Was that true? All I knew was that he'd made the decision that changed everything.

"And you blame me for not telling you until it was too late to do anything else," I said.

"I don't believe this," Eric said as if to himself.

"Take the girls and go camping, please," I said. "Get them away from all this. Give yourself a break from this."

Eric sagged, the fight gone out of him. "You're throwing us away," he said.

"I'm trying to save us," I said. "You want to get away from this thing with my brother, and I can't leave it behind. A long vacation together isn't a good recipe for the two of us right now."

His laugh was dry, bitter, and wholly disbelieving. "I give up," he said.

* * *

ERIC AND the girls planned their trip without me. Each day a new piece of shiny equipment arrived to be unpacked and displayed in the living room. A tent big enough for four in which only three would sleep. A Coleman stove with two burners. Three sleeping bags.

UPS delivered three mess kits just like the one I'd had as a Girl Scout. I held the metal cup, and remembered the pleasure of drinking from an icy stream.

"Don't ever drink from a stream," I told Lilly. "There could be germs."

This was no ordinary trip they were planning. It was an adventure to encompass all their vacation desires. Camping for Lilly, college visits for Julia, and freedom from my brother's crisis for Eric.

"How can we afford all this?" I asked, the equipment on the floor around us.

"We can't," Eric said.

I had so many worries. Ticks. Diseases lurking in streams. Lilly wandering into the wrong bathroom alone. Our family separated for good.

"Lilly's so young," I said. "I don't know if she's up to all this."

"She's eight, not two," Eric said. "If you're so worried, you can come with us."

"You know I can't." We'd been over the reasons. Except for the biggest one: I couldn't get past how angry I was at Eric for removing himself from my family's tragedy and for refusing to understand that I could not.

"YOU'RE COMING to the last day of school, aren't you? Our program," Lilly said, her arms folded. She had a new way of talking to me, with a suspicious edge, just like her older sister.

"Of course," I said, dreading the prospect. I had not been back to my former school since the day two months before that I'd cleaned out my classroom.

Lilly had been so prepared for an argument, for disappointment, that my yes had made her unsure of herself. She dropped her arms warily. I pulled her into mine, feeling her resistance slacken. She wasn't ready for the teenage thing. When all this is over, I thought, I'm going to win you back.

Eric said he'd meet me there. He wanted to get in a round of golf first. I wanted him to walk into the school with me so I wouldn't have to do it alone. But I didn't dare ask. I didn't want to give him the chance to say no.

I didn't know what to wear. The suit I'd worn on *60 Minutes* would be too much.

A teaching outfit didn't feel right because I wasn't that person anymore—someone who got up in the morning, put on a denim skirt, and thought she had a handle on the day.

I wore a pair of linen slacks, a summer blouse, and sandals, more nervous walking into the school yard than I'd been waiting to go on television. This school had been my dream, just as the University of California had been my father's. But I'd never before realized how small my dream had been in comparison: asphalt, a building with big windows, a play structure surrounded by sand.

I was early and I didn't want to be.

A boy called my name. It was Benjamin Murphy. Only two months had passed but he looked taller. The most brilliant third grader I'd ever taught, and as usual, he was somewhere he wasn't supposed to be.

I said hello and tried to act like the teacher I'd once been. "Why aren't you inside with your class?" *My class.*

"I want to show you something," he said, dashing into the building. What did I care where he was supposed to be?

I sat on the bench bordering the play structure. He returned with a notebook, the pages swollen from an excess of glue. "I made a scrapbook about your brother," he said, sitting next to me. Somehow I wasn't surprised. Benjamin loved current events, explosions, and in a third-grade way, he loved me. He put the scrapbook in my lap, watched me examine each page. He'd clipped a few articles from newspapers, some pictures from magazines, and drawn a few himself. He even had a photo of me in it.

"Do you have any stuff I can put in?" he asked.

I patted the warm sand, and thought about what I could give him. "I have some science notes that my brother made in school," I said. It was strange but I wanted him to have them.

"Notes on how to make a bomb?"

"Just regular notes," I said, surprised at how much I missed the perspective of third-grade boys, how single-minded they were in the pursuit of their interests, how easy they were in friendship, how unlike girls they still were. I watched Ben run off with his scrapbook, wondering how Bobby would take the news of his third-grade biographer. Somehow I didn't think he'd be displeased.

In the distance, I heard the unmistakable noise of children about to be freed from their classrooms. Enough parents were arriving that I thought I might be inconspicuous walking in behind them. Rows of folding chairs crammed the gym. I wanted to slip into a seat in back, but I had to be where Lilly could see me from the stage.

"Natalie, I didn't recognize you." The school secretary threw her arms around me. "How did you lose so much weight?"

So much weight? I couldn't remember the last time I'd even weighed myself.

She looked stricken, as if she'd just remembered I had a terminal illness. "Of course," she said quickly, "all the stress you've been under." She was so flustered that I got away easily to find seats for Eric and me. Most of the parents just waved as they passed, but a few stopped, the how-are-yous awkward and overly bright.

Eric slid in next to me, and we endured the boredom of watching other people's children. When Lilly stood for her small part, she scanned the audience for us. I waved and saw her relief. My eyes stung. She hadn't been certain we'd be there.

After the program, we took Lilly's picture, our second-grade graduate, and asked another second-grade parent to take one of the three of us. Lilly pushed me closer to Eric, then she clung to my other side and smiled for the camera.

chapter twenty-nine

I'D WANTED THIS STILLNESS. To move from room to room in peace. Now, with my family gone, I could not stand the silence. When the phone rang, I jumped. It's them, I thought, calling from the road, even though they'd just phoned that morning.

It was my sister. "Don't freak," she said. But freaking had become my permanent state. "It's Mom, but it's nothing."

Her doctor was keeping her overnight in the hospital for some tests. Sara had to deal with a plumbing problem at her place in Potter Valley. Could I pick up Mother tomorrow and take her home? I agreed so readily I wondered if this was what I'd been waiting for—not just a way out of the house, but a way back to my other family.

When I let myself into my mother's condo three hours later, I told myself it was just to tidy up. I emptied the dishwasher and swept the floor. Then I rummaged through every room in her house, as if somewhere within those white-walled rooms lay the answer to how everything could have gone so wrong.

I found a black-and-white snapshot in the cluttered drawer of her bedside table. My father, solid in a tailored suit, his hair still dark, stands on our porch smiling, a man's man women adored. The chubby ten-year-old squinting into the sun beside him has done something strange with her hair. I'd plastered Scotch tape across my bangs to straighten them. Bobby's on my left, his arms hanging dead beside him. In a boxy suit, he stands ramrod straight except for his head, which is listing to the side as if it weighs too much.

I put my palm over my hanged-man brother and my tape-banged self, leaving only my father. "Tell me what I'm looking for," I whispered.

I found a legal-size file folder from Bobby's lawyers in the dining room buffet. Inside were copies of interviews with Bobby's neighbors, people who now knew him better than I did.

He was polite.

He seemed gentle.

He returned his library books on time.

He looked as if he did not get enough to eat.

He smelled.

He spoke only a few words at a time, and the words didn't always make sense.

He was always alone.

Why wasn't anyone saying that this gentle, addled man could not possibly have done what he had been accused of doing? Because they thought he might have?

I went through my mother's mail and unsealed a letter from Bobby's attorney that had just arrived. It said there was a courtroom change in Friday's pretrial hearing.

Maybe I had a letter like this at home.

The guest room was littered with Sara's belongings. She and my mother had never been close. They were too much alike in their relentless self-containment. But this disaster had tossed us up in the air, and all of us had come down in different places.

I crawled into my mother's bed. My father had never slept in this house, but my mother slept on the same side of the bed as she had with him. I moved to the other side, my side in the bed I shared with Eric.

I KNEW the hospital where my mother was staying. My father died there.

"You look like you've spent the night in here instead of me," my mother said.

"Are you all right?" I asked, ignoring her jab.

"Much ado about a little rapid heartbeat," she said sourly. My mother's father had been a doctor but no one in our family ever sought one out.

I told her I planned to stick around awhile. "Bobby's hearing is in a couple of days," I said without looking at her.

She took my hand. She never did that.

"Because of *60 Minutes* people are starting to see Bobby as a human being," she said. "I want you to promise that you'll keep it up, do whatever interviews we need to do to make it clear to the world that Bobby is mentally ill."

It was shocking to hear her say it. The woman who'd denied her son's mental illness for thirty years was now ready to wage a public-opinion campaign for an insanity plea.

"I'll do what I can," I said. It wasn't the answer she wanted, but it was the only answer I could give. I had a family, too, one that was huddled in a tent a thousand miles away from me.

Sara showed up several hours after I brought Mother home. "You're relieved of duty," she whispered in my ear.

"I'm staying," I said.

"Suit yourself," she said.

I moved into the guest room, picked up Sara's clothes off the spare bed, and left them folded neatly on a chair. When she came in, she acted as if she didn't notice.

I'd brought the wrong nightgown to wear in front of her, an oversize, floral-print flannel from L.L.Bean.

"No wonder your husband's gone on vacation without you," she said.

"He took the kids off my hands as a favor."

"I wasn't implying there was trouble in *Ozzie and Harriet* land." Sara removed her shorts and sat on her bed in her small T-shirt and bikini panties.

"You and I haven't shared a bedroom in years," I said.

"We never shared a bedroom," she said. Sara pulled a lighter and small pipe from her backpack.

"Mom's in the next room," I said as Sara held the flame to the bowl. I jumped up to open the window, trying to disperse the smoke with my hand.

"If she walks in, you tell her it's for my glaucoma." Sara settled back, her arm folded behind her head, staring at the ceiling. She was so lithe. I pictured her last November, standing outside Mother's condo in her little shift, smoking her pot. She would have already read the Cal Bomber's manifesto by then.

"We have shared a bedroom," I said. "All those summers at Gold Run."

"I didn't mean to hurt your feelings," she said.

"It's easy to forget." I hesitated before continuing. "Remember when I phoned you in January worried that someone might think Bobby was the Cal Bomber? You told me you'd read the Cal Bomber's manifesto. But you never said why."

Sara shrugged. "It was in the newspaper."

"You told me you'd read every word. Why read every word of something that boring?"

"What are you getting at, Natalie?"

I wasn't entirely sure, but I pushed ahead anyway. "I don't think you're being straight with me. You couldn't possibly have read Bobby's letter to Mom *and* the entire manifesto without the thought occurring to you that they were awfully damned similar. No one could. But you always acted as if the thought had never entered your mind."

"Fix yourself a drink, Natalie." Sara reached for her pipe and I put a hand out to stop her.

"Not until you answer me."

We stared at each other, my hand poised to grab her pipe, although I already had my answer.

She looked away. In all the forty-eight years Sara had been my older sister, I'd never seen her blink.

"Go to sleep, Natalie," she said, turning on her side, her back to me. I watched her lying there, her silence not concerning me, as if we'd traded roles and I were the indifferent sister now.

* * *

IN THE MORNING, I phoned Bobby's attorney to ask about the hearing. "It's just a housekeeping thing," she said. "The only reason it'll be in open court is because of the press. Your brother won't be there. We'll argue trial dates but nothing important is going to happen."

But she was wrong. So wrong that she came in person late Thursday afternoon, direct from the hearing, to tell us about it. Debra sat at my mother's dining room table, a woman about my age with curly brown hair, dyed, I thought, lines on her exhausted face, her dark suit wrinkled.

"Bob kept journals and coded notebooks," she said. Her voice sounded tired but even. "As well as detailed diaries." A kindergartner could have gotten where she was going, but not me. I just sat there imagining that this was a good thing.

"I take it they don't exonerate him," Sara said.

"They say things like 'I mailed the bomb.'"

My mother gasped, then put a hand to her mouth. I felt myself growing pale."I wanted you to hear it from me," Debra said. "The other side made the disclosure in open court. In front of the press."

"In front of the press," I repeated thickly. "So it'll be in the news?"

"Yes," she said simply.

"You didn't know about the diaries?" Sara asked.

"We knew," Debra said. "That isn't the point. The only reason for the other side to bring up the diaries today is to prejudice the media." She sighed. "Your interview on *60 Minutes* spooked them. They want their cold-blooded killer back."

Sara put her head in her hands. I looked to the lawyer, wanting her to reframe what she'd just said in a way that would make it better. As she just sat there without answering, I grasped at an idea. "Could I read them?"

Debra's eyes focused on mine. "Why would you want to do that?"

I tried to think. "Maybe there's something in them. Things he said happened that I could prove didn't happen. That would show he was delusional."

She looked thoughtful. "It's possible," she said.

That was all we had now. The best we could hope for—that Bobby was insane.

chapter thirty

My brother's lawyers had offices in the federal building on the Capitol Mall. A slender young woman with a casual ponytail led me into a conference room. There were boxes stacked on the table, against the wall. She reminded me so much of Julia, I wanted to touch her hair.

"Did you have any trouble finding us?" she asked pleasantly.

I pointed to the window. "My father worked in the state building across the mall. My mother used to take us kids to have lunch with him."

I walked around the conference table to the window and craned my head toward Capitol Park. "We used to run around on that lawn." The three of us chasing one another, my mother on a bench lost in a book. "I had a job one summer in my father's office as a messenger." I remembered running back and forth between these buildings, proudly carrying my big brown envelope. He must have paid me out of his own pocket. For all I know the envelopes were empty.

The young assistant smiled at me in that tolerant, desperate way my kids did when they hoped they didn't have to listen to me much longer.

"So what do I do?" I asked.

Relieved, she showed me where to sit at the large table. She gave me a legal pad and some pencils. Bobby's diaries had been photocopied and also transcribed.

"I'll be here if you have any questions." She sat at the far end of the table, and got down to whatever she was working on. I was suddenly irritated. I didn't want to be watched. I eyed her surreptitiously but she never looked up.

I was overly warm, restless. I took two Advil from my purse and swallowed them with water from my plastic bottle, my fingers already shredding the label. I hadn't even been there ten minutes.

The night before Sara had told me not to come here. "Leave the diaries alone," she said. "Trust me, you'll regret reading them."

"Regret is the only sure feeling I have," I'd answered.

I opened a page. My brother's writing filled all the white space on the paper, his handwriting cramped, minuscule. When I looked closer, I saw dates. Entries ended and began on the same line without space between them. His letters from Guatemala had looked just like that. He's trying to save paper, my mother had declared, in a way that made me feel I wasted it.

The airless scrawl was nearly impossible to read. I reached for the thick binder holding the transcription. Bobby wrote about growing his own food. He measured his potatoes, his carrots, for length and circumference, fought garden pests and birds. He had a hole in his cabin floor where he stored his vegetables in the earth. He tried to be a vegetarian, but he'd trapped and eaten a rabbit that was destroying his garden.

My mind drifted. I remembered Bobby at our refrigerator, hanging on the door, staring inside, my mother telling him to shut it. "There's never anything to eat," he said, slamming the door.

"Yeah," I'd echoed in solidarity.

"Let's go, squirt," he said.

I'd burnished that memory, my big brother buying me a hamburger at a drugstore soda fountain, a boy who couldn't make himself a peanut butter sandwich.

In the diaries, my brother obsessed over his health. His stomach gave him trouble. No intestinal detail was too minor to be recorded. It seemed we both shared a tendency toward heart flutters and headaches. Bobby thought of buying a blood pressure monitor but the price was exorbitant. The young woman looked up when I laughed. I was tempted to try to explain to her the ludicrousness of my brother fretting about his blood pressure while he built bombs.

His cabin didn't have plumbing, so he built an outhouse and hauled water from an outdoor pump. There was no electricity. If his cabin had been in the city, it would have been a cardboard box on a vacant lot. What fable would we have told ourselves about Bobby then? That he worked with the homeless?

He wrote that he was unspeakably lonely, that he detested his parents. Our parents. He said that Father had accused of him being a *sicko.*

He wishes me dead because I am an affront to his tidy life, the effete liberal values he embraces to compensate for his lack of personal power . . . He is a lackey for the system and a bully at home. He uses his fists and would kill me if he thought he could get away with it.

His fists? I closed my eyes against the awful words on the page and the sense that I was falling. Who was this bully of a father Bobby claimed to know? Not mine. Sara had tried to warn me, but I'd walked right into this. I took a sip of water from my bottle, forced my eyes to read.

Although Mother is smarter, she accepts the role of hausfrau. Denied an outlet for her mind, she's focused on controlling mine . . . She claims I might feel better if I saw a psychologist. She fakes naïveté but she knows full well: the only purpose of psychology and psychiatry is to control people . . . She tries to control me by sending money that I have to accept because she knows I have no income, no other way to finance my work.

Finance his work. His bombs. What if she hadn't sent the money? Would seven people be alive today?

I looked up, glanced around as if searching for accusing stares. I'd given Bobby money, too. Small checks for Christmas, his birthday, checks he never acknowledged but cashed. Enough for packing material, bus fare, detonator wires. Enough for the postage on the bomb that killed Olivia Trinidad.

The sweat of my fingers left marks on the page I turned. The goal of society, Bobby wrote, was obedience.

Children are conditioned into obedience by parents and schools. Those who are not obedient are separated from the others and sidelined into the ill or delinquent population . . . The mechanisms of control rob us of the self-esteem we need to create our own goals.

Obedience? Who did Bobby ever obey? Who was controlling him? Other anarchists? Or was it the demons in his own mind?

I flipped a few pages ahead to a rant about the post office. They'd raised the first-class rate to twenty-five cents. *The purpose of which is not only to support the inefficiency of the post office but also to condition people to their own powerlessness. Two birds are killed with one stone, but the end result is dead birds.*

What did Bobby care about the price of stamps? He never wrote anyone. But, of course, he sent packages, and every penny counted. He kept exact records. It cost five dollars and forty cents to mail a bomb to the Stanford scientist who had his arm and half his face blown off. Fourteen dollars for the hotel room in Sacramento where he mailed the package. Twenty-six dollars for bus fare. Food on the trip totaled three dollars and seventy-eight cents.

An awful metallic taste filled my mouth. I pressed a hand against my lips. Whatever impulse had brought me to this room and compelled me to read these words wasn't healthy. I'd pushed Eric and my children away for this. A sane person would pick up her purse and run to her family. But I wasn't that person. I was sick from missing them, sicker from what I was reading, but I couldn't stop.

The most dangerous feature of modern techno-industrial society is its power to make people comfortable. Once comfort rather than survival becomes man's objective, there is no end to the comfort he craves, not just physical but mental, moral, and emotional as well . . . The autonomous person is not a comfortable person, and autonomy is nearly impossible in a system that uses comfort as a controlling mechanism.

On the surface, my brother's words made complete sense. Except the truth they told wasn't the one he intended. All my life, I'd wanted comfort. I'd wanted love without loss. So had my mother. Even Sara, possibly my father. Because the truth about Bobby had been too painful, we'd chosen to substitute the pretty pictures in our heads for the reality we couldn't face.

I skimmed pages looking for something I could stand reading. I stopped at a section about time. *Before the breakdown of a day into hours or seasons into weeks, a man might have feared being eaten by a bear, but he did not fear death itself.* Everyone cultivating his own patch of earth. No more worrying about cholesterol or paying for the kids' college. The world he described had its appeal. Except he advocating killing people to get there.

In the bitter cold of an Idaho winter, Bobby wrote about California, *a state built on the heedless rush for gold.* And who got to profit from the gold buried in the mountains and rivers of the state? *Not the indigenous population, not even the government in the name of the common good, but any asshole with a pick.* Within twenty years of the Gold Rush, Bobby wrote, four-fifths of California's Native American population had been wiped out. *It wasn't enough just to kill off the Indians. The California legislature also authorized more than a million dollars to reimburse Indian killers for their expenses in getting the job done.*

There was no California dream, he concluded, only a nightmare of avarice. The institutions of the state arose from the rape of the land and publicly subsidized mass murder. *A state built on the annihilation of indigenous man and the despoiling of the planet serves as a template not just for the country but the world.*

The California universities, too, were tainted from the start, he argued, and their goal had been to spread the contamination. *While Stanford pioneered in the field of electronics research, Berkeley smashed the atom. One paved the way for the computer age, the other the nuclear, the semiconductor as destructive to mankind as the bomb. One obliterates with force, the other with information.*

I rubbed my eyes. All those words without a single paragraph break had made them burn. I stared at the black-and-white patterns, not because the words made no sense, but because I understood them too well. Bobby and I were fifth-generation Californians. My father's great-grandfather had come here for the gold, my mother's for the land. My father was devoted to this state. The universities were his life's work. My brother had built his philosophy out of the pathology of his own mind.

Bobby wrote that he would have preferred not to have to kill anyone, but *the technological age has produced a toxic information overload that overwhelms the individual. He can no longer distinguish between the trivial and the vital, between manufactured and real desires*. Under such circumstances, he wrote coolly, the only way to be heard, the only way for an important message to make a lasting impression, was for people to die.

I felt woozy, my face clammy. The person who had written these words wasn't my brother. My brother was gone. Now there was only this killer.

The lasting impression Bobby wanted to make was not in the minds of ordinary people. It was on other radicals. The only way to bring down the system was through a sustained campaign of violence horrible enough to plunge society into chaos. An apocalypse, yes, but our earth would be saved and mankind would be freed to return to primeval liberty.

I'd hoped to uncover evidence of an insane mind, and I had. I'd also found the brutal logic of a terrorist.

chapter thirty-one

IN THE FOUR HOURS I spent reading Bobby's diaries the weather had changed. By the time I got back to my mother's place, I could smell the approaching storm. My mother and Sara were reading in the living room, Mother in her chair, Sara on the couch, two gray-haired women in half glasses. Maybe in all this, they'd found a kind of peace in each other's company.

"You must have been chilly out there without a sweater," my mother said.

"It's beautiful out," I countered. "You want to go for a walk, Sara?"

She shrugged, then got up slowly. We put on hooded sweatshirts.

"Valley weather," Sara said after we'd walked in silence to the park in the center of the tract. She pointed up. "White clouds to the left, storm clouds to the right, and in the middle a sky that can't make up its mind."

We both put up our hoods. Sara lit a cigarette and inhaled as if there were nothing better than smoke filling your lungs in crisp, clean air.

"So how was your research? I assume that's what you got me out here to talk about," she said.

"You were right about the diaries," I said, hugging my arms. "I shouldn't have read them."

She stopped, faced me. "How bad was it?"

"I was able to sit there, I was able to drive home," I said. "Bobby had his reasons. He laid them out. Industrial society has polluted the earth and dehumanized mankind, so now he thinks it's time for anarchist revolution."

"That's it? His big theory?"

"It gets better," I said. "He's had to focus his campaign because he's only one person. He picked out California universities as a symbol of what he considers the tyranny of technology. He understands he's a terrorist and that terrorism is effective. He wants to be heard and to inspire others to emulate him."

"Oh, Lord," Sara said, grinding her cigarette out on the lawn. She retrieved the butt, held it in her hand. "It's all so sophomoric. I would have expected more of Bobby."

"He's paranoid about being controlled," I said. "He thinks psychiatrists use drugs to control people who are depressed by their powerlessness, that technological society controls the rest of us with mindless entertainment and consumerism."

"Do you think that's why he keeps refusing to see us?" Sara asked. "That he's afraid we're out to control him in some way?"

"I don't know. There's not a word about either of us in his diaries. But there are pages of every mundane detail of building bombs, mailing them, even of building his fucking outhouse. Suffering a hangnail, sending a bomb—the tone is the same. It's all flat, except for flashes of rage at Mom and Dad. You and I basically don't exist."

I looked to the sky, silently willing the rain to wait. "He hated Dad. He thinks Dad wanted to kill him. Actually kill, as in murder."

"You've got to be kidding," Sara said.

"Did Dad ever hit Bobby?"

"It's hard to imagine," she said quietly. "All I know is Dad was really disgusted with Bobby after he quit his job at Columbia. He thought Bobby threw his life away to live like a bum." Sara withdrew into her sweatshirt. "Neither Mom nor Dad could ever accept that there was something wrong with Bobby. They had too much invested in him. Mom became his apologist, and Dad was so hurt by Bobby's failure to be the son he wanted that he wrote him off." She paused. "Do you think *Time* and the others were actually correct with their asinine pop psychology? That Bobby bombed universities to get back at Dad by attacking what he worked so hard for?"

"I'm sure that's in there," I said. "Not that Bobby is capable of seeing it. If he were, we wouldn't be here."

Sara resumed walking, her head down. I kept pace with her.

"Mom never asked you to clean out the cabin in Gold Run, did she?"

Sara shrugged. "She never mentioned it."

"No, she asked me. She knew I'd do just what she wanted without her having to spell it out. She wanted me to get rid of anything incriminating, and I did. I threw out a coded notebook of Bobby's."

Sara stopped to look at me. Then she laughed. "I wouldn't lose any sleep over it. There's enough evidence against him already."

"That's not my point." I put my hand on her arm to keep her where she was. "It might not have been exactly conscious, but I knew what I was doing when I threw that notebook out. Before he even moved to Idaho, Bobby was keeping notebooks in code. I found one and threw it away. I was acting just like Mother." I paused. "And like you."

Sara looked quietly surprised. But I wasn't going to let her retreat into her customary silence. I took a step closer to her. "When are you going to stop lying to me?"

"Come off it, Natalie, it's getting really cold."

But I couldn't stop myself. "You read the manifesto months before I did. You must have suspected Bobby all along. But you couldn't face what you might have to do. You let me do it."

"What *you* did was run to Eric."

"That's right," I said. "I'm no different from you. It took me two months to face up to the possibility that the Cal Bomber could be Bobby, and by that time Olivia Trinidad was dead."

"You and I aren't to blame for that," Sara said.

"Yes we are," I said. "Not for the bomb that killed her, not for what Bobby did. But for our cowardice. For our unwillingness to do anything about what was right in front of us. Until it was too late."

She didn't answer, but I knew she'd heard me. We walked back in silence, the rain falling at last.

* * *

I drove back to Berkeley the next day, and scrubbed the house as I never had before, chemicals filling my nose and brain. Eric phoned. He put Lilly on, then Julia. I longed for a complaint, a problem—a hurt finger would do—but they were like someone else's children, polite, happy, and eager to get off the phone. Eric talked about blue skies and river rafting.

I stopped him. "Bobby did it," I said. "He kept diaries. That's why the government's been so sure of itself."

"I heard," Eric said. "It's all the over the news."

"I'm giving an interview to the *Sacramento Bee*," I said. "My mother's PR adviser arranged it. I have to do it. Bobby's going to be tried in Sacramento."

He was silent. "I can't stop you," he said finally.

I WELCOMED another reporter into our home, but this time, I had no illusion that my brother was anything other than the Cal Bomber. His ruined mental state was now the only hope we had of saving him, and the point I had to get across.

"My brother's writings are full of his concerns about mind control," I said. "He lived in a tiny dirt shack that he barely left. He didn't bathe. He thought my father wanted to kill him." I told the reporter the government understood my brother was severely mentally ill. "They're insisting on the death penalty for only one reason: they're terrified of looking soft on terrorism."

LILLY LAY bloodied and motionless in my arms, rubble surrounding us. I stroked her blackened legs, her bare feet, her lifeless hands, cradled her as if she'd just been born.

I groped the sheets, reached for Eric. But of course he wasn't there. I'll forget this nightmare, I thought, knowing I never would.

In the morning, I read an op-ed piece by the maimed Stanford professor, his angry response to my newspaper interview. He'd lost his arm, his eye, his ear, his good-looking face to one of Bobby's bombs.

Still in my nightgown, I wrote to him, pleading for his understanding and his forgiveness. My brother wasn't evil, but tragically ill.

I dressed, drove to the post office, then past it. I had no right to ask that professor for anything. Eric and the girls were in Glacier Park in Montana, in the wilderness Bobby claimed to have loved. I parked in downtown Oakland near an old coffee shop, and found a booth inside. I drank coffee, staring out the greasy window.

You tell yourself a story of the place you're from, the family that cared for you, the life you've led. You perfect it until it becomes like a cape with an iron weave protecting you. I wanted to die with that cape on. I never imagined it would be torn from me.

I dabbed my eyes with a napkin from the well-fingered dispenser. My husband and two daughters were up in the mountains, the bite of pristine air in their lungs, and I was at this sordid table, an ant dead in the sugar dispenser.

IN LATE JULY, my mother and I flew to New York to appear on a special *20/20* with the ABC news anchor herself. The show passed quickly, the female host as cozy as your best friend, sympathy in her eyes. Maybe she had a brother of her own.

After the taping, I followed my mother to her room. I was high from the rush of the interview. I really believed we were succeeding, that we could change public opinion, influence the government to drop the death penalty. I said this to my mother.

She shook her head. "The administration doesn't want to look weak on the death penalty in front of the Republicans," she said.

She sank into an overstuffed chair, smaller than I could ever remember her being, her feet on an ottoman. "I'm glad your father didn't live to see what's happened to his party."

"Or to see Bobby on trial for the murder of seven people."

I didn't know what made me say it, but my mother took it in stride.

Bobby would not have approved of a first-class lounge where the privileged got to separate themselves from everyone else, but he had given us that, the opportunity to wait for an airplane in private, my mother and I each with our own glass of Scotch from a little airline bottle, saying nothing.

"He was the most beautiful child, with those long lashes,"
looking past me. "I taught him at home until your father insis
him to school. I didn't trust ordinary teachers with a mind lik

I was speechless at this mad scientist of a mother in fro
I wanted my real mother back, the one who'd sent Sara an
to kindergarten without a fuss, the one who never seemed n
moderately interested in her children's lives.

My mother did not normally use her hands when she spok
did now. "Bobby made me this picture," she said, spreading h
"He was just four. He'd poked holes in blue paper over white
me the constellation Orion. I still have it."

My face flushed. Orion was mine. Bobby had given hin
the two of us outside the cabin at Gold Run on a fall night, o
against the old picnic table, Bobby's arm raised to show me
telgeuse and Bellatrix formed the shoulders, Rigel the left foot
time, all those autumns, I'd looked up and remembered. Mayb
was just a routine he used on adoring women, women who
little in return.

A YEAR AGO, my mother could have passed for ten years young
she was—tall, strong-boned, and clear eyed. Now she looked he
eighty years as she clutched my arm, walking tentatively throu
Travelers rushed around us, toward us, heedless. Any one o
could have knocked her down.

We walked past an open bar with a red Budweiser sign, shi
dles on the tap. A television played the news. I was so thirsty. If
alone, anonymous, I could have stopped.

The television was loud, there was no way not to hear it: th
ney general of the United States had asked for the death penalty
brother.

My mother's grip felt like a tourniquet. "The attorney gene
the president are cowards," she said.

People were looking at us. We'd been on television the night b
Our walk to the gate seemed endless.

chapter thirty-two

ALL THAT DAY'S long journey from New York to Sacramento, the news reports echoing in our heads, my mother and I shared a single thought: if we couldn't stop it, Bobby would die. My mother took a cab home from the airport. I went straight to Bobby's lawyer. When Debra rose to greet me, her skirt was unbuttoned at the waist and the gray roots of her hair were showing.

"I thought we had a chance of persuading them," I said.

"It makes me furious," Debra said. "It's barbaric."

She offered me a chair opposite her desk, took the matching one next to it. She rested a hand on mine. "He wants to see you."

I almost asked who.

"Just you," she said in answer to a question I hadn't yet formed.

My heart stuttered. All I could think to say was "Why, after all this time?"

"It might have something to do with this," she said, rising. She rifled through the stacks on her desk, the back of her blouse loose from her skirt. She handed me a two-day-old copy of the *Sacramento Bee*, and put a finger on what she wanted me to see.

My brother, the man with no friends, was collecting disciples. A radical journal was calling him a political prisoner. An environmental fringe group wanted to run him for president. A few mainstream thinkers had dared to say that while they abhorred his tactics, his critique of contemporary society was dead-on.

"I don't understand," I said.

"If we lose our appeal to invalidate the search of your brother's cabin, the best defense we've got is his mental state," she said. "The more people ascribe an ideology to Bob, the easier it is for the government to claim he's a terrorist, and once you label someone that, you make it vastly easier to execute them."

My eyes stung and I turned away. Her southern-flavored voice softened. "The problem is that your brother is enjoying being thought of as the leader of a violent anarchist movement instead of the mentally ill man he is. It's given him a real lift."

"I still don't see what that has to do with his being willing to see me now," I said.

Debra looked grim, the exhaustion around her eyes magnified by her glasses, her body wearing the relentless hours she'd already devoted to saving my brother. "He wants something from you. I'm just not sure what." I must have looked stricken, because she said, "I thought it was what you wanted."

What I wanted was to have the brother back I'd lost years before. Not to be so terrified of the man he was now.

WHEN I phoned Eric from the hotel later that evening, I woke him. I'd lost track of what time zone he was in. I told him about Bobby.

"Don't see him," he said. "He's not worth it. He'll just hurt you."

"I can't run from this," I said.

"We turned him in, Natalie. It's not a good idea."

"I'll have to face him sooner or later," I said.

"You're trying to punish yourself," Eric said. "You still think it's your fault he's in that cell. It's easier than blaming him for what he's actually done."

Was that true? All I knew was that I was going to see my brother. It was inevitable.

That night, I dreamed I was home washing a stain from one of Eric's button-down shirts at the kitchen sink. As if she were one of my own daughters, Olivia Trinidad was at my side. "It's blood," she said. "It won't ever come out."

chapter thirty-three

When I was a girl, I fantasized growing up to be someone the world would notice. Now I was someone people noticed all right. Everyone in the Sacramento County Jail seemed to know my name.

I went through the metal detector, past the guard, and stood against the wall with everyone else. We could have been in line at Kmart. Inside I was searched again, the handheld detector beeping at the underwire in my bra.

The visiting room was bare except for a metal table and stools bolted to the floor. There was a mirrored window next to the door, reinforced and clearly two-way, a loudspeaker in the cement wall, then a commotion so loud, it seemed impossible that it was just a door opening. My brother was led in, his wrists handcuffed from behind, his gaze away from me. The door shut again, and I heard us being locked in. Bobby squatted with his back against the door to have his handcuffs removed through a slot. He was dressed in a red prison jumpsuit. Red, I'd been told, was the color for the most dangerous criminals.

I'd dreamed of this jailhouse meeting so many times, I could have been dreaming now except for the racket of my heart. To steady myself, I tried to move the stool closer to the table, but of course I couldn't.

Bobby acknowledged me with a slight nod, gazing not at me but just to my left. He looked like my brother but much older, and too feeble. He was shorter than I remembered, his shoulders narrow, and his legs thin. His hair was mostly gray. The strands that weren't were coal black like our father's. The fact that, after all this, he was still Bobby made my eyes sting.

"Bobby."

He sat across from me easily, as if he'd grown used to cold, immobile furniture. He squinted as he adjusted my present self with whatever idea he carried of me. "You've aged," he said. "I don't know if I would have recognized you out there." His voice sounded shockingly like my father's, the intonation, the slight Valley accent.

I nodded. "You look older, too."

"It happens," he said. He slouched, drumming his fingers lightly on the tabletop. I remembered that drumming, how I'd tried to imitate it when I was young.

"Are you doing all right?" I asked, my hands clenched in my lap.

He laughed slightly, almost inwardly. "That's funny," he said.

"Are you eating?"

"I eat," he said.

He coughed, a polite hand over his mouth. I glanced around for water, but of course there was nothing.

"I know it wasn't you who turned me in," he said. "You haven't got it in you. I know it was your husband."

"Yes," I said, shocked at how readily I curried his favor, how easily I betrayed Eric to spare myself.

"Then why are you still with him?"

"I'm not," I lied. Or maybe it was the truth.

"I didn't know that," he said, massaging his gums. "You need to publicly renounce him."

All I could think to do was change the subject.

"Sara's staying with Mother," I said.

"They're screwing with my visitor list," Bobby said.

His abruptness, his lack of interest in the family we shared, was like a slap. "Who is?" I asked, trying to sound as if I hadn't been hurt.

"My so-called counsel," he said. "I've agreed to an interview but they won't let the reporter in to see me." So, this was the reason my brother wanted to see me. He needed me to do this for him.

"Which newspaper?"

He named a Sacramento weekly, an alternative paper given away in coffeehouses and secondhand record stores.

"I want you tell the lawyers that if they don't consent to the interview, you'll bring me the reporter's questions and take down my answers to give back to him."

I was no more to him than an errand girl. "I think your lawyers are just trying to protect their defense," I said, hoping to sidestep the issue.

His hand came down hard on the metal table; it must have hurt. "It's *my* defense," he said.

"I don't want you to die," I blurted.

"You've been listening to the lawyers." The anger was gone from his voice. It was my father speaking, his tone understanding, a hint of amusement at his excitable girl. "The death penalty's a crusade with them. They've got tunnel vision."

"Tunnel vision?" My voice was high, my nervousness like a separate being, another entity to fear in the cement room.

"This is a political case." He spoke like the professor he'd once been, with calm authority. "But they're afraid to risk a political defense because it's likely to result in the death penalty. They'd rather the jury think I'm a nut job. It serves their noble cause."

"They care about you," I said.

"They care about themselves. But I won't be humiliated." He thumped his chest. "I will not have my words taken from me. I'm not afraid to die for what I believe."

I looked toward the two-way glass, anxious about unseen people listening on the other side. Bobby lowered his voice, leaned his head toward mine. "What I stand for isn't easy. An end to techno-industrial society, to formal education, to the entertainment culture. No more things to buy, no television, no Internet. It's easier, safer, to call me crazy than to grapple with the truth of what I'm saying, the danger I pose to their fat-ass system."

I took a breath. His words had a certain logic. Except it was the logic of the prosecution's case.

"Mankind's at the end of the line," Bobby said as if he really wanted me to understand. "There's no going forward, no standing still. Our only hope is return. The question is who is going to push this civilization aside—someone of my education and intelligence, who wants true anarchy, who uses violence only when necessary, or fanatics with some fascist religious agenda."

"What about the victims, Bobby? The girl, Olivia Trinidad?" My voice shook. "Was she a necessary kill?"

He looked blank.

Rage pushed through my fear. "My daughter," I said. "The baby you held in your arms. She was at Stanford the day a bomb went off. She could have been killed."

"I don't know what you're talking about," he said.

I looked away, tears burning my eyes. I tried to compose myself. "I don't understand any of this, Bobby. Not a single piece of it."

"Don't put yourself down," he said, his tone telling me he'd misunderstood. "You're smart. You can grasp this."

"There's the appeal on the motion to dismiss the evidence," I said, desperate to return to what passed for neutral ground between us.

He nodded. "It was an illegal search. Unconstitutional. The case should be thrown out."

"If it is, what would you do?"

"Come and live with you," he replied evenly.

I couldn't control my expression.

"You don't have to look so horrified," he said. "I'd go back to doing what I was doing." He smiled. "I have a few followers now."

I stared at the hole I'd dug in my thumb under the nail. I felt nothing, no pain, just surprise that I was bleeding and a kind of heat.

He signaled to the observation window that we were through. He got up and crouched against the door to have his handcuffs put back on. He looked so small in his prison jumpsuit. I hated that he still meant so much to me.

chapter thirty-four

ON THE STEPS outside the jail, a young mother poured Pepsi into her baby's bottle. I looked away. Who was I to judge? For all I knew, my children were brushing their teeth with it.

I walked to Debra's office under a sky that was colorless and flat. "We lost the appeal on our motion to exclude," Debra said as soon as I took the chair opposite her desk. She looked defeated, but she must have known they were never going to let Bobby go free on a technicality.

I told her about my visit with him, what he wanted. "No jailhouse interviews," she said. "I'd hoped you could influence him to listen to us, not the other way around." I assumed she was trying to be jocular, but her voice betrayed an edge.

"He doesn't want any sort of psychiatric defense," I said.

Debra was quiet for so long, I thought she wasn't going to answer me. "It's the only defense we have."

I didn't know what I was hoping for. My brother had done exactly what he was accused of doing.

Debra rifled through the files that overwhelmed her desk, pulled out a report, and handed it to me. "I just got this," she said. "Pancuronium bromide. It paralyzes while leaving the brain functioning and the nerves able to feel the pain of cardiac arrest. A lot of veterinarians have stopped using it."

I felt a prickling at the top of my head.

"It's one of the drugs used to execute human beings," she continued, her voice even. "It's not like we lose this trial and Bob spends his life in a prison library."

I imagined my brother paralyzed, dying in excruciating pain before an audience of witnesses. I saw it as clearly as if Bobby were dying in front of me. This was the image she wanted me to carry to keep myself focused. It was the one I was supposed to get across to my brother.

I couldn't help my last question: "What if the psychiatrists find that Bobby's not as crazy as we think he is?"

Debra took my arm. "Don't go there," she said.

I HAD TRIED to tell myself that this Robert Askedahl, this murderer, was not my brother. That he was some psychopath who'd taken my brother, made even the memory of him impossible. But I'd been wrong. They could have dug him up, a horror-movie zombie, and he'd still be my brother.

He kept me safe when I was young. He gave me his room to dream in. Without Bobby, I might have been Sara, a girl who crawled out windows at night even though no one would have noticed if she'd used the front door.

Sara had returned to her place in Potter Valley. After I left Debra's office, I phoned her from the car. I told her I was coming to see her.

"What's this, a soap opera?" she asked. "You have to show up? We can't talk on the phone?"

"It's a soap opera," I said.

I heard the shrug in her voice. "I'll leave the door unlocked."

THE DRIVE FROM Sacramento to Potter Valley took nearly three hours. Once there, I had trouble remembering how to find Sara's house. The last time I'd been here was ten years ago, with a fussy Julia on a visit to her indifferent aunt. At the end of an unpaved road of hippie dwellings, time stopped in 1968, I recognized her place. Her car wasn't outside. I went around back to a dirt yard cluttered with old patio furniture, her laundry stiff on a line.

The sliding door to the kitchen was unlocked. I stepped inside past a waist-high stack of old newspapers, a half-dozen brown bags filled with empty cans and bottles, and a sink full of dishes. No one answered when I called out. My mother's Stickley sideboard—the companion to the table and chairs I now possessed—sat against the living room wall covered with mail. I spotted a pink envelope with Mother's return address. It was a birthday card. My sister, the Gemini. I hadn't remembered.

"Hey," a male voice said. I turned, startled, my hands trying to shove the card back in the envelope. The young man—he couldn't have been more than thirty—had come from a bedroom. He was heavyset, with a wispy beard, barefoot in a sleeveless tee and baggy shorts. His long curly hair was tied back in a messy ponytail.

"I'm Sara's sister," I said.

"Jim." He extended a fat arm. "You've got a very cool sister," he said. "Helped me get on disability. She can really navigate the system."

"I'll bet," I said. I hadn't meant to sound so sarcastic, and I regretted Sara hearing me as she came through the door.

"What are you, a Republican now?" she said.

She gave Jim a list of errands. She spoke to him the way I did to my third graders.

"It's convenient to have him around since I've been away so much," she said after he left.

The "oh" must have shown on my face, because she said, "What did you think, he was my boyfriend?"

"I saw Bobby," I said. "This morning in jail."

Sara was suddenly still, without pretense, her face unguarded. We sat down on opposite ends of the blanket-covered couch. She seemed so small inside her loose sundress. We'd never been close, but she was the only person I wanted to tell this to. She listened without interruption, without a hint of impatience.

I tried to describe his mental state. "He seemed of a piece with his philosophy, as if he had no past, no other interests, as if he and it were one. There are flashes of the old Bobby, the shy smile, the quiet humor . . ." I broke off, overwhelmed by trying to make sense of it.

"Why do you think Bobby asked me to do his favor and not you? You were the more logical choice."

Sara was thoughtful. "I love him," she said slowly. "But you love differently. You put so much into it. It makes you an easy mark."

"I would have died for him, for both of you, when I was a kid, just to get invited along." Maybe, I still would.

"The curse of the youngest," Sara said.

I looked at the wound I'd dug in my cuticle that morning, now a raw, nasty red. "Bobby would rather be executed than use a mental-illness defense. He wants to go down as the ecoterrorist he believes he is, and he thinks he can manipulate me into helping him."

Sara nodded as if she'd known this all along. "So can he? Manipulate you?"

I wanted to be offended, to spit back that I wasn't twelve years old, but there was no condescension in her tone. It was a fair question. "I have to do what I can live with," I said. "I'm just not sure what that is."

"What you won't be able to live with is helping Bobby commit legally sanctioned suicide."

"Is that what all this is? The bombs, the philosophy, everything. An elaborate, years-long suicide?" I covered my face.

Sara leaned forward and touched my shoulder. "If we prevail, Bobby will go to prison for the rest of his life. He'll find a way to live, and maybe he'll even find redemption."

She made it sound so simple, but Bobby wasn't going to pursue redemption, only justification for what he'd done. The same thing I feared my sister and I were going to spend the rest of our lives doing.

I woke up stiff on Sara's couch the next morning, the house silent in the early light, and left a note that said I was taking off. The air was so clean I could smell the wild blackberries on the bush beside my car. I plucked one and tasted the dust on it, the sweetness, the sun gentle on my face. For a moment I relished the feel of a summer morning, and then it was gone.

I got in my car with its dented bumper, the suitcase I'd carried to New York still in the trunk, and headed out with every intention of seeing my mother. I would have been there before ten but I took the wrong exit in Sacramento—it was easy to do.

chapter thirty-five

I NEVER INTENDED to go as far as I did. I was just driving, away from my mother's condo, away from the jail that held my brother, south on 99. I kept the air conditioner off and the window open, letting the sun hit my pale arm. The new tracts wedged into the fields south of the city made the huge, pastel houses seem like another crop. I liked the signs rising above the plastic pennants, the absurd promises and harmless lies of their names. Country View Estates, Woodbridge Manors, Willow Heights.

I thought about the girls and Eric, the summer driving trips we used to take. The kids in the backseat lulled into a stupor of boredom, Eric and I thrilled to be in the moment, going nowhere important, the four of us together. I tried not to contemplate if we'd ever have that again.

Outside Stockton, I realized where I was headed—to Modesto, to have lunch, and walk in the old downtown. Then I'd turn around, be back in Sacramento by two.

I'd been in Modesto years before with my father. I was eight when he took me with him to a political rally. It might as well have been 1920. There were red, white, and blue banners in the park. I passed out leaflets to the crowd and sat on a folding chair swinging my legs while people gave speeches. It was so hot that my father wore a white suit. At least, that was how I remembered it.

The 99 led right into the old part of Modesto. Past the Fosters Freeze, I saw just the sort of place I was looking for: Sam's, a stucco restaurant with booths in front of plate-glass windows. Their sign said they served breakfast, lunch, dinner, and cocktails.

I waited for a seat. Nearby at the counter, two men in white shirts with short sleeves talked over iced tea. They spoke in the Okie twang of the San Joaquin Valley, and they were talking about my brother. They'd probably never been out of Modesto except to go to Fresno State, but they knew what Bobby deserved. I left before the hostess could seat me.

In the car, I drove blindly and lost my bearings. When I figured out I was driving south, not north toward my mother, I just kept going. I stopped at a Mexican restaurant off the highway. The place was so dark that when I went back into the sunlight after lunch, I couldn't see a thing. The sensation thrilled me. My mother used to drop us at the Rialto on Saturdays for the all-afternoon kids' matinee. No parents, movies end on end. Sara was supposed to stay with me, but she would run off to join her friends. The older boys flattened their popcorn boxes and sent them flying in the light of the projector. Sometimes the manager stopped the movie, threatening to turn us out on the street. But it wasn't like school. Even the good kids were indifferent. At the end, Sara always came back, and we'd stagger into the sunlight together.

I drove away in the same direction I'd been going. My window down, the air was so hot and dry it should have ignited me. But it had the opposite effect. I could have been floating in freshwater.

It seemed logical to me now that I was going to Bakersfield, that it had been my destination all along. I was riding to the end of the line.

In the late afternoon, I checked into a Sheraton with the suitcase I'd carried home from New York. Could it only have been two days before? My cell phone rang as soon as I got to my room. It was Lilly, asking where I was.

"I'm at Grandma's," I lied.

She didn't sound convinced. I had to prod her to get her to tell me why she'd called. I listened to her stories, talking to her for as long as she wanted, but I got off before she could pass the phone to her dad. Eric and I were like strangers now. I was even more of a stranger to myself.

I opened the drapes to a view of the parking lot and sprinklers revolving on the green beyond. I remembered watching the huge Rain Bird sprinklers that watered my great-grandmother's fields. I have a photo of her taken in the thirties, a bobby pin holding her white hair back, the ground parched beneath her feet. I'd always planned to make a scrapbook for my daughters, to paste in the old photographs and write down the stories: my great-great-grandparents crossing the Sierra Nevada by covered wagon; my grandfather with his class at Berkeley in front of the old South Hall; my parents with Governor Brown at his first inaugural, a long silk scarf around my mother's neck. Five generations spent building a state, and Bobby would soon be on trial for trying to bomb it all away. I knew now that I'd never make that scrapbook.

I put on the bathing suit I'd packed for the futile possibility of exercise in New York, and went outside to the long pool. I swam without thought, past exhaustion. The sky turned dark. The distance from one side of the pool to the other grew farther until it was endless. What I wanted, I could not have, and that was to stop.

I showered in my room. The logical thing would have been simply to go to bed, but I was no longer tired. I put on some makeup and stared at myself in the mirror. It was me and it was someone else entirely.

It was after nine when I headed downtown.

I'D BEEN to this Basque restaurant years ago with Eric. A large dark bar in front, a smaller bright dining room in back, and long tables with red-checkered cloths. I was surprised that I found it again so easily, even more surprised that I'd been looking for it.

The bar was as packed as I remembered, but the dining room was nearly empty, the tables still littered, a large group finishing up in the center. No one approached me. The food was served family style on platters. I was without even my own small family. What had I been thinking? It was a quarter to ten.

A waitress came from the kitchen. She was mature, sure of herself. "Dinner's over, honey, but you can get a sandwich at the bar until eleven," she said.

I glanced behind me. The crowd at the bar was three deep. I couldn't think. I stood there like a huge bird, my arms too long, the left one now sunburned.

"I'll find you a place," she said, motioning for me to follow. In a few swift moves, she cleared a path, gave some orders—you up, you over—and I was seated. The man next to me bit into a sandwich. "Tri-tip," he said, wiping his mouth with a napkin. "It's good here."

I nodded in a friendly way, and ordered a Scotch and soda with the sandwich. There was a television at the far end of the bar, but it wasn't on.

"The TV's been broken since the Carter administration," the man said.

"Longer." Another patron laughed.

"That's the way it should be," I said. All the televisions in the world broken. I was starting to think like Bobby.

"You a trucker?"

My friendliness shut off. I was offended. It wasn't the picture I had of myself. "A teacher," I said icily.

He was looking at the band of white between the T-shirt I was wearing now and the sunburn on my arm. Suddenly I understood that he'd been joking, maybe flirting, and I'd taken his comment the wrong way.

"What do you do?" I asked. I didn't care what he did, but I wanted to make up for my chill.

"I work for the city," he said.

I nodded knowingly, as if to say *yes, the city*, then turned my attention to the sandwich that had arrived. It was messy but good. I asked for a second drink and another napkin.

A band was setting up noisily on the little stage in the corner of the room, keyboard, amps, guitars. They weren't kids, but ordinary-looking middle-aged guys. Geezer rockers, as Julia would say. The tall, rangy guy tuning his fiddle looked at least sixty. The man next to me drained his beer, put his napkin on his plate, crossed to the stage, and picked up a guitar.

I stared, surprised, and he smiled at me. The lights came up a bit. The lead guitarist stomped his foot. There was a sudden punch of sound. I knew the chords. "Mobile Line."

Although his speaking voice was low, he sang high and nasal. Couples crowded the dance floor in front of the band and spilled into the center of the room between the bar and the tables along the wall. This was an old crowd, silver-haired guys in cowboy shirts, pressed jeans, and boots and their big-haired, weathered-about-the-neck dates.

He introduced the band. They were local guys. I got from the jokes that my friend—I'd elevated him to that—was a cop. At the break, they moved through the bar, shaking hands and slapping shoulders. My friend joined a table with five women. The rangy violinist flirted with the waitress who'd taken care of me. The bartender told me that the lead guitarist managed the paint department at Home Depot. Someone fed the jukebox. I ordered another drink. My waitress danced with the violinist. I saw it all from my perch at the bar, but I was invisible, crazy with relief to be outside myself.

The band played a shorter last set—or maybe I just didn't want it to end. I paid my bill, tipped the bartender, and pulled a twenty from my purse. When I got off the bar stool, I was unsteady on my feet. I sensed I was weaving as I crossed to the waitress. "Wow." She smiled, holding aloft the twenty I'd given her. Someone turned the jukebox on.

My friend glided into my field of vision. "Dance?" he said.

I wanted to for so many reasons. I loved to dance. The crowd was my age. Fear lay under my happiness and would soon be in control. I was drunk and hadn't yet figured out how I was going to get back to the hotel. It had been years since I'd danced with a member of the band.

I took my purse off my shoulder and left it on a table. Be careful of your purse, I always said to Julia, especially if you're going to be dancing.

He was taller than me, straight-postured, and still lean. His salt-and-pepper hair hit his collar. He had a beat-up, acne-scarred face and a strong grip. I guessed he'd been married a few times but wasn't now. His shirt was damp, unsnapped far enough for me to see that his chest was hairless. More than twenty years, I thought, since I'd felt a smooth chest next to mine. He pulled me close for a slow dance. "I love the way you look," he said. "Your hair."

"Thanks," I said, flattered in spite of myself. It had been years since I'd danced like this, one song after another with a willing partner. When we finally dropped at a table against the wall, I was ready for the drink he bought me.

"Is this place always like this?" I asked, drumming my fingers on the table to the hum of the room.

"This is a good night. Last week it was dead."

He placed his hands over mine, stopped their movement, and held them. He rubbed a finger across my wedding ring.

"Why are you here?" he asked.

"I was hungry," I said. "I didn't want to watch television in my room." There were so many more reasons, hundreds of them like a bridge behind me, spanning years to a place before I was even born. But I couldn't bear looking further back than a few hours.

As if I were a teenager, I rose to dance again and pulled him up, the jukebox playing a country song. I didn't know how to do the dance and he tried to show me. Soon I was laughing and falling against him. He was laughing, too. The bartender announced last call. I put up my hands. No more to drink. "What I need is a cab," I said.

"I'll give you a lift," he said as if it were the easiest thing in the world.

Outside in the cooling air, I clutched him for warmth, for steadiness. He had his guitar in his other hand and asked me to hold it while he cleared the front seat of his pickup, tossing loose papers and a jacket behind the seat. He helped me up, and I felt as if I'd accomplished something simply by managing to get inside. He got in, and rested the key in the ignition. We were parked behind the restaurant, the lot dark, no other cars around. "Where do I take you?" he asked.

"The Sheraton," I said. "Do you know where that is?"

He laughed. "Yes," he said. He looked at me, and put his hand in my hair. I reached to take it away, my hand on his too long. Then he was kissing me, the softness surprising me. No, I thought, and then I was kissing him back, not breaking it off, too greedy for the moment, this moment in which there was only sensation, only self and nothing else. As if I were seventeen, I thought all right this but not that. The cab was warm, the windows fogged. We were drunk. Our shirts were off. I didn't want to remember the thing I had to remember: who I was. Zippers, hands, fingers. I didn't care that I was getting marked, a knee banging into the dashboard, my smooth face against his rough one. It was too desperate, my franticness to stay submerged, fighting the pull of consciousness.

"I can't," I said, trying to disentangle myself.

"Your place or mine," he said, misunderstanding.

I wasn't dreaming. The panic biting my chest was true: I really had betrayed Eric. I groped for my T-shirt.

The act of arranging myself in my clothes made my breath shallow. "Oh God," I said, throwing my head against the seat, my hand a fist against my mouth, hot tears on my hot face. I couldn't stop. He grabbed me, and held me against him. He kept saying, "I've got you, it's all right." But it wasn't.

I pulled away, no longer the person I'd always thought I was. I asked him to take me back to my hotel.

He didn't argue. We drove in silence, the night air from our cracked windows stinging my cheeks. I looked at the stars hanging low in the sky and tried not to think.

Outside the Sheraton, he suggested coffee.

"My husband's camping with our kids," I said, looking at him. "I didn't go because I had too much else going on. My brother's the Cal Bomber."

There might have been a flicker of surprise in his eyes. It was too dark to tell. I supposed he was used to people confessing all sorts of things. "Jesus," he said quietly.

He offered to give me his card if I ever wanted just to talk. I thanked him but I refused. I thought of apologizing, but another apology seemed beside the point. I fled his pickup and hurried inside, a hand shielding my eyes from the awful light of the hotel lobby.

* * *

I DIDN'T KNOW where I was when I woke up, or why I ached so. When I opened the blackout drapes, the sunlight was like an assault, and the night before seemed impossible. But my face in the bathroom mirror told me it really had happened—my eyes bloodshot from drinking and swollen from hysteria, my cheek reddened from the rub of another man's face. I stood under the shower and tried to wash it all away.

I checked out of the hotel, the desk clerk looking too long at the name on my credit card. The name of my great-great-grandfather who'd crossed into California in 1848, the name I'd always been so proud of. When I went outside, I couldn't find my car. In the life I used to know, it would have been in the parking lot. In the life I'd fallen into the night before, my car was outside a Basque restaurant. I had to call a cab.

Since I first fell in love with Eric, I'd never shared so much as a kiss with another man. Except in dreams. Then I'd awake relieved that whatever I'd done hadn't been real. But last night had been no figment, a stranger's breath on mine. I'd been willing to exchange so much and we hadn't even traded names.

I got onto I-5 and headed north, toward home. I was finished with wrong turns. Outside of Stockton, the odometer on my Honda flipped to a hundred thousand miles, but I missed the event.

chapter thirty-six

I WAS FLUSHED, alive in anticipation. My children were coming home today. I picked up a magazine, put it down, went to the window and back again too many times to count. I could not be contained. When I heard the sounds of an automobile in the driveway, I ran outside waving and jumping. The right car had pulled up but the wrong family emerged. The man was too tan, too lean, too unshaven, the kids too old. The girls seemed mortified by my loud voice, my waving. Julia had chopped off her hair and put it in spikes, her beautiful long hair. She wore a tattered blue blouse that looked like she'd found it at a Laundromat. I swallowed. They'd been gone two months.

"You look so grown up," I told her. She endured my embrace the way my third-grade boys did when their mothers tried to kiss them at school.

Lilly stood next to Eric, a hand on the hem of his gray T-shirt. She was at least an inch taller, the first hint of cheekbones pressing through her chubby cheeks. I dropped to my knees, suffocating her against me. When I rose, she stepped back to take Julia's hand. Eric and I kissed quickly, his unfamiliar stubble stinging my cheek.

Eric wanted to unpack the car, to get that out of the way. Julia headed straight for her room and the telephone. Lilly flopped to the floor in front of the television. I sat next to her and touched her curly hair. I had so many questions, but she uttered no more than one-word replies. I could have been anyone bugging her. I hadn't let myself imagine how hard this was going to be.

I'd made dinner, spaghetti with homemade meatballs and a sauce of fresh tomatoes, a reliable hit. Even Julia shoveled it in. The girls dominated the dinner-table chatter. Afterward they managed to be in every room we were, as if they were afraid we might forget about them. Eric and I couldn't have had a real conversation even if we'd wanted to.

It was eleven before the girls were asleep and the two of us were alone. Eric sat on the edge of our bed, tanned and fit in jeans and a T-shirt, his gray hair cut short. He could have been a stranger.

I stood in front of him. "Good to be home?" I asked, too lightly.

He didn't answer, or even look at me.

I rubbed my arms against my sudden chill. "Have you met someone else? A campground woman?"

"Stop it," he said.

I took a breath. "Are you leaving me?"

I'd pictured this conversation, played both sides, steeled myself for it, but I wasn't prepared for how naked the words left me.

"I've driven five thousand miles this summer," he said. "I've certainly thought about it."

I felt helpless waiting for what he had to say.

"I'm not going to be the one who breaks up our family," he said.

I laughed, bitter-throated. "You're going to leave that up to me."

A few days before, I'd reached my arms out to someone else. Eric might have, too. Could he read on my face what I was trying to pretend never happened?

How had we gotten to this broken place? I didn't know. My brother had mailed bombs, and our marriage had been among the casualties.

I took a step toward him, my heart frantic. He looked at me without speaking. I drew the inside of my wrist down his face, and felt the pleasure of tender skin on hard bristle. He grabbed my wrist, his grip hard.

We stared at each other, our faces close. I didn't move.

I was shaking, my thoughts pleading. *Forgive me.*

He brought my wrist to his sunburned lips and kissed it.

I brushed his face with my fingertips as if his skin might scald me. We kissed, pushing against each other, toppling onto the bed.

"I want to forget," I said, his hands in my hair.

Our anguish made it easy. We forgot to guard old injuries, fear new ones. There was only this falling, this hanging on.

Later I put on a nightgown to defend against the morning intrusion of children. I lay in Eric's arms, licked the salt from his chest, and breathed his sweat, the scent that had once made me feel so safe.

"I don't know how to go on from here," he said.

"I don't either," I said, pressing my face against his chest.

WE'D BEEN too raw, too desperate, the night before, and now at breakfast, Eric and I were back to acting like strangers with secrets to hide. Overly polite, too careful with our words, uneasy touching. When he left on vague errands, I exhaled.

I had so much to do—laundry, bills, shopping—and I had nothing to do. It was the end of August, sixty degrees and overcast. I had my family back home and the furnace on to ward off the chill.

I went upstairs to Julia's room. She'd removed the pictures from her bedroom walls, the photographs torn from magazines, leaving only bits of tape.

"Redecorating?" I asked.

"I want my walls bare," she said.

Later, she showed me downloaded pages of the year-abroad program she hoped to attend in Ghana.

She'd picked a place as far from home as she could go. "But you'll miss your senior year of high school," I said. "Graduation, the prom."

"Not to mention having the kids over for Cokes after the sock hop," she said.

She fell onto the couch, clutching the remote.

"Why don't you phone one of your friends?"

"What do you care? It's not like you have any."

"I'm not fifteen," I said to have the last word. But she was right.

Somewhere in the miles all of us had traveled that long summer, over the days wedged together, too full and then too empty, I'd stopped thinking about the way things were *before*. I'd stopped thinking *when this is over.* I'd lost even the idea of it.

* * *

LILLY'S new teacher, the one who'd replaced me at Mountaintop, had sent a school-supply list more elaborate than any I'd ever handed out. I showed it to Lilly, who was sprawled on my bed watching TV. I played up the forty-eight pack of colored pencils. "I thought we could go buy them," I said. "Then go out to lunch, just the two of us." Leave Julia to her sulking. I was mildly excited by the prospect, but Lilly wasn't giving me the reaction I expected.

"I don't want to," she said.

I shut off the television. "Sure you do."

She sat up. "I don't want to go Mountaintop anymore. I want to go to public school."

Four months ago, I'd known her mind as well as my own. Her thoughts, her dreams, her worries. When she told me about her day at school, she started with the first bell.

I tried the old tricks, the old questions, but she'd shut herself to me. All she said was "Please."

ERIC AND I could never be truly silent with each other. We had children. "Did you know that Julia wants to study abroad next year?" I asked him when we were alone in bed.

"She mentioned it," Eric said. "I suggested Spain, and she said, 'Oh, Dad, you're always so predictable.'"

"She wants to go to Ghana."

"Over my dead body."

I petted his arm, feeling a moment of safety. Of course she wasn't going to Ghana. I told him about Lilly wanting to change schools.

"Maybe that's a good idea," he said, as if he'd thought about it.

I stiffened. "She's too young to know what she wants."

"She's old enough to know she wants a fresh start," he said. "I think we owe her that."

He'd said we, but he meant me. *I* owed her that.

chapter thirty-seven

THE ALARM went off more loudly than I could bear. Eric pulled a pillow over his head. Down the hall, Julia's alarm echoed ours. It was the first day of school.

A new year.

I went to wake up Lilly, my heavy sleeper. Her eyes were wide open.

"I was awake all night," she said.

"Were you thinking about your new school?" I tried to sound casual but my stomach was a fist.

She hesitated, uncertain she wanted to tell me. "Some of the time," she said.

The public school was too large. She didn't know anyone there. We'd helped build Mountaintop. Lilly could've had four more years where everyone knew her—and us.

"You can still go back to Mountaintop," I said too quickly. I wasn't sure she could.

"You don't have worry, Mom," she said, heading for the bathroom. "I'll be okay."

Julia came down to breakfast in her carefully-thought-out-first-day-of-school outfit: worn tennis shoes marked up with peace symbols, frayed jeans, and a sweater buttoned top to bottom. Something about the intense buttoning made me ask, "What are you wearing under there?"

She shrugged. "A T-shirt."

"Let me see it."

She stared into her cereal bowl. "Why do you have to make such a big deal out of everything?"

I wasn't sure why, or why I was starting what was bound to be a fight. "I just want to see it."

"No," she said.

I knew I should have let it go, but I was suddenly furious. I clutched the counter, my heart pounding from the fear that lay beneath my anger.

She carried her cereal bowl from the table, made a show of washing it, then tried to walk away. I blocked her exit. "Show me your shirt," I said.

"If you want to rip my clothes off, go ahead," she said "Otherwise, let me go to school."

"You're not going anywhere." I called upstairs for Eric.

"Oh, great," Julia said. "Make a federal case of it."

We faced each other, our arms identically crossed.

Eric looked tired, already fed up. I could feel his exasperation with both of us. For a moment, I feared he would not back me up, but he ordered her to do what I'd asked. She refused. All three of us were yelling, me thinking, How did this happen?

"I hate you," she said, red-faced, hysterical, glaring not at Eric but at me. She unbuttoned her sweater.

I don't know what I'd expected, but it wasn't this. She wore a white T-shirt emblazoned with Bobby's face and the words SMASH THE MACHINE. FREE ROBERT ASKEDAHL.

"Where did you get that?" I was rasping.

"It's a T-shirt," she said. "Not a bag of cocaine."

I repeated the question.

"A stand on Telegraph," she said.

"Wear something else," Eric said.

"That shirt makes Bobby out to be some sort of Che Guevara, which is just what the prosecution wants," I said, after she went upstairs to change. "My God, she can't possibly be sympathetic to Bobby's sick cause."

Eric slumped into a chair. "She didn't buy that T-shirt to upset you," he said. He sounded like a shrink with too many patients. "She's not proud of her uncle. It's about facing the other kids. I think she was being brave."

He's my brother, I wanted to say. But I was sick of saying that, sick of my own self-pity. I wished I could get outside my own head enough to see the T-shirt as no big deal. Instead, I climbed the stairs to Julia's room and tried to talk to her about the shirt, make it seem like just another fight I could turn into a lesson. She would have none of it.

"There's nothing to learn from this," she said. "Unless I have kids and Lilly grows up to be a mass murderer. And even then I wouldn't act like you did."

"Let's forget it and try to be normal," I said.

Julia just rolled her eyes and walked past me on her way to school in her second-choice T-shirt.

A FEW DAYS after the kids began school, Eric started his new job. I handed him a glass of wine when he came home, and patted a kitchen chair for him to sit. My expression must have been eager because he said, "There's nothing to tell."

He took a hefty swallow from his glass. "Except they made it clear they expected me to arrive every day at eight thirty sharp."

"Does it seem like it's going to be an okay place to work?"

He shrugged. "It's a paycheck."

LILLY brought home her new backpack filled with work sheets, some for homework, others already graded with pasted-on stars. Gold for perfect, silver for very good, red for run-of-the-mill.

"I never gave my students work sheets," I said to Eric when were alone. "Kids her age shouldn't be doing homework, especially that kind of busywork."

"You're not Lilly's teacher," Eric said. "Work sheets never killed anyone."

Lilly seemed happy at her new school, except that she couldn't tolerate a wrinkled work sheet. She stacked the graded ones in neat piles on her shelf according to the color of their star. She asked for her own box of stars. I caught her pasting red ones on her starless work.

"Why not put on a gold one?" I asked.

"That would be cheating," she said.

She constructed a behavior chart, and taped it to her wall. They had them at school, she said. I was supposed to evaluate her behavior at home with the appropriate star. We marked off the days with gold stars for her relentless perfection.

She made a friend in class who invited her to Sunday school. "They're Methodists," she said, as if that would set my mind at ease.

"Five days of school is enough," I said. We didn't need that, being pulled into some unknown family's churchgoing.

"There goes my only friendship," Lilly said.

I relented and said she could go.

In late September, a date was set for Bobby's trial. January 6. Epiphany.

The date my mother chose fifty-four years ago for the baptism of her bright-eyed son.

chapter thirty-eight

ERIC AND I slept as if we were sunburned, on guard against the pain of accidental touch. We kicked off blankets, then reached for them again because October nights in Berkeley were chilly. In the morning, the kids gave us wide berth. We had the air of people you didn't want to mess with.

Sara phoned to say she wanted to see me the next day. I told her I had to work at Lilly's Halloween carnival. The truth was, I was looking forward to it, the ordinariness of being a volunteer at my child's school fair, just another anonymous parent. Sara said she'd find me there.

The parents had trucked in pumpkins, sunflowers, and bales of alfalfa to turn the playground into a pumpkin patch. I was sent to the photo stall to take two-dollar Polaroids of kids on a bale of hay beside a floppy scarecrow.

Lilly seemed thrilled that I was in a booth with a cash box and a camera, acting like the other mothers, a part of things. She ran off to play, but she came by often to check that I was still there.

The kids posed with their friends or with their families. I preferred the kid groups. There was something creepy about the families, the way they arranged themselves in the present for a photo I could envision in a news story ten years down the line.

Sara didn't look out of place in a baggy sundress, walking through the straw on the playground, her long gray hair fastened with a barrette. She ate from a small bag of Fritos, a safety pin dangling from the temple of her sunglasses, Lilly's eccentric aunt arriving at her school fair. Except we both knew she wasn't here for Lilly.

She sat on the vacant folding chair next to mine and examined my Polaroid discards, the ones that were so bad I'd had to shoot another.

"Don't quit your day job," she said.

"I already have."

We sat together in the booth, Sara eating her Fritos. I finished a hot dog. There was barely room for the two of us. I fiddled with the cash box. Apparently everyone who wanted a photo had gotten one because there were no more customers. I wondered when someone would come to relieve me.

"Mom's going to be eighty next month," Sara said.

I knew. The real eightieth as opposed to the false-alarm eightieth of last year.

"Is that what you risked hay fever to come here and tell me?"

Sara smoothed out the empty chip bag on her lap, folded it in squares, and tucked it in her pocket.

"The prosecution is leaking evidence again." She leaned forward, the safety pin tingling from her sunglasses, and lowered her voice to a whisper. "They're going to hang Bobby with his words before the trial even starts."

My mouth tasted of the hot dog I wished I hadn't eaten. I looked around the school yard for Lilly in her princess costume. When I spotted her, standing alone and to the side of a group of girls, I felt no better.

"Our backs are up against it," she said. "You need to move back to Sacramento, pronto. Be seen there full-time, do whatever PR the lawyers suggest."

I'd expected to go back, but not so soon. There was trick-or-treating with Lilly, and a few weeks later, Thanksgiving. Lilly wasn't having an easy adjustment to her new school. She needed extra attention. Julia had just celebrated her sixteenth birthday and was talking driver's license. I didn't want to even think about Eric's reaction to my leaving home again.

A group of boys in superhero costumes chased one another past the booth, one knocking into it. My eyes scanned again for Lilly. She still wasn't playing with anyone. "I don't think I can leave my kids right now," I said.

"You're kidding," she said, her voice caustic.

Sara got up, her mouth tight. She stood outside the booth, pointed at a tilted pole. "Your house is collapsing," she said.

TWO DAYS after Sara's visit, my brother's lawyer phoned. "Are you rested?"

"Rested enough," I said trying to keep the bitterness from my voice.

"There's going to be a big story coming out in Sunday's *Bee*, an interview with the wife of one of the victims." She took a breath. "I think you should talk to the *New York Times*."

When I didn't answer, Debra said, "There's something else." She hesitated and I sensed she was taking a risk in telling me. "It's absolutely confidential. Bob has agreed to bargain a plea. Guilty in exchange for life."

For a moment, I couldn't identify the feeling washing over me. "When will he be sentenced?" I asked, my voice sounding my relief.

"The government doesn't have to accept our offer."

"But . . ." I stammered, desperate to believe an end was in sight. "I can't believe they'd go to all the trouble and expense of a trial just to get a sentence of death over life in prison."

"Believe it," she said. "It's politics."

"They lied to my face," I said, unable to keep the fury from my voice. "They used me. They made me think they cared about us when all they wanted from the very beginning was to see my brother dead."

"I know," she said, her voice exhausted.

I told her I'd see her in Sacramento.

"WHERE ARE the kids?" Eric asked when he got home from work. He knew something was up. The kitchen table was set for just two.

"I fed the kids earlier. They were hungry. Lilly's asleep. Julia's studying." It was too transparent, my nervousness, the kids out of the way so early.

He poured himself a glass of wine without offering me one. "All right, what is it?"

I told him about the plea bargain. "Bobby would be locked up for the rest of his life, and all this would be over. But that's not good enough for the government. They want him on a gurney with a needle in his arm."

"They might accept the plea," Eric said.

"And they might not," I said. "The defense team wants me back in Sacramento to be the public face against the death penalty for Bobby. They want me for the sympathy factor because I turned him in."

"You could be there for months," Eric said, sounding resigned.

"It's only an hour away," I said. "I'll be traveling back and forth."

"You're not even here when you're here," he said.

DURING THE next few days, I was singled-minded with efficiency. Eric's mother would come to stay with the kids. She would sleep in Lilly's bed, Lilly in a futon on the floor. I dusted and scrubbed. I stored enough groceries to last through an arctic winter.

Nights were a different story. In my dreams, I lost my children, forgot their toddler selves on beaches, in burning houses, in cars with no brakes. I made love with the wrong man, in the wrong place, only to face an uncomprehending, unforgiving Eric, to plead that it was just a dream. I searched endless bureau drawers without finding a stolen yearbook I'd hidden and never returned.

chapter thirty-nine

THE AIR had a bite. It was the first of November, the Day of the Dead come around again. Sara and I were back to sharing the twin beds in our mother's spare room. "She calls this the guest room, but I doubt she's ever had any but us," Sara said.

But she had, I thought, remembering my girls breathless with excitement to stay at Grandma's new house, their parents quietly giddy to be off somewhere without them. I hated the way I felt closer now to Sara than to Eric, summoned back to my tribe by my brother's bloody war.

"You're awfully quiet," Sara said.

"Do you ever think that if our great-great-grandparents had crossed into California a few weeks later, they'd have been traveling with the Donner Party? A few weeks later and they'd have been cannibals, too?"

"I wouldn't mention that to the reporter," Sara said.

"What lunacy possessed them to cross those mountains in a rickety wagon with little kids? Maybe it would have been better if they'd ended up eating each other."

"Very funny," Sara said as if she didn't think it was. But I could not be stopped. "From the start of this," I said, "I've thought, 'Why us? Why not some other family?' But after I read Bobby's diaries, I knew it *had* to be us. If our forebears had stayed put in the 1840s, there'd have been no Bobby. Normal people don't leave everything behind for a dream of utopia, of gold. They aren't willing to sacrifice their children for it. Even Dad had his sacred vision of a golden state and free higher education for everyone."

"I have no idea what you're getting at," Sara said.

"All those monomaniacs mingling their genes—someone somewhere down the line had to get it backward, carry the obsession in the wrong direction. I think Bobby was just trying to go back to the beginning to start over and get the dream of California right this time."

Sara didn't try to reason with me. Maybe she sensed I was beyond reason. Maybe she thought I was right.

IN THE MORNING, I washed my hair and applied makeup as if I were meeting a lover instead of a reporter from the *New York Times*. I didn't know what to wear. I settled on a simple skirt from J.Crew, a turtleneck sweater, and loafers, masquerading as a regular gal with subtle makeup. I told myself I had the interview thing down.

This reporter was on the early side of middle age, his face neither as babyish as I'd feared nor as battered as I'd hoped. We met in a small conference room at the attorneys' office downtown. The room was furnished with a worn leather couch, two armchairs, and a nicked coffee table. There was no pretense that this was anything other than another ploy in a struggle not going our way. We drank coffee from Styrofoam cups. He sat in a chair. I sat on the couch, facing a window that offered a view of the building where my father once worked.

He took out his notebook and turned on his tape recorder. He asked how I was doing. I wasn't expecting the question, the sympathetic tone. My eyes flooded. We'd only just begun and already I'd ceded him the upper hand. He fumbled in his briefcase, handing me a small pack of tissues.

I dabbed my eyes. "I've been better." I pointed to the window. "My father's office was right over there on the mall," I said. "He used to take Bobby in with him sometimes. Bobby was fascinated by government, how it could be used to help people."

The reporter asked if I'd ever met Governor Brown.

I laughed. "He used to come to our house for dinner." I talked about the Sacramento of my childhood. "Before the governor's mansion had a pool, my dad would join the governor swimming at the motel across the street."

The reporter prodded me forward in Bobby's biography. I gave him what I'd rehearsed, the growing signs of what, in retrospect, had to be mental illness, Bobby's move to a shack without electricity or running water.

We'd been talking for two hours before he asked when I first suspected that my brother might be the bomber. I was getting tired. I told him about my first inkling, discussing it with my sister after the UCLA professor was killed in January, and that we'd dismissed the possibility.

"Sara read the manifesto when it was published. She didn't believe it could be Bobby. I didn't either."

"Were you surprised your sister had read the manifesto?" His question was neutral but I realized what I'd done.

"If you knew my brother," I said, "you wouldn't have believed it either. We see what we want to." There was defensiveness in my tone, an intimation of confession: if either my sister or I had been braver, if we hadn't been so blinded by what we didn't want to see, Gloria Trinidad would have her daughter today.

chapter forty

I'D NEVER KNOWN my sister to waste as much as a piece of string. She never gave away her own effort, never freely spent her emotions. Her dynamism, her animation, even her early rising in the room we shared, was new. The government's determination to execute our brother, it seemed, had rewired her.

My sister who'd refused to own an answering machine now had new phones installed at our mother's condo. She commandeered the dining room for an office, and the table for our shared desk. We wrote letters, juggled phone calls from lawyers, the ACLU, and our supporters in the anti-death-penalty movements. We met with Buddhists, Quakers, and Catholics in church basements, gave interviews to the press, and appeared on *Nightline*. Every call, every meeting, every interview had a single purpose: to pressure the government into backing off the death penalty for Bobby.

I found comfort in Sara's direction, in the order of our birth. I was grateful for her willingness to forget for now that I'd been the one who turned Bobby in. I tried not to think beyond the task at hand, not to revisit the decisions that had brought me here.

Bobby would no longer see me. Secretly, I was relieved. It was easier to carry only the idea of my brother—my sweet, mentally ill brother who'd offered a plea to spend his life in prison for the lives he'd taken—unfettered by the messy reality of him. Meanwhile, my brother fought his lawyers on a mental-illness defense and refused to be examined by a government psychiatrist. We had only our conviction that Bobby had to be mentally ill to fuel our argument that he was.

As if I had a job that separated me from my family, I commuted home on the weekends. The girls embraced my guilty overdevotion—the trips to the mall or the movies, the easy yeses they got from me. In a way, Eric seemed happier, as if my absence during the week gave him the normality he craved.

THE WEAK-SOUNDING voice on the phone asking for me was so familiar, I thought against all logic, It's Dad.

"It's Bob," my brother said. "Am I bothering you?"

I leaned against the counter in my mother's kitchen, my heart thundering. The call was unexpected. I didn't know what it could mean.

"Are you all right?" I asked stupidly.

"I haven't slept more than an hour a night in weeks," he said. "You can't imagine the noise in here. Banging, wailing, other sounds too disgusting to tell you. It's affecting my health. I can't think to defend myself."

I went blank trying not to imagine what it must be like for him.

"You have to get me out of here," he said.

I gasped, I couldn't help it. "But how? Where could you go?"

"To another facility," Bobby said. "Away from the drunks and psychos. There's a federal prison south of San Francisco."

"I understand," I said, but I had no idea how to do anything about it. "Have you mentioned this to the lawyers?"

As soon as I asked, I regretted the question. Of course he had or he wouldn't be talking to me. But his voice, when he answered, was matter-of-fact. "The lawyers are trying to use this situation to pressure me into accepting a mental-illness defense. I give in to seeing a government shrink and they suddenly find a way to get me out of here."

I didn't want to think that could be true, but how did I know? I told him I'd make an appointment to see his lawyers. "I'll do what I can," I said with far more confidence than I felt.

"Thank you," Bobby said, finally sounding like the brother I remembered.

* * *

DEBRA was with her co-counsel, Mark, the two of them hunched at a table surrounded by document boxes when I arrived at their office. I hardly knew him, but instead of shaking my hand, Mark hugged me. "You look stressed," he said. "Sit."

I sat stiffly, afraid that if I responded to his kindness I might cry. When I told them Bobby's request, a look passed between them.

"We're working on getting him transferred to the federal prison at Dublin until the trial," Debra said. "We've told him that. Many times."

"He's thinks you're dragging your feet to pressure him into seeing a government psychiatrist," I said, my eyes alert to their reaction.

They both sighed. They'd heard this before. "Even if we were, which of course we aren't, there'd be no point to it anymore," Mark said.

"The government has won their motion," Debra said in answer to my confused expression. "They've succeeded in using Bob's refusal to be examined by one of their psychiatrists to get all psychiatric testimony barred from the trial. We'll have to argue that he acted out of psychiatric illness without any testimony from experts." Her face wore her defeat. She looked exhausted. "It's an enormous setback."

I tried to bring the two of them around, to share the hope I'd convinced myself was a sure thing. "But with Bobby agreeing to a plea bargain . . ."

"There's no certainty they'll accept our offer," Mark said. "They may insist on a trial to get the death penalty."

There was no way out of the restraints that bound us. If the government insisted on trial, Bobby had forbidden the only defense that could save him. In his refusal to tolerate any suggestion that he might be mentally ill, he'd all but handed the government the needle to kill him.

chapter forty-one

THE WEATHER GAUGE outside my mother's window registered a warm seventy-four as the girls and I talked of Christmas. The sun on my back through the window, Christmas vacation only a week away, I felt suddenly hopeful.

Sara was hard at work across from me in the dining room that had become our office. Her head was bent over her laptop when, a few minutes later, I answered a phone call from Bobby's lawyer.

I knew by the way Debra said my name that the news wasn't good.

"Washington has turned down our offer of a plea," she said.

"No," I gasped. Sara looked across the table at me.

"We never had a chance," I said, to her as much as to Debra.

"It's politics," Debra said. "It always comes down to politics. The administration can't be seen as soft on crime in a case like this."

There was nothing more to say. Until that moment, I hadn't realized how much I'd believed the government would do the right thing. That it would have been foolish of them to do otherwise. They could have put the Cal Bomber in prison for life and been done with it. Instead, I'd been the foolish party to believe this thing might ever end except with Bobby's death.

I couldn't concentrate. I wasn't any help to anyone. I had to get away from the condo, from my sister and mother, from the ringing phones. I got in the car intending to make a trip to the store. Instead I drove clear downtown, past the cute, new restaurants, past the Capitol Mall, past the jail where my brother must have already heard the news. Maybe he wasn't even that unhappy about it.

I turned east onto J Street. The afternoon sky cloudless, I cruised up and down the shaded streets from Thirty-Eighth to Forty-Sixth, looking at the grand houses, as if I were on a Sunday drive. Finally, I parked in front of the only house that mattered.

I left the car and walked up the driveway of our old house, the lawn verdant in the near winter. I thought I just wanted to peek around back, imagined telling my mother, *They've kept the rosebushes*. It looked as if no one was home.

I peered into the window next to the kitchen door. Our old O'Keefe & Merritt range still stood where it always had. I craned my neck to see farther into the room.

"Are you looking for something?"

I quickly stepped back from the window. A woman had opened the kitchen door. She was about my age, maybe younger, in jeans and a boat-neck sweater, her blond hair cut very short.

"I'm sorry. I thought no one was home." I kept talking, sounding more and more idiotic until I got to the fact I'd once lived there.

"You're Natalie Askedahl," she said.

"Yes," I admitted. Then I apologized for trespassing.

Her expression relaxed. "Please, come in. I'd be happy for you to see the house."

It was a bad idea and I knew it, but I followed her inside.

"It's just the same," I said, looking around the kitchen with its green tile, painted cabinets, and linoleum floor.

"We're going to remodel," she said. She discussed her plans cautiously as if I'd designed the house instead of having merely grown up in it. She pushed aside the swinging door to the dining room. I half expected to see our old furniture—the table and chairs I now possessed, the sideboard Sara had, the antique botanical prints my mother had given Bobby to sell. How many lethal components had those pretty flowers bought?

We crossed the entry hall to the living room. It looked better than it had when we lived there, cleaner, brighter, the floors gleaming and bare, the heavy drapery gone. I shut my eyes, afraid the new would rob me of the old. Or, was it that reality would blot out the dream?

There was another first-floor room. "My father's study," I said at the door. "We couldn't enter without knocking." I drew in my breath as if I expected him to be on the other side. "His desk was there. He sat with his back to the window." It was their family room—blanket-covered sofa, TV with a large screen, computer and PlayStation—but nothing could take the memory of this room from me. The bookcases with glass doors. The worn leather couch. The wingback chairs with the smoking stand in between. The smell of tobacco and newspaper.

I hesitated, surprised I was telling her so much, although she seemed fascinated. "He worked for the first Governor Brown," I said. "The governor came over sometimes. He sat right here." I tapped the air where a chair had once stood. "I was so young, I couldn't say 'governor.' He told me to call him uncle."

"I saw him in the framed photographs," the woman said. I recognized her animation, a smart woman, getting a jolt out of something unexpected in her day. "We found a box in the garage." She reddened. "I'm afraid we threw them away." I waved my hand that it wasn't anything. My mother had just left them behind, as if they wouldn't matter to any of us.

We went upstairs. She showed me the master bedroom that had once belonged to my parents. I walked to the windows overlooking the backyard. When we were kids, we used to move an old mattress out there to sleep outside in the summer heat. Bobby and Sara would tell me I'd have to go right back inside if I kicked or cried. I lay as still as death between them.

Across the hall was the guest bedroom where Adlai Stevenson had stayed when he was running for president, now a boy's room. My room, the one that had remained forever girlish while I aged, now belonged to another girl. Sara's room was a home office.

At the end of the hall, the new owner opened Bobby's door.

"My studio," she said. The accoutrements of an artist lined shelves along the wall. An easel stood in the center of the room. Paint flecks dotted the old floor. I looked at the ceiling where Bobby's airplanes had hung. The old light fixture was still there. A memory came unbidden: the fixture hanging loose, the glass broken, his planes in disarray.

"We haven't told the children that Robert Askedahl lived here," the woman was saying. She stopped suddenly as if she might have upset me, but I was paying no attention to her. I had to get out of this room and away from the picture in my head.

chapter forty-two

THE AMBULANCE had come for Bobby in the dead of a sweltering night. Lights flashed beneath my window. There were footsteps on the stairs, urgent voices. I was eleven and slept through most of it, my sheets in a tangle around my sweaty legs, the grim voices of my parents punctuating what had to be a dream.

In the morning, when I came downstairs, my mother was scrubbing the floor in the front hall. "Is today Wednesday?" I asked, confused. She only cleaned like this on the day Mrs. Sakai came, the two of them mopping and dusting.

"I'll thank you not to be impertinent," she snapped, as if I'd said something rude. It wasn't fair. My question had been perfectly reasonable. I left her to her scrubbing. No one else was around. My father was at work. Sara was away at cheerleading camp. Bobby had been sticking to his room, no longer joining us for meals, not even the time Linus Pauling came for dinner.

It was the middle of summer, stifling, endless. I had nothing to do. Cheerios in front of the TV, an aimless stroll along Forty-Sixth Street until the heat drove me inside. Sara had a uniform for cheerleading camp: red shorts with a white stripe, and a T-shirt with the camp logo. The camp girls tied up their sleeves with a ribbon strung through the collar. I used shoelaces to tie my own sleeves as I walked through the neighborhood, hoping someone would notice.

In the late afternoon, itching with boredom, I turned the doorknob to Bobby's room and peered inside. Even if he just yelled *go away*, it would put a ripple into the deathly stillness of the day. But the room was dark, the curtains drawn, the air smelling like an old person's house. I thought for a moment that he might be sleeping, but when I pushed the door open wider, I saw that both beds were made. I slipped inside, and pushed the button on the switch, but no light came on. A broom leaned against the wall. The floor felt vaguely powdery under my bare feet.

"Bobby, are you in here?" I whispered, as if he actually might be. I checked his sun porch, stacked with books, the curtains drawn against the light. It was thrilling being in his room again after so long—since he'd come home from Princeton, he'd kept the door shut to me. I opened and closed a few books, then picked up a cereal bowl from his desk, holding it aloft by the spoon that was stuck to it. I sniffed a moldy coffee cup and was sorry I did. The long desk that ran across one side of his room was so messy that I didn't notice the broken planes at first. A group of them lay in a heap, looking as if someone had torn them from the ceiling, smashed them underfoot, and crushed their wings. I glanced up to where they should have been hanging. The ones that were left hung lopsided on their slender wires. Bobby's light fixture had come loose from the ceiling. The glass that had covered the lightbulbs was gone.

I was about to climb onto the bed for a better look when I felt something sharp go into my foot. I yelped. My foot was bleeding.

I wanted to call my mother, but something told me not to. I hopped to the bathroom, my foot dripping, and turned on the light. The white-tiled room was bright after the dark of Bobby's room. I watched my foot run red under the faucet, pressing and prodding the flesh until finally I dug out the glass with my fingernails. I covered my heel with Band-Aids, then cleaned the mess of my blood from the bathroom and hall floor. A part of me was like my mother now.

Later I went to her. "Where's Bobby?" I asked cautiously, as if I already knew something I was trying not to know.

"He's in the hospital," she said.

The everydayness of her tone made my palms sweat. "Appendicitis," she said, her eyes on the newspaper she was reading. "He'll be home in a few days."

I lifted my hurt heel, shifting my weight to the other foot, and stared at my mother's head bent over her newspaper. "Did an ambulance take him to the hospital?"

My mother looked up, mildly surprised. "He went with your father," she said. Then she told me to set the table.

THE AFTERNOON Bobby came home from the hospital, my mother put out a fresh tablecloth even though the one on the table was perfectly clean. She made roast chicken and mashed potatoes, the dinner Bobby always asked for on his birthday. When he arrived with my father, he wore jeans and a short-sleeved cotton shirt with the collar turned up. He wasn't holding his side or walking funny. He looked normal.

"Did they take your appendix out?" I asked. A friend at school had gotten appendicitis and they'd removed hers.

He looked at me as if he couldn't quite get me in focus. "Ah, no," he said finally.

I couldn't help being disappointed. "They just kept you in the hospital, and they didn't take *anything* out?"

"Pretty much," my brother said.

My mother fussed over him as if he just gotten back from World War II instead of a couple of days in the hospital. The way she petted his hair and ran to get him lemonade made me feel that even if my appendix burst, she'd never adore me like that.

He ate dinner with us that night. We sat at our usual places, my mother against the door that led to the kitchen, my father opposite her at the head of the table. I sat beside Bobby, our backs to the dining room window, the curtains drawn against the summer heat. Sara's side of the table was empty. I wanted to believe that none of us missed her.

"Did you throw up in one of those little pans?" I asked, desperate for details of his hospital adventure. "Did you get ice cream?"

"Yes to the ice cream," he said. "No to the throwing up."

"Enough about the hospital," my mother said, as if she were the teacher and I was talking out of turn. I glanced at my father, hoping he'd stick up for me, but he was looking past my mother, past Bobby, past me. I'd never seen him look so tired, the lines etched so deeply in his face, and it made me afraid. I stared at my plate, no longer hungry. My brother was the one who asked me what was wrong.

"I was thinking about your broken planes," I said, although it wasn't true. I couldn't name my sadness.

"You saw them?"

I took a breath to stall—I'd just admitted snooping in his room. "How'd they get like that anyway?"

"Natalie, let's clear the table for dessert," my mother said, like one of those bossy, cheerful mothers on television.

"I pulled them down and broke them," Bobby said. "It was a stupid thing to do, and I'm sorry I did it."

My mother jumped up from the table, pushing open the kitchen door with her outstretched palm. My father stared at the door she'd left swinging, his eyes on the diamond-shaped pane of glass near the top. I looked at my brother.

"Were you angry?"

"Angry?"

"When you pulled down the planes?"

He took a long time to answer, which was nothing unusual. He took all questions seriously, as if no matter how young you were, how basic the question, it held a dignity that deserved a considered response.

"I acted in a kind of anger, yes," he said.

My father rubbed his eyes under his glasses.

"Are you going to fix them?" I asked. Bobby nodded, his hair falling over his forehead. "I'm going to get a new tube of epoxy tomorrow. You can come with me if you want."

Epoxy. The word was like a breeze blowing through me, conjuring the crazy jumble of the hobby store, the pride I'd feel at the counter beside Bobby. "Sure," I said.

"Drop me off at work and you can have my car all day," my father said. Bobby looked pleased in a quiet way. Usually, he only got to drive my mother's car.

When my mother returned, my father did something I'd never

seen him do before: he helped her clear the table. My parents stayed in the kitchen awhile. I leaned into Bobby, not wanting him to disappear upstairs.

My parents came through the door carrying big slices of blackberry pie. The pie got my father reminiscing about the berries that grew wild on his father's ranch. We stayed at the table past dessert, the way my parents did when their friends ate with them. My mother and father told us stories about when they were young, stories we'd heard before but liked hearing again. How as kids they rode inner tubes down the Sacramento, silt from the river filling their bathing suits. How my father worked one summer guessing people's weight at the State Fair, that he could still guess anyone's weight. How on a spring day at the Greek Theatre in Berkeley, my mother gave a valedictory speech of such elegance that it made my father cry. Bobby smiled, and I felt the strange vapor that had crept into the house and clung to us like the remnants of a bad dream begin to vanish.

chapter forty-three

INNOCENCE CAN BE a kind of not looking. I needed to hold on to whatever I had left, to be home with my daughters thinking about tree buying and who wanted what for Christmas, and nothing else.

Eric saw right through me. "You look so weighed down," he said after the kids had gone to bed the first night I was home. He'd taken his mother home the day before. Now there was just the two of us in the kitchen, drinking from the same bottle of red wine.

I didn't know how to answer him. It was the first private thing he'd said to me in weeks.

"Bobby offered to spend his life in prison for only one reason," I said slowly. "He couldn't face the humiliation of having to sit there while his lawyers presented the case that he's crazy. Now that the government has squashed his plea, I don't know what he'll do."

I didn't want to say what I feared: that Bobby would rather kill himself than face any kind of insanity defense.

"I don't know how my mother's is going to get through the trial," I said. "How she's going to endure sitting there while the prosecution presents the grisly details of all Bobby's done. I don't know how I can."

"You don't have to go," he said.

"I wish that were true," I replied.

* * *

As if it were nothing at all, Julia mentioned that a woman from her exchange program was coming to the house on Saturday.

"You're kidding," I said, the open dishwasher between us.

"Like, for an hour, to do a family interview," she said matter-of-factly, placing a cup on the upper rack.

"She can't come," I said, unable to even imagine it.

Possibly for the first time in her life, Julia greeted a no from me with equanimity. "I'm sorry but we are sort of stuck having to do it." She shrugged sympathetically.

"You're not going to Ghana and that's final." I shut the dishwasher for emphasis. "You're too young."

Julia looked from the appliance to me. "The program is for kids my age," she said, sweetly reasonable. "I may not even get in." She put a hand on my arm. "I know it's a drag, Mom, but please."

I'd willed the girls to freeze in place while I was gone, to greet my return exactly as they were when my gaze had left them. But Julia wasn't stopping for anyone.

The four of us sat in our hastily cleaned living room in our just-washed clothes, looking perhaps too pressed. We'd put a few flowers in a vase, set out a plate of cookies and our best cups on the coffee table. The lady from the exchange program was about my age, with blond hair making an easy transition to gray. She wore a sweater set and pearls, an enviable leather briefcase at her ankles. Eric tried to hide his exasperation. He did not want Julia going to Ghana any more than I did. He did not want to have to talk to this woman who surely knew who we were. Lilly had plastered her bangs to her forehead, a dangerous look in her eyes. Julia, taking the measure of her father and her sister, shot me a desperate look. I sent back a reassuring one, the two of us on the same team for once.

"How would you say your family resolves conflict?" The woman had a pen in her hand, the question addressed to no one of us in particular.

I'd been asked excruciating questions by people who did it for a living, answered live on television, my voice modulated, as if I'd been born to answer terrible questions in prime time. But now, in my own living room, I'd gone blank. Julia stared at me, her eyes enormous in their pleading.

Eric spoke up, friendly, assured, a dad in the best sense of the word. "Of course, our family's not a democracy," he said, "but we try to talk everything out, to explain why we have the rules we do, and to admit when there might be a better way of doing things." The woman looked too brightly at Eric, but I didn't care. I was busy wishing we really were the people we were pretending to be.

We managed a few easy questions. Lilly grimly but politely answered a query about what she was studying in school. The woman smiled indulgently at her, then looked around at the rest of us. "What kind of things do you do together as a family?"

Was she kidding? I caught Eric's glance and we both looked away, afraid that if we maintained contact, we'd burst out laughing.

"We go camping," Julia said, eyeing us. "We went to Yellowstone and Glacier National Park this summer,"

"Mommy didn't go," Lilly said, clearly fed up with the pretense.

Julia looked as if she'd been shot.

"That's true," I said in the same open-but-in-control tone I'd used on *20/20*. "I couldn't get away. But we do a lot as a family." I babbled about movies, museums, hiking, and board games, all but the movies a stretch, but no one stopped me.

"SHE'S GOING," I said to Eric when we were alone.

He sat next to me on the couch. "Unless we stop her," he said.

I shook my head no. "She can't wait for college to leave. Maybe if . . ." I stopped myself. What was the point of saying one more time, *if this hadn't happened*? "I think we have to let her go."

Eric looked at me without speaking for a moment, then he asked: "Do you wish you could go to Ghana?"

"Ghana?" I didn't understand.

"Go someplace where no one knows you," he said. "Where you could do what you wanted without having to consider what everyone else needs you to do."

"Are you taking about yourself?"

"Maybe," he said.

I CHECKED on Lilly in bed, bent to kiss her. Her face was hot, flushed. I put a hand on her forehead. "Do you feel all right?"

She looked hopeful. "Can I have Popsicles for breakfast tomorrow?"

"How about we try a cooler nightgown?" I unbuttoned the heavy, flannel gown, and helped her out of it. There was a gold chain around her neck. I lifted it, and saw the small cross.

"Grandma gave it to me."

"It's very pretty," I said, fingering it. "You never wore it before."

"Grandma said to keep it against my skin."

I brought her another nightgown, helped her change into it, but I kept looking at the cross.

"I hold it when I pray," she said.

I sat beside her, trying to keep the suspicion from my voice. "Did Grandma tell you to do that?"

"No, she told me not to put it in my mouth."

I read Lilly's face. She was debating whether to confide in me. I picked up a stuffed bear, smoothing its fur. "What kind of things do you pray for?"

Lilly shrugged. "I just talk to God." She hesitated. "What happens if you pray for something bad?" She tried to sound as if she had no stake in the answer.

How would I know? I didn't pray. When I was young, Bobby had taught me not to.

"Did you pray for something bad?"

"No," she said. She looked down. "Once."

"What bad thing? You can tell me."

She sucked on her knuckle. "I asked God to make Uncle Bobby go away," she said.

Her secret seemed so small, I was relieved, but Lilly's shoulders shook. I pulled her into my lap.

"God understands it's normal for a little girl to want things the way they used to be," I said.

"But God answers our prayers." Her chest heaved. "He might make Uncle Bobby die, and then I'll be a killer, too."

I clutched her against me, my face in her hair. I had a secret, too, one that I couldn't reveal to Lilly, or anyone else. In these past weeks, I'd wished my brother dead. I'd half pictured it, some peaceful death. All this over.

"If Uncle Bobby dies it's because of what he's done," I told her. "You won't ever be a killer."

I rocked Lilly the way my mother rocked me when I was small. The way she must have once rocked Bobby, whose trial for the murder of seven people was three weeks away.

chapter forty-four

THE SUNDAY before the trial I took down our Christmas tree, as if it were any year, any dead tree. Then I drove to Sacramento and my mother's spare room.

"I'll never sleep tonight," I told Sara. The half-filled tumbler of Scotch in my hand was doing nothing for me.

Sara pulled a small plastic vial from her backpack. She dumped two tiny white pills into her hand, took one with a swig from her water bottle, and handed me the other.

"What is it?" I asked.

"Ativan."

I downed it with a large sip of Scotch, the normal rules no longer applying.

"You're not supposed to drink when you take it," she said.

I rolled my eyes. "Did you go to a doctor for this?"

"I haven't been to a doctor in years."

For some reason, I found the way Sara circumvented the standard channels comforting. I looked at the ceiling, the table lamp casting a low glow between us.

"Have you ever noticed that Bobby looks a little like Lee Harvey Oswald?" she asked.

"He does not," I said too loudly.

"His size," she said. "The expression around his eyes."

"I thought this stuff was supposed to make us fall asleep," I said.

Sara turned off the light.

My limbs felt weighted but my mind was floating. "Sara?"

"What?" she said sleepily.

"If you had your life to live over, what would you do differently?"

She was quiet for so long that I thought she'd fallen asleep.

"I would have been an only child," she said. "But I'm not and here we are."

I wasn't hurt. I admired her honesty. I'd played the good girl, kept my rebellions secret to reassure my parents that our family was all right. But Sara had done more. She'd given up on her own life so Bobby wouldn't look so bad.

I DREAMED it was the next day at Bobby's trial. The judge interrupted the courtroom proceedings to make a swift ruling. I was to die the following day in the gas chamber and never see my children again.

"You look terrible," Sara said when she saw me in the morning. "Didn't you sleep?"

I wrapped some ice in a towel and held it to my puffy face.

I put on the green silk suit I'd worn on *60 Minutes*. It was all wrong, the jacket too big, the color unflattering against my blotchy face. I couldn't believe I'd ever looked good in it. I changed into the charcoal skirt and sweater I'd packed.

"You're wearing black," Sara said. "What kind of message are you trying to send?"

"It's charcoal," I said. She was wearing a camel shirtwaist I'd never seen before, her hair pulled into a bun. "You look like you just got a job as a high school principal."

"I'd have made a good one," she said. It wasn't true. She would have made an awful principal.

Sara drove my mother and me in the car my mother hardly used anymore, dropping us off before she parked. This was the day I'd dreaded for so long. I expected the relief that comes at the end of waiting, the specificity of finality. Instead, my knees were so weak that I feared I might fall with my fragile mother on my arm. The people around us seemed to hang back, making a path for us as if we might be contagious.

The federal courthouse was a newer building of blond wood and natural light. We walked so slowly from the sidewalk, up the stairs, through the heavy doors, and the metal detector that it seemed possible we would never reach our destination, that there would be only this inexorable journey.

Outside the courtroom, club chairs faced a wall of glass overlooking the city in which my parents, Bobby, Sara, and I had been born.

"It's so gray out," my mother said.

The marshal must have known who we were because he let us inside without checking his list. I kept my eyes straight ahead, but still I saw them in the front row on the prosecution side. The Trinidads, George and Gloria, with Olivia's beautiful sister seated between them clutching their hands. How many other victims and families of the dead were here? I was afraid to imagine.

We sat in the first row on the left behind the defense table, my sad, shrunken mother next to me, both of us staring into the distance. Sara slipped in on her other side. She took Mother's hand. My own were clenched in my lap.

Although people moved about the courtroom, no one approached us. I let myself believe it was out of respect, but more likely it was disdain.

I stared at my dark sweater, afraid of what Bobby might be wearing. Sara was wrong. Bobby looked nothing like Lee Harvey Oswald, but I still didn't want to see him in a sweater like Oswald had worn.

He wore one, a too-large crewneck over a white shirt, the collar showing. His defense team had dressed him, tried to use soft yarn to soften him.

The courtroom fell silent as he came up the aisle. He looked straight ahead, glancing at no one, not at me or Sara, not at Mother, whose eyes were overflowing. It was the first time she'd seen her son in years.

Debra came behind him, stopping to hug each of us. Mark clasped our hands. Bobby took his seat, his hands on the defense table, a slight twitching at his shoulders.

There were no cameras, just the slight shuffle of papers, and whispers that made no sound. I wanted to glance at my watch, but even that felt like a betrayal of most everyone here. How could people sit so still? I couldn't. Bobby never could. I saw us in the kitchen of our old house, still kids. Bobby was sitting on the tile counter, swinging his legs. Sara and I were at the table. Our mother was standing by the sink. It was the first day of summer vacation, breakfast was over, and all of us were just waiting. Bobby said, "Now what do we do?" We all laughed. It was one of the few jokes I remember him making. Maybe he was serious.

Bobby's lawyers sat on either side of him. Debra turned to adjust his collar. See how harmless he is? Maybe it wasn't calculated, maybe it was just nerves on her part, maybe his collar needed straightening.

I wanted badly to shift in my seat, to exchange glances with Sara, but I didn't dare seek the slightest comfort. I was the bomber's sister. The bailiff announced the arrival of the judge. Everyone stood, then sat. I glanced at my watch on the way down. Eight twenty-two. Eric would have already dropped the girls off and be almost at work by now. He'd offered to come with me today, although we both knew he couldn't. The defense team didn't want him there. They couldn't risk how Bobby might react.

I PULLED at the neck of my sweater. The day outside was cold and gray, the courtroom cool, but I burned as if I were the one on trial.

The prosecution table was stacked with boxes, evidence of the crimes my brother had committed. There were no boxes on the defense table, where Bobby sat between his lawyers, a legal pad in front of him.

When the jury took their seats, I resisted looking, staring at nothing with such fervor that I stopped seeing. I listened as they were sworn in, their voices too loud.

I'd imagined courtroom proceedings moving slowly like a football game, all starting and stopping, but the lead prosecutor was already on his feet. Tall and blandly good-looking, he could have been any kind of professional—a doctor, an accountant, a school administrator. A man who got the job done without having to raise his voice.

His voice was even, his tone flat as he addressed the jury. He didn't need drama for this story. He had my brother's bombs and the names of the dead.

Anyone could have understood what he was saying. Overwhelming evidence would show that my brother constructed and mailed bombs with the intent to kill as a way of furthering his political agenda. He was a terrorist, plain and simple: patient, methodical, unwilling to die for his cause but coldly willing to let others die for it. He had been caught virtually red-handed in his remote cabin, which was little more than a bomb factory. Federal agents had recovered live bombs on his property that matched the bombs he'd used in fatal attacks down to the identical markings on the components. The prosecutor pointed to the boxes stacked on his table. In one of them was the typewriter Bobby had used to type his manifesto.

And the government had more. They had my brother's own words detailing his crimes in the journals he kept.

My mother and sister slumped in their seats, but Bobby sat ramrod straight. Not tense but proud, as if he'd been awarded top prize at the science fair. He looked like he hoped they'd let him demonstrate how he built a bomb, the meticulous precision he used, the way he specially marked them.

There was so much evidence against him you could almost laugh. I put my hand to my mouth to make sure I wouldn't. My mother dabbed her eyes, but I'd gone numb under the weight of the government's case.

The prosecutor's tone remained flat, but his switch from the evidence to the story of Bobby's victims was as dramatic as anything I'd ever seen on a stage. I was prepared to be stunned by the facts of the case, but I wasn't prepared for Olivia Trinidad's lovely face on an overhead screen, in her cap and gown. In a click her face was replaced by a crime-scene photo of her limbless body, the clothing and flesh torn from it. I heard gasps, a second click to remove the shot from view, then the muffled sobs of her mother and sister. I felt myself go white, but I didn't faint. There was no way out of this.

Sara had found a tissue for my mother, who'd shoved it to her mouth.

In a steady voice, the prosecutor read my brother's journal entry following the bombing that killed Olivia: "'I aimed at killing only the professor,'" he read. "'As a bonus, I got a grad student and an undergrad. All bodies completely blown apart, as well as massive damage to building. Pleased with efficacy of steel fragment attachments.'"

The prosecutor looked up from his papers. "Steel fragment attachments," he repeated. "The bits of nails and razor blades he taped to the bombs to make them more lethal."

I'd thought the hardest thing for my mother to bear would be Bobby's death, but enduring his own words might even be worse.

I jumped at the new picture on the screen. It was a family group—a father, mother, gangly son, and daughter with braces, a daddy's girl leaning against her long-legged father. He was killed in front of them. There was no crime-scene photo, only a written description from his wife, of her husband's arms blown off at the elbow, his throat ripped open, his children staring, his wife vainly blowing air into his mouth. Then the prosecutor read Bobby's words: "'Satisfied at last with the igniting mixture.'"

I heard crying and understood: the wife and her children were on the other side of the aisle. I'd seen them when I came in without grasping who they were.

In a way, the repetition of the horror made it easier to bear. The handsome UCLA professor survived by the sister who adored him. Then the others. The prosecutor did not have to show a photo of two of the victims. They were in the courtroom: The Stanford professor who'd lost his right arm and half his face to one of Bobby's bombs. A UC San Francisco psychiatrist rendered deaf by another. *I am a failure*, Bobby wrote of the bomb that had deafened the psychiatrist. *I cannot seem to make a bomb that kills.*

The prosecutor was finished. His opening statement had taken a little more than an hour. The judge called a fifteen-minute recess and rose from his bench. Bobby walked past us, his eyes averted, flanked by his attorneys. The prosecutors left their table. Only the spectators remained, like an audience stunned by the play they'd just seen.

Slowly people rose. There were whispers, then louder voices. Sara got up. My mother and I remained seated, not looking at each other, silently staring at Bobby's empty chair. A woman approached and tried to speak to me, a reporter. I waved her away. The clock read ten ten. Eric would be at his desk, the girls would be dealing with just another Monday morning at school.

My mother was crying softly next to me. I reached for her shoulder but she recoiled. She didn't have it in her to even pretend she could be comforted. Sara leaned over me when she returned. "Seven men, five women, one black, two Asian, the rest white," she whispered. It took me a second to realize she was talking about the jury. She handed me a couple of cough drops, a Kleenex. "Just in case," she said, squeezing past me to her seat on the other side of our mother.

I tried to think about the jury, whether more women would have been better, but what did it matter? We were on an airliner going down. I just wanted it over, to feel the impact, then nothing.

chapter forty-five

I SENSED TENSION when Bobby and his lawyers returned to their table, Bobby clutching a manila envelope to his chest. Debra was going to give the opening statement.

I shifted, crossing and uncrossing my legs. I glanced to my right and saw the sister of one of Bobby's victims, the UCLA professor, take her seat. She was petite and dark haired, wearing a light-colored dress. My opposite. Would they call us to testify back to back? Sister to sister? The spectators returned, yet the courtroom was unbearably silent. I clutched the Kleenex and cough drops Sara had given me. The judge climbed to the bench. My brother gulped water from a glass. It was so quiet I heard the gulp.

A thin, calm voice, utterly familiar, broke the hush. "Your Honor, I need to discuss an important matter regarding my legal representation."

The judge looked stricken. The prosecutors shot concerned glances at one another. The spectators seemed confused, unsure who had spoken. But I knew.

The judge stared at the defense table a moment before ordering my brother and his lawyers into his chambers. One of the prosecutors turned to the Trinidads. "Don't worry," he said. "We'll handle it." Then he left the courtroom with the rest of his team.

"What?" Sara mouthed to me. I shrugged slightly. At first the spectators sat like schoolchildren expecting their teacher's imminent return. Across the aisle people whispered, then spoke openly. I sensed a kind of relief, as if they'd just been set free from having to watch an autopsy.

On the prosecution side, people began moving around, talking genially. Bobby's victims were introducing themselves to one another. Sara left to smoke, returned, then left again. An hour passed. No one crossed the aisle to speak to us. My neck and shoulders ached from the tension of staring straight ahead. I tried to touch my mother's hand but it was cold. She was gone, somewhere I could not imagine.

I couldn't sit any longer. Outside the courtroom, people paced the hall talking on cell phones. They glanced at me, then quickly averted their eyes. I didn't want to believe my reflection in the restroom mirror. *Sippenhaft*, a German word I'd come across. It meant punishment for the crimes of your blood relatives. I was wearing mine on my face.

In the courtroom, I sat silently with my mother and Sara. We waited another two hours. Finally, at one p.m., the bailiff announced that court was adjourned until Thursday morning. He gave no explanation for the two-day delay.

Our long-anticipated play had been cut short in the middle of act one. No one seemed ready to leave. Sara, my mother clinging to her arm, walked behind a group heading reluctantly toward the elevators. I crossed the hall to the window, but reporters appeared at my back: Why had Bobby stopped his trial? What did I think?

"No questions," I said. I headed down a corridor, and found a fire escape. I'd wait for Debra at her office.

The door to the stairwell closed hard behind me, my shoes noisy on the steps. When I was two flights down, the same door slammed above my head. I heard a man's impatient footsteps, his irritated voice echoing into a cell phone.

"He's a cockroach," he said. I knew he meant Bobby. I didn't want to hear more, but he was gaining on me.

The easiest thing would have been to hug the railing and let him barrel past. Instead I turned, and saw the half-ordinary, half-ruined face, the prosthesis showing beneath his sleeve. As if I were a fan agog at a movie star, I just stood there staring, him above, me below blocking his path on the stairs.

I gripped the railing, said his name, then spoke my own.

"I know who you are," he said.

He ended his call. I saw from his clumsiness with the phone that he'd been right-handed.

"I tried to write you," I said. "To say how sorry I was."

"Save it for *Oprah*," he said.

He brushed past, his angry "excuse me" like an assault.

My rage came out of nowhere. I reached to grab the arm that had bumped into mine. How dare he? My fingers felt the tweed of his jacket. I was about to clench when I came back to myself so suddenly I had to sit. I held my head, his footsteps reverberating in my ears. The stairs beneath me were cold, but I felt unable to rise. I thought of phoning Eric, but there was nothing he could do. There was no way to erase Bobby's words, no going back to before I'd heard them read aloud to a courtroom full of his victims.

The hood of my raincoat over my head, I walked the three blocks to Debra's office, letting the rain sober me. She didn't arrive until four. She had on fresh lipstick. She'd been talking to the press. "Bob's trying to fire us," she said, sitting wearily at her desk. "It's the mental-illness issue."

Bobby had been arguing for months that he didn't want a defense that even implied he was mentally ill. "I thought you'd resolved that," I said.

"So did we, but at the break he suddenly objected to our compromise."

I asked if they'd be able to work it out.

"We have to."

"I could try to talk to him, if he'll see me."

"Sure," she said without enthusiasm.

I knew why Bobby wanted his lawyers gone. He preferred the prosecution's picture of himself to theirs.

MY MOTHER'S PLACE was dark at five o'clock, the curtains drawn, the porch light off. I stood outside staring at the last sliver of blue-gray sky. Inside, the only light came from the lamp above my mother's chair in the living room, an unread magazine on her lap. My sister had gone running.

"She doesn't let anything stop her," my mother said.

I turned on a second lamp and sat across from her, repeating what Debra had told me.

My mother's eyes were damp. "Why does he do these things?"

"You mean fire his attorneys?"

I hadn't intended the sarcasm, but of course it was there. My mother's back stiffened. "He was sick when he wrote those horrible things."

I'd made her mad, and I relished her anger. I wanted this reduced to the familiar: me the cheeky daughter, and my mother giving back as good as she got. But when my mother spoke again, she was pleading.

"I hope Debra reads from his letters, the beautiful passages about his love for nature." She wrung her hands. "I gave her a wonderful photo of him from when he first moved to the cabin. He's wearing a good-looking pair of corduroy pants, a nice sweater." She searched my face. "Wouldn't you think she'd show it so the jury can see how he looked before?"

"He doesn't want before and after pictures," I said. "That's what the fight with his lawyers is about."

My mother got up to peer between the curtains. "I worry when Sara runs in the dark," she said.

WE DIDN'T HAVE to get up early. Still, Sara and I were in our twin beds by nine thirty. Sara lit her small pipe. I held my tumbler of Scotch, no longer caring if my mother smelled what Sara smoked.

"Had you read that horrible stuff in the diaries?" she asked.

I shook my head. "They just showed me what they wanted me to see. They spared me the truly hideous passages."

"I keep thinking this will end sometime," she said. "That I can go home to my tomato plants, take a bath in my own tub. But I'll never be clean again."

I took a long sip of my drink and told her about the professor in the stairwell. "I was me and then I was someone else ready to yank this guy's other arm off."

"This thing has made us all someone else," Sara said.

We were quiet for a long while. I tucked my nightgown under me and raised one leg into the air.

"What kind of weird exercise is that?" Sara asked.

"When I was kid I used to look at my leg like this," I said. "I thought from this angle, my leg looked like yours, and that I could be a cheerleader like you one day."

"You need to ease up on that drink," Sara said.

"I'm serious," I said. "I was fascinated by you. You were always hopping in or out of a car full of kids. I never had that kind of high school life."

"You didn't need it," Sara said. "You didn't care. You only thought you did." It seemed like a compliment, but I didn't want to press and find out that it wasn't. I lowered my leg and settled back into bed. Sara turned off the lamp.

My head felt suddenly light. A tune ran in my head. *"Look, look, my heart is an open book,"* I crooned. "Carl Dobkins Jr. Bobby gave me a dollar to buy the record for him. I was nine. This grown-up errand. I remember the feel of that forty-five in my hand."

"And look at us now." Sara said quietly. "We're still running Bobby's errands."

BOBBY CONSENTED to see me late Wednesday afternoon. I waited for him in the cement room. I could go there every day and I'd never get used to it.

As if it were something too personal to watch, I looked away as Bobby squatted against the steel door to have his handcuffs removed. He sat at the table bolted to the floor, not quite looking at me. He crossed his thin legs, slouching. I remembered the posture: as if he were boneless. Trade the jumpsuit for a tweed jacket and you'd have a professor too shy to look a student in the eye.

"I didn't know if you'd see me," I said, my voice betraying my nervousness. "You never look at us in court."

He sighed as if I were a tiresome child. "I'm on trial for my life. I can't be distracted."

There was something different about him. A stillness. His hands on the table didn't move. His wrists were so small, like a woman's.

"This thing with my lawyers is nothing personal." His voice was mellow. "We disagree fundamentally about my defense."

I listened with an alertness I knew too well, as if I'd lived my entire life with my ear to the lips of a dying man.

"I got a fax on Monday from an attorney willing to give me the political defense I want," he said.

My mouth went dry. *A political defense?* As in: *I did it to save the planet?*

"But the judge won't allow it."

Thank God, I thought.

"It leaves me no choice but to put on the defense myself."

For a moment, I just stared dumbstruck. "Defend yourself? That's suicide," I said.

"No, that's *Faretta*." He smiled, but I didn't get the joke.

"*Faretta versus California*. It says a defendant has an absolute right to defend himself."

"The judge isn't going to let you put on a political defense," I said, flailing. "It's the same thing as admitting guilt. He'll stop the trial."

"Obviously, I have to be careful," he said calmly. "But the fact is I'm being prosecuted for my beliefs. If I didn't believe in anarchy, in an end to technological society, I wouldn't be on trial."

I just kept staring at my brother. No, I thought, you wouldn't be on trial if you hadn't killed those people. It was all so crazy, yet he seemed calmer, more pleasant, more like his old self than I'd seen him in years.

"I wish I were younger," he said. "I don't have the stamina I had even five years ago." He squinted. "How old are you now?"

It was the first time in all this that Bobby had asked me a personal question. I was so disconcerted, I had to think. My birthday had passed like so much else since all this began, uncelebrated. "I'll be fifty next year."

He looked genuinely surprised. "My baby sister fifty. I can't believe it."

It was the warmest thing he'd said to me in fifteen years, and it made me desperate.

"They're going to say you can't defend yourself because you're crazy."

"Let 'em try. I'll prove them wrong."

"You'll let their shrinks examine you?"

"If I have to. Plus I've got you to testify to my sanity."

I laughed as if it were a joke, but there was no trace of humor in his expression.

"You can testify that you've met with me, and you've seen no evidence of anything wrong with my mind."

I rubbed my throat to calm the pulse beating there. "I won't help you get the death penalty."

He smiled. "I might get myself acquitted."

I assumed he was kidding, but I wasn't sure. "You should know by now that the government isn't your friend," he said as if I were still ten years old. "If they want to put you away for crimes you didn't commit, they'll plant the evidence to do so."

My astonishment must have shown but he didn't react to it. He looked thoughtful. "Besides, there are worse things than death," he said. "I'm not just some guy on trial for shotgunning a family and their dog. I'm a threat to the United States government. You know where they're going to send me?"

"No," I said.

"To the supermax prison in Colorado. Solitary confinement in a cement cell, seven by twelve, meals shoved through a slot in the door. Twenty-three hours a day without fresh air or natural light, without a glimpse of the sky, of anything green. They'll censor my mail, restrict my reading. There will be a camera in my cell. I'll be constantly monitored, not a single private moment, even on the john, for the rest of my life."

I opened my mouth to say something. What? That it was preferable to death?

"I'm better off on death row," he continued easily. "The conditions are much more pleasant and they can't refuse you law books. I might even appeal. There are larger issues here." He shrugged. "I could tie them up with legal maneuvers for thirty years. They won't know what hit 'em." There was real joy in his smile.

I pictured Bobby, white-haired in a cardigan sweater like my father wore, hunched over a desk in a normal-size cell, surrounded by law books.

"I won't do it," I said. "You'll have to get someone else."

He was quiet before answering. "I don't have anyone else."

He leaned forward, a cavity at his neck. "Do you know what my lawyers were going to do?" He didn't wait for me to surmise. "They were going to use the cabin I built with my own hands to call my sanity into question. They had my place taken apart, shipped here. They were planning to display it in the courtroom."

I tried to picture how a cabin could fit in the courtroom. Then I got it. How insanely small it must have been.

"The home I built," Bobby said, a finger hitting his emaciated chest. "The life I freely chose. The skills I acquired to survive on my own in the wild. My defense team was going to use my every accomplishment, everything I'm proud of, care about, to argue that I'm crazy."

In a flash like a backhand to the face, Bobby's tone, his expression, darkened. "You're saying you want to save me, but how? By destroying me?"

My eyes darted from his glare, my gaze going from the floor to walls. There was nothing to break up the cement that enclosed us, not a splotch of paint, a shelf, a venetian blind, or even a drain in the floor to distract me.

"How about you?" he asked. "Would you want to live in this world if technology took away everything you valued? All the children, for example. Wouldn't you do whatever it took to prevent that?"

I didn't answer. He wasn't interested in what I had to say. He was shaping his defense.

My eyes watered. "You have your values, your principles that you don't want taken away. But you have no regard for mine or anyone else's."

"And, what principles would those be, Natalie?"

It was the first time in all this that he'd used my name, and he'd used it against me.

"For a start, choosing life over death. Standing up to injustice, to the wrong the government is trying to commit."

"Natalie." This time he repeated it gently. "If you listen to the lawyers and the others," he said, "you will spend the rest of your life talking in a monotone about the mentally ill and the death penalty. You will have a cause—you will please Mother—but you will lose yourself."

Bobby looked just to the side of me. "People will do whatever they can to keep their illusions intact," he said. "Then they justify it with a philosophy."

Was that all I was doing? Or was my brother revealing the truth about himself?

It didn't seem to matter that I didn't answer him. He signaled at the two-way glass that we were done.

There was the sound of locks turning in the metal door. "Bobby, when I was young," I said desperately, "you were everything to me." I searched his eyes for recognition, that he knew what I was trying to tell him.

"You didn't have anyone else," he said as he turned toward the door.

AT EIGHT the next morning, Debra rose from the defense table to request on Bobby's behalf that he defend himself. I heard the murmur in the courtroom through the rushing in my ears. My mother turned to me. "Why?" she asked before covering her eyes.

The judge conferred with the attorneys. He ordered a psychiatric evaluation, and set a competency hearing for the following week.

Later, we told one another what we wanted to hear. "The competency hearing and the rest are merely pro forma," my mother said. "The judge will never allow Bobby to defend himself."

"Unless he's an idiot," Sara said.

"Which he isn't," I said. "He isn't going to let this case become any more of a public spectacle than it already is."

"The judge has had it, that's for sure," Sara said.

I phoned Eric and told him I'd be back in Berkeley in time to pick up the girls, that there was nothing left for any of us to do but wait.

* * *

I PUT TOGETHER dinner and opened a bottle of wine. When Eric came home, I managed to ask how he was doing before blurting: "You don't think the judge would really let Bobby defend himself, do you?"

"Depends," he said. "You don't have to be sane to be competent in a legal sense. If Bobby's symptoms don't interfere with his ability to put on his own defense, the judge could say yes." He paused. "But I can't imagine him taking a chance on losing control of his courtroom in such a big case."

It was what I wanted to hear. I was worrying about something that was never going to happen.

ON MY ninth day home, a Friday, Sara phoned. "The shrink report came in," she said immediately. I drew in my breath.

"Paranoid schizophrenia, preoccupied with a systemized delusion about education and technological society, with otherwise minimal impairment and periods of remission. Meets criteria for legal competence."

I sat in a kitchen chair, my knees suddenly weak. "This is good, right? The government will have to agree to a plea now, won't they?"

"Fuck if I know," Sara said.

"Has the judge ruled?'

"Not yet."

"The judge is never going to turn his courtroom over to a schizophrenic," I said.

"A paranoid schizophrenic," Sara corrected.

"And that's as crazy as it gets."

"Sorry to have to tell you," my former-social-worker sister said. "They are more functional than schizophrenics. They can pass as normal, sort of. Until you spend enough time with them."

"Oh God," I said.

"All I know is Bobby has been found legally capable of standing trail and representing himself," she said. "That and we're back in court on Thursday."

* * *

WHATEVER I did, no matter how pleasant—a movie with the girls, an hour to myself—I wanted it over. Yet I dreaded going forward. I missed my daughters even as they sat next to me.

I dallied too long at home on Wednesday and got caught in afternoon traffic. I heard about the judge's decision on the radio outside of Davis. I cut into the right lane, pulled off the freeway, and parked beside farmland, frantically searching for Debra's number on my phone.

"It's legally sanctioned suicide," she said, acknowledging my worst fears.

"Maybe it's a ploy to force a plea," I said, as if I were the attorney.

"Bobby pulled that off the table. He has what he wants."

I gasped, wanting to beg: *Give me* something, *anything*. "You'll be there, though? You'll help him."

"I'll be in court as an observer," she said, "but I've made it clear to him, I won't be a party to this." A court-appointed attorney would replace Debra and her partner at my brother's side. "The most we can hope for is grounds for an appeal."

THERE WERE news vans outside the gates of my mother's complex. Inside, we disconnected the phones to keep them from ringing nonstop. My mother went to her room early, less, I suspected, from a desire to rest than a need not to talk. Even with Sara and me.

I phoned Eric. He spoke to me as a doctor to a patient about to be hospitalized. He was trying to use his expertise to comfort me, and I clung to every word.

The next morning, there were more demonstrators than usual outside the courthouse. Placards supporting us, damning us, having nothing to do with us. We sought out friendly faces, hugged the anti-death-penalty demonstrators who'd been out there every day. Normally, we did not speak to the press outside the courthouse, but that day we made an exception.

"We are devastated by the judge's ruling," Sara said. We looked it, I thought, my mother too small in her clothes, Sara's face worn, me sleepless and dazed.

Bobby did not look up as the courtroom filled. His head hunched over a yellow legal pad, he was writing madly. He'd been given only a day, but in a sense his whole life was preparation for this.

His sweater was gone. He was a lawyer now. He wore a thin sport coat, a button-down shirt, a tie. There was something in addition to the usual tension in the courtroom. I felt it in my stomach, the kind of sick excitement you get at the first news of a disaster.

chapter forty-six

AT EIGHT TEN, the jury filed into the box, the rustling of their clothing the only sound in the courtroom. The judge explained that Bobby would be acting as his own attorney. It was his turn to make an opening statement.

It shocked me when Bobby stood. I was so used to his movements being restricted that I feared they'd reprimand him. He looked pale, timid, his clothes loose and mismatched, a teacher afraid of his class. I felt the same fierce protectiveness toward him that I felt when my daughters performed in front of an audience.

Bobby walked to the far end of the jury box, paused, looked a juror in the eye, and said hello. He moved down, and said hello three more times.

Had someone told him to do that? He shoved his hands in his pockets. They were shaking, but his thin voice was even.

"The last time you were here, you heard about a man who built bombs and sent them to people he did not know," Bobby said. He spoke slowly, deliberately, without notes. "A man the FBI could not find for twelve years despite his being among their most wanted." He paused. "Now I'd like to tell you about *me*."

He promised to be brief and he was. He'd left his job as an assistant professor of mathematics because he found the relationship between the government and the university dispiriting. "The old scientific values have been replaced by the amorality of the marketplace," he said. He'd built his own tiny cabin on a parcel of land in Idaho and learned to become self-sustaining. He'd still be there now if weren't for the misplaced anxiety of his sister and her husband.

I sat there next to my mother and Sara, but I felt utterly alone.

According to Bobby, we'd given the FBI—frustrated after twelve years of looking for their man—a plausible bomber. Only thing was, the FBI had no evidence on which to get a search warrant. No problem. They lied. They staked out his place, arrested him, and then spent days searching his cabin.

Bobby paced off an area about eight feet by ten. "Days," he repeated, "to search a place this big. Did they ask for help from the local sheriff? No. Was there anyone outside the Bureau there to supervise what they were doing? No, again."

Bobby stood in front of the jury and placed his hands on the box. I looked to the judge. He let the gesture pass.

I'd never known Bobby to look anyone in the eye, but he was now, making contact with each of the jurors. "You think it can't happen to you," he said. "Your constitutional protections cast aside, crimes you didn't commit pinned on you. I'm here to tell you that it can."

I finally understood. Bobby couldn't put on the defense he wanted, but he knew he had to have one. *The police planted evidence* might have been his only option. Maybe he was arrogant enough to think he could get away with it.

Bobby looked at the clock in the back of the courtroom. "Fifteen minutes," he said. "No one should have to listen to anyone for longer than that."

Yes, I thought with a shameful thrill. I was rooting for the killer.

I LEARNED you can sit through anything, have the horrific become routine. After a few hours, the prosecution's evidence numbed me: chemicals, wiring, a pipe bomb, handmade nails, three-ring binders containing diagrams of explosive devices, logs of bomb experiments written in my brother's hand, a draft of the manifesto and the typewriter it was written on. Experts testified how materials found at Bobby's cabin precisely matched fragments at the bombing sites. There were books from the cabin on bomb manufacturing written in three languages. English, Spanish, and German. Bobby was fluent in all three.

But the prosecutors had so much more. They had the bomber's surviving victims and the families of the dead. They had their silent presence in the courtroom.

IN THE FIVE DAYS it took the prosecution to make their case, Bobby made no objections, cross-examined no witnesses. He never conferred with the court-appointed attorney. "I can't stand it," I said to Sara during the lunch recess on the fifth day. "All this devastating testimony and Bobby just sits there scribbling notes as if he's at a math lecture."

Sara nodded grimly in the small room the court offered us for our breaks. My mother said nothing. Sara tore off most of the bread on her sandwich, then ate half. I took a bite of potato chip but the salt burned my mouth.

At three forty-five that afternoon, the prosecution rested. The judge adjourned court until eight a.m. on Monday. Debra bent over me, and whispered that she wanted a word. She signaled a bailiff. He led us through an empty courtroom across the hall into a jury room.

"Is this the same setup our jury has?" I asked, although it was obvious that it was. The courtroom we'd just passed through was identical to one where Bobby's trial was taking place.

Debra nodded. I looked around as if I'd just been granted access to the Oval Office. A large table and chairs took up most of the room. A sink and counter with a coffeemaker stood against one wall, next to a pair of vending machines. The room was so cramped I could barely maneuver. I couldn't imagine twelve people wanting anything other than to get out of here as fast as possible.

"I've just learned that Bob has you on his witness list," Debra said.

I stared out the window at the leafless trees. What had I been thinking? That Debra had taken me into this little room to give me a tour?

"He asked me to testify that his mind seemed clear the times I'd visited him in jail."

"And you said?"

"I said no, I wouldn't do it."

She sank into a chair at the jury table. "Apparently he didn't take your no for an answer. You should have told me."

"It didn't occur to me," I said. "I'm so sorry."

She nodded wearily. "So far Bob's doing a decent job of building a platform for his ideas," she said. "My sense is he wants to use you to make him—and by extension his ideas—seem rational. Even sympathetic." Her voice hardened. "But if you get on the stand and answer even one question for Bob, you'll leave yourself open for cross-examination. If you so much as hint that his actions might be rational, you'll lose every ounce of sympathy the jury has for you."

She patted my hand. "We need you to testify for us during the penalty stage," she said. "Even more than his mental illness, you're our best argument for saving Bob's life. You'd never have turned him in if you knew it would lead to his death. The jury doesn't want to make you pay for that."

I lowered my eyes, and nodded that I understood.

"We're still all right," Debra said. "The judge hasn't ordered you to appear. You haven't been subpoenaed. Bob must assume you'll be in court on Monday. All you have to do is not show up. Disappear for a few days."

I said I would. I phoned Eric from the parking garage, crouched against the wall, my coat around me, the hood drawn up. "It's almost over," I said.

"I know," he said. He told me he was going to spend the weekend at his mother's with the kids. "The TV people are back camped out in front." Eric's tone was the same one he used every time ants invaded our kitchen.

MY MOTHER'S HOUSE was dark, too silent. The door to her room was shut, a dim sliver of light underneath. When she didn't answer my knock, I opened it. She sat in the upholstered chair next to her bed, her hands folded in her lap, her body motionless, her eyes blank and staring.

"Mother," I said, my voice frantic. I rushed toward her.

Her eyes flickered. "I'm not dead," she said.

I sat on the edge of the bed next to her chair, my father's side of the bed. I glanced down. My legs were shaking.

"You frightened me," I said.

"I was lost in thought," she said. There was an old-fashioned glass on the table next to her, half full of amber liquid, the ice nearly melted. The only light came from the low glow of her beside lamp.

"Sara's out running?"

My mother nodded. "She's always been so disciplined, so self-possessed. I'm surprised she never made more of her life."

"What about me?" I asked. "Have I made of my life what you imagined?"

She smiled. "You've made of your life exactly what I imagined. You've been a good girl."

"Maybe too good a girl," I said. "Or not quite good enough."

My mother narrowed her brows. "Just what are you trying to say, Natalie?"

"I stopped at the old house. The new owner gave me a tour." Weeks had passed since I'd been there. I didn't know what possessed me to bring it up now. Perhaps I'd simply passed the point of no return.

My voice shook as I told her about the sudden rush of memories that had come to me in Bobby's old room, memories of that hot night when I was eleven and Bobby seventeen. I hesitated, but I knew if I didn't bring it up now, I never would. "Bobby tried to hang himself, didn't he?"

My mother took a long swallow of her drink, her hand clutching the glass. I glanced away from the bones prominent in her thin flesh, the dark spots on her translucent skin, her arthritic fingers.

"But you were asleep," she said.

"I thought what I heard that night was a dream," I said. "But now I know it wasn't." I braced myself. "Mom, we have to talk about it."

I waited in agony for her to begin. When she finally did, she started with the heat of that August night. Every window in the house was open in the hope of a breeze. My mother had fallen asleep with the electric fan blowing on her. Sara was away at camp. Bobby was in his room. I was asleep in mine. My father was out. He came home much later than he should have, an elegant man, in elegant clothes.

"He'd snuck in the house with his shoes off like a boy," she said.

"But why?" I asked without thinking.

"He'd been out with a woman," she said.

I felt wild, sick. I wanted my father there to tell me it wasn't true, that none of it was true, to silence my mother, and restore my dream of him. But I wasn't a child, and my parents had built their little kingdom together, just as Eric and I had built ours.

"He was often out at night," my mother said.

I'd pushed her, and she was going to push me right back. She was going to leave me with nothing, not even a shred of fantasy. Maybe that's how she felt.

"Mom," I said gently. "I need to know what happened with Bobby."

My mother did not answer for long time. When she finally did, she spoke without looking at me, as if from a place I couldn't imagine to somewhere beyond my presence. I bore her words silently, in stillness.

MY FATHER had climbed the stairs, shoes in hand, his thin black socks slippery against the dark wood. At the top of the landing, something made him turn toward Bobby's room instead of his own.

There was an odd banging sound coming from inside it, a band of light under the door. My father knocked, his fist pounding his alarm, his powerful voice demanding Bobby answer. When the knob wouldn't turn, he flung his shoes aside and took his still-strong shoulder to the door. The wood splintered and the lock broke. But he had to heave twice more to dislodge the bureau his son had used for a barricade.

Bobby's body swung in front of him. The sound my father hadn't been able to identify came from his son's shoe banging against the foot of the bed.

My father righted the stool Bobby had used, and climbed onto it. He lifted Bobby's slack body, trying to loosen the silk noose around his neck. He used the gold pocketknife Bobby had given him for his forty-fifth birthday to cut him down.

My mother awoke, thinking she was dreaming. She heard my father yelling for an ambulance, and knew immediately it was Bobby. Later, she wouldn't remember what she said to the operator, only the feel of the dial on her shaking finger as it made that awful circle.

She ran barefoot down the hall. My father was on his knees pounding his fist into Bobby's chest. She thought there'd been a fight, that my father was pummeling Bobby, and she screamed for him to stop. Then she saw my father leaning over their son's mouth to blow air into his lungs.

As if she were somewhere outside herself, she took in the remnants of a silk scarf, recognizing it as her own. It was a special scarf, the blue-and-gold one she'd worn to the governor's first inaugural. Blue and gold because those were the state colors of California.

My mother saw the bits of ceiling plaster and broken glass on the floor, the smashed model airplanes on their tangled wires. She had to move around my father to glimpse Bobby's face. His eyes were rolled back in his head, his skin a gray she had never seen on a living person. His mouth was open, his tongue was black, and she knew he was dead.

When the ambulance attendants brought their gurney inside, they scuffed the wall. She thought there must be something wrong with her for noticing. When my father left to ride with the ambulance, she handed him his shoes. The sidewalk under her bare feet was still warm from the heat of the day. Alone in the dark, she realized she didn't even have her robe on.

On her way back into the house, she heard me calling her. She climbed the stairs to my room. I asked what all the noise was.

She sat on my bed, stroked my hair in the dark, and said, "It's nothing. You were dreaming. Go back to sleep." She waited until she heard the rhythmic breathing that told her I had. Then she shut my door and went back to Bobby's room. She picked up what remained of the silk scarf he'd taken from her bureau. She returned the furniture to where it belonged and placed the model-plane wreckage on his desk. Later, she brought her broom upstairs and tried to sweep the room clean.

"If your father hadn't been out with one of his women and come home just when he did," my mother said, "I would have lost my son."

All I could think was that she lost him anyway. I asked her if Bobby had seen a psychiatrist after he tried to kill himself.

"He didn't want to," she said.

"He was seventeen," I said too loudly. "You gave him that choice?"

"We took care of him at home," she said.

I heard the front door open. My sister was back from her run. "And you never told Sara?"

"It was no one's business," my mother said. "We brought Bobby home from the hospital and we never spoke of it again.

chapter forty-seven

IT WAS RAINING when I left my mother's, but I didn't bother with an umbrella. My hair wet, my face bloodless, I drove as if in a trance, my hands clenched to the wheel.

I longed for Eric's warm grip and the chatter of my children, but the house was cold and dark when I arrived. My family had gone to visit my mother-in-law, to the embrace of an uncomplicated grandmother, to a tidy house without news vans and sightseers parked outside.

I poured some Scotch into a tumbler and took it into the living room. I'd selected or inherited every piece of furniture in the room, positioned each lamp, every photo in its pretty frame. The colors were my colors, warm and easy, the style my style, the Oriental carpet on which my children played their board games was the same one I'd played on as a girl. Yet I couldn't shake the sensation that at any minute another woman would emerge to ask what I was doing in her house.

I'd pushed my mother for the truth, and when I'd gotten it, I was horrified. Princeton had sent Bobby home because he'd broken down mentally, and my parents hadn't gotten him help. Ten months later, he'd gone through my mother's scarves and my parents never asked why he'd chosen the one he did. Instead, they sent him to finish college under the blue-and-gold banners of Berkeley. He never saw a psychiatrist even once.

My parents had sacrificed Bobby out of pride or fear or reasons I would never know. But they could have done everything right, and still lost him.

My brother had been a math professor at Columbia. A few years later he was living in a dirt shack. I had blamed myself when Bobby wouldn't have anything to do with me. My sister shrugged it off. My father couldn't hide his disgust with him. My mother gave him money. We chose, each of us, not to listen to the ticking at the edge of our lives.

The Askedahls weren't so different from other people. We tried to hold our family together by ignoring what could break us apart. Except our delusions cost seven innocent people their lives.

I wrapped myself in an afghan and drained my Scotch. On the street outside, a car slammed on its breaks to avoid—I hoped—whatever small animal had run into its path. I must have been six when I followed some other kids to look at a run-over cat. The animal's black fur was ripped wide, flies crawling on the glistening insides. I remembered staring, transfixed. This was death, and it was profoundly interesting.

I didn't understand then that I could die. In school, when we dropped to the floor, one arm over our heads, the other against our eyes to shield ourselves from a nuclear blast, what I was afraid of was everyone else dying. Being alone in the world with no one to take care of me.

Bobby was a year older than Julia when he climbed onto that stool in his bedroom and made a noose out of my mother's silk scarf. Is that how he felt when he kicked away the stool, utterly alone in the world with no one to take care of him? He had me. I would have kept him company throughout that long night, taken care of him when I was older. But he couldn't wait. Or I wasn't enough.

Nothing was ever the same after that night, despite the years we would all spend pretending that it was.

I WALKED in bitter rain and gray mist, up before my neighbors, my only chance to be outside before the news vans reappeared. I kept my gaze on the slippery sidewalk, on my worn-out shoes in the rain. Once when I was twelve I'd gone to buy a movie magazine, wearing shorts. A man on the sidewalk outside the drugstore—maybe he was drunk, maybe he wasn't as old as he seemed—said, "I'd like to lay you on that big butt of yours and screw you good."

I'd walked away fast, looking only at my shoes, my eyes hot with tears. My shoes were brown, scuffed and stupid looking. When I got home, I didn't say anything to my parents. I went straight to Bobby's room. I took off my shoes and hurled them against the wall, satisfied when one left a mark.

Suddenly Bobby was there asking what the hell was going on. He'd come in from his sun porch. I had no idea he was even home.

"I hate my shoes," I said. "Mom forced me to buy them. I hate her, too."

Bobby sat on the other twin bed. "Understood, but why didn't you throw the shoes at your wall instead of mine?"

It was a reasonable question. Why was I in his room? He was supposed to be away at Berkeley.

"Why are you even home?" I said to deflect attention off me.

"You didn't answer my question."

"A guy outside the drugstore said he wanted to screw me," I said as if I were used to strange men talking to me like that.

"What guy?" Bobby asked quietly.

I couldn't keep it up. I started to cry. "Some guy. He said my butt was big."

Bobby stood. "I'm going to the drugstore," he said. "I'm going to find that guy and make him sorry he ever bothered you." He pointed at the shoes I'd thrown. "Give those to me," he said. I didn't ask questions. I gave him the shoes.

I read from his collection of old comic books until he returned, a shoe box under his arm. I asked him if he'd found the guy. He said he had and that man would never bother me again.

"But if anyone ever says anything like that to you in the future, you scream 'pervert' at the top of your lungs. As if you're really angry, you keep screaming 'pervert,' as loudly as you can."

I asked Bobby what a pervert was. "It's what that guy is," he said. He made me promise I'd do what he said. Then he gave me the shoe box. It held a cool-looking pair of red Keds that I would wear until they fell apart.

Years later, a guy came out of nowhere to threaten me on a dark street in Oakland. I was alone. I didn't see anyone else around. He backed me against a brick wall. I looked him right in the face and started yelling as loud as I could, "Leave me alone, you pervert." He ran off.

AT HOME, I did laundry at six a.m. In the mess of dirty clothes on Julia's floor, I found an old yearbook from Berkeley. We had a bunch in the attic, Eric's, mine, my mother's, my father's, my grandfather's. This one had Sara's name on it—I didn't know why we even had it. I flipped through the pages. Sara had been a blonde in a Peter Pan collar when she posed with her sorority sisters. But she'd also been a princess in the court of the Lambda Chi Daffodil Queen, something I'd never known. Sara's accomplishments were not the kind that got noticed in our house.

Bobby was in the book, too. He was nineteen and a senior, photographed in a sport jacket, smiling shyly, next to a plaque on the wall. He had earned one of the top five scores in the nation in the Putnam Mathematical Competition. *That* was something everyone in our family knew.

Nowhere in the yearbook was it mentioned that for the first time students had to pay tuition that year to attend the University of California.

"It's just a small fee," I remembered Sara saying to our father.

"No," he'd said. "It's the beginning of the end of everything we worked for."

My father had his timing wrong. The beginning of the end of everything he'd worked for had come earlier, on the summer night he cut his only son down from the ceiling.

WHEN ERIC and the girls came home on Sunday, they were so happy to see me I would have bargained away everything to stay like that always. It was late before Eric and I had a chance to talk. I knew it was dangerous. There was the possibility of a fight that could last all night when I needed my wits about me on Monday. I might not be able to hang on to my fragile decision.

"I don't want a drink," I said when he offered me one. My husband looked surprised. This was something new.

I explained the situation as simply as I could. Here is what this person, that person, and these people wanted from me. This was what I was going to do: I would be in court for my brother on Monday morning.

I steeled myself for Eric's anger. But he sidestepped what I'd just said. He spoke to me as a lawyer, his voice matter-of-fact, his feelings hidden.

"Bobby seems to be in control of himself in a way I didn't foresee," Eric said. "He got his opening statement right. He understands that he has to offer a defense. If he'd tried to take credit for his bombings or claim they were justified, he'd be admitting guilt and the judge would have stopped the trial."

I said I understood that.

"But he's going to get his philosophy in at some point, and for that to have any sort of credibility, he needs two things." Eric held his fingers up to tick them off. "One, he needs to appear somewhat sympathetic as a human being. And two, he has to seem sane. If he's evil, then so is his philosophy. If he's crazy, same thing."

I'd already heard this from Debra. A fight with Eric would have been less painful.

"To do those two things, he needs you," he continued. "He needs you to humanize him, to make him seem reasonably sane." He paused to make sure I got the point. "He's *using* you, Natalie."

"I know that," I said, because I did. I looked toward our large living room window, the pane streaked with rain. The news crews would be back in the morning and the curtains once again drawn. "Bobby can't endure the humiliation of being depicted as crazy in that courtroom. One way or another it would kill him." My voice broke and I waited to regain it. "If I did what the defense and everyone else wants, I would be the one doing that to him."

Eric was thoughtful for a moment. "I understand," he said. "But, if you give Bobby what he needs, you risk hurting yourself. It might be brave, but it's also foolhardy. You're going to make people angry, including Sara and your mother. Some of them might go after you publicly. They'll question your motives, even your sanity."

"I know," I said quietly.

We sat together without speaking, listening to the rain, and then I said good night. I had to be up at five the next morning. A few hours after that, I would have to walk into a courtroom and sell out my mother, my sister, and the attorneys who were trying to save my brother's life.

chapter forty-eight

My hands clenched, I gazed at the judge's bench and the flag behind it, as one might an altar, a cross. But no prayers would be answered for me. Debra looked stricken when she saw me in my usual seat, her eyes pained and disbelieving. I looked away from her. There was no point in trying to explain. I rose to let my sister and mother sit, neither of them guessing what it meant for me to be here in my spot. I clung to the aisle seat, as if I imagined I could run.

The prosecution lawyers came down the aisle, their steps light, every shred of evidence on their side. Bobby brushed past me in his borrowed jacket, his head down, his narrow shoulders hunched, his legal pads clutched to his chest. The mismatch would have been heartbreaking if Bobby had not done all he was accused of. My brother did not look at me. He had so trusted I would be here that he hadn't even thought to subpoena me.

There was silence tinged with dread as we stood for the judge, and saw the jury enter. This was it, my brother's big moment.

As if we didn't know, the judge explained that it was my brother's turn to put on his defense. Bobby rose and in a thin, nervous voice called his first witness. It wasn't me.

A quietly dressed, slightly built woman came forward, her curly hair streaked with gray. She put her hand on the Bible and stepped into the witness stand.

Bobby stood behind the lectern, his hands thrust into his pockets, an intense, shy academic. His witness was the librarian from the tiny

Idaho town closest to his cabin. He was one of her hundred or so patrons. She'd known him about ten years.

"How often would you say I came into the library?"

"At least once a month," she said, a tremor in her voice. "More often in the winter when you could get a ride into town with the mailman."

The mail bomber hitching a ride with the mailman. If we'd been anywhere else, someone would have laughed.

Bobby asked the librarian how much interaction they had.

"Quite a lot," she said. "I helped you obtain books and journals from other libraries, to locate academic publications, to hunt down obscure volumes."

"How would you describe me in our interactions?"

"You were always polite and appreciative." Her voice had grown more certain. She seemed to really like Bobby. "I enjoyed the professional challenge you gave me."

"In our work together over ten years, did I ever seem crazy or mentally impaired to you."

"No," she said, this answer coming more slowly than the others.

Sara tapped my knee and shook her head almost imperceptibly in disbelief. We'd learned to communicate in court with the barest of expression. We could have been spies. I closed my eyes in shared concern.

"Do you have computers connected to the Internet at the library that anyone can use?"

"We have three for public use."

"Did you see me using those computers?"

"Yes I did."

"Could someone use one of your computers to publish his ideas online, making them available for anyone to appropriate?"

The lead prosecutor objected. "Calls for speculation," he said. The judge agreed, telling the jury to ignore the question. But Bobby had gotten his point across. Anyone could have cribbed his ideas. Even the Cal Bomber.

Bobby thanked the librarian and went to his seat, a look of quiet satisfaction on his face. The prosecutor said he had no questions for the witness. He could afford to let the mouse scamper awhile before he pounced.

Sara leaned across our mother, whispered in my ear, "Bobby's got to have more than this." He does, I thought.

The judge addressed Bobby: "Mr. Askedahl, on Friday you made a request to call a witness who has been in court for the trial. Generally, witnesses are excluded from being present during the trial. However, since neither side has invoked Rule 615, which would have barred the witness from testifying, and there has been no objection from the government, I'm going to allow it."

There was a slight stir as the spectators tried to connect the dots, but Sara got it immediately. I felt the burning of her shocked, incredulous glare. Then Bobby rose, and in a clear voice called my name.

The courtroom murmur sounded like blood in my ears. The judge pounded his gavel. I thought I heard Sara whispering "no" as I rose too quickly from my seat. When the bailiff opened the gate for me, I wanted to take his arm to steady me on the walk toward the witness box. But he was not my father, and I was no bride.

My hand on the Bible, did I swear to tell the truth? My throat was so dry, I wanted to ask for water, but I didn't know if I could. My brother asked the judge if he could approach me.

"Are you nervous?" he asked.

"Yes."

"Don't be," he said. When he smiled, I felt a rush of affection.

He asked my name, my occupation.

"Natalie Askedahl. Third-grade teacher and mother."

We established that I was his younger sister and that I did not use my husband's name. My brother's face seemed the only friendly place in the room.

"In your own words, would you describe what kind of brother I was to you?"

"Loving, gentle, patient. You never talked down or brushed me aside." My voice was shaky, too emotional. I took a breath. "You taught me to tell time, to appreciate nature, to recognize constellations, to play chess. How to ride a bike. You listened when I talked."

Bobby held up his hand as if in modesty. "Did you ever see me hurt anyone or anything?"

"Never."

"To show prejudice toward any group?"

"No."

"In recent months, you visited me on two separate occasions in the Sacramento County Jail, is that correct?"

I pressed my hands against my trembling legs. "Yes," I said.

"Did I act in any way mentally ill or impaired on any of the occasions you visited me?"

I heard the breath come out of me, quick, sharp, and painful, magnified by the microphone at my side. Bobby looked at me suddenly uncertain. I was taking too long.

"No," I said. It was the truth, as well as a lie.

"In the last fifteen years before I was arrested, how many times would you say we saw each in person or spoke on the phone?"

"Once."

"Did we correspond?"

"I wrote you a few letters, sent some cards, but you never wrote me back."

"Do you think your husband liked me?"

"I don't think so."

"But if we were not communicating and your impression of me was as you described, why would you contact the FBI about me?"

I tried to think, to say it simply. "You wrote a letter to our mother that had some similar ideas to the Cal Bomber's manifesto. When a bomb killed three people in Berkeley, I needed to know that it couldn't have been you. That I wasn't hiding anything that could help catch this person."

"So what did you do?"

"I took the manifesto and the letter to my husband at his office."

"At the law firm of Sterling, Talbot where he was a partner?"

"Yes."

"Does his firm represent the University of California among other well-known clients?"

"Yes."

"What did your husband do?"

"He read what I brought him, then he consulted with another lawyer from the firm."

"What did this lawyer do?"

"He arranged for the FBI to meet with us at the firm."

"Hmm," Bobby said, as if there was something ominous in what I just said.

"Did you speak to them alone?"

"My husband and his partner were present."

"Did you identify me to the FBI as the Cal Bomber?"

"I did not," I said, strength in my voice at last.

"Did the FBI indicate to you that they thought the bomber could be me?"

"No. They said they were pursuing many leads in the case. That you didn't fit their profile."

"Did you speak without any preconditions?"

"No," I said. "We needed the FBI's assurance that if our information led to your conviction, the government would not pursue the death penalty."

"Why was that so important to you?"

"We were coming to them freely without any obligation to do it. We were providing them with information they couldn't get anywhere else. I knew I wouldn't be able to bear it if that information were to lead to your death."

"Did the FBI agree to your precondition?"

"They gave us their word."

"Their word," he repeated. "Did you have any other preconditions?"

"Yes, that our tip would remain completely anonymous."

"Why was that important to you?"

"I wanted to protect my family, and safeguard my children. I didn't want to break our mother's heart. I didn't want you to bear the hurt that I could have suspected you."

Bobby flinched ever so slightly at my last sentence, his eyes showing surprise or maybe it was anger. Then he regained his footing. "Did you remain cooperative with the FBI after I was arrested?"

"No."

"And why was that?"

"Because they betrayed us. They'd lied to our faces."

"The government lied," Bobby repeated.

I looked at my brother and he smiled. "Thank you. That's all."

Bobby walked back to his table. I tensed, waiting for my cross-examination. The lead prosecutor looked up. "No questions, Your Honor," he said. He didn't have to ask me any. I'd already given him everything he could hope for. I'd made Bobby seem perfectly sane.

I went back to my seat. I had nowhere else to go. Sara refused to look at me. My mother was crying quietly.

My brother called his next witness. A trim, bald man in a dark suit took the stand. He was the FBI special agent who had written the affidavit for the warrant to search Bobby's cabin. Bobby asked for permission to read from it.

"In other words," he said after reading aloud a brief section, "you claimed here that you possessed definitive DNA tests pointing to me as the Cal Bomber?"

"Yes."

"Does it say anywhere in your affidavit that seven million Americans might also be the Cal Bomber based on the same DNA tests?"

"No," the agent said.

"Does it say anywhere in this document that the FBI had other suspects for these bombings?"

"I don't believe so," he said.

Bobby read from a section that said Eric and I had provided strong accusatory statements that Robert Askedahl was the Cal Bomber. "But in fact, my sister and her husband did not identify me as the Cal Bomber, correct?"

He hesitated. "Yes," he said.

"In other words, the government lied to get their search warrant."

The prosecutor was on his feet objecting. The judge had the statement stricken.

"No more questions, Your Honor," Bobby said as if he were a lawyer on television.

The prosecutor, tall and steadfast, his light-colored, thinning hair combed back, rose from his seat. He held up the full bound document that Bobby had read from so we could see just how thick it was. He showed the file to the agent to establish that it was the affidavit used to request the search warrant in question.

"How many pages long is it?"

The agent knew without looking. "It is ninety-five pages long."

"Ninety-five pages of probable cause that implicate Robert Askedahl as the Cal Bomber." The prosecutor showed the agent a section, and asked him to describe what was detailed on the page.

"It is a list of canceled checks made out to Robert Askedahl from his family, and the dates he deposited them."

My mother stiffened beside me, her gasp so quiet I barely heard it.

The prosecutor went through the checks one by one. My mother had sent the majority, but I had sent two and Sara one. Each check was posted a few weeks before a device was planted or a bomb went off. I had sent the last one. My brother had cashed it six weeks before the Berkeley bombing.

The lawyer worked his way through the other documents, one by one, each more damning than the last. He ended with my own statement to the FBI of when I'd last seen my brother before his arrest: the accidental meeting at my mother's with the girls in their fancy Christmas dresses. A mail bomb had been sent from Sacramento the same week.

My neck ached from holding up my head. I glanced at my watch. Ten forty-five.

Bobby called his next witness, the sheriff of the county where my brother had lived. The sheriff, a big, rugged man with a silver mustache—he could play his own role in the TV movie of the trial—testified that the FBI had kept his department in the dark when they staked out Bobby's cabin.

"Is it unusual that an outside law enforcement agency would not inform local enforcement of a stakeout of this kind?"

"Unusual? Disgusting is more like it. They violated law enforcement protocol."

"So the FBI could have done anything they wanted at the cabin without being observed?"

The prosecutor objected and the judge agreed, but it didn't matter. Bobby had finished with his surprisingly sympathetic witness.

The prosecution declined a rebuttal and it soon became clear that Bobby had no other witnesses to call to the stand. The judge brought down his gavel against the buzz in the courtroom, then ordered both sides to be ready with closing arguments at eight the next morning. Moments later, he adjourned the court.

The room seemed overly bright. There was commotion all around me, a reporter appearing at my side.

"I can't talk," I said, wondering how I would make it through the rest of the day.

chapter forty-nine

RAIN STRIKING the windshield, I drove my mother home in silence, my body aching as if I'd taken a fall. When we got there, my mother hung up her coat and put a chef's white apron over her dress. I watched as she measured coffee into the percolator she still used, and made little sandwiches out of soft dinner rolls.

"How did everything go so wrong?" she asked, her back to me.

I didn't know if she meant Bobby's defending himself, my testimony, or something much greater.

"Bobby was only a year old when Sara was born," she said. "It wasn't good for either of them."

I didn't answer because she wasn't talking to me.

"His brilliance meant too much to me," she said.

An odd relief flooded me. She wasn't blaming me for what I'd done.

"Your father had his life's work establishing the educational system of California," she said. "I made Bobby my life's work."

Yes, and Bobby made his life's work destroying what both his parents had built.

I asked her when she first suspected Bobby might be mentally ill.

"Things were different then," she said. "People didn't have the understanding of mental illness they do now. There were these tragic souls in asylums, and there was everyone else." She looked away. "Your father was so disappointed in Bobby," she said quietly. "He had such high hopes for him. Maybe I went too far in the other direction."

"But when did you first suspect?" I pressed.

"The day they arrested him," she said, her voice breaking. "When I saw his picture on the news."

A part of me thought she couldn't possibly be serious. She had to have known something was wrong with Bobby long before then. But what right did I have to judge? I'd spent a lifetime choosing the story I wanted to be true over the one that was. If the ground hadn't collapsed beneath the life I lived, I never would have stopped.

My mother set three places, poured coffee for the two us, and set a sad little ham sandwich in front of me. She sat down in her white apron, her long legs still shapely, and took a dainty bite. I wanted to say something, to protect her somehow, but I had nothing left to give. We sipped our coffee and picked at our sandwiches in silence.

I sensed Sara's arrival before I heard it, my mother and I both looking toward the door. Then she was in the kitchen, her curly hair damp around her face, her coat wet.

"Get out of that coat," my mother fussed, but Sara's eyes were on me.

"You tell me," she said, "because I don't understand."

I'd braced myself for her rage, but this was something else. I rolled my eyes in the direction of our mother in a plea for Sara to wait, but she'd have none of it.

"How in the name of God could you get up on the stand and ambush us like that? How could you undermine everything we've done to save Bobby's life?"

Still in her wet coat, she sat down next to me. I forced myself to look at her, her face drawn, her mouth set in a thin line of pain.

"I did it because he asked. Because he didn't have anyone else. Because he's our brother."

"You did it because he asked you to?" Sara slapped her head. "He's a paranoid schizophrenic. He may be holding himself together right now but it won't last. You gave the government just what it wanted. You handed them Bobby to kill."

My mother stifled a sob. I stared at the barely eaten sandwich on my plate. Mother pushed back her chair. "I'm going to my room," she said.

"Did you ever think of her," Sara said after she'd gone. "Or just yourself?"

"You didn't meet with Bobby in jail, Sara. You didn't have those conversations."

"Bobby saw you because he knew he could manipulate you," Sara said. "You had all that guilt he could play on."

"I know that," I said.

"You know what you've done? You've destroyed any possibility we had of saving him."

"We blew any chance of saving him years ago."

"So that's it?" She flung her hand against the air.

"Sara, I used everything I had to reason with him. But Bobby's brain doesn't work like yours or mine. He's not going to get treatment. He's not going to find redemption. His whole philosophy is an elaborate defense against knowing that his perfect mind is gone, that his possibility for greatness is gone, that he's no more than a pathetic, crazy killer." I looked in Sara's eyes. "There's no way I could save him. His delusions are all he has. I could only help him keep his dignity."

Sara's jaw was rigid. She must have been cold in that wet coat, her eyes overflowing with tears, but she ignored it all. "Don't you get it?" she said. "The government is condemning a mentally ill man to death just so a bunch of politicians can act tough on crime. You could have stood up to that."

"Yes, but the only way I could have done that was to humiliate Bobby." I grabbed Sara's hand. Even as she tried to pull away, I held her in my gaze. "I knew what I was doing. And if it comes to that, I'll be there with him when he dies."

Sara dropped her head. She was crying. We both were. I put my arm around her, and leaned my head forward until it rested next to hers. "I will not stop fighting," Sara said. "I will not stop until the death penalty is overturned in every state in this country."

"And I will do everything I can to support you," I said.

* * *

We moved slowly, inexorably, leaving the house before the sun was up the next morning. We parked under the courthouse and went through security. We rode up in the elevator, Sara and I on either side of our mother. The bailiff opened the courtroom for us. The first to arrive, we took our places behind the defense table, looking straight ahead.

At eight ten, the lead prosecutor, looking confident in a fresh suit, walked over to the jury. He paused before speaking, as if weighed down by the burden he carried. His voice steady and commanding, his words plain, he spoke for the victims in the courtroom, and he spoke for the dead, the seven innocent people who had been fully alive one moment, gone the next. When he spoke about Olivia, I heard the muffled sounds of weeping. I did not move for fear of sounding my own grief.

When Bobby stood to give his closing statement, his eyes sought me out. Without thinking, I nodded. My reassurance was a gift I'd offered all my life to the people I loved.

"Something's gone wrong in the government of the people, by the people, and for the people." He faced the jury without notes, speaking with quiet passion, the great professor he might have become.

"You know it," he said, looking in turn at each of them. "You feel it in your exhaustion as you work harder and harder just to stay in the same place. You see it in the disappearance of the outdoor life you knew as a kid, and every time a green pasture gives way to another concrete store selling junk from China." His voice was not angry but grieving. "You feel it in your home as the assault of mindless television and the gadgets of technology rob you of your family life. You know it in your own mind when so much information comes at you from so many sources that you can't make a clear decision."

He paused. "And, you've seen it in this courtroom."

My father had delivered his speeches in a rich baritone. He could thunder if he had to. But apart from Bobby's tenor voice, the rest was all there: my father's cadence, his choice of simple words, the passion held in check, the argument from the heart delivered in the second person. Like my father, he knew just when to pause to look his listeners in the eye.

I wasn't the only one who noticed the resemblance between son and father. My mother shook beside me, a tissue pressed to her mouth.

"My home was a cabin I built with my own hands on land I purchased in the Salmon River Mountains," Bobby said. "I raised my own food, got along with my neighbors, and returned my library books on time. I went to sleep one night thinking about my corn plants and woke up to a federal posse at my door. You've heard the government's story. Now I will tell you the truth of how I got from there to here."

He put a hand shyly in the pocket of his borrowed jacket. He looked younger than he was with his slender build, his full head of unruly hair. His whole demeanor seemed to say, *Look how harmless I am.*

"My crime is that I share the same antitechnology attitudes as the so-called Cal Bomber. I expressed these ideas in a letter I wrote my family and on the Internet at the library." For the first time, Bobby looked away from the jury. "You heard my sister Natalie's testimony," he said, pointing in my general direction, "that she did not believe the Cal Bomber was me, but to dispel any doubt, she showed my letter to her husband, a partner in the law firm of Sterling, Talbot. You've heard testimony that the University of California, a target of the Cal Bomber, was a big client of his."

For the first time, Bobby referred to his notes, reading the names of Sterling's other marquee clients: the oil conglomerate in the news because of a toxic spill; the chemical company accused of leeching toxins into the soil of a California farm town; the mining and logging concerns. "Some of the biggest polluters in the United States," Bobby added, seeming to know and not care that the prosecutor would object.

"My sister never phoned the FBI about me," Bobby said, his voice rising. "She did not make that call. The law firm of Sterling, Talbot did." The prosecution objected but the judge let it stand. Technically, it was true.

Bobby went through the high points of my testimony, ending with the FBI's promise to safeguard my anonymity. "And how did my sister's faith in the government's word turn out for her?" Bobby's voice was tinged with outrage, a brother unable to protect his little sister. "The FBI announced her name to the world and destroyed her private life."

Bobby's lawyers had wanted to use any sympathy the jurors might have for me to save his life. Instead, I'd allowed him to use it to make himself and his philosophy appear perfectly reasonable.

In a voice pure with conviction, Bobby accused the government of planting the evidence against him. Federal agents had brought a caravan of vehicles to arrest one man. Large vans that could easily hold whatever the FBI wanted to plant. No local or outside law officials were permitted to observe what they were doing. Agents spent days searching his cabin unsupervised. More than enough time to create whatever crime scene they wanted.

"And why, you might ask, would they go to all that trouble?" Bobby's tone was helpful, as if the jurors might be thinking just that.

"The answer is simple: because they couldn't find the Cal Bomber. They couldn't find the man they'd been hunting for twelve years, a man with his own FBI task force." He paused for dramatic effect.

"And why couldn't they find him?"

This was it, my brother's big moment. The one I enabled him to have.

"They couldn't find him," he said, "because he doesn't exist." He waited as if to let his words sink in.

"Yes, there was violence to further a cause of vital importance. And yes, there was a manifesto for that cause. But there never was *a* Cal Bomber. The phenomena the FBI has named the Cal Bomber is not a man but a movement."

The courtroom seemed impossibly still.

"It is a movement consisting both of individuals and organized groups in Montana, in Washington State, in Idaho, in Northern California and throughout the West. The groups have different names: First Earthers, Monkeywrenchers, Eco-Anarchists, Green-Anarchists. But what unites them is the sure knowledge that the earth we love is being destroyed by an out-of-control industrial, technological, political system."

I couldn't help it. I looked to the jurors, but I could see no reaction.

"Some of these individuals advocate violence," Bobby said in his best professorial tone. "Others do not. But they all agree that something must been done to prevent a future in which the wilderness we once knew exists only as a simulation on television."

I wiped the blood from my lower lip where I'd bitten it. He was doing it, using the courtroom as a stage to get his views out.

"I freely admit I share this philosophy. However"—he paused to look at each juror in turn—"sharing a philosophy with these people does not make me the fictional Cal Bomber."

His voice rose with emotion as he thanked the jurors and told them, "Never give up hope that this world can be saved. The movement continues. The techno-industrial-financial system that has enslaved all of us will come to the end it deserves."

His admonition was familiar, familiar at least to anyone who'd read the Cal Bomber's manifesto. Was it hubris or madness that made Bobby quote from it? Or had the words simply rolled off his tongue.

He was finished by ten thirty.

For their rebuttal, the prosecution turned down the lights, lowered a screen, and projected the faces of the dead. Bobby watched, resting his face on two fingers, exposing his small wrist. I grabbed my own, and held it against my stomach to calm my secret disgust at his small wrists, his placid staring, his furtive pride.

My mother, Sara, and I went to Debra's office to wait. The blinds drawn against the city, we sat, barely speaking, for more than an hour, my mother frail and lost to me. When Debra and Mark joined us, collapsing into chairs, looking pale and exhausted, I had the sense of being at a funeral that was never going to end.

"How long do you think it will be?" I asked.

"There's a lot of evidence to go through," Debra said, as if she didn't believe the jury was really going to go through it all. It was the most she'd said to me since the day I enabled Bobby to call me as a witness.

"Days?" I asked.

Mark shook his head. "But longer is better for us," he said. "Usually."

"We'll never be able to thank you enough for everything you've done," my mother said. Sara added to the words of thanks. I could only nod. I doubted Bobby's counsel wanted to hear anything more from me. I'd made their job much harder, but they would leave this case and go on, their enviable certainty intact. Whatever I would have at the end of this, it wouldn't be certainty. It wouldn't be ease.

Mark ordered lunch in for the five of us, a lunch I suspected only he was interested in eating. Sara had booked us a room at the Sheraton a few blocks from the courthouse to wait out the verdict. We'd just called a cab to take us there when Debra got the phone call from court. The jury had a verdict. It was barely three o'clock.

My mother, Sara, and the attorneys took the cab the short distance to the court. My coat pulled tight, I walked alone, savoring the crisp, winter air as if I feared I'd never breathe it again. I lifted my eyes. Bobby was coming toward me, his jacket unzipped, a chessboard under his arm. I nearly waved before I saw it was just a boy carting a skateboard.

I passed city hall, the county jail. Bobby would have returned to the courthouse by now. A crowd had gathered in front. I fixed my gaze, the stare I'd perfected these past weeks, the one that took in only what was necessary to keep pushing ahead.

In our familiar seats, we knew the verdict before the jurors came in. Everyone did. It had taken them less than four hours to convict Bobby of seven murders.

As if he were really a lawyer and the verdict belonged to his hapless client, Bobby calmly requested that the jury be polled. "Guilty" rang out twelve more times, like the sounding of chimes at midnight.

We split up after the verdict. My mother and Sara went with the attorneys, and I headed home alone.

chapter fifty

ON THE WAY BACK to Berkeley, as I'd done so many times before, I stopped in front of the old house on Forty-Sixth Street. The lawn was lush from winter rains, but I remembered grass scorched from summer sun, the pleasure of stiff blades spiking my bare feet, the three of us running wild with a garden hose, gleefully on the edge of violence, water shimmering in the vivid air. Had it even happened? I didn't know anymore.

I'd dreamed my young dreams, plotted my schemes, told my lies, and tried to find the truth in those tree-shaded rooms. I'd been carried up this walkway in a receiving blanket and walked down it as a bride. I'd sat on those steps and waited for the people I loved to come home.

My gaze traveling the length of the house, I did something I thought I never could. I said good-bye.

I MADE a sharp turn past the news vans and into my driveway. In all this I'd become a better driver, my reflexes heightened, my confidence assured. As I dashed from the car to my back door, my neighbor saw me and pretended she didn't.

The clock on the living room mantel, already old when it sat in my father's study, chimed four, but it was nearly six. To pass the time until my family came home, I built a fire against the chill.

I was on the floor, mindlessly staring into the flames, when Eric and the kids came through the door. Julia's overweight backpack hung from one shoulder. Lilly wore a too-big raincoat that I realized had been her sister's. Eric carried a briefcase splotched with rain.

"Mommy, you're home," Julia said, as if in my absence she'd become the one who did the welcoming. I rose to my feet. Julia dropped her backpack. I held her with one arm and Lilly with the other, planting more kisses than they wanted. I lifted my face to Eric, our kiss awkward and off center.

He left to change his clothes, but I wasn't going to let the girls go anywhere. "I got into the program," Julia said as if she didn't know how I'd take it. "You know, to study in Ghana."

"I'm going with her," Lilly said.

"I'm sorry but you can't," Julia said kindly.

Lilly shifted away from her sister. "You can't stop me," she said.

I didn't want to hear about Ghana, this country I knew nothing about. I wanted to forestall all talk of anyone leaving. But I kept my expression agreeable, trying to talk over Lilly's growing tantrum.

"I hate you," she yelled at Julia, but I knew the sentiment was really directed at me. I reached my arms out to Lilly and she fell into my lap sobbing. "I still hate her," she said.

"I'm going to miss Julia, too," I said. "But I'll be home, and we'll just have to bake a lot of cakes and eat lots of ice cream."

I told each girl how proud I was of her. "I know this hasn't been easy for either of you."

"We're proud of you, too, Mom," Julia said. "The way you stuck up for your brother and kicked the FBI's butt in the trial."

Her remark was so unexpected, I laughed. Eric returned, dressed in old khakis, and a flannel shirt open over a T-shirt with holes at the collar. We called for a pizza and ate it on the floor in front of the fire, the kids in no hurry to leave when they finished.

I PUT THE GIRLS to bed under extra blankets. When I came back downstairs, Eric was putting more wood on the fire.

"Why's the house so cold?" I asked him.

"The furnace is going out," he said as if it were no big deal. He was too much of a gentleman to bring up that night what we both knew. That we'd have to sell our house. That we couldn't even count on making the move together.

Eric poked at the fire some more, then retrieved a bottle of wine and glasses from the kitchen, joining me on the couch.

"I was impressed with Bobby's defense," he said. "It had a perverse brilliance."

"That's Bobby," I said.

"He was masterful in using you on the stand."

I dropped my gaze, quietly humiliated. "I know that I've failed pretty much everyone," I said. "You more than anyone."

He looked away, as if he did not know what to say. Or, as if he did not want to say what he knew.

Eric and I hadn't made love, or spoken freely to each other since that night in August. We were speaking now, but a part of me longed for the distance that we had become accustomed to. When we'd deferred all talk of the future to make it through the present.

He turned back to me. "What you've been is brave," he said. "Far braver than I could ever be."

I suppressed my urge to counter, to assuage the pain I heard beneath his thoughtful tone. I needed too badly to hear what he was saying.

"I thought I was saving our family by putting up a wall between us and that nightmare," he said. "Instead, I drove us apart."

"Don't," I said, reaching to touch his arm. I remembered us young, parked outside my college apartment, the caress of his corduroy coat, what I felt for him even then.

We didn't speak, drinking our wine and staring at the fire. It wouldn't be long before a new day started with its confusion and demands.

"Sometimes I think you married me for your parents," Eric said, breaking our long silence. "To give them a normal child."

"But that was years before all this."

Eric shook his head, his face lined with fatigue, or maybe it was sadness. "Bobby was on his way to becoming a bomber when I met you. Sara was already wasting her life and being self-righteous about it. You were your parents' only hope and I was . . ." He searched for a word. "Suitable."

I thought of my father's easy companionship with Eric, the son he never had, Julia climbing in and out of her grandparents' laps, all of us in their backyard, limes from the tree by the fence in the drinks we shared.

"No," I said. "You saved me when you married me." It was the truth. "You loved me for who I was, and you gave me my own family."

"I wish . . ." Eric stopped himself. Maybe it was pointless to say.

I offered a dry laugh. "You can't imagine the things I've wished: that I was different, that you were different, that I hadn't done half the things I've done in the past two years. I've wished my brother dead. I've wished him never born."

I'd felt flat for so long that I'd begun to believe I could take anything, any punishment. But this afternoon, in the courtroom commotion, Mrs. Trinidad and I had accidently exchanged glances. In that brief instant, her eyes told me: *you know nothing of grief.*

Eric was the only person I could tell this to. He flinched when I did.

"Her eyes told the truth," I said. "Our children are alive. We only imagine we've been grieving."

Eric looked down and so did I. "Because of what my brother's done, there are people whose children are gone," I said. "Yet, only a part of me can hate him. The rest still loves him."

"I should have been with you," Eric said. "But I was so frightened of losing everything, so ashamed of not being able to protect us. So ashamed of being the bomber's brother-in-law. So worried about how it would look to the firm . . ." He raised his eyes to mine. "I'm sorry I wasn't at your side when you needed me to be."

I didn't know what to say. I was astonished. This man I'd been with for more than twenty years, this man I'd thought I'd known better than anyone. I'd understood his fierce protectiveness toward us and his anger over what Bobby had done to our lives. But I'd been so full of my own shame, my own sense of ruin, that I hadn't been able to imagine his. What it must have been like for him to go to work every day, to look for another job, facing all those people who knew what they knew about him. I hadn't even guessed his humiliation.

Eric looked back at me. "You've given your life for love," he said. "I couldn't even come close."

"You stuck with me," I said. "There's more than enough love in that."

I started to say something else, but Eric put a hand out to stop me. He pulled me against him, his flannel shirt smelling of our laundry soap. I didn't want to consider tomorrow, or the days after, or even moving from the couch. There was only this moment, in which nothing more needed to be said.

About the Author

Stephanie Kegan grew up in Southern California. She attended UC Berkeley and the Masters in Journalism program at the University of Southern California. A freelance writer, she is the author of the *Places to Go with Children in Southern California* guidebooks and a previous novel, *The Baby*. She lives in Los Angeles with her family.